Unexpected Revival

by

E.L. Roux

Revived, Book One

The Wild Rose Press, Inc.
PO Box 708
Adams Basin, NY 14410-0708
Visit us at www.thewildrosepress.com

Publishing History
First Edition, 2024
Trade Paperback ISBN 978-1-5092-5548-1
Digital ISBN 978-1-5092-5657-0

Published in the United States of America

Dedication

I'd like to dedicate this book to all those who have supported me on this journey. To those who helped shape the book in the early revisions to Sandra Ramsey who continued to push to deepen my novel. I'd also like to thank everyone at Wild Rose Press, especially my editor Morena Stamm who took a chance on me. Lastly, I'd like to thank my family and friends who constantly supported and encouraged me.

Chapter 1

Employee Name: Shannon Troy-023.
Date of Birth: Unknown. (Edit 201 AV: Age estimated between 25 and 27 years.)
Date of Death: Unknown. (Edit 201 AV: Early 21ˢᵗ century.)
Location of Body: Kro-Gen Facility Hanford. (Edit 201 AV: Kro-Gen Facility Old Russia.) (Edit 701 AV: Kro-Gen Koi Island.)

The black box buried deep in her psyche was a gift, created with the intent to help Shannon cope with all the shit in her life. She used it as a chest of sorts. A way to hide away emotions she couldn't deal with until she had the mental capacity to pull one painful item out at a time and process it. It'd been damn helpful, too. She'd been able to forget about it for a time because she'd learned to cope with whatever life threw at her. But now the black box slipped out of the long-forgotten mental closet she'd shoved it in after college likely due to the body lying in front of her, offered up like a sacrifice on an altar of white.

Cold air whispered across the room. Shannon's skin pimpled and she shivered. A soft beeping started behind her from the platform she'd just crawled off. The sound increased in volume the longer she remained standing. Shannon brushed a curl out of her eye, interested in more important things, like how she got here. The prone body in front of her, draped head to toe in a sheet thin enough to see through. Hands shaking, she lifted the edge of the cloth and peeked under. A bald head, square jaw, and strong bushy eyebrows stuck out on an unimpressive face. Even with the pale undertone, their skin was darker than her own light brown had ever been. She raised the sheet higher and jerked upright. He was naked.

"Sorry," she whispered and rolled her eyes. "Good job, Shannon. It's not like they're awake to know you looked."

Another cold burst of air. Shannon tightened her own threadbare white sheet to ward off the chill. Clothes were at the top of her to do list, right after she figured out what she could from this body. He was the only other living being in this room of floating platforms she could find. The bed she woke on lay three rows away, flashing red and beeping louder. Shannon refused to acknowledge it.

She folded the sheet at his waist and tucked the loose ends under his legs to keep it in place. Despite everything, he didn't look dead. His skin was clear of any scars, damaged skin, or bruising that could hint at the cause of death. She poked his arm. The flesh dimpled, slow to recover. His cold skin was warmer than her father's the night she'd found him dead on the couch.

A whisper of a sound emanated from the white walls. The scent of mint drifted past, followed by the harsh bleach of industrial cleaner. God, she hated that astringent smell. Had hated it ever since she'd pulled a stint as a janitor to help pay for school. The scent of bleach had refused to leave her skin that summer, no matter how much she scrubbed.

She eyed the only exit as the alarm grew louder. It

loomed dark and ominous twenty feet away. Shannon needed to figure out where she was and what the fuck was going on before the shit hit the fan. Since she awoke, her ability to move without pain had increased, but she was still weak and unable to stand for a period of time without support. She wanted to get the hell out of this room, but there wasn't any way she'd be able to escape without a crutch. Her legs wobbled.

"Fuck."

She braced herself on his floating bed before she collapsed. What the hell had happened to her? She remembered an argument with her boss about an upcoming research trip—but a trip to where? And now she was here. Wherever here was. She squinted at the corners of the room and searched for something familiar, but it was nothing like the hospitals she remembered. It was more like a bright light washed room out of a sci-fi movie. How long had she been out of it? She tried to remember more and slammed into a black void.

Shannon rubbed at her throbbing temples and glanced at the kinda-dead man's bed, needing answers. A red-heart icon flashed on the platform's surface, beating once every minute. So, this place wasn't a morgue, but some place else? A digital clock counted down next to it. Mentally doing the math, she calculated the timer would hit zero about a week from now. And then what?

Shannon hesitated. Wiping her damp hand on her makeshift dress, she lifted the mostly dead male's arm off the table and laid it across his stomach. She shoved his shoulder, grunting from the weight, but managed to roll him on his side. More bare skin and the smooth bumps of his spine greeted her. His back was free of wires or tubes that would supply nutritional support or health metrics for a body. He must be getting nutrients some other way. Maybe through the table?

She rolled him onto his back and visually swept the room once more to check for anyone else. The uncanny emptiness of the space grated on her nerves. The rows of tables were too perfect and all carbon copies of each other. She checked for leg supports earlier when she'd fallen off her own bed but found none. They had to be magnetized somehow to stay afloat.

She wet her lips. "How long—"

The alarm from her empty bed peaked, loud enough to wake the dead. Shannon glanced at the bald man. Nothing.

Shifting her weight, she drew the sheet back over the body and patted it in place. She glanced at her empty bed, uncertain if she should stay or leave this strange medical center. The alarm would call someone who could either answer her questions or could make her situation worse.

Lights flickered on at the door. A lean figure strode in, triggering a wave of light down the room. Bright white scalded her vision. She blinked back tears as the blob grew bigger.

Her heart stuttered as it separated into two. Light glinted off the head of the lean human shape on the left, but Shannon's vision sharpened on the second figure.

With broad shoulders and narrow hips, they loomed a head taller than the bald human figure. Their lips were pulled up at the corners. Sharp teeth flashed.

Shit. Shannon's fingers twitched as horror movie after horror movie played through her mind. Something shifted near the floor. A long *tail* twitched at their feet.

Adrenaline pounded through her veins. Shannon

pressed back against the occupied bed, the cold body hard under her hands. She'd suspected there were aliens somewhere out there in space, but this predator was no little green man. Instead, they were a weird cross between an Abyssinian cat and a human. They had golden hair with pointed ears that peeked out of the strands on the side of their head.

More details became clear as the alien continued to close in. Dark clothes hugged the muscular planes of their body. A well-muscled chest and long torso narrowed to a thick black belt wrapped around their hips, securing the sidearm strapped to their thigh. A knife handle stuck out from the top of their scuffed black combat boots. They rested a palm on the butt of a weapon at their waist. Armed to the teeth, everything about them screamed male as they boldly blocked the door.

His oval pupils dilated to saucers as his pointed ears rotated forward.

The small hairs on the back of her neck rose as the alien flashed a sharp-toothed snarl. "Why is Troy-023 awake?"

Shannon clutched her throbbing head as his garbled voice resonated sharply within her skull. She brushed her fingers over her left ear and paused at a pea sized bump tucked behind her lobe, the skin sore to the touch. "What the hell is this?"

The bald human, encased in a silver onesie, wound their way through the mass of floating beds toward her. "I don't understand."

That made two of them. Shannon focused on the human as they walked past her. The lab coat was a pillar of sanity as Shannon's world spun out of control. People in lab coats always had answers. She tracked the doctor as they stopped next to the bed Shannon had woken on and silenced the alarm. The red light flickered off.

The doctor shoved their hands into their pockets. "How could this have happened? I used all the standard calculations."

The doctor's occasional out-of-sync lip movements were distracting enough to start Shannon's mental spiral all over again. Shannon focused on the similarities between her and the doctor. They both had two eyes, a set of ears, a nose, and a mouth. The hands, before the doctor had tucked away, had five digits. Neither had a tail.

The predatory alien male growled and stepped closer. "That's no excuse."

Shannon's heart slammed in her chest as her fingers trembled. Was the alien coming for her?

"Calm down Troy-023." The alien took another step.

The path to the door cleared. Shannon bolted.

Her limbs jerked erratically. Her muscles responded half a second too late in an uncoordinated flurry of movement.

Hard arms wrapped around her waist as her back hit the alien's chest. Her feet went out from under her. His touch was firm and unbreakable. Terror tore through her. The urge to freeze increased. Frantic to escape, she hurled her terror into the black box and slapped on the lid. Adrenaline burned through her veins. She slammed her heels back into her captor's legs. Sharp pain shot up her ankles. Shannon might as well have kicked a rock. The bastard hadn't even grunted in response.

"Let me g—" His callused hand clamped over Shannon's mouth. The taste of salt permeated her lips.

His fingers bit into her waist as she twisted.

Kicking wildly, Shannon struggled to bite his flesh. Her teeth hardly dented his rough skin. He wasn't going to take her anywhere without a fight.

His palm ground harder against her jaw. "Stop." His deep growling words were a thick syrup in her ear. "Unless you want us to call for backup support."

Two against one were bad enough odds. More of this type of alien would tip the scales even further in their favor, but she couldn't stop. She struggled harder, the sheet kicking up around her feet. There was no guarantee they wouldn't call more recruits later, and she'd end up in the same situation, completely out of control and with no idea what was going on.

Shannon twisted and his belt buckle dug a divot into her back. His thick tail wound tightly around her hips. Hot breath skated across her neck, uncomfortably close to her jugular.

She froze. One quick bite from his sharp teeth and she'd be dead again. Or had it been a coma? Shannon's breath rushed out of her. She needed to figure this out.

Arms tightly wrapped around her chest, he swung Shannon around until she faced the doctor. "Dr. Grates." At her back, a growl vibrated through her organs. She froze as her heartbeat pounded. The menacing sound came from him. "My'len specifically requested Troy-023 remain unconscious until my team arrived."

A dull throb pulsed behind her left ear. His deep rumble no longer distorted his words. He sounded furious. A whimper escaped her as fear shot a spike of adrenaline down her spine. How had her life gotten so far out of control?

Shannon wiggled in his grasp. She needed to get

away.

"D'lane, I—" The doctor looked up from the bed's controls. Their hazel gaze flickered past Shannon to the mostly dead body in the corner of the room. "I take full responsibility. I must have misjudged the dosage of the drugs I administered. The older bodies are always temperamental. The dose should have started the awakening process, not completed it."

"You mean to tell me Troy-023 awoke from a cryo-coma—"

The room spun. Bodies gestured like marionettes with invisible puppet masters. She went limp, letting D'lane deal with her weight, and she focused on shoving all her uncertainty into the black box. The tightness in her chest lifted. Shannon struggled to bring the conversation back into focus.

"You do realize how painful the process can be without medical assistance?" D'lane said. "I could have you fired from Kro-Gen for this error."

That would explain her paralysis upon waking, and her continued lack of coordination. Although not the nakedness. Clothes would be a damn fine barrier right now against whatever the hell was going on. Was her loss of memory somehow tied to the coma, or from something else?

"Let's not get too hasty." Dr. Grates gaze skipped around the room. "Troy-023 appears to have satisfactorily survived the transition."

She needed to get some control of the situation. Shannon swallowed, trying to wet her raw throat. "Put me down," she croaked at D'lane. Neither paid attention to her with their eyes locked together in an intense staring contest. Shannon twisted about as best she could in the alien's hard grasp. "Put. Me. Down."

She remained tightly held. Growling, the sound nowhere as terrifying as D'lane's, she kicked her heels back again.

D'lane dropped her before she connected. Her knees hit the ground. The hard impact shot up to her skull. Her jaw snapped shut. She blinked sparks from her vision and struggled to stay upright. She brushed her hair out of her face and clutched the slipping sheet to her chest. Blood rushed to her head and Shannon swayed. Her arm swung out. She connected with a solid muscled pillar. Warmth radiated up her palm. A tail twitched out of the corner of her eye. In horror, she slowly turned her head and glared at her hand braced against the alien, fingertips remarkably close to the gun strapped to his thigh.

She snatched her hand back. The room was a few degrees colder now that she wasn't clamped against D'lane's chest. Fingers clenched, she struggled to absorb the residual heat from him, even as she cursed the need to.

D'lane cleared his throat. Shannon glanced up from where she knelt, but he refused to make eye contact. Instead, she focused on the tufts of his pointy ears that moved to catch every sound. D'lane cleared his throat again.

"What?" Shannon glared.

His tail tapped her shoulder.

"Quit it." Shannon brushed it aside. She grazed her sternum, touching more of her bare flesh than expected. She flushed and pulled her sheet up higher to cover her overexposed skin. Shannon struggled to her feet and glanced between Dr. Grates and D'lane. They held all the answers. But what should she ask first?

Shannon focused on the doctor, ignoring the furious alien in the room. "How long was I in a coma?"

Dr. Grates cleared their throat. "Over a thousand years."

Static rushed over Shannon. "A thousand years?" She sucked in a breath. "As in it's now the year 3010?"

"No." The doctor fidgeted with the edges of their white jacket.

Shannon's shoulders sagged. Of course, this was all some gross misunderstanding. As soon as she got whatever this was figured out, she could go home, contact her friends, and they could all have a big laugh. "What a relief. I—"

"It's closer to 3075 by your archaic calendar." Dr. Grates's hazel eyes locked with hers.

Mouth agape, Shannon sucked in a breath. "That can't be possible. How am I even alive?"

Shannon frantically patted herself down. Chest, stomach, ass, head, and crotch were as expected. They were still there and remained the same since she completed puberty. She changed her clenched cloth to her other fist and moved on to other areas.

The doctor's hard grasp on her wrist stilled Shannon's flailing hands. "Cryogenic freezing, along with genetic restoration, has ensured you are, in fact, alive."

A thousand years. She was in the *future*? How else could she explain the floating beds and the alien—unless it was some sort of prank with a lavishly expensive budget? A program that included hovering beds and realistic cat-people... no. Somehow, ending up on a punked show seemed even less likely than being thawed out in the future.

10

What happened to her friends and family? Her apartment? And more importantly, who'd taken care of her cat, Kiki? Her little orange fur baby had relied on her ever since he'd been abandoned in the alley between her work buildings. Shannon flashed a glance at D'lane and swallowed. If she had disappeared...

Chest tight, Shannon struggled to breathe. How had she ended up here? Pain dug its nails into her chest as she realized everyone she knew was dead. She was utterly alone. The room spun. She shoved this issue into the black box with all the other shit she couldn't deal with right now. The black box groaned, already filled with too many unresolved emotions.

She needed to stick to simple questions. Simple questions with straightforward answers. She could handle that—she hoped.

But what questions were simple? She looked around the hospital morgue, trying to confirm basic information about her surroundings. But nothing made sense, nothing except the antiseptic smell of cleaner she knew she hated. Why, after all these years, did that horrible scent remain the same?

"Are you okay?" Dr. Grates took a step toward her.

A sharp laugh escaped as Shannon stepped back. "Why wouldn't I be?"

D'lane frowned and held out a hand. Five fingers and an open palm offered her support she couldn't take. "You should sit down."

"Where? On one of these death beds?" She inched away from the alien and focused on the doctor, the one person who seemed to understand what was happening in this white-walled room. "Am I even on Earth?"

D'lane's tail twitched at his feet. Shannon's gaze

trailed up the alien's black boots, tight pants, and form-fitting shirt to his offended scowl. She scowled back. She wasn't there to placate anyone. She'd gotten rid of that atrocious habit when she left home for college.

"Hold on a second," Shannon said as the doctor's earlier statement sank in. "If my calendar is archaic, what calendar are you using?"

"It is the year 743 AV." Dr. Grates smoothed a hand down the front of their white lab coat and cast a quick glance at D'lane. "And yes, you're on Earth."

What happened to CE? Shannon shook her head, attempting to clear the cobwebs from her thoughts and reminded herself to keep it simple. "AV?"

The doctor's sympathetic gaze met her own. "After Victory."

Chapter 2

Reason for Cryogenic Freezing: Body salvaged from Arctic tundra. DOA.

Cost of Revival: Above normal (115%). (Edit 201 AV: Below Average (85%).)

Reason for Revival: None. (Edit 201 AV: None.) (Edit 501 AV: None.) (Edit 742 AV: May have additional information on impending Anunnaki attack.)

Everyone and everything Shannon knew was gone.

Pain sunk its teeth deep into her chest. She stared at the blue Kro-Gen insignia imprinted on the doctor's jacket as she tightened her own flimsy cloth wrap. Somehow, the design was familiar in all this chaos.

D'lane had abandoned her with a stiff bow a few moments ago. His golden hair had slid over his shoulder in a silken wave as his catlike ears flicked clear of the strands. The tufts at the end rotated back as they straightened. The alien visage was somehow more comforting than the doctor's as the heavy load of her new reality began to settle in.

Wrapped in her sheet, Shannon had followed the doctor out of the room filled with vacant beds, and now they stood alone in a long stretch of empty white hallway, no doors in sight.

The dry air held no scent, although she occasionally caught a whiff of bleach and mint, something she was beginning to associate with Dr. Grates. She squinted down the hall in either direction, the ends stretching tight like a rubber band. The small hairs on the back of her neck stood on end. It was too quiet. Where were the other people? Had she ended up in a time where most of the world's population was dead? Dr. Grates's silver jumpsuit flashed brightly as she resettled her white jacket. Shannon shivered and pulled up her sheet. What would she do if she had?

Dr. Grates cleared their throat, their hazel gaze direct. "I'd like to apologize. The revival process is usually a pleasant experience as Kro-Gen has perfected it over the centuries, but my miscalculations brought you pain."

Shannon's limbs ached deep in the center of her bones, as if the marrow itself still throbbed from the stabbing pain of her nerves awakening. "I don't see how the experience can ever be easy, Dr. Grates."

The doctor touched Shannon's shoulder and smiled. "Please call me Hellen. I use she/her pronouns. Dr. Grates is too formal, especially as you'll be in my charge until you're medically cleared."

"I also prefer she/her, and it's nice to meet you." Shannon trailed off, the sheer normalcy of the introduction painfully at odds with the fact she found herself a thousand years in the future wrapped in a bed sheet.

Shannon cleared her throat. "Why'd we stop here?"

Dr. Grates placed her hand on the wall, about shoulder height. A black line oozed to the surface as a door formed and slid open. A gust of cold, unscented air brushed against Shannon's skin. Goosebumps crawled up her arm. How many of these doors had she walked past without knowing, and what hid behind them?

Hellen stepped through the doorway, gesturing Shannon forward. "Kro-Gen assigns a room to every revivee. This one has been assigned to you."

Shannon licked her parched lips and tucked the sheet tighter against her body. She followed the doctor into the room soaked in deep gray tones, a welcome relief to the sea of so much damn white.

A gray metal-framed bed sat snuggly in the far corner without a head or footboard. Beside it stood a dark gray desk with a paper-thin computer pressed up against the wall. Two doors sitting on the opposite side of the room were light gray and had silver inset pull tab handles. It looked like Kro-Gen left the fancy electronic doors for the hallways.

Dr. Grates crossed to the closest gray panel and opened the door. Three sets of silver jumpsuits hung on the wall. A pair of black slip-on shoes were placed directly underneath the first suit. "Kro-Gen has provided you with clothing adequate for this time. Assimilation is the key to thriving while on the island."

Shannon leaned forward. The closet was excessively large for the limited number of items it held. Did the current population attire only get as exciting as the jumpsuit and how many of them did a typical human or Kro-Gen employee need? "Are socks and underwear hidden around here somewhere?"

"If you're looking for traction socks, I can arrange for a pair to be delivered tonight."

"No thanks, I'll just go commando." Shannon moved to the foot of the bed and ran her hand over the smooth desk, and across the black computer screen sitting atop it. Despite her current situation, the potential information it housed on the last thousand-plus years called her. How many secrets would she discover delving into the data? Was Google still a thing?

The doctor left the closet and opened a second door. "Your bathroom."

Curious, but not yet needing to use the facilities, Shannon crossed to the far doorway and leaned against the frame. A small white sink bulbed out of the wall and a segmented half-shell reminiscent of a rolled potato bug sat a few feet off the floor next to it. A tiny, curtainless shower stall filled the other half of the room, recognizable only as the doctor arced her arm through the space. Water hit Dr. Grates sleeve, fracturing into tiny droplets before rolling off the jacket.

"Kro-Gen attempts to keep the showers similar to your era but remodeling it for every new revivee's initiation decade gets expensive. Because you woke early, you've been provided the previous revivees bathroom setup with a motion activated unit." Hellen shook her wet hand and water sparkled in the air. "You might find the temperature controls confusing at first, but I trust you can figure them out."

"Sure. How hard could a shower be?" Shannon scratched her nose and remembered when she'd struggled with the camp's shower on her first dig, she'd been caked in an ever increasing layer of dirt for days until a friend had helped her out. Shannon promised herself she'd ask for help before it got that far.

"Here's the toilet." Hellen pulled on the top of the segmented shell. It uncoiled into a high seat with no visible water in the receptacle. When released, it coiled back into the wall.

So simple and so utterly foreign.

Shannon fingered the Kro-Gen insignia on the

blanket she still wore. She cleared her throat. "Is there toilet paper?"

Hellen tapped on the wall next to the rolled up segmented toilet. "Aside from the bidet, we have these shells. I recommend watching the informational on the NAV to get the full range of usage."

Freaking shells? Shannon wandered back to the bed. So much in this time was different and yet the same. Her mind in a fog, she sat down, and the mattress perfectly conformed to the shape of her body. The mountain of information she'd have to absorb to operate in this era was overwhelming, but it wasn't an option. This was her future now.

Water ran and Hellen reappeared with a glass. "Drink."

Shannon sipped the cool liquid. Her parched throat screamed for more. She tipped the glass up and chugged. Fluid pooled in Shannon's stomach and silenced the hunger that had creeped up on her.

"You'll need to drink a few more of those before you retire tonight but go slowly. You're not approved for food until tomorrow. We have to wait for your digestive system to settle before introducing broths and soft foods. If you find you're having problems eating, we can fall back on intravenous fluids until the issue clears."

Shannon's stomach rolled. "I've never been a fan of needles."

"We generally use a hypospray to provide medications through the skin, but we still use needles from time to time when a long stay in the med bay is required."

Shannon ran her free hand across the blanket and gave the mattress a bounce. How many people had slept in this room or on this bed, and where had they all gone? She toyed with the bottom of the empty glass. "You said I'm not the first person to use this room?"

The doctor leaned against the bathroom doorframe. "And you won't be the last. We try to make the space as unique to the individual as possible, but there is only so much Kro-Gen—or I—can do."

Shannon took a moment to study the doctor who was currently her only support. Hellen's bald head was nicely shaped, but the smooth surface was something Shannon was used to seeing on men. Did humans now look like Hellen, or was the doctor an exception?

Thin, graceful eyebrows arched over wide hazel eyes. Hellen's gaze reflected a calm Shannon couldn't share. Plump lips spread into a small, yet friendly, smile creasing the cheek with a skin tone more olive than Shannon's own. Was she someone Shannon could trust? Hellen said Shannon was her ward, but what did that mean? Whose side would Hellen take if it came down to choosing between Shannon's health or Kro-Gen?

Hellen snapped her fingers, the sound loud in the quiet room. "That reminds me. You'll need to watch the Kro-Gen orientation video after you've rested. It'll help you navigate the facility, and key you into mealtimes. When you turn on the NAV, our online navigation system linked to everything Kro-Gen, it'll be the first thing to pop up."

Shannon leaned over and placed her empty glass on the desk and eyed the computer, ready to dig into what the hell was happening, and why she was here, alive, a thousand years in the future. She'd figure it all out, as she had every other time in the past. If this was anything like the psychiatric facility her father had stayed in during his twenty-four-hour emergency observation, it would be under constant surveillance, and she had no idea what cameras in the future looked like to even begin to identify their locations.

In the end it didn't matter if Kro-Gen was watching and evaluating everything she did, Shannon wanted the information Dr. Grates had promised. The sooner she understood what was happening, the better she could process her situation and understand what she needed to survive in this new time. This piecemealing process had worked in the past and enabled her to put away the black box of emotions she used to cope with once she'd mentally unpacked everything. The technique had gotten her through her high school and college years and was only meant to be a temporary fix.

Shannon wanted that box gone and slid into the back of her mind where she'd never need it again.

Shannon tapped her finger against the desk. "Where are we?"

Hellen's brow arched from where she leaned against the wall.

"You said I'm on Earth, but I haven't seen any windows to see outside. We could be buried underground, perched on a cliffside, or smack dab in the middle of the desert."

The doctor chuckled. "Nothing that dramatic. You're on a Kro-Gen run island in the Pacific Ocean. For safety reasons, you won't be allowed outside or near anything that might be used as a weapon until your orientation period is over."

Shannon's hand clenched on the soft blanket she sat on. The little details she'd picked up like the lack of headboard or doorknobs began to make sense. The room had nothing she could hurt herself with, other than the sheets. She doubted the weird Z-shaped hangers in the closet could hold any real weight, and the lack of a shower curtain or rod and the fact that the shower drained instantly sunk in. Hell, even the toilet hadn't stored any real amount of water. All these weird items she'd equated to being in the future, not to being under a mental health watch.

It'd be hard, but not impossible, for someone to take their own life in this room. The slight tensing of Hellen's shoulders when she'd mentioned the lockdown led Shannon to believe revivees weren't too pleased with that decision, and the monitoring might be more for the safety of the Kro-Gen employees working at the facility, than for the revivalist themselves. Shannon wiped her damp palms on her wrap around sheet. The doctor hadn't even mentioned therapy to help cope with the drastic time change.

Hellen stuffed her fists into her lab coat pockets. The cobalt blue insignia on the breast drew Shannon's gaze again as it finally clicked. It was different from what she'd remembered in her life before, but the basics were the same. The name had been longer back then: Krogenic Freezing. Spelled with a 'K' to be more eye-catching, she supposed. The tendrils of memory dug deeper as she struggled to remember why that name bothered her. She rubbed her temples.

"Normally I'd give you some pain meds for the translator integration," Hellen said. "But I don't have the full medical results on your genome graphed to determine how your body will interact with our current medicines."

How advanced were their medical therapies that her

biology would react differently than humans of this time? Shannon touched the spot that ached like a particularly atrocious pimple buried deep below the surface. "Will I be able to understand everyone?"

"Kro-Gen installs a basic model during the first phase of revival, meaning you'll understand all languages spoken on the island and Earth, including the alien races present. Once you have your tribunal, you'll be upgraded to an appropriate translation unit. You'll need training on written languages if the digital translators aren't available where you're transferred."

Shannon plucked at the edge of her sheet. Each answer only added more questions to her list. "I still don't understand how I got here."

Hellen propped her heel on the wall, her silver coated knee sticking out from the middle of her lab jacket sparkled in the room's low light. "Like most of our cryogenically frozen employees who have been transferred from other sites to this facility, I'm still in the process of reviewing your file." Hellen's lips ticked up at the end. "I thought I'd have a few more days to get through it. As to how you originally got put on ice, that'll take more digging. I can tell you this, you're one of the oldest ones I've been tasked with reviving."

Shannon frowned at the dehumanizing edge of excitement that slipped into Hellen's voice. "Yeah, I remember you mentioning something like that."

The doctor glanced away, perhaps realizing how inappropriate her enthusiasm was. "When you're feeling better, I'll help you fill out your employee history request. It should contain all the information you need."

"That's funny." Shannon straightened. "I don't remember agreeing to work for Kro-Gen."

Hellen raised her shoulder in a half-shrug. "You would not be here otherwise."

Shannon shoved herself off the bed and traveled the five steps to the closet. Irritation nipped at her soul. What she wanted to do was take a shower, collapse into bed, and be alone to process what had happened, but that didn't look like it was going to transpire any time soon. Instead, she stepped into the closet and grabbed the nearest jumpsuit.

Shannon closed the door, grateful the light stayed on. Alien golden eyes flashed in her mind as she dropped her sheet. "What about D'lane?"

"What about him?" Hellen's voice rang through the paper-thin door.

"Aliens." Shannon toed the sheet further away from her as she opened the silver jumpsuit. "When did we discover them and how long have we been intermingling?"

Hellen cleared her throat. "They found us. Well, the Anunnaki did when they decimated Earth's population and its resources during the War of Resurrection."

"What?" She shivered as the thin fabric slipped through her fingers and pooled at her feet. "How long ago did this happen?"

Anunnaki repeated in her mind. The name pulled on the shredded strings of her memory. Each loop was accompanied by a painful throb in her head. Information surged forward only to slip through her grasp. Why was that name familiar?

"If I remember my history classes correctly, it began around 2030 ACE and lasted for roughly three years."

Shannon sucked in a breath. How close had she come to seeing the Anunnaki attack or had she died just as it started? She shoved that thought aside, hard. That black hole would drag her into oblivion. Instead, she pushed her worry deep down into her already-full black box. Bending over, she picked up the cool puddle of shimmery fabric and re-opened the jumpsuit. She stepped through the limp fabric of the legs and slid the garment up to her hips. Instantly she was enveloped in warmth as it molded to her body. Goose bumps pebbled the rest of her exposed skin. She quickly slipped her arms into the shiny suit and held the seam together. She jerked her hands away as the fabric sealed on its own. Amazing. She tugged at the joint, and it remained closed. Hopefully for bodily fluid sake, she could get it open again.

The jumpsuit was formfitting, supportive, and temperature regulating. Shannon ran her hand down the silky front of the outfit. Did the clothing use self-organizing microstructures?

Shannon cleared her throat and drew her wandering mind back to the issue at hand. "Is D'lane one of them? An Anunnaki?"

"No. Like Earth, the Anunnaki attacked and ravaged the Chriw'rian home world, where D'lane is from. They are just one of many the Anunnaki have harassed over the ages."

Shannon's fingers trembled as she hugged herself. "Where are the Anunnaki now?"

Hellen's sigh was muffled through the closet door. "During the war, once we figured out their coding system and started shutting down their harvesting ships, they disappeared."

Shannon curled her toes on the warm floor. She had so many questions, the likes of which would be easier to answer once she got her hands on some historical information. "How many types of aliens are there?"

"Kro-Gen does business with a few dozen companies from other planetary corporations involving different species. This facility only interacts with My'len, the conglomerate D'lane works for. If it helps, most aliens are friendly, and only interested in business transactions, not destroying the Earth."

She found that hard to believe. Hell, Earth had never hit a period of global peace in her known history, and it was filled with only humans. Her thoughts bounced from subject to subject, and she fought to get her mind under control. She took a calming breath. As long as she didn't focus too long on any one issue, she'd get through the rest of the day.

Going shoeless, Shannon slid the door open and asked the question she'd been dreading. "How bad was the Anunnaki attack?"

Hellen's eyes locked on hers. The doctor gave her a complete once over, likely cataloging the fit of the clothing before answering. "They destroyed most of the surface of the planet and the life that existed on it."

Shannon blew out a shaky breath. "What did they want?"

Hellen shrugged. "With the type of damage done, our current specialists believe they were here to harvest the carbon."

"I don't understand." Shannon brushed her hand down her hips and searched for pockets to shove her hands into. There were none. "Did they raze the earth?"

If she remembered correctly, carbon made up about eighteen percent of the human body. Earth's crust had less than one percent of it stored within it, but earth's surface life had it in abundance. How much did the Anunnaki need if they were willing to destroy an entire planet?

"It's just one of the prevailing theories." Hellen chucked humorlessly. "We're still not certain why they do anything."

"They didn't take any slaves, or stay to conquer part of the planet?" The need for forced labor and resources had been some of the driving factors for most wars as well as the desire for more land and power.

"If they did, they left no witnesses to their atrocity. Most of the missing were counted as dead during the attack."

Shannon rubbed her pounding temples. Questions filtered through her mind one after another, but she'd save most of them for another day. She circled back to the most important one. "Why can't I remember how I died? I remember my youth and childhood along with most of my adult life. But I have a gaping blank spot where the most important information should reside."

She did have a fuzzy memory of the conversation with her mentor, Steven, as they prepped for an expedition. Shannon frowned. Or were they having an argument?

Hellen straightened her lab coat. "Memories leading up to cryogenic freezing are always the hardest to retrieve. I imagine your rough awakening hasn't helped the situation."

"But why was I frozen? I don't remember agreeing to it."

"Kro-Gen wouldn't have kept you on ice without your signed consent. Nor waste precious resources to keep you in stasis if your knowledge or skills weren't needed in the future."

Soft paper on her fingertips. A Krogenic watermark splattered across the signed documents in her hands. She tossed it atop the memos scattered across her boss's desk as they packed up to leave for—

Static slammed into her mind as the memory slipped from her grasp. Shannon bit her lip. She needed someone she trusted to talk through what was happening here, but all her family and friends were long gone. Her eyes stung. They'd been dead for a thousand years, possibly dying a horrible death as they were harvested by the Anunnaki. She shoved that ugly thought deep into her mental black box.

Shannon took a deep breath and sat on the bed. She braced her elbows on her knees. "Why me?"

"Most Kro-Gen cryo bodies are revived on behalf of the League. They'll explain everything once they meet with you."

"You don't know why I'm awake?"

"Even as your case manager, I'm not privy to that information."

Shannon squinted as Hellen slid her hands into the lab coat pockets. "What do you do as my case manager?"

"I'm your point of contact and will be monitoring your integration into the community."

Shannon hands clenched together as another layer of anxiety settled over her. "When will I find out what the League wants from me?"

Hellen grimaced. "The length of time varies."

Shit. What if she didn't know what Kro-Gen revived her for? Would they put her back in the cryogenic tube or kick her out into the universe with nothing more than the clothes on her back, if they even let her keep those?

She straightened. One way or another she would make herself indispensable to this League. She wasn't going to be placed back into a cryo-coma to wake up at some other uncontrollable point in the future. "That's not the answer I was hoping for."

"I know." The doctor's smile was sympathetic. "But I doubt the League will keep you waiting long."

Chapter 3

Revival, Day 4
Doctor's note: Shannon's physical will confirm her language implant assimilation and psychological status. Report will be provided to the League and Kro-Gen for evaluation.

Leaning against the wall, Shannon tugged on a pair of flimsy black shoes that conformed to the shape of her foot and hardened on her soles. She straightened and stroked a hand down the silky soft arm of her jumpsuit, still weirded out with the formfitting clothing and the lack of underwear but *c'est la vie*.

She grabbed her glass from the desk and headed into the tiny bathroom. She tucked the transparent cup against the wall of the sink. Her finger brushed the gray paint, and a mirror activated over the sink. Catching sight of herself, Shannon stilled. The mass of brown curls haloing her face was not nearly as chaotic as she'd expected.

She fingered a ringlet, unable to recall the last time she'd left her hair undisturbed. She'd kept it either straight or braided for most of her adult life. She gripped the end and pulled it tight, her fingers brushed her clavicle. Releasing the curl, it kinked back into shape mid neck, the length longer than she remembered by an inch or two.

Shadows caught on her lean cheeks. Whatever they

had done to her during the revival process, it had left her bonier than she preferred. The extra muscle she'd needed on dig sites no longer padded her arms and thighs. In between bouts of research on revival processes, she'd only been able to get in a handful of push-ups before she'd collapsed on shaky muscles.

She leaned forward and squinted at the mirror. Her dad's green eyes still stared back at her above her mom's small nose. She at least had those facets to remember her parents' appearances now that all her photographs were out of reach. Paler than normal, her skin remained the same blend of her mother's brown and father's white. She tucked a curl behind her ear and noted the holes she pierced in a fit of rebellion at fifteen were gone. Frowning, she tugged open the seam of her jumpsuit and stared at her hip, the bare skin missing the colorful phoenix tattoo she'd gifted herself when she moved out of her father's house.

She fingered the spot on her arm where a broken bone had pierced her skin when she'd crashed her bike to avoid getting hit by the family car. She'd noticed the pucker of damaged skin had disappeared, along with the scars and calluses on her fingers from working in kitchens and shoveling dirt. Even her tinnitus was gone.

She rubbed the tips of her fingers together. She'd earned those marks at the expense of summer vacations and the loss of her free time. She'd paid her way through college in community centers and afterward at dig sites around the city. Those scars had been her badge of hard-fought independence. Pain bit at her chest. Kro-Gen had erased everything she'd done to survive her past.

Blinking to clear her vision, Shannon sealed up her suit and turned from the mirror. As much as her body had changed, the basics remained the same. Her chest, hips, and ass were as rocking as ever, although who she would be rocking for, she didn't know.

Back in her room she scratched at the itching bump behind her ear. The NAV, as Hellen had called it, stated soft tissue didn't survive well in prolonged cold, which was why she thought her body had been fixed. But had the neurons in her brain been rewired over time to survive the freeze? She looked at the computer screen, certain there was at least one monitoring camera hidden there and wondered if her thoughts were her own after all the years and 'care' provided by Ko-Gen. Had brainwashing improved over the years alongside cryogenic systems?

She still vividly recalled the love-hate relationship she'd had with her father when he'd been drinking and the joy she'd shared with him when he'd sobered, along with her struggles to keep in touch with his family after he died. She glared at the computer and the oversight it represented.

At least her drive for knowledge, and desire to understand the world around her hadn't changed. The NAV had offered little information on what had happened to her close friends and relatives other than listing the large global casualties that occurred during the initial Anunnaki attack.

The informational video Hellen had mentioned Shannon should watch featured a perpetually smiling woman who'd walked her through an unhelpful introductory explanation on cryogenic freezing and the regeneration process. Shannon didn't care about the how, she needed to know *why*. The fact humans had reverse-engineered alien technology leftover from the

Anunnaki attack to freeze and manipulate genes, create space-faring ships, and repopulate the world was an interesting notion. But how did it all play into what Kro-Gen and this mysterious League needed from her? When the video had ended with the Kro-Gen's company slogan "Exploring the Possibilities," she snorted.

The possibility of what? Lunacy? What else would drive a company to dabble with cryogenic freezing when the process had a one hundred percent failure rate back in her time? How many people had they attempted it on before success and was the -023 after her last name on the Kro-Gen file an indication of those failures? Was she the twenty-third attempt at cryogenic freezing or the twenty-third success? Her fingers twitched. There were some questions she didn't want to explore.

Shannon suspected there was some sort of parental lock on the NAV, as the computer had supplied little information on much of anything else. She'd had enough skill with programming to get herself into trouble back home, crashing systems and fixing the fallout. But here, whatever hacking skills she thought she had only triggered a tampering safeguard and got her locked out of the system for half a day. The timer still silently counted down the minutes in large red numbers behind her until she could access it again.

She approached the automatic door in her room, and it opened like it had every time she'd retrieved the food Kro-Gen delivered in the hall.

Shannon stilled. Large golden eyes pinned her in place.

D'lane's lean body stood framed in the doorway armed to the teeth. He still wore a pair of tight black pants and a dark T-shirt. His two-piece uniform was an item she now envied. The silver jumpsuit was comfortable but was reminiscent of a Halloween costume rather than everyday clothing. And the lack of pockets was starting to annoy her.

No longer high on adrenaline from waking in a strange place, Shannon reevaluated him. His rectangular nose was a bit wide at the base, and his skin the color of desert sand she hadn't seen on a human yet, darkened to gray as it neared his temples. The tuft of his ears stuck up through his hair, an interesting trait comic con attendees in her day would have envied. With his high cheekbones and sharp chin, D'lane called to her in a way only a handful of people had in her lifetime, even with the knives and guns strategically strapped to his body. Her hand brushed the soft fabric of the jumpsuit at her hips. Should she be armed?

He arched a brow. "Has no one illustrated how to operate the doors?"

She cleared her throat, thrown off by his gruffness as she closed the distance between them. "What do you mean? I walk toward the wall, and it opens."

There wasn't any way she was doing it wrong. It was an automatic door that opened and closed as she approached.

He stepped inside. The vibrant force of his presence pressed against her skin even though they didn't touch. He stopped beside her. The scent of hot sand and something otherworldly filled the space between them and placed his palm next to the door. It closed. Lifting it, he repeated the process, opening it again.

D'lane's tail swayed back and forth. The long line of its length drew her gaze up to the profile of his beautifully shaped ass. Man, she was a sucker for magnificent butts.

"Do you see?"

She jerked her attention up and flushed. "I think so?"

He shifted to make room for her. Swallowing hard, she pushed back the curly hair in her face and stepped forward. Her shoulder brushed his arm. The vivid memory of being in D'lane's grasp in medical, her feet dangling above the floor as the top of her head brushed his chin reminded her again just how tall he was, and how strong. Even as she feared for her life, his powerful arms had held her firmly against his muscled chest. Now on her own feet, his sternum landed at her eye level.

Copying his earlier motion, she placed her hand on the cool light gray surface of the wall.

Nothing happened.

He chuffed. D'lane's warm, callused palm pressed down atop hers. His fingertips extended an inch past hers ending in dark, unexpectedly thick nails. He shifted her hand closer to himself against the wall. The door swooshed closed.

Releasing her, he stepped back and gestured for her to try again.

Her cheeks burned. She fought a shiver at the loss of his body warmth and brushed the flat, smooth surface. She searched for something. Perhaps a raised portion of the wall indicating where the palm reader was imbedded, an indented button, or even tactile lettering. Huffing in irritation, she dropped her hand as the door opened. How the hell did this door work? She placed her hand in the exact same spot. The door closed at her touch, but nothing on the surface indicated why this spot and not another.

D'lane tapped the wall above her fingertips. "If you wish to lock it, once you enter the room, hold your palm on the pad for a few moments, and it will only open at your request."

"Thanks."

He nodded in response.

Her stomach gurgled, the sound lasted entirely too long and was unnervingly reminiscent of a dying animal. It reminded her of why she'd been heading out in the first place. She cradled her stomach as she sized him up. "I was getting ready to find food." She hesitated. "Care to join me?"

It never hurts to make new friends, especially ones that might have the answers to her questions.

He nodded and rested his hands on his hips, inches away from his weapons. "I'll ensure you eat before your visit with Dr. Grates."

Confused, she propped her shoulder against the wall. "How did you know I had a meeting with Hellen?"

D'lane's tail twitched at his feet. "By accepting the mission set forth by My'len, I became responsible for all personnel assigned to my ship. Until the League considers you unfit to be assigned to my team, you are by default under my protection."

Her thoughts spun. She closed her eyes and focused on breathing. She didn't want to touch that mission statement with a ten-foot pole, at least not until she'd silenced the ravenous creature in her stomach.

She sucked in a breath. "Your ship?"

Did this mean she was going into space?

"The T'grevis." He arched a brow. "Perhaps I'll show it to you later."

Of course he had a ship. How else would he get from

his home planet to Earth? Unless teleportation was a thing...

Lifting her lashes, she focused on the knife that followed the powerful line of his right bicep and changed the subject. "Why wear all those weapons?"

He crossed his arms and flexed. She stared at the muscles that had so easily lifted her. He brushed over the handle of the weapon strapped to his right arm. "This is the normal required armament for when a Chriw'rian is stationed outside of My'len regulated spaces."

Her stomach growled again. His ears flicked forward as his lips pinched. The corners twitched as if he was holding back a laugh. The gurgle had been loud enough that someone three rooms down could have heard.

His stance relaxed as he headed toward the door. "Let's get that beast fed before it decides I'm not too bitter for its taste."

She slapped the wall, opening the door for him before he could slam into it and followed him out. "Brave of you to assume I'd get it activated in time."

He flashed her a smile. "I trusted in you figuring it out."

Her cheeks warmed as she hurried to catch up. After two days of being fed multicolored bread, which she initially thought was moldy, that had been slathered in a peanut butter-like putty, she was more than ready to try something new.

"Do you like working for My'len?" she asked to fill the silence as they passed a silver-suited human in the hall. She followed the human's progress until they disappeared through a door. Was D'lane the only alien at Kro-Gen? Hellen had indicated not when they'd discussed the translator, but Shannon hadn't come across any others in her short time here.

Before being locked out of her computer, she'd researched Chriw'rians and how they'd initiated contact with Earth. They'd been key to ensuring Earth interacted with the rest of the galaxy—even when they had to drag humanity kicking and screaming into that contact after the Anunnaki attack. The restricted NAV hadn't provided much more information on other alien types and their relationships with Earth, but she hoped D'lane would be able to provide some insight.

"My'len is one of the largest companies on my home planet. They have project ventures and stations positioned across the galaxy."

Shannon glanced up at D'lane when he quieted. His lips were pressed together as if he was physically stopping himself from saying more. Damn, had she managed to insult him, or was he not allowed to share any additional information? She sighed, frustrated again at what she didn't understand in this time.

His ear flicked in her direction. Gold peeked at her out of the corner of her eye. "Your quest for information is admirable, but the restrictions have been put in place for safety."

"Yours or mine?"

Chatter from a large group echoed down the hall. Her heart skipped a beat. Finally, she would see more of the people who worked here. Her pace sped up, overtaking D'lane. The smell of hot food hit her full force. Her mouth watered. She was so ready for a meal that wasn't in the form of protein paste.

She rounded the doorway. Rows of pale gray tables lined the white mess hall. She hesitated. She'd expected people, perhaps a few of them smattered around the space, but not the sea of bald faces that stared back at her. There were so many people in here, too many people. Did this account for everyone on the island, or a shift change?

The intense scrutiny settled heavily on her. More inquisitive than hostile but remained uncomfortable all the same. Every single one of them was missing the facial hair she'd come to take for granted in her time. Her hand crept up. She touched her curls. The halo of hair an obvious difference between her and the current population. To top it off, she was a full head shorter than those lined up for food before her. Her curvy frame an abnormality among the lithe bodies all wrapped in the same shiny jumpsuits.

She forced her attention away from the people around as their conversations picked up. The walls were plastered with art posters in unreadable text splattered across a variety of unfamiliar scenery. Multicolored skies and complex angular cityscapes hinted at far away destinations the likes of which she'd only seen in science fiction movies. They pulled at her to discover their meanings, but she had bigger fish to fry. Namely, the buffet spread out at the back, with Kro-Gen workers serving the masses.

"Table or food first?" She turned to the alien next to her for his input, except he was gone. Her shoulders slumped.

"Great." One of the few people she knew had left her alone in a crowd of strangers. It wasn't a new situation, but it would have been nice to eat with an acquaintance this first time instead of trying to create small talk with a population she had little to nothing in common with. She settled her shoulders. It looked like she'd have to fend for herself.

She'd done it before, after her parents had split, and again when she moved closer to college. What was one more time? It wasn't like she was living a thousand years in the future, with aliens, and no clue what Kro-Gen wanted from her.

Hunger propelled her forward.

The trek across the mess turned into a test of patience as she nodded back at superficial greetings and wove around those people not paying attention to the space they occupied. In some sense the mundane routine action soothed her nerves. Finally, she had something she could relate to. She made it to the back of the room unscathed.

She gripped a tray at the start of the line, the same tan tray from every lunchroom she'd ever eaten in and stared at the bald human head in front of her. This close to others, an occasional flash of an earring or tattoo peeked out from under the jumpsuit and hinted at the differences in personality that existed from person to person.

She reminded herself not to lump everyone together. Her own experiences and school studies should have wiped that kind of prejudice from her mind, but fear continued to pull that ugly reaction forward.

She tried to smile at the hairless server holding the weird ladle.

They smiled back. "What can I get you today?"

"Uh…" She glanced at the food spread before her. None of it was familiar. The colors were off, and the shapes resembled bricks more than any meat she remembered. The smells flooded her in a blended pungent pool. Even the labeling was unreadable. She'd gotten used to the NAV in her room translating everything. How was she supposed to know what she was eating?

She cleared her throat. "Does anything taste like chicken?"

"Chicken?"

She opened her mouth to explain and closed it. How did you describe a food that was used to express the taste of other foods? She searched for the familiar unappealing speckled sandwich she'd survived off of and couldn't find it. Her grip tightened on the tray; she put a smile on her face. *Here goes nothing.*

She held her tray out. "I'd love a small sample of everything."

They pulled out a gridded plate from behind the counter like something you'd give a picky child, but with a lot more pockets. "New here?"

She laughed, her throat tight, as they began to add bits of food to each pocket. "Am I that easy to peg?"

"Nah." They chuckled as their gaze landed on her curly hair. "You don't stick out from the usual population at all."

Her brittle smile transformed into something natural. She nodded at the buffet. "Anything you'd recommend."

"Hmm." They tapped their spoon on the counter before moving on. "I won't give you any names this time around but remember what you like, and I'll fill you in the next time you come through."

She followed them as they dished more food onto the plate. A purple cake made it into a pocket, and with a smile they piled a little bit more atop. "Cooked fresh this morning, and one of my partner's favorite foods."

"I can't wait to try it."

She followed them all the way down the counter watching what they did and didn't add to her tray until they reached the end.

"A word to the wise," they said as they handed the tray over the top, "a suitable topic of conversation around here is asking what job they've been assigned to by Kro-Gen. Small talk here is all about current project favoritism. The silverware is under the counter."

She nodded her thanks, grabbing a chopstick-like spork. As she turned toward the tables and the thinning crowd, Shannon contemplated their advice. Corporate favoritism wasn't anything new, but she did worry about how it might have warped this far in the future.

She chose an empty table near the middle of the room. It was close enough to overhear nearby conversations and far away enough she could explore the taste of her food without offense if she spit something out. She set her tray down on the white table and sat on the cold bench seat. She pulled her food closer. The multipocketed tray held a weird assortment of white blobs, purple sticks, and unusually colored fruit. The large blue apple was particularly interesting.

She fiddled with the silverware that had a pair of long thin chopsticks that led to a diagonally cut tip. It was a mix of a knife, spoon, chopstick, and fork all wrapped into one. *A choppork?* She snorted.

A growl of a cleared throat drew her gaze upward. Golden eyes pinned her in place. Her heart fluttered. He came back.

His ears twitched from side to side independently as he tracked the noise in the mess. The sharp line of his jaw and the flattened shape of his nose became more familiar on his humanoid face each time she saw him. His tray was held mid-stomach, too high for her to see what was on it. With a grunted nod, D'lane indicated the seat across from her. "May I?"

"I did ask you to join me earlier." She tucked her napkin in her lap with a smile. "The offer still stands."

He placed his tray down and took a seat with a slight grimace. Instead of a multitude of pockets, his plate was partitioned into three equal areas and filled with items the Kro-Gen employee had chosen not to supply her. "My crew will enjoy eating without me for once."

"Are they here?" Excited, she shifted in her seat as she searched the crowd. More aliens! Would they all look like D'lane, as homogenous as the current human population in the mess, or would they reflect a wider variation of physical characteristics?

"They're prepping for my next mission as we speak." He took a vicious bite out of what she assumed was a chunk of dried meat.

"How many crew members do you have? Will I get to meet them? How big is your ship?" Desperate for information, she'd peppered him with as many questions as he would answer.

His chewing stopped. "Eat and I'll answer your inquiries."

Her neck heated when she realized she hadn't taken her eyes off him since he returned. She grasped for her choppork and scooped a pile of sticky oat-like goo. Half of it plopped back onto the plate. She shoved the rest into her mouth.

Flavors burst across her tongue. Sweet and tangy married over the grainy texture of Malt-O-Meal. She went back for more until the metal pocket had been scraped clean. She moaned and held herself perfectly still until pleasure ebbed to a small quiver in her stomach. She sat on her hands to keep from licking the residue from the tray.

D'lane cleared his throat. Back straight, he sat rigidly across from her and raised an eyebrow. His expression was a cross between annoyance and intrigue.

"What?" she asked as he continued to stare.

His clenched fists relaxed from around his plate. "You're causing a scene."

"Am not." She licked her lips and picked up her choppork. She scooped up a random food item and shoved it in her mouth just to irk him. Dry bitterness coated her tongue. Sharp pain stung her jaw. She coughed, food spraying into her hand. Her eyes watered as she wiped her hand on the napkin in her lap as she swallowed what remained in her mouth. She wouldn't be going back for more of whatever the hell that was.

D'lane laughed as his stance relaxed. The sound was rich and deep. Her stomach tightened even as she coughed up the rest of the bite. His laugh should be illegal. She scooped up another item and gave it an experimental lick. She moaned. It tasted like dulce de leche. She hadn't had anything this rich as far back as she could remember. Which wasn't saying much with her chunk of memory missing.

He leaned forward and his shirt pulled tight across his chest. "Can you eat quieter?"

The power display was impressive with his sheer definition of muscles. She forced her gaze up from the distorted gray My'len insignia on his right peck. The gold in his eyes glinted in the overhead light. She wet her lips and shuddered when she hit a spot of bitterness. "How are you not tasting what I am?"

He straightened and rubbed the back of his neck. "From my conversations with others in your position, a heightened sense of taste is a side effect of the revival process."

That would explain the paste she'd been eating over the last few meals. Wouldn't want to overexcite your new employees with exciting food right after thawing.

"In a week food will taste normal again." He frowned. "Well, normal if you are from this era."

"Right." Her shoulders slumped as she fiddled with the choppork. "Thanks for reminding me."

His head angled to the side, exposing more of his catlike ear. "You were alive. You died. Now you live again."

He shrugged. The action smoothly rolled from one shoulder to another like a cat prepping to pounce. The motion was something she couldn't replicate.

Was it that easy? She focused on D'lane, an alien that would have blown the mental capacity of any human back in her time and yet here she sat, calmly talking about food across the table from him as he bristled with weapons. How did he wear them comfortably?

"In my culture, names have strong meanings." He pulled the curved blade strapped to his arm and cut up the meat he'd been eating earlier into small precise pieces. "They're meant to impart wisdom and advice throughout our lives."

She straightened and tucked her hands onto her lap. This was an interesting conversational change. "There are, or at least used to be, cultures on Earth that believed the same. I've always loved that philosophy. What does yours mean?"

"Mine is a powerful name." His lips were roguishly tipped up at the corner, exposing sharp eye teeth. He settled into his seat, as if preparing to lecture a student. "I am named after one of our past kings. A mighty Chriw'rian who fought valiantly against the *Hissat* or, as you humans call them, the Anunnaki. He's credited with their first defeat on our planet."

She locked her fingers together. "Really?"

He placed the curved knife beside her tray. "For your protein."

Shannon glanced around the room. Surely someone would jump in to stop him from offering her a weapon. When no one did, she picked up the knife and cut up the last bit of food on her plate, a wrinkled sausage link in an off-putting green color. The blade cut smoothly through the dehydrated chunk. "Thank you."

She fingered the metal handle. Smooth and warm in her hand, she tilted the blade far enough to see her reflection on its surface. She wanted to keep it. She placed the knife beside her tray and glanced up as D'lane consumed the last of his jerky.

He pushed his empty tray to the side. "The previous D'lane crashed his warship into the Anunnaki fighter set to bomb our most vulnerable. His actions disrupted the mothership and allowed the rest of the fleet to destroy them. If not for his heroic actions, my planet wouldn't have survived their last attack."

She ate a bite of the sausage and winced. It fought her with every chew. Mouth dry, she discreetly spit it into her napkin. A few brows arched in her direction, including D'lane's. To give herself something to do, she handed the knife back, handle first. He wouldn't have let her keep it anyway. "Have you figured out how your name dictates *your* future?"

"Yes." His fingers brushed hers as he accepted its return. The silver metal blurred when he holstered the blade. This male moved quickly.

She was afraid to ask about his future. She kind of liked this particular alien and didn't want to see him dying any time soon. "And?"

He grinned and flashed his sharp canines. "One belief is I will be a great benefit to my people, but unable to participate in the ultimate victory of my path."

"Does that mean you expect to die?" Shannon asked, undecided on if his smile edged from sexy into frightening.

"It is a possibility."

She picked up her sausage, put it back down, and frowned. "You said one of the meanings. Can you choose another path?"

"There are many possibilities that exist for an individual. The Namegivers do not choose lightly when gifting a child at birth with their destiny. I could follow another D'lane's path, or I could forge my own fate and provide a future for another down the line as the previous D'lane did."

"Which destiny is yours?"

"I follow the path of the king."

"Ah." She ran her finger over the smooth surface of the table. Did that mean he expected to die or was there another path within that destiny he would follow? How did someone know which one to follow?

It had taken her months in college to discover she wasn't interested in chemistry. Six long hellish months. The frustration alone for losing that small bit of time seemed inconsequential when compared to the possibility of traveling an entire lifetime down the wrong path.

He tapped the table. "What does your name mean?"

She huffed, knowing her name meant little when compared to his. She'd looked it up once after an unpleasant conversation with her father. "It means possessor of wisdom."

Her father had wanted to call her Clair after his sister, but her mother had gone with Shannon after hearing it on a show during labor. The uncomfortable conversation on how he'd hated her name had been a slight peek into her mother's past, even as her dad lay drunk on the couch. He'd apologized later, but the damage had already been done. She forced a laugh to lighten the mood. "If you take it to mean I went to school, then I've lived up to the title."

"It is accurate." His nail pressed down on the table's surface. A bit of plastic curled in its wake.

His nails were either extremely durable or the tables were flimsy. Shannon flattened her hand next to her tray and curled her fingers. She scratched at the table and winced as her nail bent back. "How so?"

"You were revived for information that will save billions of lives and stop a war."

Chapter 4

Doctor's notes: Shannon is exhibiting increasing curiosity into the situation around her revival. In my professional opinion, I do not believe she will accept the original explanation provided in the official report. I recommend additional incentives to ensure subject compliance.

Shannon swung her foot back and forth under the floating medical bed she sat on. Unpleasant memories of nerves stabbing like needles deep into her skin as she slowly regained consciousness lurked at the edges of her mind. She slammed her heel on the underside of the bed. The pain snapped her attention outward as Hellen rounded the end of the platform, her lab coat gaping open with every step to expose her silver jumpsuit.

Hellen smiled in greeting. Her teeth were a bright contrast to her tan face in the harsh overhead lights. The unpleasant scent of mint wafted in her wake. "How are you doing today?"

"I'm well?" Shannon's voice cracked. She cleared her throat and tried to ignore the still full box in her mind containing everything she hadn't dealt with since waking in this time. The clinic's sterile white walls were adorned with three more floating beds equally spaced around the circumference of the room. Was this where she'd find out what else she'd lost during her freeze? She shivered. Her hands clenched on the end of the bed. The edge bit into her palm. "I don't know what exactly I should be feeling. I only have you and the limited research on the NAV to gauge otherwise."

"If you've reached this stage of information frustration, you're right on track."

Hellen stopped in front of Shannon. The cobalt Kro-Gen insignia crystal clear on Hellen's jacket pocket. The pointed toe of Shannon's shoes brushed the floor on her next swing. "What other option is there?"

"Some people don't cope well with the thaw and need more intense integration methods."

Hellen pulled a hand length thin tube from the end of the bed. Light glinted off the three prongs at the top. Shannon froze. Fear spiked as it came closer. The three prongs moved like a snake, the heads lurching out for her as they curled and uncurled. Shannon's knuckles whitened. "What the hell is that?"

Hellen held up the device. "This is a medical scanner." She brushed the wall at the head of the platform. The white surface flickered on with medical screens. "I use this scanner in combination with the bed's reading to get an accurate update on your physiology."

Shannon flinched as the scanner halted before her face. A slithering worm of blue light blinded Shannon as Hellen scanned her head. She blinked bright spots from her eyes as Hellen lowered the scanner to her chest before slowly traveled up one arm and starting down the next, it's tentacles writhing all the way. Shannon scrambled for a subject that would pull her attention away from the snake wand. "Where are the other revivalists? I'd like to meet them and ask how they've coped with the time change, maybe join a support group."

The NAV, or really Kro-Gen, had kept that data from her, scuttling her ability to plan for her future at every turn.

"You can't, at least not yet." The scanner lowered to her abdomen. The blue light followed half a second behind. "Kro-Gen goes on complete lockdown during the revival process. Everything, including the orientation and reassociation periods you are experiencing, are for the safety of the patient."

Basically, Shannon was shit out of luck on answers until Kro-Gen decided she could handle it, but who at Kro-Gen decided this? Hellen's wording tugged a mental string. Shannon frowned. "What do you mean by safety? Does this have anything to do with the risk-proofing of my room?"

Hellen sighed and tapped the scanner on her thigh. "Kro-Gen has learned over the years not to overwhelm revivees with too much information so close to waking up."

Shannon snorted. "Aliens and new technology aren't considered overstimulation?"

Hellen met her gaze with a small smile and shrugged. "Yes and no."

"Let's have you lie so the bed can do its thing." Shannon followed the slight pressure Hellen placed on her shoulder to lie back. "Since you've awoke, Kro-Gen has kept you under surveillance."

Shannon tensed. She had guessed that was the case, but having it confirmed still left an unpleasant taste in her mouth. She made a conscious choice to relax. The quicker this physical was over, the better.

"Aside from limiting your access to information, Kro-Gen also keeps outside forces from interacting with your integration. As a rule, no one's allowed to enter or leave the island without special approval during this period."

Shannon nibbled at her lip. Bad actors had previously been limited to people and countries with internet access and the mindset to spread false narratives, but misinformation on an interplanetary scale was a horrifying idea. She had no way to orientate herself within it and determine fact from fiction if she jumped in without a touchstone of truth. Reduced access to an intergalactic internet system suddenly sounded like a great idea, no matter how frustrating she found it.

Shannon's gaze tracked to the wall filled with data from the scanner. She hadn't been a fan of medical dramas, but she did recognize the pulse line in the far right corner, otherwise she had no idea what any of the five sections were monitoring. The middle screen beeped and flashed yellow. Stomach sour, she half-heartedly joked, "So, am I going to live?"

Hellen chuckled as she helped Shannon sit up. "Everything checks out, but I'll need to see you once a week to make sure the more delicate parts of your regeneration remain on track for a full recovery."

Shannon went rigid. "What do you mean? And could you please change the data so I can read it?"

Information was going to be key to her integration in this time. The NAV hadn't indicated there were any general problems associated with the revival process, but in truth she knew nothing about what was happening to her and wasn't sure how much she trusted Kro-Gen to give her the truth.

"Right, sorry. I thought it best not to show you until I completed a full scan. I didn't want you to draw any inaccurate conclusions." Hellen tinkered at the wall. An additional line of text scrawled out under the existing one. Heart rate, blood pressure, weight, and height paraded across the screen. The other windows weren't as easy to understand. Possibly metabolism and brain wave activity?

Hellen moved to the end of the bed and tucked the scanner away. "You are one of the oldest people Kro-Gen has successfully revived."

Shannon sighed. "That's the third time I've heard that."

The repetition possibly indicated a meaning she didn't fully understand, other than perhaps she required more work to effectively recuperate. "How many unsuccessful attempts at reviving someone of my "age" has there been?"

Cryogenics in her time hadn't been anything more than pumping bodies full of antifreeze, chopping off their heads, and storing them in lockers. Unsurprisingly, none of them were ever successful. Although they had started to make progress in hibernation aimed at long term space flight.

"At least three that I can remember." Hellen pressed a finger on the top of the bed. "There may be more, but in school we only focused on the famous ones."

Shannon pinched her arm where her scar from a bike ride used to live, the memory of her father's raised voice lingered in the silence. "Am I in a totally new body?"

"As the presiding expert on reviving the dead—"

Her vision tunneled, ears ringing. How the hell could she keep forgetting she'd died in this process?

"—I want to assure you, your current body holds as many of its working parts as I could keep. I pride myself in going above and beyond the requirements Kro-Gen supplies for a full and thriving regeneration."

Shannon thought her translator might have had a misinterpreted when D'lane spoke earlier, but now… What did that make her, the walking dead? Would she suddenly crave the flesh of her fellow humans? The heart rate machine beeped in warning as it spiked. She took a steadying breath. Chest tight, she held her breath for the count of three and shoved all her fear into the already-cramped mental black box.

She slowly exhaled through her nose, using the breathing technique she'd learned in her youth while she fought for control. She needed to change the refrain. Instead of death, she pictured herself taking a long relaxing and rejuvenating spa vacation at a fancy resort instead of wherever her body had been found. She imagined the soft scent of lavender wafting by as she dipped her toes in a stream. The alarm on the wall stalled. She wrinkled her nose as mint crept back in and overwhelmed everything.

Reality left a sticky residue as another thought punctured her oasis. Her father had taken immunosuppressants after his kidney transplant. The drugs had worked to keep his donated organs alive until others began failing. Unless they'd slipped medication into her meals, she wasn't on any and Hellen had mentioned organ fabrication. She wiped her damp palms on her thighs, the suit absorbing the excess fluid, and asked the most pressing question. "How likely am I to reject regeneration?"

Hellen tugged at the end of her jacket sleeve. "On average, less than two percent."

"But not zero?"

Hellen waved away her concern. "You have nothing to worry about. Your readings are great." She pointed at the data scrolling horizontally in a constant stream of information. The text was black on white with the occasional red and green phrase thrown in, the jargon too quick to get a handle on. "All your biological markers indicate your body has fully accepted the replicated internal structures."

Shannon wet her parched lips and worked up the courage for her next question. "What needed to be repaired?"

Hellen pulled up a generic human figure on the wall. Red and yellow covered the majority of the body with a speck or two of green. "Your initial examination found four broken ribs, fractures at the base of your skull, a shattered ulna, and various soft tissue injuries normal with accepting a body posthumously into our cryogenics program. These were successfully repaired during your first installation in the revival pod. However, several organs failed over the years and had to be replaced when they transferred you here about three hundred years ago."

"Which one of those original injuries was the cause of my death?"

"If I had to hazard a guess, likely a head injury."

Shannon ran her fingers through her hair and rubbed at the back of her head searching for any residual scarring on her smooth skin. There were too many ways to get a head injury in her job. People were always leaving their tools around and trip accidents were high. A fall into a deep enough hole at the dig site would do it. But what could she have been digging for in the icy tundra she kept getting flashbacks of?

"I know you haven't regained all your memories." Hellen gave Shannon's arm a comforting squeeze. "I wouldn't worry too much about it. Even in extreme cases, a revivee's memories returned before the end of their employment period. You should get yours back soon."

She hugged her stomach. "How long was I dead before Kro-Gen retrieved me?"

Hellen closed the screens and the data-filled wall shifted back to white. "The answer might be uncomfortable to hear."

Shannon's breath stilled. Holy shit, this was bad. Had it been decades?

"Kro-Gen policy requires this information be shared only when you are in a mentally sound and comfortable space."

Shannon bit her cheek to remain silent. That meant she wasn't going to get any information now and any outburst would prove she couldn't handle the secrets her file contained. Her foot twitched. She wanted to know what was in them. Were these safety features as universal as Hellen stated, or had an increased watch been put on her and her mental state because of her bodies age? She hated being singled out.

A knock sounded in the hallway. The sound drawing Shannon's attention away from the test in front of her. Her teacher rolled to the door, hands making quick work of the wheels. It creaked open. Scratching pencils stilled. Was it for her father again? Please let someone else's name be called just this once.

Hellen's hand firmly squeezed Shannon's shoulder. Pain spiked. She sucked in a sharp breath. White static obliterated everything as Hellen's thumb pushed into a pressure point. A sharp sting nipped at her neck.

"That should help keep your anxiety down." Hellen slipped the hypodermic syringe into her pocket and gave it a pat. "I can prescribe a couple of doses of it if you continue to have problems."

"Not yet." Shannon rubbed her neck, unsure how she should feel about being dosed with something without her permission.

"It's here if you need it."

The silence stretched. Hellen cleared her throat. "Would you like help filling out the Kro-Gen form to officially release your employee file and artifacts obtained around your death location?"

"Sure." Normally, Shannon would have figured it out herself, but she wanted the information quickly. A grim smile crossed her lips. How many people could say they got to research their own deaths? It was every archeologist's dream. Her boss Steven would have been over the moon. Her smile slipped.

"Were there any other bodies retrieved near mine by Kro-Gen?" If the Kro-Gen paperwork had managed to keep her alive, maybe he had been with her at the time? There wasn't a dig she went on that Steven wasn't in charge of.

"No." Hellen leaned back against the bed across from her. "Kro-Gen processes all viable bodies found on site and yours was the only one noted."

A lump stuck in her throat. Steven had been the father she'd wished for growing up, even after her relationship with her own dad improved, Steven had been the one she leaned on and now there was no one. She had to form new connections all over again. A terrifying task. Cold sank into her bones.

Icy wind bit sharply at her cheeks. Numb fingers wiped the tacky wetness sticking to her lashes. Blinking the snow clear, the sky cut vertically through her vision. Black-booted feet crossed into her field of view.

Motion pulled her outward. The doctor moved closer. Shannon's mouth opened. She blinked. What had she wanted to say? The shot had detached her from her emotions. The black box was now a dark smudge outside of her reach. Did she need it right now?

Sympathy softened Hellen's expression. "Your employee file may have the information you need to help you remember more of your past."

She jerked a nod. Hellen stepped away from the bed and toward the office in the middle of the room. Shannon hopped off the platform. Her knees wobbled, and she braced herself against the bed. What exactly was in the shot Hellen gave her? "Do you know where I can get another towel, and a razor?"

Shannon didn't have a lot of hair, but the light dusting on her legs, and bushier-than-normal hair in other areas, needed to be contained or at least shaped.

Hellen crossed back to the bed and opened a cupboard. She pulled out a black cloth similar to one Shannon had found in her closet. "You were assigned a self-cleaning towel. You can leave it out under the room's lights which allows the nanofiber to deconstruct the organic material accumulated on it or give it a flick." Hellen snapped the towel. "The energy supercharges its coating, and it's instantly clean. Your clothing can be refreshed the same way."

"Thanks." Shannon accepted the extra towel and flipped it over her shoulder. She waited until Hellen turned around to give her own shoulder a sniff.

Shannon's nose wrinkled. Could D'lane smell her body odor during lunch? First thing when she got back in her room, she'd clean this suit and the other two in the closet. "And the razor?"

Hellen's bald head glinted as she shook her head. "Kro-Gen hasn't needed to issue one of those in ages. I doubt we even have one on file for our replicators. I can put a request through for upper management to approve the acquisition of one, but I won't be able to replicate one until Kro-Gen ratifies your status."

Shannon's brow arched. What else was off-limits until Kro-Gen gave her the all clear? She was surprised they gave her the second towel. She mimicked Hellen's relaxed lounge against the bed. "Can I ask you a question?"

"Sure."

She fiddled with the fringe of the absorbent cloth. "Why do you have eyebrows?"

Not something she would normally ask, but the medicine made it easier. Out of all the people she'd passed in the hall and seen in the mess, few had eyebrows as thick as Hellen's, and hers were delicate when compared to Shannon's own thick bushes.

The doctor quirked one in response. "The facial hair does a great job of redirecting water away from our eyes. With all our technological gains, there was a time when people questioned if the brows remained as a benefit to our genetic tree. I either have a 'naturalist' in my familial past who decided to keep them, or they remain through a quirk of genetics."

Shannon crossed her ankles. "How long have humans been genetically modifying themselves?"

"For a few decades after society stabilized, it was

socially acceptable to tweak genes to a certain extent. We thought we were speeding up evolution. People altered their bodies by removing body hair and axilla sweat glands, among other things. Eventually the modifications became so commonplace there were chop shops on every corner peddling their editing techniques."

"Everything came to a head when corporations outlawed the modification practice in general. Earth's evolutionary groups argued that by stopping the gene editing we were reducing human evolution to a snail's pace." Hellen rubbed at her ear, the top of which ended in a soft point. "The modifications were not without their problems. I won't bore you with the details, as we've since removed those unpleasant mishaps. And in most cases, the practice of gene editing is still illegal, except in specifically League-approved instances."

"Do you agree the tampering should have stopped?" Shannon recalled the tech developer who had injected himself with trial gene-editing medication and had died months later as a result. But doctors had also managed to find a cure sickle cell anemia and AIDs.

Hellen straightened and tidied her jacket. "I do wonder what evolutionary gains we might have lost as a population since we've stopped. However, that's a conversation for another time, and over a drink."

Shannon rubbed her forehead as frustration gnawed at her. She kept circling back to the NAV's *ERROR* message every time she searched for more information on any topic not approved by the group that requested her revival in the first place. Was it this League that she'd worked for or Kro-Gen?

A tall man stood in front of her, dark glasses shielding his eyes, hand held out in greeting. Steven stood, palms braced on the other side of his desk, refusing to meet her gaze. What exactly was going on here? The man's handshake verged on painful. So at odds with the beautifully embroidered Krogenic's on his dark jacket.

Her lashes fluttered. She dug her nail into her arm and focused on the pressure as her temples throbbed. Why did she keep seeing that man and was he important? "Who or what is the League?"

Hellen's shoulders rose in a shrug. "They're the group tasked with directing the path of Kro-Gen and the sanctioned revival, orientation, and job placement for all revivees."

"I see." Shannon focused on the wall over Hellen's shoulder, disturbed by the idea she would still be unresponsive and frozen in a silver coffin they used to keep everyone in stasis until someone had decided it was important enough to revive her. That idea was terrifying, no matter how eloquently the Kro-Gen information video had stated it.

"Without them," Hellen continued, "I wouldn't have a job and you would still be frozen. So, don't think too badly about them."

Shannon pulled the towel off her shoulder and held it bundled against her stomach. "What exactly am I supposed to do until I speak to the League?"

"Rest. Your body won't be at full strength for at least a couple more weeks." Hellen turned off the last of the computer systems still running on the bed. "I'd recommend eating regular meals and adding light exercise to your routine for the next week or so. Then you can return to your normal regime."

Normal? Shannon laughed. The sharp bite of

bitterness stuck in her throat. "D'lane says I was revived to stop a war."

A heavy silence settled between them.

"When the time comes," Hellen shoved her hands into her pockets, "try to answer all their questions."

What would happen to her if she couldn't?

Chapter 5

Kro-Gen Cryogenics Lab Memo: Per League request to cut costs by 5%, no new cryogenic chambers will be purchased. All techs are required to supply five chamber IDs holding employees with limited financial gain to Kro-Gen. Once approved, selected canisters will be purged for new inhabitants.

Desperate for freedom and color—damn, she was exhausted of endless variations of white and gray—Shannon fled the clinic in search of the outdoors. A handful of wrong turns later, she slowed as she neared another bend in the hall. The smart thing would have been to check a map before heading off in a direction she'd assumed was correct, but it was too late now.

She tapped her thigh as she took the corner. How lost could someone get on an island? Kro-Gen could likely find her through the hidden cameras they had set up in the halls if she was gone from her room for too long.

She walked past an open door.

The sound of flesh meeting floor echoed around her. Intrigued, she pivoted and peeked through the doorway. Her breath caught.

D'lane, stripped down to his pants, sparred in hand-to-hand combat with a dark-haired member of his species. Their movements were quick and dangerous. Two other Chriw'rians stood to the side of the mat-covered floor, tails idly flicking at their feet. An enormous pile of weapons sat near the far wall. Where they all D'lane's?

Drawn to the action and the naked expanse of D'lane's well-muscled chest, she ventured farther inside. Sweat glistened on his exposed skin. A few discolored scars marred the sandy muscled surface. Golden eyes met hers. He grunted as he failed to block a kick to the knee. He broke her gaze and turned back to his sparring partner. Tails, fists, and teeth flashed as the pair tried to beat the shit out of each other.

D'lane's fist slammed into the side of a more delicate face. Their block of the swing a half a second too late. They went down. Hard. D'lane hadn't landed a gentle tap.

D'lane dropped to his knee and went in for a mock-killing blow. His tail raised for balance drew her gaze to the juncture of his hips and she questioned how it attached to the top of his backside.

Her hand twitched. She could almost feel the warm flesh of his back as she mentally ran her fingertips up his spine. Her fists clenched. The desire to discover how different their skin textures were fought with her need to understand who she was in this time.

Her attraction to D'lane didn't feel wrong. The emotion was honest and true in a way nothing else could be. It was something that came from deep inside herself and wasn't influenced by Kro-Gen or being held to a ledger by the League.

D'lane's tufted ear rotated, followed by the rest of his glorious body as he shifted his focus on her. He stood.

Heat crawled up her neck as she dragged her gaze up from hip level to meet his gaze. "Hello."

A gray eyed Chriw'rian, an inch shorter than D'lane, helped the groaning Chriw'rian off the floor while another with curly hair took a wary stance behind D'lane, arms crossed over a black clothbound chest. Shannon fought to keep her hands still. There were so many tails in this room. She struggled to keep her gaze up from their twitching tips. The group confirmed what Shannon had learned on the NAV; that Chriw'rian's diversity mimicked humans from her time.

Shannon tensed as D'lane stalked toward her, both turned on and afraid by his primal display. Should she not have interrupted?

She dropped her gaze and stared at his chest. An oval, off-color scar sat near the waistband of his low strung pants, right where a human's belly button would be. Narrow hips arrowed down to cup the hardening shape of him. His energy was a gravitational pull that pooled low in her belly. He stopped a hands breath away.

His tail flicked between his braced feet. "Was there something I could help you with?"

Flustered, she jerked her gaze up. "I, ah, was planning on stepping outside when I stumbled upon you. Figured I'd say hi to one of the few people I know."

"I see." He searched her gaze, his expression unreadable.

She suspected he knew she was lost. Perhaps her fidgeting gave it away?

His rested his hands on his hips, drawing her attention to the thickly corded muscles of his forearms. Even without his weapons, he flustered her on an instinctual level.

A warm hint of sweaty male and the sweet scent of dates washed over her as the air moved around them. She wet her lips, practically tasting the salt glistening on his skin. Her nipples peaked. She crossed her arms over her chest, uncertain if the jumpsuit would hide the pointed tips. No way was she going to let him see how she reacted to him, especially since she had no idea what to do about it.

A grunt, and the slap of flesh meeting mat caused D'lane to turn.

She focused on the rolling ball of fists and legs sliding across the floor. The ball slammed into the wall. Grunting, D'lane shook his head and motioned for her to join him at the pile of tangled alien bodies.

"Let me introduce you to some of my crew." He indicated the sleek dark-haired Chriw'rian leaning against the wall he had downed earlier, no worse for wear. "That's J'rax. They run engineering on my ship. T'rev is the male currently picking himself off the floor after losing his sparring match with our medic and resident cook, V'ren."

V'ren laughed, hair curlier than Shannon's own tucked neatly behind their ears. "He still hasn't learned to duck properly. Hi there." V'ren offered a hand. "I prefer she/her pronouns and it is nice to meet you."

"Nice to meet you too." Shannon clasped V'ren's offered forearm in a brief shake. "I'm she/her as well."

V'ren leaned in, the light smattering of freckles dusting her forehead and continuing down the sides of her face bright against her flushed skin. "Don't let D'lane give you too much trouble."

V'ren's gray eyes twinkled as she straightened and headed over to the pile of weapons and armed herself.

T'rev remained where he stood as his green gaze pinned her in place. He bowed with his fist pressed to the open palm of his opposite hand as they met at the center of his chest.

Her own palm met her hand as she returned the bow. D'lane had introduced her to this bow the first day she'd been revived. It was a traditional Chriw'rian bow she'd watched on repeat in her room until she felt comfortable returning it.

T'rev straightened and Shannon followed suit. D'lane arched a brow, and a smile tugged at the corner of his lips. She thought he approved of her response. T'rev went to retrieve his own armament.

Shannon approached the short-haired J'rax to deliver a similar handshake to the ones she'd received from V'ren. The Chriw'rian stepped out of reach and bowed. Shannon hastily reciprocated. What rules had Shannon missed in her studies that would explain when to bow and when not to? As Shannon straightened, J'rax's bright blue eyes fixed on her. "So, the ancient human ventures forth."

Shannon brushed imaginary lint from her jumpsuit, unsure if she should take offense to the blunt statement. "Why wouldn't I?"

"I've never met one before." J'rax's head tipped to the side as they checked out Shannon's body. "I'm surprised you have hair like us, not like those baldheaded Kro-Gen employees."

Shannon shifted her weight and reached for a curl. The statement not wrong in its accuracy.

"J'rax…" D'lane's tone carried rebuke as he stepped closer to Shannon. "As a representative of My'len, you must show respect to our allies."

J'rax glanced at their wrist. A slim white bracelet lit up to display a message. With a smirk, J'rax gave a short, flourished bow to D'lane. "I must return to the ship, my captain. Perhaps you can lecture me on protocol another time."

D'lane growled. The sound was both stimulating and frightening as her skin pebbled. She rubbed the back of her neck as J'rax laughed and headed over to the shrinking pile of guns. The crew saluted D'lane as they left. Now only she and D'lane remained in the room.

Shannon fished for something to say. She didn't want to leave just yet. The closeness of community between D'lane and his crew was something she was starting to crave. "I hope I didn't offend J'rax with my offer of a handshake."

"I doubt it." His tail swished at his feet. "J'rax and T'rev haven't had as much exposure to alien cultures outside of my home world of Chriw'r. They aren't comfortable providing a more universal handshake greeting."

Shannon wandered over to the mat. She pressed down with the tip of her shoe. The material begrudgingly dented under her weight. No wonder they'd hit the ground so hard. "Is there a way to know when to give a bow or handshake so I don't mess up again in the future?"

"You can either wait for them to initiate a greeting or default to the bow." D'lane came to stand beside her, his physical presence so much larger when he was shirtless. She recognized he outweighed her by quite a bit. Even V'ren, the smallest of the group, had still been a head taller than her.

D'lane rested his hands on his hips. His tail flicked back and forth at his feet. "How was the exam?"

She tucked her hands behind her back as the urge to

touch him became a compulsion. "How does one react to the knowledge that your organs could start failing at any moment and that they won't let you near anything dangerous any time soon?"

Silence stretched to a tension so tight she could reach out and twang it. She shifted her foot off the mat. She needed to leave before she blurted out something weird, like asking whether his tail was prehensile. The limb in question tapped against her booted ankle. Did he want her attention?

They both stared straight across the dark blue mat until D'lane cleared his throat. "Do you miss your old time?"

She huffed. Mentally flickering through one response to the next. How in the hell was she supposed to explain everything she'd lost? "I miss the mundanity of driving to work every day and dealing with city traffic. I miss being able to understand what was happening around me and calling up my friends and family to chat." She clenched her trembling fingers. "Most of all, I miss my goddamn cat."

Hopefully someone had taken care of Kiki when she hadn't returned. She still felt the phantom weight of her orange furball at the end of her bed every night when she fell asleep.

Shannon ran a hand down her cheek before dropping it to her side and peeked at D'lane. Had she unintentionally insulted him? Did humans still have house cats? Had he seen one? Or worse, did he think that it looked like his species?

She took a deep breath and held it for a few seconds. D'lane kept his attention forward, likely waiting for her to continue. She slowly breathed out. He hadn't taken offense. "It's not like I can go back."

"You can talk to me if you have a need."

Her heart fluttered. She had hoped the bond building between them would result in a friendship of sorts, and his response confirmed he felt the same. "Thank you."

He gave a sharp nod as his tail wrapped around her ankle. The weight heavy and warm through her jumpsuit. "Has the transition been a hard?"

She laughed unsure what to do about his fifth limb. "Can't say. I've only done it once."

She tucked a stray curl behind her ear and reminded herself to ask for a headband or hair tie—at least until she was allowed access to scissors. "I'd hardly call what I'm doing a transition. I haven't even been awake for a week and I'm still dealing with the time shock." Her gaze lingered over his tufted ear and sharp jaw line. "And aliens."

He laughed, and a smile lingered, one she took as an invitation to continue. "The hard part is how different this place is. Outside of my room, which is more advanced than I'm used to, nothing is familiar. The food is different, the clothing is weird but comfortable, and the other humans don't look like me. You and your crew, even with the tails and tuft pointed ears, are more comforting for me to be around."

It might have something to do with D'lane's desirable body, sexy walk, and the partial hug his tail still gave her. Or perhaps how his bare chest called her to run a finger down the center until she hit his black pants. She rubbed the side of her nose wondering why her attraction to D'lane didn't bother her as much as she expected.

D'lane turned toward her. "Through My'len, I have been on missions where I was the only Chriw'rian."

"It's not the same." She crossed her arms and stared at the center of his chest. Small hairs laid in intricate lines all over his skin, similar to what Blaschko's lines on humans looked like under UV light. "You have an entire planet to return to and can reach out and talk to anyone who has lived your shared experience. I can't even do that, at least not yet."

If she was one of the oldest humans Kro-Gen has revived, she likely didn't have anything in common with the other revived. She pressed her arms hard into her stomach. The almost hug felt nice even if she gave it to herself.

His voice, when it came, was harsh and rushed out like an order. "You will create a new home."

She glared. "Are you commanding me to get over myself?"

He nodded.

"Unbelievable." Anger spiked. Trembling, she spun on her heel and headed toward the door. "Of all the ridiculous things to say."

He moved to block her path. She stalled mid-step. His ears flicked forward as he stared. How the hell had he gotten there so quickly?

She stepped to the side to go around; he mirrored her move. Her jaw clenched. "Get out of my way."

"I apologize if I offended you. That was not my intention." His gaze dropped to her ankles as he frowned. "You're hard to read without a tail. I don't know if what I've said will upset you until you respond."

She propped her hands on her hips and tapped her foot. Like him, she floundered at reading his body language. His flexible ears and extra limb threw a whole new set of body posture into play.

Her foot stilled. Despite her frustration, she wasn't ready to be alone. She craved the extended interactions between them and would need to learn quickly to move past any frustration from cultural and physical differences if she wanted to stay friends with this male. She rocked back on her heels and fished for something to say. "Do all Chriw'rian's know martial arts?"

"Only those deployed off planet." D'lane nodded at the mat. "Do you spar?"

"No. I've never had the time."

He shot her a hesitant glance. "I can teach you, if you'd like?"

She played with the collar of her jumpsuit, and it slid open an inch. Her stomach clenched. The thought of any of Kro-Gen's repairs reversing, even after Hellen's assurances that everything had taken, had her second guessing and playful interactions. "I'll need to get approval from Hellen before we start anything physical."

"That would be a great idea." D'lane stepped to the side as he prepared to move away.

Panic tightened her chest at the thought of his leaving. She stared at the expanse of naked skin in front of her, unable to deny herself the pleasure of possibly touching him and being touched by him in return. She dampened her lips. "Maybe you could show me a few defensive moves? Something that doesn't involve contact? I'm sure Hellen would be okay with that."

D'lane strode to the mat, his feet sinking an inch into the padding. Her spirits fell. She stayed only to selfishly watch him arm himself, but he paused in the center, and he pivoted to face her. Her arms dropped to her sides as he gestured for her to join him. She didn't hide the joy tilting her lips. The mat barely gave under her feet as she walked to where he indicated and stopped an arms-length away.

"There are twenty-six basic forms of defense taught to all students at My'len. Everything after is based on variations and combinations of these moves. I will show you the first three I learned at the beginning of my training."

Her hands fidgeted at her sides. "How old were you when you started?"

His smirk revealed a bit of side fang. "Old enough. Now pay attention."

He shifted into a more alert stance. "You want the weight of your body centered toward the balls of your feet, stand with your heels shoulder width apart. Your tail..." He cleared his throat and glanced at her hips. "We'll focus on body posture instead."

Her spine tingled as if in complaint of its missing limb. "How much help does your tail provide?"

The tip flicked about his ankles before settling. "It provides a counterbalance and stabilizes my center of gravity. We may need to adapt some positions to fit your smaller pivot point."

"Let's deal with that later. Now, about these three moves." She mimicked his stance, bending her elbows, hands spread out to either side.

He circled, the scent of desert and dates whispering past as he modified her body position one small touch at a time. Fire ignited and heat built with every physical interaction until her body sang with each brush of his warmth. She could move in any direction without effort, but she only wanted to move in one. She fought the urge to step back until she pressed against his front. Nothing indicated he would reciprocate her advances, and she didn't want to ruin the relationship they were building.

"You are currently in position one. Feel the balance of it in your bones. Use your mind and muscles to memorize this stance. This position links all the others together."

At D'lane's request, she straightened and stepped out of the stance, returning to it time and again until D'lane no longer had to shift her body into the form he wanted. She contemplated raising a shoulder or dropping an arm so he'd touch her again, but refrained.

The second move involved a quick sidestep to evade a hit or grab. A seamless slide from one place to the next and required an awareness of the body moving toward you. In essence, it was a quick shift to return to the first position. The light sweat she had worked up doing those two simple moves cemented how much stamina she'd lost during her revival. Before, she could do her morning jog without getting out of breath. Now here she was, not even ten minutes into a lesson, and already panting.

"The last move is one you cannot practice on your own but will prep you for your next lesson."

Using her forearm, she wiped the sweat off her forehead. "Okay, what is it?"

"A fall. Knowing how to relax when you are taken down reduces injury to your body. The first throw will be quick, to remove anxiety."

He came up behind her and she fought a shiver at the warm heat of him. "Should I stand in first position?"

"No." The air brushed her neck as he moved.

"I don't think this is a good—"

Her feet went out from under her. Air grunted from her lungs as she slammed into the ground.

Thick clothing hindered her movements as a

screaming cold wind bit at her face. She shifted on the ice as a rock bit sharply into her back. Muffled grunts flashed feet from her too quickly for her to catch. Adrenaline punched through her. Would he come for her next?

She blinked as D'lane came into focus above her, the icy tundra nowhere to be found. She shuddered as fear settled deep, wishing these memories would never come back.

Chapter 6

Kro-Gen Internal Memo: Management has determined the sooner the asset is away from Earth, the better. Please expedite mission and provide full support.

Shannon dug her fingers into her hair, ready to pull every strand out with her bare hands. Why couldn't she remember more from her earlier flashback?

She paced the length of her bedroom floor and tore apart what little she'd remembered during her sparring session with D'lane with a frustrating lack of progress. She did not know how her last clear memory of arguing with her boss back in St. Louis turned into dying on the arctic tundra.

The information provided by Kro-Gen had been carefully blank on what revivees were meant to do after they'd been re-awakened, or how they transferred from this facility to the external world. What would happen to her once she met with the League? Chest tight, she struggled for air. Would the League leave her to rot until they needed her again? Darkness crept into the corners of her vision.

The door chimed. Slowly she turned to stare at the seamless wall. She sucked in a sharp breath as her heartbeat calmed. Who would be visiting her now?

The access request chimed again. She tugged her sleeves straight and took a mental gamble on it being Hellen at the door. She wasn't quite ready to deal with

D'lane yet, not after their last physical interaction. It took her a moment to find the correct hand placement and open the door.

D'lane, armed and stony faced, stood framed in the entryway. Backlit, his silhouette was broken by the occasional weapons handle, screamed strength and virality. His gold eyes gleamed as they surveyed the room. Tufted ears swiveled. His nostrils flared as his tail twitched erratically at his feet. Dressed in black, the My'len insignia bright grey on his chest, he looked ready for action.

More than a little turned on, she asked, "What is it?"

He stepped into her room, sharp tension following in his wake. Her lips twitched as the door snicked closed. She wanted to pet the tension out of his frame. Would he let her?

"We need to leave."

Shannon arched a brow. "Not the response I was expecting."

She didn't know what she expected of him, but not the need to leave. Maybe some more one-on-one time sparring with additional skin contact?

He scanned the space as his tail stilled. "Grab anything you value and let's go."

Apprehension tightened her back as she glanced at her bare walls, made bed, and empty cup she'd failed to put away on her desk.

No stranger to fleeing homes in her youth, she wanted to ask why, but understood time was of the essence. She pushed aside the spike of anger at her father and the chaotic life she had when she was younger, shoving the memories back into her mental black box, and focused on whatever the hell this fresh problem was.

She glanced down and wiggled her toes in her shoes and debated what to do. The question was if she trusted him. If he thought they needed to leave now, then she'd do so. Her gut said yes, and it hadn't led her wrong before. She squared her shoulders and met his gaze. "Let's go."

The door chimed and D'lane grimaced, sharp canines exposed as his expression tightened. He fingered the knife strapped to his thigh, the tick a nervous one she'd caught him doing before. "Forget what I said." He stepped closer, tail twitching erratically between his feet as he grasped her shoulders. The warm weight of his hands was comforting as one of his ears rotated toward the door. "If you have any feelings toward me, do not mention my lapse of judgement."

Shannon touched her throat, soothing a small wrinkle in her collar. She needed a moment to center herself. She closed her eyes. Encased in darkness, she had to rely on her other senses and mental state. She wasn't sure what she felt for him. She knew she was attracted to him, but he was so different from everything she'd ever known. His culture and strength had been poured into a body and mind that drew her in.

His warm fingers wrapped around hers and squeezed. She struggled not to read too much into his actions, but her mind kept whispering he was going to kiss her, and she didn't want to stop him. He pulled her closer. She shivered. It was going to happen. She dragged in a deep breath filled with his rich scent. His nails caught on her shirt. She stepped forward. Her chin tipped up as she pressed against his firm chest. No press of lips greeted hers. Her lashes fluttered and her heart sank. He wasn't going to kiss her.

She opened her eyes, pulled into his golden gaze as a soft brush of a tail whispered over her suit leg. They might not be friends, but if he trusted her to keep what he said close, that had to mean something. Warmth spread in her chest. "I won't say a word."

He stepped back and bowed. One she hadn't been given before. His elegant neck arched to the side, exposing a long smooth line of skin. The move was quick and yet remained seared in her mind as he straightened. She'd only seen that bow in her research on D'lane's culture regarding courtship. Her cheeks warmed. It was all the confirmation she needed that he wanted her too.

His golden gaze held hers. "You have my gratitude."

Heartbeat pounding in excitement, she returned the bow.

"No." His nails bit into her shoulder as he stopped her.

She gasped. Pain dug deep. His sharp rejection was disorientating and devastating. Apparently, she had misunderstood his customs again. The one where he'd initiated a deeper emotional relationship. She jerked away from him and stared at the wall. The door chimed again. She refused to show how much his denial hurt her.

Shannon straightened and kept her gaze averted as she walked past him toward the door. She swiped at the irritating sting in her eyes.

"Shannon—"

"Nothing I ever do is right." She bit her lip and gave her head a hard shake. She needed more time to work out her feelings before dealing with D'lane again.

"You don't understand."

Shannon laughed. The sound bitter and harsh in her chest. "You're right. I don't."

77

She slapped the door open. Her palm stung, but the pain was nowhere near as deep as his rejection. The door opened. A pair of silver clad guards stood rigidly on the other side.

Compared to D'lane, the unarmed guards presented an ominous front. Their stiff demeanor and bulkier build stressed the seams of their jumpsuits. D'lane growled behind her. Were they why D'lane had changed his mind?

"Troy-023." The guard on the right spoke, "You've been called before General Fernández and the League."

Chest tight, her mind raced with the biggest question centered around the guards. Paranoia, a long-armed coping mechanism from her youth flared. Why were there two of them? Was the League worried she would run? She bit back a snort. She had nowhere to go even if she could, although—she cast a sidelong glance at D'lane beside her—perhaps she did. All things aside, he *had* wanted her to go with him.

She glanced between the guards. "I thought I had more time?"

D'lane gave a subtle shake of his head. Her anger at him fizzled out. This was what he'd been trying to spirit her away from. She didn't understand why. She frowned at the guards when they didn't respond. D'lane's warm hand settled at the small of her back and moved her out into the hall.

Her life from before wasn't what the League wanted. Who the hell cared about twenty-first century sciences and digging techniques? Not when life had advanced so much since she died. No, they wanted information seated deep in the black hole of her death, out on a frozen tundra where her boss fought for his life.

She'd have to delve into her mental black box and dig through emotions she wasn't ready to deal with yet to give them what they wanted.

Apprehension tightened her nerves as her door closed. She truly had nowhere to hide. Shannon crossed her arms. Hidden from view, her nails dug into her palms. She needed to tackle this obstacle head on to get a handle on the situation. History had taught her that no one wanted to deal with emotional outbursts, especially vulnerable ones.

Fighting for a nonchalance she didn't feel, Shannon stalked behind the shorter guard as they led her to an area of the compound she'd never ventured into. The warm heat of D'lane at her back and the occasional jingle of him fidgeting with his knives grounded her in the sea of white.

The walk was both incredibly long and blindingly short. They passed no one else in the hall either because no one lived or worked in the area, or the rest of the population knew to steer clear of the League and this general. The lead stopped short. Only D'lane's firm grasp on her shoulder kept her from running into the guard.

She briefly rested fingers atop his. "Thank you."

His touch slipped away as he retreated. "We've arrived."

The shorter guard palmed open a door. The room beyond was dimly lit. A lone light shone on a chair in the center of the room. Darkness ate at the corners. The guards were silent sentinels to the gaping entrance of doom. She drummed her fingers on her thigh. She couldn't escape this. Breathing out, she straightened her shoulders and stepped through.

A commotion started behind her. The guards barred D'lane from entering. "You are not allowed past this point without express approval."

Growling, D'lane loomed over them. "She is part of my team."

The guards remained in place. "The order stands."

D'lane made eye contact over their shoulders. "I will wait for you."

The door closed, and she was alone.

She turned back to the room as ready as she'd ever be to face what was coming. An oblong, curved table cut the space in half. Four empty chairs were equally spaced on the far side. The single seat she saw earlier sat ominously in the center of the half-circle the table created.

She rubbed warmth back into her chilled hands, disturbed by the entire situation. She headed toward the lone chair and rested her hand on the back. Her fingernails scraped against the hard plastic.

She rotated the chair side to side. What would happen to her if she couldn't give Kro-Gen what they wanted? Would they freeze her again, or cut her loose? Or worse, what if she *did have* what they needed?

Unease tugged at her nerves. She rolled her shoulders and shook out the tension in her fingers. Whatever happened in here would determine her future and there was nothing she could do to prepare for it other than explore the curved desk.

No name tags or visible identification marked who sat where. The chairs were white, plush, and conformed around her when she sat. Shannon brushed a finger across the tabletop. A glowing blue handprint illuminated the underside of the surface as if awaiting a command. She tapped the glass table, the handprint flashed red.

She raised her hand. Nope. She wasn't going to set off any alarms, not today. She sat back in her chair and contemplated changing it out for one of the nicer ones, but it was bolted to the floor.

The door behind the table opened. She froze and her heartbeat exploded. This was it. She clambered to her feet and escaped to the front of the table.

Three older humans entered wearing copper jumpsuits, taking up the seats on the left, which left the far right seat empty. One face held hints of eyebrows. Silver stylized upside-down V's rested on their right breast, similar to the Greek capital lambda. And then a brown-haired human entered.

Shannon's breath caught, and she dropped into the plastic chair. The mop of light brown hair hazardously styled brushed the top of their olive gray shirt and pants that hinted at more of a military cut than the shiny suits most humans wore. They took the last seat at the table without looking at her. Their sleeves were pulled back to reveal the start of a tattoo on the forearm as their palm pressed against the table. The screen lit up, and they swiped through the windows.

Shannon's fingers clenched on the arms of the chair. Who was this brown-haired person?

At the table's apex, the bald human's fingers danced over the glass. The surface's edge lit up in a brief flash. Sharp blue eyes landed on Shannon, and they stood. Shannon swallowed the phlegm stuck in her throat. The meeting had officially started.

"I am Ash, currently she/her. I've been charged with leading this review panel." She spread her arms out.

"And we three are representatives of the League, charged with monitoring and reviving cryogenic assets across the globe." She hesitated, a slight grimace tilting her lips as she gestured to the last human at the end of the table. "General Fernández is here at the request of the Global Council. He's meant to be an impartial judge of your character."

Shannon shifted in the suddenly uncomfortable chair, terrified to ask the question bubbling within her. "Am I an asset?"

"Yes." Ash said, retaking her seat. "Kro-Gen maintained your body at the League's request. As you can imagine, the maintenance and upkeep of your body and cryo-chamber has naturally incurred a hefty cost."

Shannon flinched.

"Everything from your body's retrieval and maintenance to the clothes you're wearing, and the water you drank at your last meal, have been tallied and tracked over the centuries." Her bald head glinted in the light as she leaned back. "I'm sure you can appreciate this isn't an easy or cheap operation to manage."

Shannon's fingernails bit into her thighs through the thin fabric of her jumpsuit. Anxiety battled with panic. "How much debt did I *accumulate* while at your disposal?"

The room grew silent.

The general cleared his throat, drawing her attention from the glowering League member. "Seeing as you have no grasp of today's currency you wouldn't understand the amount even if they were to supply it."

She needed more information. Any shred of control she could grasp would give her options, and small choices inevitably lead to control of larger ones. At least that methodology had in the past. "How can I be held accountable for something I don't remember agreeing to?"

A tight-lipped smile lingered on the general's lips. "Kro-Gen includes a caveat in their contracts for retaining any knowledge they may need at a later date." He glanced at the League, "It's often a surprise to all of us."

She lifted a fork filled with silky lo mein and pointed the white plastic at Steven as she said, "It's not worth it to remove a single line from the contract, especially if we need to leave in a week."

She ground the sharp point of her elbow into her thigh. The sharp stab of pain brought her back to the present.

"To help you understand the precariousness of your situation," Ash said as her fingers danced over the table, and the wall beside Shannon shimmered with information. "We've translated your debt into the years required to work them off and based on the average salary and cost-of-living expenses, you'll find we've estimated the total of your debts would be paid off in 130 years. As a curtesy, we'll additionally reduce your outstanding balance to allot you a retirement package for the last 10 years of your life and all mandatory holiday pay."

Shannon straightened as panic began to set in. How long did they expect her to live? This setup sounded suspiciously like indentured servitude.

"Which puts you at around ninety-five years to work off your debt."

The general's chair squeaked as he resettled his weight. "As I'm sure Ash was about to enlighten you before jumping right into the interrogation, the League evaluates the value of the information you'll provide and may reduce the duration of time required to pay off your debt." He leaned forward. "I would advise against embellishment to increase the apparent worth of your answers. The penalty for each untruth is a year added to your service."

Ash leaned back in her chair. "These policies were put in place to protect both your independence and the League's ability to recoup its losses. As a part of this procedure, your vitals are being displayed on the table in front of us. We'll be notified when you utter a lie."

The general tapped the table, turning to face Shannon. Their intense hazel gaze met hers. "Do you require a demonstration of the mechanism?"

"No." Shannon needed no additional proof of her lack of control over the situation.

Ash's lips flattened. "You will stay seated during this entire meeting. Removing yourself from the seat will add five years to your service."

She gingerly straightened on the uncomfortable device masquerading as a chair—Why couldn't it be as soft as the med bay beds?—and waited for her first question.

Ash leaned forward, "We believe you have knowledge about the start of the last Anunnaki war."

"I thought the attack was the result of random intergalactic chance?" Or at least that's what Kro-Gen's NAV perpetuated as Shannon read up on it. Perhaps it wasn't. Why else would the first thing they ask about be how the attack occurred? Shannon gripped the armrests, hard plastic biting into her palms. "You think it was planned?"

"Two years will be added to your sentence for each evasion." Ash's voice echoed harshly. "This is your only warning."

"I wasn't evading, merely attempting to better understand the situation. Besides, a question hadn't actually been asked." Shannon shivered as the cold from the room seeped into her bones. She couldn't see the online world *not* exploding during an alien attack. "Wouldn't the internet have most of the information you need on the first Anunnaki attack?"

"We lost vital information during the War of Resurrection. However, it is rumored that we had no clue as to how the technology existed to call them to Earth for the harvest even before the war. This is just one of the many reasons why the League decided to maintain your body in stasis over the centuries."

The general drummed his fingers on the table and swung his hazel gaze toward Shannon. "Our history is convoluted, but we've always known the location of the beacon that summoned the Anunnaki to Earth."

Shannon froze as she searched each person across from her. Her mind scrambled to connect the dots.

"You were revived because of your proximity to the signal." The general swiped his hand across the table. The wall beside her lit up with information. Shannon refused to look at it.

"We know you saw the Anunnaki being called to Earth. The question is how much involvement you had in initiating the attack."

Shannon's vision blurred. Her heart rate spiked. Sweat seeped from her at a rate too quick for her jumpsuit to cope with. Shannon slammed open her mental black box and shoved every emotion she had into it. How could they think that she had anything to do with the attack on Earth that killed billions? She wanted to toss the box into the far reaches of her mind, but she needed it close if she was going to argue her case of non-involvement. But a thought still lingered—had she played some part in it?

Kro-Gen had sponsored the expedition that had killed her. The contract she and Steven argued about, the trek into frozen tundra…

Heat burned her cheek as it throbbed. The painful bite of ice against her bare face added to the pain. She clenched frozen fingers. A man dressed in black slammed Steven into the ice a few feet from her sprawled boots. Black metal glinted.

She blinked rapidly as the room came back into focus. The painful memory settled deep in her chest as she struggled to put together the sequence of events leading to her death. The hawkish gleam in Ash's eyes along with the apt attention of the rest of the silent League on her vitals splashed on the wall weren't helping her focus.

What did they want from her that they didn't already know? They had her file, it was plastered all over every available surface, they had to know how Kro-Gen played a part in her death and was likely involved in initiating the attack.

She shifted slightly in the chair, struggling to get comfortable in a device meant to share all her secrets. "I've gotten glimpses of someone with Krogenic's stamped across his shirt on the tundra."

"The League is aware of the Kro-Gen employee that accompanied you on your dig." Ash sat back in her chair. "They were there to provide protection and assistance while you were searching for the artifact."

Shannon had a hard time calling her memories with the Kro-Gen employee beneficial. "Why question me now if you have all the answers? If the League needs the missing bits of knowledge my mind holds, you'll need to reschedule this meeting until I have all my memories back."

"We can't wait." The general answered as the group across from her shifted in their seats. "We believe another attack is imminent."

Her vision tunneled until all that remained was the flash of the League's silver insignia on Ash's suit. Chest tight, she ruthlessly fought for focus. "Why would someone direct the Anunnaki to attack Earth now?"

"Our answer may lie in the past." The older human on the far left leaned forward, the shadows deepening the grooves in her cheeks. "Hijacked Anunnaki transmissions during the war confirmed they'd been summoned."

Well, fuck.

The older human tapped on the table. "We need to know if the beacon used to call them had been left behind from one of their previous attacks...or if we have a whole new communication system to worry about."

Shannon's mind circled back to the man on the tundra intent on killing Steven. Why had they been fighting? Had they found what Krogenic's had paid them to search for?

Ash leaned forward as her voice cut through the silence. "We have reason to believe they are planning on destroying more than just Earth."

Shannon's mouth dried. How many people, or beings, would die in this galactic attack? How could anyone ever stop a war set to destroy everything? Did they really believe she had the information needed to stop the Anunnaki from harvesting again?

"You were alive before the war started," Ash stated.

She straightened. "I don't remember aliens attacking."

But the flashes of danger in the tundra had her second guessing herself. If she'd lost the memory of her death, what else had she forgotten. Slivers of memory bubbled out of rock-hard ground, and the loud thunk of shovel hitting ice.

The general asked, "What *do* you remember?"

Ash settled their palm on the table. "Anything about a beacon?"

"I'm not a specialist on technology by any means." Shannon rubbed her forehead, temples pounding as a headache roared to life. How could she help them, and herself, if she couldn't remember anything about the trek that killed her?

If the name Anunnaki was familiar, what other ancient names might pluck another mental string? She ran through a gauntlet of every culture she studied until she landed on one that stuck. "I think we might have been looking for an undiscovered Indus artifact."

Was that the beacon they asked about?

The general pinched the bridge of his nose. "The Kro-Gen employee reported nothing had been found at the site."

Shannon twitched in her chair. The information sounded wrong. "Was he the only one who survived the trip?"

"These questions should have waited until the recommended duration of time after arrival," the youngest human on the end said.

"And as you know," Fernández turned toward them, "We don't have time to follow proper procedures."

Shannon's gaze jumped from the general to each of the League members. Whatever was happening, it didn't bode well. The intense weight of their scrutiny pressed heavily on her shoulders.

"She knows nothing." Ash stood and braced her fists against the table. "We don't have time for this. We're wasting precious time that could be spent locating useful information."

"Wait!" Shannon focused on the general. She had to have *some* information to get time knocked off her sentence. She didn't want to spend the rest, what little may remain, working herself to the bone for people who couldn't care less about her dreams and desires. "I've been getting brief flashes of memories."

"What kind of flashes?" Ash straightened, her blue gaze as sharp as the rest.

Shannon hesitated, unsure how the information she was about to disclose would be taken. She raised her hand to touch her cheek the fantom throb from what she suspected was a result of a fist. "Steven and the Kro-Gen employee were fighting."

Wind howled in her ears as her hood flapped around her neck. The struggle over life and death happening feet away.

Chapter 7

Intercepted Memo: Weapons will be in place and ready at a moment's notice.

Shannon blinked rapidly to bring the League's interrogation room back into focus.

"Disagreements are of no importance," Ash said, drawing Shannon's attention back to the group standing on the other side of the table. "We need to know what happened right before your death."

"More precisely," the general added, "how it relates to the Anunnaki attack."

She fisted her hands on her thighs. The black box creaked as she decided to breach the surface of the emotions she'd hidden away, but all that came out was anxiety and a crushing fear of abandonment. "If you gave me more time, I'm sure I could remember more information."

"We don't have the time."

The finality of Ash's statement was a solid punch to the gut. Why revive her for her memories but not allow them to surface before questioning? She didn't understand what was happening and pressed harder for answers. "What happened to the Kro-Gen employee?"

"He died before completing his report." Ash tapped the table, the sequence quick and decisive. "Why else do you think you're alive."

Ash's turned to her counterparts and her tone when

she spoke next was harsh as her arm cut sharply through the air. Her words were all garbled up in nonsensical ways. Nothing made sense. Shannon tapped on the bump behind her ear. When that didn't work to clarify the words, she forced a yawn and popped her ears. Shannon trembled. Her clammy palms clenched on her knees as terror set in. They turned off her translator.

The League's clamoring voices were abrasive in tone as they spoke over each other. Panting, she shoved this fresh hell into her mental black box to deal with later. Her shoulders relaxed as the lid closed. She focused on their body language to try to gain an idea of how the conversation was going. Her new number one priority was learning the universal language of Earth, so she never had to experience the utter lack of ability to communicate. Shannon's limited attempts at the written language on the NAV when not translated into her English also jumped to the top of her list.

She let their words flow over her as the general stepped closer to the trio. Is this what Earth's universal language sounded like now? A hodgepodge of words slammed together, partially sexed if the *el* and *das* being tossed out along with the recognizable pitches of Korean and the tonal languages, she wasn't sure were rooted in African dialects or Indigenous American ones.

Shannon's gaze jumped from one speaker to another as arms crossed and an occasional glance sent her way. Earth's lyrical language occasionally interrupted by the general's harsher syllables hung heavy in the air. It appeared as if his translator was still functioning. Shannon rubbed at the small bump behind her ear and shivered. What else could be turned off with a flick of a wrist?

Even if she'd had her memories right before death, Shannon doubted the information she could provide would satisfy the League. The general glanced Shannon's way. Shannon briefly made eye contact before his gaze skittered back to Ash who continued to be the loudest in the bunch.

She sat up straight and relaxed her grip on the chair. Shannon would not be cowed by them. Who did they think they were standing up there with her life in their hands? She'd been in this situation once before. Her younger self just as terrified as she was now, except Shannon knew she would survive no matter what. The real question was, what would be the cost?

Shannon raised her chin as a cold sweat pooled at the base of her spine. Her anger simmered at the total loss of control. She never agreed to commit her life to them in servitude, even after death. Her nails scraped plastic as the general's gestures grew more forceful.

The action across the room culminated into some form of agreement. They turned to Shannon. The three humans stationed themselves behind the chairs they'd previously occupied as the general stormed out of the room. The League's expressions ran the gauntlet of frustration to sorrow. Ash's held indifference, their lips twitching at the edges before they pressed into a line.

Ash's fingers quickly traveled across the table. "As it stands, we had two possible options for your future. Teaching about the ancient history you lived in or studying a potential piece of the puzzle to stop the Anunnaki attack creeping in at the edge of our conglomerate space."

Shannon sucked in a sharp breath. Panic set in. "That's it? What other choices are there? Your conversation was too long for only those options."

Ash tapped the table, and the wall of monitoring information cleared. "You're free to go back to your room. General Fernández will update you on the terms of your repayment once we've had time to finish the official contracts."

The group silently began to file out of the room.

Shannon jumped to her feet. "You can't do this!"

Ash paused at the door and raised her brow ridge. "We already have."

"Fuuuuccccckkkkk!" Anxiety surged. She hugged her stomach and leaned forward.

The door swooshed open behind her. The heavy shared tread of the guards came closer. Taking a fortifying breath, Shannon turned to face them.

The shorter guard met Shannon's gaze. Was she imagining the hint of pity in their eyes?

"Please follow us."

Her feet dragged with each heavy step toward the gaping door. What the hell was she supposed to do now? Could she trust the League to keep their word? If she did or said something wrong in either of their choices, would they ship her off to somewhere worse? She'd seen the news articles on the NAV while researching her new environment, of workers who were sent to mine a rocky body and could never afford to leave their contracted location.

D'lane's growl pulled her from her misery as she crossed the threshold to the hallway. Her heartbeat quickened as he gave her a careful once over. She blinked away wetness.

His deep voice cut some of the tension from Shannon's shoulders as he spoke to the guards. "I will escort her to her room."

The guards paused. The shorter of the two responded. "The League was quite specific."

D'lane growled. "I will take her."

The larger guard's hand clenched. Fabric creaked. "What were you doing in Troy-023's room earlier?"

D'lane's shoulders squared as the rest of his body relaxed. Shannon shifted to the side. He'd taken up the initial position he'd taught earlier, and she didn't want to be in the way when he moved.

"You are not in a position to inquire into my movements."

Shannon bit back an anxious laugh. What the hell was happening right now?

The shorter guard shifted their weight. "Your word, captain, that Troy-023 will be returned to her room."

D'lane stalked forward hands flexing. The guards tensed.

Shannon cleared her throat. All eyes focused on her. "I'd actually like to see Dr. Grates."

There was something Shannon wanted, and Hellen was the only one who had the solution.

D'lane walked around the guards in the direction of medical. "Then let's be on our way."

The guards stayed rooted in place and Shannon took it as a positive agreement to her request and followed D'lane until they were clear. She sped up to his side.

He looked down at her. "What happened in there?"

Hopelessness settled deep in her chest as Shannon's shoulders sank. "I didn't have the information they were looking for."

"How bad is it?"

"I can either teach or use my experience to help

catalog a ship."

D'lane stopped. Shannon took a few more steps before following suit. "Did they give you any information on it?" he asked.

"No, but the general is supposed to lay everything out after the League has finalized the details."

"Hmm." D'lane began walking. He didn't speak until she had caught up to him again. "It is fortunate that the League gave you options."

"Go me." Shannon brushed a curl away from her cheek. "I take it that most aren't given that opportunity?"

"No," D'lane said as they closed in on the medical bay.

So why were they giving her a choice? Was there something she was missing? Shannon desperately needed to get her memories back to get a handle on her situation.

She stared at D'lane's back as she slowed. As much as it pained her, she knew which option she was going to choose, but there were a few matters she wanted cleared up before she truly made up her mind.

Shannon hurried to catch back up to D'lane. "About earlier."

She caught the glint of his gold gaze from the corner of her eye. He made her feel all the feelings, and she wasn't sure if she liked it. She had so many questions about what had happened in her room before the meeting. Why he had come to her in the first place, and what exactly had happened after his bow. "Was this—"

His lips pressed into a line and cut his gaze forward. "You gave me your word."

Shannon hummed and swallowed the rest of her question. His tone was firm but not angry, which gave her hope in understanding what exactly was meant to go down before the guards interrupted them.

Shannon's arm brushed his as they walked. He didn't shift away. She struggled to remain nonchalant as they neared the medical. Where they friends or moving toward something more? Would her decision change anything? She needed to do more research on touch in the Chriw'rian culture.

When they arrived at the clinic, Hellen was seeing another patient. They had their arm clenched to their chest as Hellen ran the scanner over the limb. When Hellen caught sight of Shannon, she waved to a bed across the room.

Shannon hopped up onto the floating surface, her nose scrunching with the puff of mint that wafted up. D'lane propped his shoulder against the wall and crossed his arms over his chest a few feet away. His gaze constantly scanned the room.

"You don't have to stay." Shannon stilled her fidgeting fingers and struggled to sound indifferent. She wasn't sure if she wanted him here when Hellen came over. "I'm sure your crew might need you."

He arched a brow. "You won't get rid of me that quickly."

Shannon was missing something from his body language or social cues to understand what was happening between them. She'd expected him to leave at the first opportunity.

Antiseptic greeted Shannon before Hellen rounded the bed. "Is something wrong?" The doctor frowned as they fished for the scanner from the end of the table. "Are you in pain?"

Shannon gripped the edges of the bed and braced

herself for what she was going to ask. "I want a deep synaptic brain scan."

Hellen froze. "No."

Hard corners bit into Shannon's hand. Desperate frustration rose. "You don't even know why I want it."

"I can guess." Body rigid, Hellen carefully put the scanner down. "And I won't attempt the procedure."

"What is the problem?" D'lane straightened, tail lashing between his feet. "Explain the issue to me."

Hellen propped her hands on her hips. "She wants to force a synaptic re-connection."

"It's a common procedure," Shannon stressed. "It's done all the time for stroke and coma victims."

"What exactly is she asking for?" D'lane asked.

"She thinks that we can reboot her memory pathways to gain those she lost in the regeneration process." Hellen frowned and glared at Shannon. "What your NAV results failed to disclose is the synaptic re-connection can cause severe brain damage with revivees. Your regenerated soft tissue needs to create those connections naturally. You cannot force the recovery."

Shannon shoulders hunched as the last shred of hope left. "But I'm already remembering bits from right before my death."

"*Exactly* why we need to have this process happen naturally," Hellen countered.

"Besides," the general cut in as he stalked through the door, the mop of light brown hair still a shock to see on humans. "It won't change the League's decision."

Shannon tossed her arms into the air. "Then why wake me at all?"

The general sighed as he stopped at the end of the bed. "They have their reasons."

"I could be of so much more help in stopping the Anunnaki attack if I could remember everything that happened before I died."

D'lane placed his hand on Shannon's shoulder. "Which is why you want the synaptic re-connection."

Her shoulders slumped, and she rubbed her dry eyes. "Yes."

It would also reduce her building anxiety on leaving the research to those who had more knowledge on this time. Especially if she could confirm her memories held nothing of importance.

The general's features sharpened as he placed a small tablet on the bed and spun it to face her. "Have you had the chance to read your revival report?"

"Hellen and I started the request processes earlier, but we hadn't heard back yet." Shannon's fingers clench. That handheld contained more information than she knew about herself. If Hellen was to be believed, it would still be weeks before she got her copy of the official report from Kro-Gen.

He tapped the device. "This is a complete breakdown of your employee file."

She wiped the sweat off her palms and plucked the PDA from the bed. Smooth to the touch, the handheld was so light she almost dropped it. Her fingerprint unlocked the screen.

She rapidly flipped through the screens, disturbed by what she read about herself. Among other things, the Kro-Gen agent thought she had been a bit of a menace. That didn't bother her. Her fingers clenched around the edges as more information scrawled across the nonporous clear surface. He had extensive notes about her emotional state and the possibility of manipulation through positive interactions with authority figures.

She snorted. If that was true, she likely wouldn't be sitting here today with an alien cat man standing at her back. Instead, she'd have been stuck in a boring job her high school counselor recommended and prematurely dead like everyone else she knew.

The PDA tipped forward. "Three pages? The League kept me on ice for over a thousand years for three pages of halfway accurate notes?" Shannon glared at Fernández. "What the hell had the League expected to get out of me with nothing more than the location I died and the contract I'd signed?"

It felt like some big cosmic setup, and she was the punch line.

She opened the next file and flipped the device around to present her heavily redacted Kro-Gen contract to the general. "Why is this information blacked out? I've already read this document. My name is signed at the bottom."

Why wouldn't she have full access to the contract she signed that supposedly consent to keeping her body on ice? D'lane's palm settled on her shoulder. She struggled to rein in her frustration.

Fernández shrugged. "This is the copy available to high level Kro-Gen employees. The League has the full unedited version."

Which meant she might get the full copy weeks from now, after all the decisions had already been made. Shannon glanced up at D'lane. "Do you have full access to this information?"

His lips tilted up at the end, a bit of fang exposed. "It arrived moments before your League meeting."

Shannon hummed, understanding a little more on

why he came to her before the League meeting. She turned to Hellen. "I assume you do as well?"

Hellen leaned over the device and scrolled down the document. "This is above my clearance level."

Shannon cradled the PDA in her lap. There was no way she would give it back, not that anyone was trying to take it from her. She sighed. "Let's hear it."

The general sat at the end of the bed. "The first basic repayment option involves teaching about pre- and post-war Earth."

Her fingers clenched and unclenched on the handheld. She had already decided on the option she wanted but needed to get as much information as she could. "And the other?"

Fernández cleared his throat. "There is a ship encroaching at the edge of the League's conglomerate space."

D'lane's hand tensed on Shannon's shoulder.

"It's a remnant of an Anunnaki attack, abandoned after being unable to make the trek back after their retreat. We believe it might hold the answers on how to stop the impending attack." The general gestured to the handheld. "The information on both options is stored on your device."

Shannon swiped right. The image of the ship was blurry. The dark hulking beast had long bulging curves coiled down the long length of it. The scale was incomprehensible without reference but was something out of her nightmares. D'lane tipped his head to read over her shoulder. Hellen braced her hand on the bed as she leaned over for a look.

"The League has decided your previous contracted skills with dig sites, language research, along with your knowledge of pre-war times will provide an edge in understanding this ship and how it might play into the coming attack."

Reluctantly Shannon focused on Fernández and asked the question biting at her nerves. "Where are all your Anunnaki specialists? The persons who have spent all their lives waiting for this moment?"

The general sat back and tracked Hellen as she straightened. "We have so few of them and they're either occupied with other potential leads or no longer contracted with Kro-Gen or the League."

D'lane growled and flipped through the images on her device, his rough finger occasionally tapping against hers. What had he seen that had made him so furious? Or was it something Fernández said?

"If you choose to teach," the general said, "you'll undergo two years of training before being transported to the farthest school in need. Every five years you'll be transferred to a new location until eventually you have worked your way back into the inner conglomerate space where you'll spend your later years."

She flicked a quick glance at D'lane, noting his attention focused solely on her. What was he thinking? She cleared her throat and glanced back at the general. "And the derelict?"

"You would leave immediately to research the Anunnaki vessel on the T'grevis with D'lane and his crew. You will spend a week on site studying the ship and return with a full report."

Hellen remained close by, sanitizing the area around them. Shannon frowned when the doctor crept closer and began working on the bed Shannon was still sitting on. The smell of bleach overriding everything else.

Shannon peeked up at D'lane and he arched a brow in response. "A week?" She turned back to the general. "That wouldn't be much time to discover much of anything."

If this was her original time, that'd be enough time to set up camp, canvas the area, and start setting up markers. Not enough time to do anything but an initial survey of the site and plan the rest of the dig.

Fernández flicked the screen to the next page on the handheld. "This is a list of tools available to help map the ship, and a complete list of what Kro-Gen will require you to report on."

It sounded more and more like she was a last-ditch effort on the derelict. "Neither option tells me how much time I'll be compensated to reduce my debt."

"As stated earlier, teaching will require a full ninety-five years of service for the repayment. If you marry, Kro-Gen will allow some leniency on location, otherwise you'll be moved to positions Kro-Gen determines to be a good fit." Fernández nodded at the PDA. "The contract for that option has been loaded into the portable NAV, and ready for you to review and approve. Unlike the teaching position, if you choose to accompany D'lane, the remaining duration of your work quota will be modified once your return and submit your final report. The derelict contract resides in there as well. I suggest reviewing both to determine which is the best fit for you."

She tapped the PDA against her palm. "What if I remember how I died while traveling to either location?"

The general shrugged. "There's no guarantee your memories will hold any valuable new information."

"So nothing would change." At least they'd given

her a choice. The option to have some control over her future, and her path.

D'lane leaned his hip against the bed. "Even after cataloging and reporting the information the League and Kro-Gen has requested, she may still be required to work for them in order to pay off the remaining debt?"

"Her contract will be re-evaluated and could be considered paid in full upon return, but that is rarely the case." The general tugged his sleeves straight. "There is no guarantee with the League. I did everything as requested upon revival and am still in the process of repayment."

Hellen's brow ridge rose. "How many years do you have left?"

Hazel eyes narrowed. "You know it's not polite to ask that question."

"You're right." Hellen packed away the sanitizer wand and tipped her chin down in a small nod. "I apologize."

Shannon filed that *faux pas* away for later review as she scrolled down the list of "required" items to include in the report. Damn, the list was long, and they expected her to get everything done in a week? "It's been years since I've attended a class that required this level of writeup, and I haven't maintained my language skills in the interim."

D'lane brushed up against her back. His comforting warmth seeped through her jumpsuit. "My crew and I will also be there to help collect this information."

He must have noted her apprehension, but it didn't fix anything. "Will they count that help against me?" she whispered to him.

The reality of the situation was, she could head out

to the ship and find nothing or collect every iota of information they wanted, returning to earth to still be forced to teach for another ninety-five years. But if she chose the derelict, she'd get the opportunity to explore her relationship with D'lane. The struggle was she knew nothing about the previous wars, the Anunnaki, or even the current time period. There had to be someone else they could ask that could contribute more information on how to stop the attack headed this way.

"What option do you choose?" The general straightened from the edge of the bed.

Her fingertips clenched around the handheld. Nerves tingling, more afraid of D'lane's reaction than anything, she straightened her shoulders. "I'd like more information on the teaching position. The description of duties wasn't included in the contract."

D'lane shifted away from Shannon, removing his warmth and support with the action. Her chest panged, and she refused to look at him, instead she took comfort in the fact that he remained even if it was feet from her. She wasn't rejecting him and their relationship as it was, but she was rejecting the whole absurd saving the universe tied to the derelict situation. The League had to have other people lined up who could resolve this situation regardless of what the general said.

Fernández sighed. "Hellen, if you would pull it up on screen?"

Hellen moved to where the wall met bed. "The usual revival starting point?"

"Please."

Shannon smoothed out a small wrinkle on her leg. Hellen's statement was a reminder that nothing Shannon was experiencing was either new or exciting to anyone but herself. Every step of her process had already been repeated time and time again with other revivees. Why did she keep thinking she was unique or that her experience was any different from others, especially with another revivee in the room?

Hellen activated the screen at the front of the bed where Shannon's medical information had been previously displayed. An information graphic popped up with space station information, reminiscent of the pages that had popped up on the NAV when she searched about Chriw'rian history and anatomy. Although she couldn't read the page, it was laid out the same way the Chriw'rian home world Chriw'r had been on the NAV with demographics information and population densities on the right, current location and history on the left, and a depiction of the space station top and center.

The floating metal landmass was large and shaped like a tube. Shannon had no idea on scale, but if the five-year duration was true, she'd likely get the chance to explore all of it regardless of size. "How old is this place?"

"The Gunnel was built over 500 years ago. The League purchased it over a hundred years ago from the My'len corporation."

The room stilled. The text wasn't large, which is why it had taken Shannon time to locate it, but the symbols in the right-hand corner flashed a bright red. The same warning light her bed had given off when she first woke up here in this time. "What is it?"

"When was the last time the Gunnel reported in?" D'lane asked.

"There is no need," the general said as he pulled out a tablet from his back pocket and frantically typed. "That marker information is set to constantly report its location."

"Could it have failed?" Hellen asked.

Shannon glanced at everyone in the room, their gazes locked on the screen.

Hellen shook her head and answered her own question. "No. The redundancies built into the medical system make it impossible."

"What's going on?" Shannon straightened, her hands weaving together tightly in her lap.

Shannon tensed as D'lane squeezed her shoulder. "The station is gone."

Her heart began pounding. She doubted stations just up and disappeared, especially with the technology they had today. "How is that even possible?"

"My'len has been tracking the rumors of the start of an Anunnaki incursion." D'lane wiped a hand down his face. "My'len thought they had more time to share this information, but I only found out this morning where they were headed."

Everything slammed into place. D'lane's entrance into her room. His demand for her to leave with him as well as his command to remain quiet about his request. He knew the Anunnaki were starting their attacks, and that she'd likely be sent to a station in their raid route. But why withhold that information from the League or Kro-Gen?

"Over half a million lives gone." Hellen leaned against the bed. "How did no one know?"

"The League knew." The general rubbed his temples. "They wouldn't have offered the teaching option in the first place if the station still existed. Fucking politics."

"Why didn't the League warn that station?" D'lane growled. "They could have saved some of the population."

"That's information I don't have access too." The general grimaced. His expression relaxed as his gaze met Shannon's. "All of us are operating in the dark here and with this latest attack, the situation is more dangerous than you can imagine."

Shannon clenched her knees and rocked. The League had sat there and lectured her on telling the truth all while lying their asses off. Shannon glanced up at the general. "What does this mean? Will I be offered a position at another station?"

She kept herself from asking where the Anunnaki were headed now. The answer was one that wouldn't help her current situation.

D'lane's nail lightly trailed across her skin as he tucked a curl behind her ear. "No station will be safe."

Dread pooled in her stomach as the appearance of control shattered at her feet. Right. Everyone was going to die. All the outer reach stations were likely high on the list of those first attacked. Shannon had hoped that there was one on the other side, away from all this that they might send her to, but that was a long shot.

"You leave on the T'grevis tonight." Fernández's gaze hit all three of them, before settling on Shannon. "You no longer have a choice in this."

The general stood and turned toward D'lane. "Do you have any other information you can share with me?"

"No."

The general waved at the device in Shannon's lap. "Several memos from both the League and Kro-Gen, dating back to a time around your death, have been included in your file. Please read through the material during your trip. I shouldn't have to remind you that the more information you have going into this, the greater the likelihood of success. For all of us."

Chapter 8

Intercepted Missive: They know about the mission.

Warm salty ocean air filled Shannon's lungs. The fresh scent of grass swirled around her with every step. D'lane lead the way to his ship parked in the distance, his tail idly swaying at his feet. The soft stroke of sea breeze brushed her cheek. She gripped a small bag holding all of her meager possessions as her steps slowed. The sky stretched far and wide as the courtyard opened up. The deep hue holding more purple than she remembered. Tufts of crabgrass stretched to the edge of the island before abruptly dropping off as a wide expanse of water took its place. She clenched the soft fabric sack and fought the urge to run back to her room.

This was the first time she'd been outside the Kro-Gen facility since she woke. The open sky and unending ocean stretched in all directions and left her floundering for purchase. She zeroed in on D'lane and the emotional anchor he provided even as the distance between them grew as he continued to the T'grevis. She took a bracing breath and place one foot in front of the other until she caught up with him.

The ship sat squarely in the center of Kro-Gen's courtyard like a dark shadow. The flat black surface stretched high above her and wider than expected. The dull skin of the ship ate all the light that fell upon it. It reminded her of the blackest of black paint that absorbed

99% of light.

If she had stumbled across this massive object in the field, she'd have no idea how to even catalog it. With no windows or visible engine structures the shape reminded her of a huge angular boulder with legs sticking out of it. The weight of it sunk the landing feet half a foot deep into the soft grass. It likely had thick walls that she doubted X-Rays could penetrate if it was meant to prevent space radiation from harming the crew within.

"Why paint the ship black instead of white?" Shannon asked as she came to stand beside D'lane at the back end of the T'grevis, her bag tucked under her arm. "Wouldn't you want to reflect instead of absorb radiation?"

D'lane flashed her a smile. "It's easier to hide your position with black instead of the white."

Shannon crouched and ran her fingers through the waxy wild grass a few feet from the ships legs. She closed her eyes as a cool breeze ruffled the hair at the side of her face. "So, broadcasting your position isn't high on your list of to-dos?"

D'lane chuckled. "Generally not."

A door rolled up on the bottom third of the ship as an entrance ramp descended. The smooth motion of extension was eclipsed by the chaos at the end of the ramp, as a large gouge the length of a table runner dug into the dirt. Grass rolled up the gangway as it extended fully into the dirt. D'lane moved to the foot of the metal gangplank and up toward a familiar male brown haired and green eyed Chriw'rian who lounged against the inside of the ship.

D'lane's boots rang sharply on the metal ramp. T'rev's mouth tipped up at the side as he straightened at

D'lane's approach. The last time she'd met T'rev, he'd been nursing a sore jaw, wearing less clothes, and had a stiff attitude. But all that negated the one thing that the metal plank feeding up into the ship meant. She struggled to hide her excitement as she caught up to D'lane.

Even with the attack looming, experiencing something new and exciting and entirely removed from her old reality overrode everything else. She skipped the last bit of distance as she matched D'lane's pace. She was going into space!

D'lane stopped at the top of the ramp and flashed her a smile. "The T'grevis isn't the fastest ship in its class, but it's a close second. Its unique design is a hybrid of a small cargo ship and luxury vessel."

He gestured to the other Chriw'rian. "You've met my first mate T'rev earlier."

"I have." Shannon gave the Chriw'rian greeting bow and T'rev returned it.

As they straightened, Shannon noted T'rev's skin tone was slightly darker than D'lane's, more of desert sand at dusk than the sun-soaked skin of D'lane. The bridge of T'rev's nose had a sharper point to it, and his close-cropped hair exposed ears a bit more rounded at the tips under the tufts. Instead of the loose black pants he'd had on during the sparring match, he wore a matching two-piece uniform to D'lane's, except in a dark gray. Around his hips rested a tool belt holding devices similar to the doctor's scanning wand, and a few odd-looking screwdrivers. There was even a mallet. What the heck did you need a mallet for on a spaceship?

T'rev's tail swished lazily back and forth behind his legs. He kept his green eyes on her as he directed his question to D'lane. "She'll be joining us?"

D'lane's hand touched her lower back. "She belongs to our ship now."

Shannon fidgeted, unable to deny that there seemed to be some secret meaning behind those words.

"Yes, Captain." T'rev's tail twitched at his feet as he nodded at D'lane before disappearing into the bowels of the ship.

"Do I get a personal tour of this badass ship before takeoff?" Shannon followed.

"Of course, but…" He stopped her with a hard grip on her shoulder. His fingers flexed. Nails pricked her skin. Whatever it was he wanted to say brought up a lot of emotion. A blush heated the skin at his jawline instead of his cheeks. The tip of his tail twitched rapidly.

"I wasn't denying you earlier." He flicked a glance over her shoulder before meeting her gaze again. Was he checking to make sure they were alone? He gave her shoulders another squeeze and released her. "I was asking a question of sorts."

Shannon froze. He was talking about the bow he'd given her earlier and the one he'd rejected when she returned it. Her palms dampened as excitement pulsed through her body.

His golden gaze locked onto hers. "The bow is a request not to harm. It creates an open and weak position to the giver by exposing the sensitive line of the jugular. It's a show of trust and starts a dance I should not have indicated interest in with how new you are to this world."

His rigid body indicated he was uncomfortable with this line of conversation. She wanted to push, to fully understand the start of a dance the steps of which she was just learning about. But if he wanted to pull back and not discuss what might be developing between them, she would let him keep his secrets. At least for now.

His ears slowly rotated back, then flicked forward. He gave her shoulder a rough pat. Turning, he waved her into the ship. "Let me show you where you will be staying."

She wiped her palms on her jumpsuit and tucked her disappointment down where it wouldn't distort this moment and hurried after him, craning her neck trying to take everything in. The square lines of the ceiling and light blue-gray tinge to the wall felt like a warehouse, but it and the bitter scent of metal in the air was a welcome change to the boring all white of Kro-Gen facility.

The bottom of her shoe caught on the ship, and she glanced down. The floor was lined with a dark gray friction mat worn down the middle from repeated traffic. More like boarding an airplane than popular science fiction in her time led her to believe. The spaceship lacked the pizzazz she expected. Where was the shiny equipment, the flashing lights, or the solid wall of touch screens?

She caught up with D'lane as he placed his palm on the back wall. The ramp behind them began to roll up as the door started to close. The room darkened. She clutched the bag to her chest and bounced on her toes as the overhead lights flickered on. "I'm on a spaceship."

"We'll need to get you situated in your room and prepped for lift off as soon as possible. Once we're in space, I can give you a personal tour of the ship."

The square corridors were smaller than Kro-Gen's halls but wide enough she could walk shoulder to shoulder with D'lane. The smell of freshly destroyed grass disappeared as she entered the bowels of the T'grevis. They passed the curly haired medic V'ren on their way up an internal ramp. V'ren currently wearing a purple two-piece uniform waved and flashed Shannon a quick smile as they passed.

On the third floor, they passed an open door. A quick peek inside hinted at a dining area. D'lane halted in the middle of a hallway and used his palm print to open an invisible door. She suspected they had passed a few of them on their way here, but how was she supposed to know where these rooms were? Was there a marker she was missing? At least with the smaller ship, she'd have an easier time finding her door compared to the long hall at Kro-Gen.

D'lane cleared his throat and shifted to the side. "This will be your room."

She stepped into the space and quickly glanced around. It was small, half the size of her room at Kro-Gen and lacked a closet. Her fingers twitched as her gaze caught on the lush set of dark red pillows piled high on the dark grey blanket covered bed tucked into the wall. Plush and welcoming, she wondered if the pillows would be soft to the touch or rough as a counter texture to the bedding?

She glanced at D'lane where he remained by the door with his gaze intensely locked on her. Usually that deep of a red color brought up connotations of lust, passion, and desire. Did the rich red tones hold the same romantic meaning in his culture as they did hers?

Giving in to her need, she ran a hand over the silky soft pillows. Did D'lane have the matching ones in his bed? Her fingers lingered as she visualized him sprawled out on them hot and sweaty after an intense workout. Fanning herself, she drew her attention away from the bed and peeked into the bathroom.

Small, with a sink sticking out from the far wall and the familiar toilet cocoon sitting next to it. No bathtub or visible shower sat in the room. Hopefully she'd be able to figure out how to bathe with the help of the NAV. Then again, asking D'lane how to shower might not be a bad thing. Her cheeks heated as she turned back to the room.

D'lane kneeled on the floor at the end of the bed. He waved her forward. Her thigh brushed his as she crouched next to him. Warmth seeped through her jumpsuit. He glanced at her. She flashed him a smile but didn't move. She'd let him decide what he wanted to do.

His tail curled around his ankle, slowly tapping against the ground at the tip of his scuffed boots. "In leu of a closet, you have three storage compartments under the mattress."

His thumb was tucked against the flat gray panel directly under the mattress pad, his nail beds flat and narrow like her own although they held an olive undertone. He pressed his thumb pad against the wall. A small door swung open, exposing a tiny storage space.

"Stowage for your duffle." He moved her bag inside before closing the door. His tufted ear rotated toward her as he stared straight ahead. "The other two lockers hold towels, and standard cleaning supplies."

Palm spread on the bed, he turned to face her. His fingers slid to the edge of the mattress wrinkling the grey bedspread. "Should I run through accessing the locker again?"

His face was close enough for Shannon to catch the subtle change of skin tone around his lips. She wet her lips and shook her head.

He stood abruptly. His hips now at eye level. "There

is little free or unused space on my ship."

Shannon stifled the urge to reach out and touch him, to establish a connection as she sat at the feet of an alien male, on a spaceship a thousand years in her future. His fingertips drummed out a brief beat on his thigh near the knife secured to his pants. He cleared his throat as his tail twitched. Opened his mouth. Closed it. Was she making him uncomfortable?

She tilted her head to get a better view of the dark ribbed handle poking out near his hand. She bet the metal was silky smooth, maybe even warm to the touch.

His fingers stilled.

"Ensure loose items are secured at all times." A deep growl underscored his words. "A steady trip is never assured, and you could get hurt by flying hardware."

"Okay." God, what was wrong with her? He was literally giving her a flight safety brief while she sat at his feet, her mind wandering from one interesting point to the next. Like why he still stood so close to her and how interesting it was that her face was perfectly level with his—

"Once I've granted you access to the My'len system," he took a step back, far enough away she could no longer touch him, "You'll have access to your personal property and different areas of the ship."

"Great." She dragged her attention away from his pants, and what they may contain. "Is there anything else that needs to be secured?"

She tipped her head back. His golden eyes trailed down to her exposed neck. She noted the heavy bob of his throat as he swallowed. His cheeks darkened. He gestured toward the bed. "I'd stow the pillows under the bedding and anything else that can't be stored in the cabinets. The blankets have a locking feature that secure themselves during evasive maneuvers."

Standing, she tucked everything in under the grey comforter and followed him into the hall. They passed an open door containing the same type of mess hall tables as Kro-Gen before heading down a ramp and hitting a long hallway she suspected held more hidden doors. "How much of the ship will I be able to explore?"

He flashed her a smile and walked down another ramp. "Most areas."

She pressed her lips together to suppress a laugh. How much trouble could she actually get into on a ship?

D'lane palmed the wall, opening a door. She blindly followed him in and froze.

Was this the bridge? Back to the all-white of Kro-Gen, three chairs spread out across the room, with a bench seat along the closest wall. In the back of her mind, she'd entertained the idea of the bridge reflecting that of a popular show from her time with shiny consoles people would sit at. She was wrong.

The cockpit was no larger than her small childhood living room.

There was a captain's chair, if the object centered in the middle about a third of the way into the room was anything to go by. It was the only concession to her dashed expectations. Another two seats sat on opposite sides of the room and faced blank walls. At the back, a three-person bench seat sat atop the same type of storage compartment as under her bed.

To top off her disappointment, there was nothing to see. The big screen peering out into the unknown remained a white wall.

"No window to see outside?" she asked as D'lane

led her to the seats in the back. "Where are all the terminals with the blinking lights or surfaces to work on? Are these ships run on mind control?"

Chuckling he helped her into her seat. His hand lingered on her hip. "Calm yourself and watch how I close and open the clasp."

The straps came across her shoulders and connected to a five-point harness buckling in the middle of her sternum. His actions were quick and efficient, but the placement of the straps had the backs of his fingers brushing against the sides of her breasts. Her breath hitched, and she flushed as goosebumps traveled up her arms. Gold gaze met her before they returned to the task at hand. Flustered, she watched him open and close the lock a few times, braced for another electrifying stray graze. Her lip pouted when none came.

"Did you see how this is done?"

He stepped back, and she glanced down and noted the color coding on the buckles that matched the plugs on the latch. Looking up, she nodded at him.

"Now," he said, unbuckling everything, "Let's have you do it."

She fumbled with the buckles, cursing under her breath until the last clasp clicked into place. "Tada!"

He checked everything, tugging at the straps, and arranged the metal center to rest in a more comfortable position on her sternum. "It's required to be securely seated during takeoff."

She tensed her thighs, rising up slightly to check the play in her harness before settling back down. She'd been strapped tighter into amusement park rides, but knew she wasn't going anywhere.

"Windows are a huge safety risk, especially in

battle," he said picking up their earlier conversation. "The projection surfaces are keyed into the stations. You'll see them once the rest of the bridge crew arrives."

"Navigation," he indicated the seat to the right of the room, "and operations," his arm swept to the left, "use the same type of technology as the handhelds." He rotated the chair in the center around and sat facing her. "The walls alter to display information as needed."

He tapped the space above his chair's arm and his voice echoed throughout the ship. "All personnel secure loose items, and head to surface-to-air stations. Our estimated departure window is in five minutes."

He tapped a few more times above the arm of the chair before buckling himself in with the same five-point harness she wore. T'rev entered shortly after, still in his gray uniform from earlier, minus his interesting tool belt. He sent her a brief nod before taking a seat at operations and securing himself for liftoff.

The wall in front of T'rev rippled. Images and shapes scrolled across the display in what might be Chriw'rian or another universal language she'd yet to be exposed to. His hands typed away in the air in front of him. Windows popped up and instantly closed. Multicolored lights flashed before turning green. She scratched at her cheek before wiping her damp palms on her knees. All this advanced technology and they still needed her archaic knowledge to help stop an attack?

T'rev rotated to face D'lane. "All operations normal, Captain. We will be ready to depart at your stated time frame."

"Good." D'lane's ear rotated toward the door.

Mint wafted in moments later as Hellen stepped into the room.

Shannon twitched. The unexpected shock briefly drew most of her attention away from the third Chriw'rian dressed in a blue two-piece uniform. The only member of D'lane's team she'd yet to be introduced to. Out of the corner of her eye, she caught the flourished flick they gave their tail to move it out of the way before taking the remaining navigation station.

"Shannon." Hellen smiled as she slid into the empty seat beside Shannon. "Are you excited for your first space flight?"

"I am." She turned toward Hellen as much as the harness would allow. "But I didn't know you'd be coming with us."

"I never travel with the thing." Hellen finished buckling herself in with a strained smile. "And you're likely as shocked as I am at this last-minute transfer."

The doctor's warm hand settled on Shannon's knee. Her muscles jumped uncomfortably under Hellen's personal touch. In the mess, after one too many people sat uncomfortably close to her, she recognized that people now-a-days were more comfortable with physical contact than she was used to. Accepting and giving more casual touches was something she was working on. But the lingering touches from Hellen always seemed to last a little too long.

"Fernández and Kro-Gen wanted to ensure your health, both body and mind, while on this mission. So here I am, along for the ride."

Unsure about this 'helpful' side of Kro-Gen, Shannon shifted her knee out from under Hellen's touch. She'd hoped to escape from under the watchful eye of the League on this trip, but with Hellen in attendance, Shannon doubted she would be out from under their observation until she paid off all her debt. She swallowed the thick knot of frustration and forced cheer into her voice. "I'm glad to have another familiar face around, even if I'm only familiar with two."

Hellen laughed and drew her hands back to her lap. "On a ship this size, you'll get up close and personal with the rest of the crew in no time."

The navigation officer who had come in during their conversation, turned and winked in Hellen's direction. Hellen responded with a warm smile, before giving Shannon's leg a tap. "It's scarcely a hardship. The Chriw'rian's have always been intriguing bed partners."

Shannon bit her lip and glanced at D'lane. The definitive answer to human and Chriw'rian's relationships wasn't something she'd had the time to research, but Hellen's statement indicated at least short-term relationships weren't taboo. She took in the straight line of D'lane's back as he worked, his posture strong and sure as he interacted with the rest of his crew. Was that where they were headed, or was she reading too much into their interactions?

D'lane's voice cut across her thoughts. "Q'aid, status?"

"Navigation is a go," the new member stated. Their grey eyes met Shannon's briefly before returning to D'lane. "We've received approval to exit the atmosphere and are ready for lift off."

D'lane sent another message ship wide. "Liftoff in sixty seconds."

Shannon's fingertips tingled as the reality of the situation began to set in. She was headed into space in less than a minute! She gripped her knees, nails digging into the sensitive skin. Her breathing sped up.

The ship rumbled. Despite the harness, Shannon's shoulder jarred into Hellen's. Shannon straightened as much as the restraints would allow as the large blank wall in front of her rippled. She gasped.

The Kro-Gen yard came into crystal-clear view; she could almost smell the grass. The 180-degree image was tinged red by the T'grevis's flashing lights. Not a single person was in view. Where were the barricades to keep the building from being destroyed by the engines?

The ship lifted off without a shudder. Clouds of steam distorted the view. They were airborne as the land mass behind them shifted. Nauseous, she pressed her heels hard against the metal under the seat. Everything was happening quick, too quick to fully process.

"Space bound in three minutes," Q'aid called from their station.

The T'grevis swung out over the water, and further away from the island she'd called home these last few days. Blue sprawled out as far as she could see as they climbed. There wasn't anything for miles around the island.

The nose tipped up slightly straining her neck as she kept it off the back headrest and focused on the screen. Acceleration punched her back into her seat.

Hell yeah! She'd always loved rollercoasters, and this felt like all of them combined.

A conversation started up between D'lane and Q'aid, discussing possible flight paths and trajectories, but her attention was solely focused on the steadily darkening sky in front of them. The ship banked sharply to the right. She grunted as her straps pressed into her chest. The small island Kro-Gen operated popped back into view as the image extended to a 360-degree representation of their surroundings. It got smaller as the ship continued to move up through the atmosphere.

Holy crap, she was going into space!

A red light flashed out of the corner of her eye. She jerked her gaze to T'rev. His tail was twitching on the floor as frantically as her heartbeat. Then it stilled.

Red wasn't always bad, right?

An alarm blared and was cut off as a countdown began.

"Take evasive measures." D'lane braced a hand on his chair. "Increase acceleration. We need to be space bound before that missile hits us."

Fuuuuuuuuckkkkk. Shannon's nails bit into her palm. "Why are they shooting at us?"

"Taking evasive measures," Q'aid repeated.

The ship rolled to the left. The restraints bit sharply into Shannon's shoulder as all her weight crashed into it. What the hell was going on? Why would anyone send a missile after them?

The ship rolled right. Her hand slammed into Hellen's face. Pain shot through Shannon's knuckles as Hellen cried out. The ship dipped. Shannon went weightless before slamming back down into the seat.

The room spun. She broke out in a cold sweat. Her stomach heaved. She was going to throw up. She swallowed bile and gripped her thighs tightly.

"Land doesn't know where the projectiles originated," T'rev stated, his voice calm amongst the noise. When did he have time to talk to anyone in all this chaos? "Kro-Gen no longer carries any land-to-air missiles to assist."

D'lane gritted out, "Then lose those damn things."

There was more than one? Shannon's fingers

twitched. How were they going to escape them?

"I am trying to, Captain," Q'aid said, "but they're locked on."

"Raise shields."

"Advise against it, Captain." T'rev flipped through the windows at an even faster rate. "It'll be viewed as an offensive act and Earth's defensive shield would rip us apart."

Hellen gripped Shannon's hand. "In either case, we're dead."

Shannon pressed her hands between her knees. "Great, so it' get destroyed by missiles, or save ourselves and die by Earth's defensive measures?"

"It'll be a close one." Q'aid's harsh voice cut through Shannon's growing panic. The ship rolled again. "But we should be able to shake it."

"Impact in ten." T'rev started the countdown.

"Brace yourselves." Q'aid wiped sweat off their face.

The ship dipped once more, slamming Shannon's head into the seat rest. She blinked away stars.

"T'rev," D'lane shouted over the warning siren. "Raise those shields at the first possible moment."

"Four. Three—" T'rev counted.

Hellen's hand shook in Shannon's grip. Shannon tightened her grasp. Her knuckles throbbed in pain.

"And…we are out!" Q'aid banked right.

"Shields up! Counter measures in place." T'rev's hands frantically moved across the counsel.

D'lane growled, "Destroy those damn missiles, and get us the hell out of here.

Chapter 9

Intercepted Notification: Target eluded obstruction measures. Will attempt again.

Hand throbbing from slamming into Hellen's face, Shannon attempted to loosen the tight harness straps. She fumbled with the release as Hellen quickly unbuckled next to her. Why the hell couldn't she figure this shit out? Shoving her fingers between her shoulders and the straps, she tried to alleviate some of the pressure still pinning her in place. The damn things had tightened on her at the first tip of trouble. Her chest heaved as she sucked in air. It was getting harder to breathe.

Hellen leaned over and freed Shannon from the strangle hold with one push of a finger.

"Thanks." Shannon rolled her shoulders to release the tension. "And I'm sorry about the cheek."

"It couldn't be helped." Hellen lightly poked around her eye. "It wasn't like you meant to hit me."

Shannon's uncomfortable laugh died off as she glimpsed D'lane heading over to ops. He rested his hand on the back of T'rev's chair. "Damage?"

"None, sir." T'rev flicked his hand across the screen in front of him. "Counter measures destroyed all missiles. Shockwave damage is negligible."

"Why is no one freaking out? You're all acting like a missile attack is normal." Shannon shrugged out of her harness straps but remained seated. She didn't want to miss anything. The artificial gravity she'd read about had kicked in, but the weight of it seemed heavier than on Earth.

"That was anything but normal." Hellen said rubbing her puffy cheek.

"I've revised our target trajectory to match our current location," Q'aid interjected.

"Good." D'lane patted Q'aid's shoulder.

Shannon blinked and found D'lane crouched in front of her. He settled his hand gently on her knee as his tail grazed her ankle. "A bumpy first ride," he chuckled and brushed his thumb against her thigh, his dark nail beds jarring against her silver suit. "I hope it hasn't deterred you from future space travel."

"I trust you and your crew." Shannon added wearily, "although I'd like to remove the possibility of blowing up for the rest of our flight."

His golden eyes lit up. "I will see what I can do."

Q'aid swiveled to face them, a smile spread across their youthful face. "Every takeoff involves some risk."

"Yeah…" She struggled out of her seat as D'lane backed up to give her room. "But I'd prefer for it to not include missiles aimed at the ship I'm currently residing in."

"You asked too much." Q'aid laughed, winking at her before turning back around.

She could see why Hellen was interested in them. They were an attractive Chriw'rian with a skin tone that had an ash undertone that was unique among D'lane's crew. D'lane shifted at her side. Shannon's gaze caught and held his. But Q'aid wasn't as attractive as the ship's captain even as D'lane's earlier comment came back to her. "Did you know this would happen?"

D'lane rubbed his lip. "It wasn't unexpected given the secrecy of our mission."

She swayed as the blood rushed to her head. Why hadn't she been told? There had been plenty of time before takeoff when they'd been alone that D'lane could have mentioned it. She clenched her hands as pain settled in her chest. Didn't he trust her?

Hellen stretched, Q'aid's gaze tracking her long, lean lines. The doctor's arms dropped. The sharp slap of Hellen's palms hitting her thighs cut through the room.

Shannon glanced back at D'lane. "Do we know who or where the missiles might have come from?"

D'lane's bright gold eyes held Shannon's. "Trajectory tracing on the weapons launched is currently in process."

Hellen cleared her throat as she glanced around the room. "Why would someone want to stop us?"

"Hopefully we'll have those answers soon." D'lane's gaze became unbearably intense, and she fought the urge to fidget. "Because I doubt this will be the last attempt."

Shannon's heart shuddered. She glanced at her hands, wanting a break from everyone but she'd take fewer people in the room as the next best option. She stepped away from D'lane and smoothed her hands down the top of her thighs, ready to return to her room.

"Wait," D'lane commanded. He had the full attention of the bridge, including her own. "Let me show you around the ship and finish getting you settled in."

Shannon's heart skipped a beat, and she fought the urge to grin. Whatever this was between them, he wasn't trying to hide it. Not after that declaration.

"Commander." Hellen stopped beside Shannon,

close enough that her hand brushed Shannon's side when she placed it on Shannon's shoulder. "I need to complete another physical on Shannon to ensure her soft tissue regeneration hasn't been affected by the rough takeoff."

Given the choice, Shannon would choose D'lane over yet another scan. Shannon caught Hellen's frown and smiled at her. "I'll stop by later."

D'lane gave a firm nod to the doctor, and stepped forward, pulling Shannon along with him.

The bridge door cut off Hellen's response.

Alone together, Shannon turned toward D'lane. "Why didn't you warn me about the possibility of an attack?"

His ears flicked back. "It hadn't occurred to me."

Sharp pain cut into her chest as her excitement died. He didn't trust her. Why else would he keep that information from her? He'd said she was now considered part of the T'grevis crew; was that just lip service to get in her good graces or did it actually mean something? "Is it because I work for Kro-Gen?"

"It's not that at all." D'lane placed his hand on her hip.

She sighed as D'lane's tail curled around her calf. There must be something she was missing. Shannon placed a fingertip over the 'y' on the My'len patch on his shirt. "Then why?"

"I have a hard time trusting people, especially when they know the meaning of my name."

Shannon spread her hand over his chest, his heart beat a gentle thrum under her palm. "Do they expect to profit from your path?"

He'd spoken of being a great benefit to his people, even if he thought he was going to die in the process. She could see how some misconstrued that to mean he'd be involved in something profitable or something that they'd use as a steppingstone for themselves.

D'lane pressed his hand flat against hers, conforming her palm to his muscles underneath. "Would you forgive me if I promise to keep you in the loop from now on?"

Shannon stared up into his golden gaze. His sincerity was plainly visible on his face. "I forgive you."

He leaned close and pressed a kiss against her cheek. "Thank you."

Her skin tingled, and she fisted her free hand to keep from capturing the sensations from where his lips touched. What did it mean?

Stepping back, and with a gentle grip on her elbow, he steered her down the hall. "The T'grevis is a Chriw'rian Class 5 cruiser and has three levels."

Shannon trailed her fingers across the wall as she followed. The metal was cold and smooth under her fingertips. "How many ships have you been on before?"

D'lane flashed her a smile. "A few, but the T'grevis is my favorite."

"Are you just saying that because we're flying on it?"

"Captain's rule: Never badmouth the ship you're currently assigned to." D'lane activated a screen on the wall at the juncture of two hallways. A map of the T'grevis popped up. He tapped the red dot in the middle of the ship. "We're on the second floor with the bridge, conference room, and security. The third floor above us contains the mess, infirmary, and crew quarters." He slid his finger down. "The engine room and storage are below us."

"From outside, I thought the ship had more levels?"

The tip of his tail tapped against her heel. "The T'grevis has a large storage bay normally used to haul small loads. Missions like ours would normally be carried out on one of the faster cruise vessels, but the T'grevis was the only ship available on such short notice."

Shannon fought a shudder. Where would she be if another captain had been called in by the League? Her connections to others were rooted directly in her growing friendship with D'lane and the confidence he made her feel in this time. Would she have connected as much with a different Chriw'rian?

Shaking off that unpleasant thought, Shannon focused back on the map and the lack of labels in each room. She pointed to the vacant space in the middle of the picture. "Is this the bridge?"

"Yes." He lightly touched the screen, and the image zoomed in. "The rooms aren't identified for security reasons, but you can usually guess what function each one serves based on its size and location.

"Security, or the arms room, is on this floor along with a conference room off to the right." He cut the image to a side view of the ship with all floors visible in a schematic of red and blue lines. "The bottom, Level 3, aside from the engine and maintenance rooms, we also have a gym with a large sparring room."

"Is there anything else on the top level I need to know about?

"Who's sleeping quarters are where, perhaps?" He arched a brow and her cheeks heated. He cleared his throat. "In case you might need to locate them in an emergency?"

She hummed, wondering what exactly constituted an emergency. Was it only life or death, or were there other, more interesting needs that might qualify?

D'lane closed the screen, and the wall returned to the bluish gray it was before. They continued down the hall and up a ramp. The sharp incline had a rougher gripping surface under her thin shoes than the main deck. Her thighs strained slightly with each step. She'd gotten more exercise walking the T'grevis than she had her entire time at Kro-Gen. "Why not use stairs?"

"It is easier to move supplies and people up and down levels without worrying about a misplaced step breaking a bone, destroying cargo, or limiting the potential pool of crewmembers. The larger ships tend to have lifts built into them to further reduce movement restrictions."

He led her to the ships mess. If there was a door, it remained constantly open. Three rows of darkly colored tables stood in the center of the room. Bright yellow and green cushions covered the gray metal seats. On the right wall a video ran constantly of a brightly colored forest with unfamiliar plants. The buzzing of insects and rustling wind softly played in the room. She toyed with the latch on her mental black box of issues still waiting to be resolved. She wanted to come back here and relax while unpacking one item at a time and soak up the peace the room presented.

A kitchen nook spread out against the far wall, with an open door off to the right.

Metal clanged. Shannon twitched. Her nerves were still raw from their takeoff. She moved closer to D'lane. His warm arm pressed firmly into her side. Her view of the small room was restricted by large cans and bags of unknown items hanging on the wall. What fresh terror was hiding back there? Not that she thought D'lane had anything dangerous on the ship, other than himself.

A Chriw'rian backed out of the room, tail held still as they held a large tray stacked with cooking staples. Body tall and slender, with close cropped dark curly hair, Shannon thought it might be V'ren who'd given her the non-Chriw'rian handshake earlier. They wore a purple two-piece suit V'ren had on earlier.

"Idiot men. Don't know what they're doing."

Shannon blinked at the southern drawl she hadn't caught in V'ren's earlier introduction at Kro-Gen. Could aliens have accents with the translator buried under her skin?

Without turning around, V'ren placed the tray on the counter and unloaded the stacked supplies, slapping each item down on the surface. "Throwing ships around like they haven't got people and things inside them. I didn't sign up for this and I know whose fault it is too, and don't think I won't take it up with himself in the meantime."

D'lane cleared his throat.

V'ren froze with a can of something unidentifiable in their grasp. Slowly the can arced down to land next to the other items on the counter. She spun around; a hand braced against their chest. "Why captain," V'ren drawled. "I didn't know you were here."

"I'm sure you didn't." D'lane lips pressed together as they twitched at the edges. Shannon didn't fight to suppress her chuckle. She loved the repertoire between D'lane and his crew. Each one had a snark that meshed well with the others. J'rax with their witty comebacks, V'ren with her playful parenting, and Q'aid with their outgoing youthfulness.

Shannon froze as D'lane's hand rested in the small of her spine. "V'ren," he said, "you remember Shannon from our sparring match at Kro-Gen. She's been assigned as our ancient cultural expert for this trip."

"Of course I do." V'ren carefully wiped her hands on a nearby towel before tucking it into a wall holder. "And the human doctor replacing me on the ship?"

D'lane arched a brow. "Elsewhere."

"Just so long as she understands I'll be handling the Chriw'rian on this vessel." She winked in Shannon's direction. "Now, what can I do you for?" V'ren turned and headed back into the pantry.

What else could V'ren need beside the six cans and three gallon size bags of items on the counter? Shannon stifled the urge to explore the pantry to see what it held.

"Recog is in the corner if you can't wait." V'ren waved to the right, "Otherwise I'm making some fixins for the crew."

"Recog?" Shannon glanced at the machine in question. The device was set deep into the wall and looked like a cross between a vending machine and a handle-less microwave.

"I'm lucky to have V'ren as part of my crew. Most ships of this size don't have a cook on board, although that isn't her primary position," D'lane said as he guided Shannon toward the closest table. "Unless it's a long mission, or a large number of crew on board we're usually relegated to reconfiguration machines, or recogs." D'lane gestured at the microwave vending machine. "It saves on ship space and resources."

"Us cooks can be hard to find," V'ren said as she moved back to the kitchen. "We tend to get the first pick on desirable destinations. With the extra benefit of being a medic, I'm one of the first to pick from the upcoming assignment lists."

"And you chose this mission?" Shannon asked as she took a seat, the green cushion soft and welcome reprieve from the hard seats in the bridge.

"It's a riveting destination." V'ren chucked. Her sarcastic drawl was strong in that statement. "But I'd go anywhere D'lane asks of me. I wouldn't be alive if it wasn't for him."

Shannon pivoted to D'lane.

D'lane appeared uncomfortable with Shannon's sudden attention. "You make too much of it, V'ren. All I did was ensure you arrived at your destination."

"It was more than that." V'ren didn't elaborate further.

Shannon shoved all her questions aside until a more receptive time and returned to the previous conversation to keep the conversation flowing. They'd been on the cusp of 3D printed food back in her time, but the final print designs tended toward amorphous blobs, which worked well for cookies and pizza, but not for much else. Although artificial meat hadn't been far from commercial production. "Why not rely on canned food? The area required to store the raw fabrication material must consume a lot of space."

"Recog's collect material scrubbed from discarded food scraps, ship recycling systems, and particles scrubbed from the air, store them in powders and hyper compressed spaces, then rearrange the components into what's been requested. Or at least the nicer ones do." D'lane chuckled and Shannon shuddered.

Finally, something that sounded like science fiction come alive. If the astronauts on the space station could drink recycled urine, upcycling food shouldn't have been too far behind. The reduction in food waste alone would be worth it. "It might take me a bit to get over the repurposed garbage aspect of the machine."

"The machines never go bad and can be a useful tool for meals used in conjunction with fresh food, which is where I come in." V'ren leaned her elbows on the table. "Cooks, along with providing exciting conversations, support crew relations and a mentality of belonging. Which is why we're needed on long trips."

V'ren winked. "There's a lot less mutiny when cooks are around."

"The recog on the first ship short term mission I crewed on used to spit out nutrition bricks. Horrible, gross, nutrition bricks." D'lane chuckled as his tail thumped against her ankle under the table. "As unpleasant as that trip was, the recog's haven't killed anyone in ages."

"Which is longer than some people I know." V'ren glanced at D'lane and chuckled. "But I'm sure that guy deserved it."

D'lane tapped the tabletop. "The courts determined that was the case."

"Wait." Shannon glanced between the two. "You killed a guy?"

"Not me," V'ren said as she straightened.

Shannon cleared her throat. "D'lane?"

"It can be a hazard of the job, but no. I believe she's talking about P'ret, my brother."

V'ren flashed a smile that was all teeth. "Why don't you two keep yourself company while I make us a meal."

The clink of plates and dishes flickered deep and plucked a buried thread.

The soft sound of conversation filled the late-night air of the group camped around the community fire. A harsh laugh drew Shannon's gaze to the right. Steven's forced smile sat tight on his lips as he stared up at the Krogenic's man. As she watched, the company man delivered a jarring slap to Steven's back before leaving the fire for his lone tent off in the distance.

She shivered, tracking his progress as he disappeared into the darkness. There was something wrong with the whole situation, but she couldn't do anything about it now.

"Shannon."

Her gaze slammed into D'lane's. V'ren's hand rested heavily on her shoulder. Blinking rapidly, she locked onto D'lane, needing an anchor as her memory lured her back. Two tails wrapped around her, one on her ankle, the weight familiar, and another lighter one around her waist. She wasn't ready yet to visit the imagery hovering at the edge of her mind. She wanted answers, but not to the events that led up to her death. No one cared how she got where she died, only what had happened once she was there.

She must have lost a bit of time in her flashback, long enough that V'ren had pans out and had been in the process of making food before coming to Shannon's aid. She cleared her throat. "Thank you for your help to pull me from an unpleasant memory, but please don't let me stop you from making the crews meal."

"Let me know if I can help. I may be trained on Chriw'rian mental traits, but I'm sure they're translatable to human emotions as well." V'ren patted Shannon's shoulder, unwound her tail, and headed back to the kitchen.

Shannon glanced at D'lane. "I'll keep that in mind."

The offer was one she would think on. Hellen hadn't offered any counseling or therapy on Shannon's transition to this period in her life. Likely the failure was a result of the time constraints and not how Kro-Gen and the League had their revival program set up considering all the other planning that went into revival.

D'lane rested his elbows on the table and clasped his hands together. His tail still wrapped around her ankle gave it a squeeze. "Where did you go?"

Hands shaking, Shannon tucked them into her lap. "Based on the environment, it was a camp site on our way to the beacon."

The weather had been too warm compared to the memories of her aching cheek and frozen packed ground.

"This memory disturbed you?"

"I've had other flashbacks, brief moments of time captured in crystal clear cinematography. Usually, they involve violence and danger where I've been hurt, or my friend and boss Steven has been."

D'lane's nails bit into the table. Their black tips added to the multitude of scratches that already marred its surface. "But not this time?"

Shannon played with the end of a curl itching her cheek. "No, I mean, there was aggression by the Krogenic's man, but mostly it was the feeling of anxiety and something being off. Knowing *now* what is going to happen, how Steven and I are going to die, I want to rush to that moment of death. Instead, my mind is jumping all over the place, from one time to the next. I even had a memory from my childhood. And everything is vivid, extremely clear, and too exact. I've never had memories this clear before my death."

D'lane rubbed his chin. "Perhaps it's a result of the regeneration process?"

"I haven't asked Hellen, but that could be the case. In my research, the side effect of *hyperthymesia* wasn't listed as a possibility. Could I even have an eidetic memory if pieces of my life are still missing?"

"Food's ready," V'ren called as D'lane's ear rotated in her direction.

"Something to ask Dr. Grates during your visit." D'lane stood and helped V'ren bring the plates to the table. Shannon stood to help, but D'lane waved her back. "We've got this."

A white plate was set before her with small side dishes spread across the table between them. D'lane retook his seat across from Shannon. She looked up at V'ren as she stopped beside Shannon. "Thank you for the food."

V'ren squeezed her shoulder. "Let's eat before the rest of the crew realizes there's food, and the mess gets rowdy."

Shannon picked up the choppork, her knuckles stinging from where they'd hit Hellen's cheek, and pulled her filled plate closer. Savory and rich, her mouth watered as she smelled the dish. She dipped her cutlery into a cross between curry and stewed vegetables. Chewing slowly, she got a sense of taste and texture of the slurry before swallowing. The flavor combination, another unique experience of savory spices she was unfamiliar with, left her with a hint of too much heat. Something she was willing to work with to fill her empty stomach. She ate three helpings. Comfortably full, she leaned back and rubbed her stomach as she waited for the others to finish.

D'lane had rolled up his black sleeves at some point. The muscles under his skin flexed as he went to place a portion of the curry into her bowl. She waved him away. He topped off V'ren's instead, before serving himself.

V'ren used a bit of bread Shannon hadn't caught sight of until now, to scoop up her stew. "Will P'ret be meeting up with us as planned?"

D'lane's gaze flickered to Shannon. Was this something she shouldn't know?

"I'll know more about his arrival when My'len sends the next brief."

V'ren pointed the last bit of her curry-soaked bread at D'lane. "If you see him before I do, tell that bastard he still owes me a bottle of *Allieae*."

D'lane chuckled. "You need to stop taking advantage of that man."

"Someone has to, or else he'd get too comfortable up on his pedestal."

She turned to Shannon. "Come see me next time you're hungry," she said as she cleared the plates off the table. "And I'll whip something up or show you how to work the recog if I'm too busy."

Shannon smiled as she side-eyed the intimidating machine across the room. "I will, and, thank you."

V'ren headed toward the recog, dirty plates in hand. D'lane stood, and Shannon followed him out into the hall and stopped next to the clinics open door next to the mess. She was anxious about possibly mixing up the two locations, but the floating beds were an easy indicator of which room was which.

"Well, this is my stop." Shannon leaned against the wall. D'lane stopped just within reach, expression serious. The silence stretched between them. Her stomach soured, and she shifted her weight. Was this when he told her whatever was between them wouldn't work out?

He stepped closer. His fingertips grazed her cheek as he tucked a stray curl behind her ear. "About that bow?"

She straightened. "Yes?"

"It is something private."

She touched his belt, the dull material surprisingly rough under her fingertips. "You'd said as much earlier."

The NAV hadn't gone past basic details on what intimacies were involved with other cultures, and even then, nothing more than what a first date might be.

"It is hard to remember you lack the knowledge of those who have been born into this time."

Did that mean she was integrating into the current human culture better than she thought, or were her old school social interactions more on par with Chriw'rian culture than her own?

"If you gave the bow to Hellen, she'd know what it meant and how to respond?" She stomped down on the spike of jealousy her own questions caused. She needed information on how this interaction between them could move forward, not rile herself up.

"Possibly." D'lane stepped closer. His chest brushed the tip of hers with each breath.

She curled her fingers into the top of his pants. The warmth from his skin seeped through the thin layer of his tucked in shirt.

His gaze intensified. "But I would never ask her."

She wiggled her fingertips. "But Q'aid would?"

He smiled, and her heart warmed. "Caught that did you?"

"It was kind of hard to miss," she whispered into the inch of space separating them.

"I don't think they'll move past flirting." D'lane's golden gaze settled heavy on her. "But I'd like to explore what's between us, further. If that's something you would like to delve into?"

Chapter 10

My'len Memo to D'lane: Agent is ready for pickup at Lagrange One. Ensure cover remains in place.

She tipped her head back and rested it against the wall. Finally, they were discussing the possibility of a relationship between them. D'lane's kissable lips were close. A shiver of anticipation settled her nerves as muscles twitched under her touch. "If I wanted to answer, how would I respond to your request?"

Starbursts of gold flickered in his eyes, the black oval pupil dilating as a flush settled over his cheeks.

"If you wanted to deny a suitor, you'd return the open bow with the closed one you've been giving. Traditionally, it could be a strike or dagger to the neck if they found it particularly unwanted, but we've moved past such actions. Many are glad it is not so anymore."

She snorted. "Probably not great for the general population either."

"It wasn't."

Shannon dampened her lips. "And if I wanted to accept?"

He smiled, canines flashing. Her fingers slipped from his chest as he stepped back.

"After the bow is initiated, the position is held until the question has been answered." Slowly he bent forward, hands at his side, and neck arched gracefully to expose the artery pulsing against his skin.

"For a yes," he said gold eyes flashing up at her from under tan lashes, "a hand is placed on the back of the neck, and a gentle grip is applied while the suiter is guided back to a standing position."

Fingertips tingling at her sides, the powerful line of his neck called to her as he returned his gaze to the floor. He left the choice of the next steps of their relationship entirely up to her.

Fear nipped at her. What if he decided she wasn't enough, or if her newness to this era was too much work for him in their relationship? She'd be left alone, again, disconnected from everyone who had come to mean something to her.

Her hand rose and hovered. She wasn't sure why he'd changed, unless she'd misunderstood his customs again, but if he is willing…Heat churned low in her core as her gaze raked over his still form. Even his emotive tail remained frozen at his feet. It was all or nothing for her, always had been. Decision made: Her arm lowered. His silky-smooth skin, warm and firm, shivered under her tentative touch.

Her grip tightened as his pulse fluttered against her fingertips. His hands clenched at his sides, dark nails divoting his skin. She swallowed thickly, rocked at the level of trust displayed by the viral male vulnerable in her grasp. Footsteps rang out on the curved metal rampway, but he remained in place undeterred by the possibility of exposure to his crew in this helpless position. She guided him up.

Gold irises were blown wide as his chest billowed. His gaze pinned her in place. Heat flared low and deep in her pelvis. He leaned down, and she closed her eyes. The rich scent of dates filled the air. He pressed smooth lips to the corner of her mouth and slowly followed the line of her lips. His hands curled through her hair. She gasped at the slight tug, her lips parted. Their breath mingled.

A brush of air came from the right followed by mint. A throat cleared delicately beside them.

A flush warmed Shannon's cheeks as they separated. Hellen stood in the open doorway of the clinic.

D'lane smoothed a thumb over the arch of Shannon's cheek. "I will leave you to your exam."

He fled, leaving her alone in the awkwardness of being caught making out in the hall. The bastard.

Hellen waved Shannon over. "Let's get you looked over so you can get some rest."

The clinic shared a wall with the mess, both situated in the center of the ship with hallways on either side of them. But unlike the mess, the med bay had a door that closed behind Shannon as she followed Hellen inside. They headed toward the first of three beds mounted to the room's outer edges. A glass enclosure with a single desk sat in the middle with a panoptic view. A hint of mint puffed into the air, a scent Shannon was really starting to loathe, as she hopped up onto the diagnostic platform.

"Medical aboard the T'grevis isn't as up-to-date as the tech at Kro-Gen, but it will suffice." The wall at the end of the bed lit up as Hellen activated the sensors. "Please lay back, and we'll get a quick scan done as I ask you a few questions."

A white stick about three inches wide emerged from the wall. It ended right above her stomach. Shannon reached out to tap the stick.

Hellen pushed Shannon's hand back down. "Please keep your arms down as the scan finishes."

Shannon sighed and drummed her fingers on the mat. She kept her legs straight, not wanting another rebuke for crossing her ankles and messing up her heart rate.

A yellow striped quilled animal waved cheerily down at her from the ceiling where it'd been painted. Long claws curled over the end of its fingers and a wire thin tail wrapped around its feet. An interesting choice to paint on a ship with an adult crew. Did this animal exist on the Chriw'rian home world?

Shannon focused on the cartoonish alien animal and answered the routine questions Hellen asked, the same ones Shannon had answered every day this week. They ran the gauntlet from how she was feeling, if she'd gotten any more of her memory back, and her current stress levels.

The scanning wand retreated into the wall. Shannon sat up, her legs hanging off the side of the table and fought the urge to swing her legs under the bed. Fidgeting would only expose her anxiety, and she wanted to keep her emotions off her medical charts. "Everything where it should be?"

Hellen chuckled. "No red flags from our bumpy lift off."

Shannon gestured at Hellen's healed cheek. "Your bruise disappeared so quickly. Is that normal?"

"No, but I have specialized ointments that help speed things along."

Shannon brushed her thumb over her knuckles that were starting to discolor. Should she ask for that ointment or would it be too awkward? Hellen pulled up

Shannon's latest diagnostics on the wall and she missed her opportunity to ask.

"Because I know you like to see the results of your scan, you'll note all the green is within the acceptable ranges, and the pre-revival repairs have mostly been accepted by your immune system. It'll be a couple more weeks until everything has fully healed, but I believe you're past the rejection stage of regeneration."

Hellen crossed her arms and propped herself against the edge of the bed. "I know you want to jump headfirst into studying and brushing up on your language skills, but please take it easy," Hellen stressed, "in all things."

Was Hellen warning her away from D'lane, or suggesting she slow things down? "What's birth control look like in this century?"

Hellen coughed.

"Are we still using condoms, or taking the pill?"

Hellen straightened, her jumpsuit shining under the light, and pulled up Shannon's medical record. "During the revival process, all employees are inoculated against the standard STI's. A full record of your boosters is available in your NAV and on your handheld. As for birth control, your body's chemistry is still in flux. You should expect your period in six to eight weeks and then we can discuss various types of chemical birth controls. As for physical barriers, we have a variety of options depending on the sexual organ of the user. The recogs are the best location to acquire these items."

"Any particular body fluid no-no's that could expose me to dangerous bacteria or viruses?"

"If you're asking about Chriw'rian and human sexual interactions, nothing of note has been reported. Although I recommend any sexual relationships with alien species be researched prior to coupling to remove any unpleasant surprises."

Shannon hummed, briefly distracted by what quirks she might find. "Any problem signs I should be looking for as my body equalizes?"

"Blurred vision, migraines, dizziness. In severe cases, the translator can malfunction due to stressed neuropathways," Hellen said, clearing the data on the wall. "It's why you'll continue to come see me every other day."

Shannon groaned.

Hellen smiled. "That's exactly what I want to hear from my patients."

Shannon laughed.

"If it helps, think of our visits as a break from your hours packed with research." Hellen rested a hand on Shannon's shoulder. "A way to break up the monotony and give your soft tissue time to absorb the information."

Hellen's hand lingered, her grip on the ball of Shannon's shoulder a little too firm. Shannon's gaze tracked around the room, settling on the other beds and empty office. How was she supposed to slip out from under Hellen's grip without seeming rude?

"Shannon," D'lane's voice echoed overhead, "Please head to the conference room."

She hopped off the bed as Hellen stepped away and tried not to run to the hall. Shannon slowed once she reached the doorway and glanced back. "Hellen?"

"Yes?"

"Thanks for answering my questions."

Hellen nodded, her head gleaming under the light. "Any time."

Shannon took the closest ramp to the second floor,

pausing when she walked past a room as the door opened. D'lane leaned against the door frame, flashing her a smile.

Frustration simmered, overriding any pleasure she might have had seeing him again. "Why the hell aren't these doors labeled?"

"They are." D'lane's ears flicked back briefly as he pointed to an area of the wall that looked like, well, a wall. "Here in intergalactic standard color and letters. It reads Conference Room."

"I don't see them." She rubbed her forehead, frustration settling in as she recognized even if she could see the lettering, she wouldn't comprehend it due to the language barrier.

"This is a serious problem D'lane. I could be in real danger during an emergency." That ship wide map meant nothing if none of the doorways were visible to her. She would end up spending precious minutes slapping the length of the wall looking for the access keypad.

She traced her fingers over the wall where he'd indicated the text resided, unable to feel the lettering. Did they not have any form of brail? The light reflected off the paint might be in a spectrum she couldn't see or, perhaps the color wasn't around in her time? "Hell, maybe it's like magenta, the color that doesn't exist, or a new color my brain isn't trained to recognize?"

"It's a possibility." D'lane's tail caressed her calf as he stepped back.

She followed him into the conference room. A white oblong table sat in the middle, its long length encompassing most of the room. Ten chairs, four on either side and a pair on the ends, were weirdly shaped. Their standard form was stylized with a V-back cut to more comfortably hold Chriw'rian bodies with their tails.

D'lane rotated a chair for her to take. She took a seat in the chair slightly off-center from the door.

Her breath caught as he kneeled at her feet. His head now level with hers, he flashed her a smile and pulled something out of his pocket. In his grasp lay a small off-white bracelet, a delicate match to the gray one every Chriw'rian wore.

"This is what will help you find your way around the ship."

She held out her arm. His rough fingers brushed against the sensitive skin of her wrists as he pulled her closer. Excitement warmed her core, as her body revved up to where they'd last left off. The bracelet gave a small clink as it closed. The soft material was cool against her skin.

"This is a portable NAV device, called a Navigation Integrated Control or NIC, similar to what was available on the data pads at Kro-Gen but linked to My'len network through the T'grevis." He brushed his thumb over the sensitive skin of her wrist. "I have programmed the important locations on the ship for you, including your room. I was going to give this to you once you got used to being on the ship, but I think you'd prefer it now."

She fought a shiver as he pulled away, falling for him a little more. "Thanks." She smiled hesitantly, rotating the bracelet nervously around her wrist. "I couldn't remember which room you put me in earlier."

"You are in Cabin 3. There are large numbers next to the doors." He trailed off and chuckled, shaking his head. "I understand now why you were constantly getting lost at Kro-Gen."

She flushed and spent a few seconds poking at the device to get herself under control. Once the heat prickling in her cheeks subsided, she smiled up at him. "Thank you for this."

His tail twitched. "It's waterproof, so there's no reason for you to take it off."

She fiddled with where it latched, picking a nail under the clasp to check if she could take it off. "Good to know."

He stilled her fingers. "I will show you how to program the NIC manually, and then store your setup information into the T'grevis and link it to your bracelet."

He stood, and she locked in on the bulge in front of her. That was twice now that she'd been teased by how he reacted to her. She wet her lips. The green light to explore what awaited beneath his pants had her hands clenching. She wanted to touch him, but her brain deviated from her body's plans. Now was not the time to touch him; they had bigger issues to tackle. She turned her chair toward the table as he tapped the glass surface.

"Once we get the NIC programmed, it'll automatically change the setting on any device you're using to your preferred language."

He leaned forward, his palm resting on the back of her chair as his thumb brushed the base of her neck. She stilled. The touch excited her more than a brush against her skin should have. She focused on the rumble of his voice, and the soft growl within his words as he walked her through the home screen. Did Chriw'rian's have some type of pheromone that pulled in their chosen sexual partners, or was her sexual attraction all because of D'lane?

A chime sounded. She glanced at D'lane; his profile was close enough she could move the soft hair surrounding his face if she breathed just right, and she could distinguish the individual strands of hair patterning his skin.

With a rumbling breath he activated the comms.

"Commander," T'rev voice entered the room. "A reminder that you have a call waiting."

"Please route it through."

He kept his hand on the back of her chair as the far wall rippled. The general's image emerged. Sharp hazel eyes landed on D'lane. "Any damage?"

"No."

"Good." Fernández ran a hand through his hair leaving light brown spikes pointed in every direction. "The Global Council has initiated a formal investigation on who launched the attack. I will have an answer shortly and pass it on when it arrives."

D'lane shifted next to her, his hip brushing her arm. She took comfort in the action when he failed to move away. His tail brushed her back through the hole in the chair. "Who knows about our mission?"

Fernández steepled his fingers in front of his lips. "Currently both of you, myself, the remaining seven League members, and a few other individuals within Kro-Gen fully understand what your mission is about. A slew of others, including Doctor Grates and your crew, know the basics to some degree what the T'grevis, with the assistance of Kro-Gen—"

"And My'len," D'lane added.

The general nodded in agreement. "—is attempting to do."

E.L. Roux

Shannon tucked her elbows tight against her sides. "That's a lot of people to keep our task secret."

"It's as much as can be expected, considering how many planets, governments, and corporations will be affected if you fail."

The sheer number of people who knew about their trip would only increase exponentially as they traveled to their destination. Which would lead to more leaks if the theory of conspiracy secrecy remained true. Her mental black box creaked as the consequences associated with failure began to settle in. She wet her lips. "What's the likelihood we'll be attacked again?"

D'lane's tail curled around her calf. "We are taking every precaution to ensure we arrive safely at our destination."

A chill snaked down her spine. Would it be enough?

"I don't want to say it all rests on you, but it's a close thing." Fernández met her gaze. "Stay alive."

The call ended abruptly. The silence lengthened. The flippant remark by the general circled her head, increasing in strength with every turn it made. Panic tightened her chest. What if she couldn't read anything on the vessel or work the machines needed to map the space? How could she live with herself knowing she failed so many?

D'lane turned her chair to face him. Crouching down, his knees bracketed her legs on either side and clamped them tightly together. His warmth permeated her cold limbs. The rattling lid of her black box quieted. She took a deep breath and buried it deep in her mind. She focused on D'lane, and the calm he radiated. "Was the call with Fernández the reason you brought me in here?"

"Yes."

She mentally tallied the time he'd taken to show her how the NIC worked, and their earlier conversation. The corners of her lips tipped up as she fought to keep her expression blank. "How long was he on hold for before you took the call?"

He flashed his teeth. "Long enough to be a bother."

She traced a raised vein on his hand still grasping her knee and tiny silky smooth hair moved gently under her touch. "Will you finish walking me through the system? I'd like to get some research in today."

His ears flicked forward. "What do you plan to research?"

"I want to read up on the Anunnaki battles and how they ended." She ran her touch over his dark hard nail. "You don't happen to have something I could take notes on?"

He reached past her, his arm a scarce inch from her chest, to pull up a program. "Place your palm flat on the surface."

The bracelet clinked as it hit the table. She spread her fingers out and pressed down. The surface blinked; the pads of her fingertips warmed. The surface reminded her more of a glass top stove right now, more than anything else.

The temperature became uncomfortable. D'lane held her hand in place. "Almost done." The table flashed again, and he slowly released her. His lingering caress raised goosebumps on her arm. "You are now keyed into the T'grevis, and your user settings have been logged." He pulled up the search bar. "Did you want to type, scribe, or speak your notes?"

She shook out her hand and checked out the light

pink tips of her fingers. "Type."

"A bit archaic." He smiled at her. "But easy to do."

The screen split in half. One side displaying the search bar and the other a blank document.

"If you decide to record, press here." He indicated a series of dots at the bottom of the screen. "This will also toggle to scribe, and with another tap, back to keyboard."

Needing to ground herself, she settled her hand on visible portion of his skin exposed by the rise of his shirt just above his wrist. "Thank you for your help."

His soft smile drew her attention to his full bottom lip as he stood and slipped through her grasp.

"I leave you to it. And Shannon," he said hesitating at the door, "I'll see you at dinner."

Chapter 11

Intercepted Memo: Second attempt imminent. Contact agent to arrange details.

Shannon tossed her PDA on the mess hall table. The room was empty and free of prying eyes as she stalked over to the recog. She wanted tea. She'd memorized the icon from the NIC—a circle overlayed with stylized numeral three crossed with a rotated T—before coming here. She flicked through the drop-down menu in search for the right glyph.

Her first attempt yielded a piece of jerky. Chewing on the dried bit of meat, the salty taste flooding her mouth, she hovered above the next icon uncertain if the curl on the bottom half of the three was pointed in the right direction. A soft tread at the door had her straightening away from the screen.

A flash of silver in the corner of Shannon's eye preempted Hellen as she stopped by her side. "Anything I might be able to help with?"

Shannon's thumb snagged on the roughly dried meat as she pulled it from her mouth. "I'm hoping for a cup of tea?"

Hellen flashed her a smile. "Ah, a woman after my own heart."

The doctor flew through a few menus before landing on the symbol Shannon had been looking for. A blue light pulsed in the recog. In the center of the machine, a ball of liquid rippled encased in some mysterious membrane to keep its shape.

Shannon tucked a curl behind her ear and studied the ball. "No cup?"

Hellen laughed as she headed into the kitchen. "I totally forgot. I've been living on that island too long. It's been a bit since I've used one of these machines."

Shannon made a mental note of the location Hellen pulled the cups from and accepted the mug Hellen handed over. "Thank you."

She stared at the steaming ball floating there, hesitant to reach in and touch it. Would it burst at the first brush of her skin?

"The recogs will provide an edible casing if you don't have a vessel in place when you activate the screen. When that happens, you can place the entire ball into your mouth and pop it with your teeth or you can break the wax and drop your tea into the cup."

"Thank you." Shannon shoved the jerky back into her mouth and took the ball Hellen offered. She tested the waxy surface with a soft tap. Hot, but not scalding, she placed the squishy orb in her mug.

She watched as Hellen ordered herself a cup of tea herself, with the cup inside the machine this time. Shannon wandered back to the table holding her data pad and leaned against it, tired of sitting.

Hellen paused on her way to the door, a bowl of snacks in her grasp. "I know you can't disclose everything but let me know if there's anything I can help you with."

Shannon pinched the skin of the sphere and tore, hot liquid spilled into the mug. A slightly sweet scent of honey with a soft hint of lemony apples filled her lungs.

"How much do you know about this mission?"

She picked up the cup and blew across the surface of her mug. Her first sip was a taste of strong leaves and spices. Her jaw clenched to keep a grimace off her face. It needed more water to cut the taste, or some milk and sugar.

Dropping her fingers into the snack bowl, Hellen pulled a purple pretzel like stick from the heap and crunched down on it. "Not much more than I overheard in the med bay on Kro-Gen. My mission statement had a lot of redacted material. I know that I've been charged with doing everything I can to ensure you succeed in your mission goals. As for the exact details on what you're meant to be doing on this assignment," Hellen shrugged, "it's of no importance to me. Frankly the less I know, the better off I'll be in the end."

Shannon frowned. Half-formed questions and frustrations swirled in her mind as Hellen left. Sighing, Shannon plucked her handheld off the table and buried everything except her research from her mind.

Sipping her tea, she sat and scrolled through the data the general had provided her with before they left. The oldest memo contained numerous blacked-out sections. The document was reminiscent of military documents she'd requested in the past for dig sites on old government bases. One memo had a single un-redacted line remaining that read like atrocious poetry. *The ground is not sufficiently thawed enough to provide the information needed.* The location read Arctic Shelf, 63°— It was dated three years after her estimated death.

Leaning back, she rubbed at her burning dry eyes. Both the human and Chriw'rian wars with the Anunnaki were complex topics with large amounts of data to sift through. Alongside those historical records were documents written hundreds of years later by authors insisting the wars were a conspiracy dreamed up by large corporations to siphon more money from the population to fund special projects that weren't actually meant to protect them. Some questioned if the war had ever happened. Those comments were in line with the discussions on historical cultures and buildings too old for people to even imagine. Instead of looking for ancient pottery or buried buildings, the internet, or what was left of it, provided enough expert proof and jarring video content to verify the alien invasion was real.

Grunting at the last comment she read stating the attack was nothing more than a combination of reflective mirrors and space balloons, she turned her handheld face down on the table and nabbed her cup. She needed more tea before she could deal with much more of this.

Other articles dissected plausible theories about why the Anunnaki attacked. The authors tried to assign different motives for the reason behind their destructive harvesting. Her favorites were fuel for some type of super solar machine, and the social rite of passage. Realistically, no one had any idea as to why they attacked, even after reverse engineering all of their equipment they could get their hands on.

Shannon placed the cup in the recog and mapped back the page Hellen had landed on. Despite how quickly Hellen had navigated, Shannon ended up on the screen she needed, found the glyph for tea, stuck her cup in the machine, and selected that option.

While she waited, she thought about one particular post by an anonymous reader: *"You all have got it wrong, the powers that be are the powers that act."* The long list of responses demanding more information remained unanswered. The comment originated over a hundred years ago. She doubted they'd be responding any time soon.

Blue light flashed. She brought her steaming mug of tea to her chest and breath in its warm scent.

She tapped a nail on the cup as she returned to the table. Even with her pages filled with notes, she still had too many unanswered questions. Questions like why the Anunnaki attacked around every forty-five thousand years or so, skipping back and forth between our planet and a few others. Admittedly, the data was based on worlds with confirmed harvestings, there might be more unreported that skewed the data, but a pattern had emerged which just raised more questions.

She set her cup down and flicked to her rough timeline. Why were the Anunnaki attacking earlier than expected? Both the last attack on Earth and the impending one were outside the harvesting pattern of the Anunnaki. She did understand a bit more as to why Kro-Gen and the League had kept her body on hand. She'd want to have a possible ace in the hole if the Anunnaki were planning to attack out of sequence again.

Rubbing her temples, she struggled again with the desire to have all her memories returned. She wanted to know what happened to her to help with the current situation, but not at the expense of watching her mentor and friend die at the hands of someone they trusted. She'd be able to answer her questions about the last attack, or maybe what led to it. On the other hand, she might have died before anything important went down and then where would that leave her?

Ready for a break, she saved her work to her

personal folder, and cleared the search screen. She took a sip of her tea and eyed the open door. Her curiosity pulled her in a direction that might be slightly shameful. Holding her breath, she listened for footsteps outside the mess. No one approached.

Flexing her fingers, she pulled up the Chriw'rian database, and slowly typed out Chriw'rian mating habits.

The screen filled with naked tailed bodies. Some embraced in varying degrees of intimacy while drawings were used to describe the differences between the sexes. They were primarily a species with lean bodies, with those who could give birth bearing small breasts. Those who could impregnate had a permanent external limb that aided in impregnation. They weren't too dissimilar to humans in regard to sex organs.

Overall, the length of their body hair remained short, except for their head, their skin darkened the closer it got to the armpits and crotch. The figure spun around, and she noted a lighter line of skin color traveled down the center of their spine, and pooling at the base of the tail. Most images had the primary sexes at the same height and build which meant no divergent trends of dimorphism. Something she'd also noticed with the current human population.

Driven by a curiosity and a desire to know how an alien penis was different than a human's, she zoomed in on the privates. She rotated the three-dimensional image. Were those rings under the skin? She squinted at the hint of two bumps sequentially placed just under the head?

A throat cleared behind her.

Slowly, horror spreading through her, she lifted her head.

D'lane dropped into the seat across from her. His

brow arched as he took in the screen. She glanced down. She must have touched something because, naked twisting bodies, of which there were at least three, engaged in a bout of energetic sex. Fortunately, the sound remained muted.

Her cheeks heated. She tried to speak but nothing came out. Finally, she croaked out, "Off!"

The screen blackened.

D'lane smiled, his body slightly turned away, his closest ear turned fully toward her as his tail swayed in large arks at his back. He growled, "Are you learning all you need to know about my culture?"

Her laugh came out a bit manic. "I wasn't watching that video!"

"Then what were you doing?" He crossed his arms and met her gaze head on.

"Ahhh." She flushed. "I was curious about what…uh, Chriw'rian's might look…" She cleared her throat. "I wanted to see if Chriw'rian's and humans were compatible. *Not* watch a video of the finer points of intercourse."

At least not in a public place.

His tail tapped, tapped, tapped against her thigh. "You could have asked me."

"I wasn't going to ask to see your junk." She ran a hand through her hair, fighting the urge to pull it out at the roots. Her cheeks burned. "At least not yet."

He arched a brow.

"Besides, your culture has a complex mating ritual, way more complex than mine."

A frown pulled D'lane's brows into a stronger 'v' than expected. "How did people court in your time?"

She peered at the gray table and the solid white back

E.L. Roux

of the handheld, trying to find the best answer to the complex question. "It usually involved finding out if the other party was interested and spending time together to determine compatibility."

"That is not much different from what we've already done."

She sighed, cheeks warming as she remembered their earlier interaction in the hall. "But yours is so much more intricate."

Laughing, he came around the table to straddle the bench beside her. Her heart fluttered.

Hands resting palm up on his thighs, he tilted his head down slightly to meet her gaze. His hair swept forward as his golden eyes locked on. "Lesson one."

The heat in his gaze held her captivated, and she struggled to respond. "In what."

This was nothing like their sparring lesson from before.

"Shhhh." He placed his hands on her knees, thumbs slowly stroking the inside of her thigh as his tail draped over the top of her shoe. "After the bow is given and received, interactions between the pair can be instigated by either party."

He drew a random pattern over her thigh, his dark nail scratching at the surface of her jumpsuit.

His tail lazily curled around her ankle and gave a squeeze. She pulled her gaze up from his fifth appendage, across his form-fitting pants outlining the hard shape of him, and struggled to keep the images of alien genitals out of her mind. She blinked a few times as she realized he'd worn no weapons. This was the first time he'd done so in her presence.

He was sexy beyond belief, but it was his soul that

162

pulled her back to him time and again. He continued to lay bare his desires and let her choose when and how she wanted to respond. Her need to know all of him grew stronger with every interaction. She wet her lips, meeting his molten gaze before responding, "I'd like to kiss you."

His grip tightened on her thighs as he maneuvered her to face him, straddling the same bench as him. She fought a shiver. He widened her stance, sliding first one leg and then the other over his to make room for his body. Tipped backward, her knees clamped against his sides. He leaned forward slowly, giving her another chance to rebuke his advance.

She remained still, hardly daring to breathe. His lips halted inches from hers. She fought the urge to lean forward and claim them, letting him continue to lead their dance.

He smiled as if he'd read her mind. "Well?"

Their breath dampened the air between them. In a smooth glide, she pressed her lips against his. The touch was too brief. She returned, and sucked lightly on his upper lip, before sipping from his lips.

Heat from his chest radiated between her legs and lit a fire in her core. Raising her hands, she slowly stroked his ears, exploring their tufted pointed shape with her fingertips.

He shivered, breath ragged on her cheek. Her tongue dampened the length of his lips, seeking to deepen the kiss. He opened instantly. She swept in, tangling with him in a silky caress. His heady taste, a mixture of male and alien, sunk deep and branded itself on her soul. It was a savory flavor she would never forget, and she fought the urge to lean forward and press her body against his. The mess was not the place to start removing clothing.

His fingers clenched her thighs. His face was a silken caress against her own as she tilted her head for a deeper angle and discovered how well they fit. Her moan was nothing compared to the deep rumbling purr which vibrated his chest. Her nipples tightened. The stiff points rubbed against the fabric of her shirt; pleasure clenching deep within.

He licked across her lips before pulling back.

She fisted his shirt. "Wait."

Leaning forward, she pressed another kiss to his lips. The kiss was meant to be brief but turned raw and demanding. He settled his palms flat against her back and leaned forward, trapping her against his firm hands and the hot length of his chest, branding her from shoulders to hips. His rumble was a solid vibration against her sensitive skin. Groaning, she tightened her thighs and clutched him closer. His tail slid up her calf to wrap around her thigh, the tip tapping so close to where she desperately needed contact. He thumbed the hard point of her nipple. Her empty core clenched in demand.

Growling he tucked his nose under her jaw and licked at her pounding pulse. Her skin tugged lightly in his tongues wake. Shivering, she tilted her chin to the side. His breath gusted across her damp skin as his hand traveled down to the safer territory of her knee.

He pulled back, and she braced her hands behind her as she focused on the fluttering heartbeat at his throat.

D'lane's lips kicked up at the corners, the raw nature of it doing little to calm her. He rubbed his palms against the top of her legs, nails bunching the silky fabric. "We need to move somewhere less public."

"Agreed."

Smiling, he stood and offered his hand. Unwilling to let the moment pass, she slipped her fingers through his. Standing, she brushed up against the hard evidence of his arousal. She took a step closer. His arms wrapped around her, pulling her to his chest.

Shannon traced a pattern over the My'len insignia on his shirt. "Your place or mine?"

"I've got the bigger bed." His lips kicked up at the edges. "One of the perks of being the captain."

Shannon's hand made a slow trek down his shirt to the edge of his pants. "Then lead the wa—"

"Captain to the bridge." T'rev spoke over the comm. "Incoming urgent message."

Shannon's hand fell to her side. "Fuck."

He growled. "Not quite."

Chuckling, Shannon tipped her head forward. The steady beat of his heart was a loud drum in her ear. Her racing heart calmed, and exhaustion pulled at her.

He rubbed her arms as a deep sigh slipped from him. "Regrettably, I must return to the bridge."

"Don't you need sleep?" she asked, still catching her breath. He'd been awake at least as long as she'd been, and she'd like to be there when he went horizontal.

"I will not take my rest for a few more hours." He stroked her back in a soothing motion. "I need to ensure the ship is running smoothly, and we stay on track to reach our first destination."

She leaned back and struggled to focus on his damp lips. "We aren't heading straight for the derelict?"

He caressed the side of her face. The rough pad of his thumb brushed over her lip; the sensitive skin tingled from the touch. "We have a rendezvous at a space station to pick up our last crew member who was unable to make the rendezvous on Earth."

She perked up. "Will I get a chance to look around?"

"Perhaps on the way back."

If they had anything to return too. The Anunnaki were still moving forward with their attack and the League had already released a bulletin suggesting stations be on alert. It'd popped up while she'd been drinking her tea.

"There's not much to see in the hangar, but you might enjoy people watching." He leaned over and brushed her cheek with his in a smooth stroke. The fine hairs on his face were a silky counterpoint to the rough lick he gave to her ear. He took a step back. "Join me on your next meal?"

"Definitely."

He bowed to her, tail flicking at his feet. His ears swiveled back toward her as he left. Was he checking to ensure she stayed put or wanting her to call him back? He rounded a corner and disappeared from sight before she could decide.

She dragged her gaze back to the table and handheld sitting atop it. She chewed her lip, worried there might be some hidden reason for her extreme fascination with D'lane. Was she subconsciously revolting against the current human population by focusing on him and his sexy body? Had she latched on to the first person she connected to in this new time? She snorted as she fondled the PDA. If that was the case, would she be hooking up with Hellen too? Her hand drifted up to touch her lips. She doubted Hellen could kiss as well as D'lane, or that she'd want to hunt Hellen down to find out just how well they'd fit together.

****

The punch came out of nowhere. Pain slammed through her side. "Damn it!"

V'ren chuckled and danced back. "I told you, you need to watch your right guard."

Shannon took three deep breaths, forcing the air and fading pain from her ribs. "I heard you the last three times."

"Not enough to change your stance," V'ren drawled.

"There are so many to remember." Shannon twisted slowly from side to side. Her muscles twitched, constantly on the edge of a cramp. Hell, even with V'ren at half speed and quarter strength, Shannon could barely keep up. "Can you show me your stance again?"

Shannon wandered down here an hour ago, hoping to get some stretching in. She'd been working through the first two sparring transitions D'lane had led her through before they'd left Kro-Gen, when V'ren had joined her, and offered to teach Shannon more.

"In the basic guard," V'ren said as she got into position. "Your dominant hand sits loosely near your chin, and you keep your elbow close to your chest. Your secondary hand, the one you keep dropping, needs to remain up and close to your chest as well."

Mimicking V'ren, Shannon struggled to keep her body relaxed and ready to move at a moment's notice. She phased back and forth between initial position and basic guard until V'ren gave a nod of approval.

"Soon we'll have you trained up to our Ortus level students."

"High level training then?"

A chuckle came from the doorway. Warmth shivered up her spine.

D'lane stopped beside her. "It's our level one

training regimen for Chriw'rian youth."

Shannon chuckled. "So, some top tier students."

V'ren bowed to D'lane. She flashed a close-lipped smile at Shannon. "You learn quickly and will be giving the captain trouble in no time."

Shannon muttered a thanks before moving off to the side to stretch as D'lane and V'ren held a quiet conversation.

Without any type of workout equipment in the ship's gym, she was left with using her body weight or walking the length of the ship over and over again. Both of which were extremely boring without music. Rising to her feet, she fiddled with her NIC. It had to have access to music; next she'd need access to headphones. Shannon eyed the pointed Chriw'rian ears. What did headphones look like now?

The conversation wrapped up. Shannon glanced up. V'ren's tail twitched at her feet as she flowed into a smooth bow before leaving. Shannon's brow arched as D'lane waved her over.

He held out a bent arm. "Break my fast with me?"

She laid her fingers against the inside of his elbow. "I can always eat."

His ear flicked at her as he turned them toward the exit. "Excellent. I need caffeine, it's too early to think properly."

She chuckled. Apparently, he wasn't a morning person. He must've gone to sleep later than he'd estimated as she'd been awake for several hours. "I take it your conversation with V'ren went well?"

The dim lighting of the engine room enveloped them as the training room door closed. "It went as I expected, especially as we close in on Lagrange One."

The trek up to the third floor went quick and stressed her already strained thighs. She mentally added traversing the ramps to her warmup. The mess held half the crew, with T'rev and Q'aid possibly still on the bridge. There was actually a line at the recog. V'ren gave her a wink as she passed with a plate filled with unfamiliar foods.

When it was her turn, she pulled out her PDA and scrolled through her saved symbols. D'lane fed a plate into the machine as she painstakingly located the food she wanted. Blue light flashed.

Grinning, she pulled her dish from the recog, breathing in the warm sweet and salty smell. "Pancakes and bacon!"

D'lane dubiously eyed the food choices. His tail curled around her ankle. "Cured porcine and carbohydrates? An appropriate choice."

Her stomach rumbled. The first piece of bacon disappeared before she sat. The hickory smoked flavor flooded her mouth. The spongy texture barely phased her as she swallowed her first real taste of home.

D'lane's choppork stopped, and he stared at her with each shoveled bite. Hell, she'd get stares eating this way back in her time, but she didn't care. She swallowed her mouthful of masticated quick bread. "I haven't had this in ages."

Shannon paused as she dug into another pancake, realizing it had literally been centuries instead of only the months from the last time she'd made these. She dipped the fluffy confection into warm, runny syrup D'lane's language had translated to *sap* stored in a mug. "Just like Mom used to make."

The idiom rolled off her tongue before she'd thought

better of it.

He played with what was left of the green pudding on his plate. He'd eaten it quickly enough that it had to be good. "Can I try a bite of that?" she asked.

He scooped up a small oval on the very end of the choppork and extended it across the table. Shannon leaned closer and locked eyes with him. Her lips surrounded the end of the utensil. His pupils flared as he pulled the choppork from her lips.

Her lashes fluttered. The taste of a malt breakfast cereal hit her tastebuds, but the flavor was slightly more bitter than she'd like in the morning.

D'lane cleared his throat as she sat back. "Do you miss her?"

She licked the last of the syrup from her utensil to sweeten the aftertaste in her mouth and pushed away her empty plate. "I didn't remember much of my mother."

Her father had burned all the photos he'd had of her when she'd left. After college, Shannon had briefly debated searching her out. She wasn't looking for answers but had more practical concerns about her family health history. She'd put everything on hold when the Kro-Gen contract came through.

"I'd come to terms a long time ago about possibly never seeing her again, but if you're asking if I miss anyone from before..." His sharp nod moved her to continue. "I do. How could I not? I wasn't close to my family, but I still had people I could count on, friends who would drop everything to help me out, and vice versa. I miss that security." She swallowed hard, terrified to say she already considered him part of her new close-knit group which included him and Hellen, although she thought her acquaintance with V'ren was starting to become more.

Having a personal network wasn't the only thing needed to make this time feel like home. "I miss having a purpose."

He touched her arm. "You have a purpose."

"No, I have a goal, a brief direction in which my life is headed."

She had no safety net, no place to call home if the League determined that she'd repaid all her debts. If she was dropped from Kro-Gen support, what jobs would she have to get in the meantime to make ends meet? Did they have human social services in the future? It was one more item to add to her list of research items.

"My'len might have a spot for you." D'lane finished the last few bits of his breakfast. "And if they don't, I'll help you find something."

She fought a smile as picked up her tray and followed him back to the recog. "I appreciate your offer to help."

"What will you fill your time with today?" he asked as he slid his tray into the return slot.

"I'm continuing my research on the wars." She waited for the machine to clear before feeding her tray in. "I'm hoping I'll be able to dig up more information on the Anunnaki and their war ships."

He brushed a soft caress over her cheek in clear view of his crew. "Have you discovered if other information systems have additional information?"

She blinked in shock. "I didn't think I had access to that information on the T'grevis?"

"It's limited this far in deep space, but you have access."

Her mind raced. The amount of information at her

fingertips was larger than she thought. Excitement and trepidation warred within her as her fingers twitched at her sides. How was she going to sort through it all before they got to the derelict in just under six days?

She tipped her head back and maintain eye contact. She wanted a kiss but wasn't sure how to initiate it. She'd heard that physical contact between people who had an emotional connection was a great stress reliever. The only problem was whenever she and D'lane kissed things quickly got out of control. "When do we meet up with the space station?"

"In four hours." He stepped closer and wrapped his tail around her ankle. "Would you like to watch us dock with Lagrange One?"

She perked up. "Does it look anything like the Gunnel?"

She hated bringing up the station that had been destroyed, but it was the only reference she had.

"Lagrange One is a chaotic mess of metal that at one point had been a bevy of ships with their docking ports permanently attached to each other. It eventually molded into one solid mass that still continues to grow."

She smiled. "I can't wait to see it."

"I look forward to seeing you then." The silence stretched heavily between them, and she realized he wasn't going to kiss her. Hiding her disappointment, she stepped back.

He arched a brow. "You're not going to kiss me goodbye?"

Heat flooded her cheeks, but she laughed through her embarrassment, joined by some of the crew. Pushing up onto her toes, she wrapped her arms around his neck, and whispered, "If you insist."

Their lips met in a leisurely exploration. She ran her fingers through his hair, unable to resist the silky texture of it. The low rumble in his chest pressing against hers, slid to her core. She squeezed her thighs tight, enjoying the friction.

A cough sounded behind them.

Laughing softly, she pulled away. His smile bared a bit of fang as he glanced at V'ren.

"I'll be needing a moment of your time, Captain," V'ren drawled, her southern accent thick. "I doubt it will be as pleasurable as what you were just doing."

V'ren winked at her. Shannon laughed and waved to D'lane before heading to the conference room.

Chapter 12

Transmission to Kro-Gen: Contingency plan in place. Implementation imminent.

The dark greenish-brown metal blob of Lagrange One stretched across the cockpits screen. Haphazardly put together, the space station had oddly shaped circular protrusions covering the exterior. As D'lane stated earlier, it was a mix-match of scorched plates patched together from old spaceships that had definitely seen better days. She shuddered. It reminded her of a rusty ship being swallowed by the sea. How many holes did they have to patch a day to keep this station alive?

D'lane sat alone front and center on the bridge. When he'd commed her through her NIC, she'd been worried that something had gone wrong on their approach to the station, but everything appeared normal. Shannon closed the few short steps between them. She rested her hand on the back of his chair, her fingers close enough to touch the smooth skin of his neck. The tightness in her chest slowly relaxed. He'd armed himself again with knives strapped to his calf and arm. Glancing down, she found he'd added a few more guns to the straps on his hip and thigh.

"Should I be worried?"

He flashed her a smile. "No more than normal."

The door opened behind her. She shifted closer to D'lane. "Is that a yes or a no?"

"It's an always."

Q'aid nodded as he passed and took up the seat at navigation. D'lane split the screen and zoomed in on a portion of the station, while their approach remained on the other screen. Cannon like armaments stuck out at all sorts of angles. The view closer to a listing cargo ship's hull than a space station.

Pock marks too regular to be anything but planned, were splattered across the surface. Shannon leaned closer, futilely hoping for a better look. "What are those?"

"They're laser scars left over from Lagrange's pirate skirmishes over a hundred and sixty years ago." D'lane leaned back into her hand. "A testament to how long Lagrange One has survived against attacks in case anyone else decides to raid the station."

"Have they?" The view tilted as they banked, taking her sense of balance with it. She clutched at the back of his chair.

"Not in the last thirty years." D'lane gestured at the screen which rotated again as they wormed their way past the debris sliding by. "They destroyed the last ship that tried."

A large piece of dull metal gleamed on the corner of the screen. Did it once belong to a ship like the T'grevis perhaps destroyed in an attack or docking accident? The deep freeze of space wormed its way into the pit of her stomach and sent a shiver up her spine.

Shannon shifted to the side of D'lane's chair and leaned her hip against it. The firm touch of hardened plastic was a point of balance as her world titled again. A glint of twisted metal entered the screen. She squinted, trying to decipher the splash of a red lettering as it blurred past. "Why leave the destroyed pieces of the ship floating around? Seems like it's a flight hazard."

The walls of the ship were suddenly too thin for comfort. One solid strike from the debris floating around the station and everyone on the T'grevis would die within seconds, unable to swim or crawl to safety as the harsh vacuum of space sucked the life from all of them.

D'lane turned toward her, his hair brushing across the top of her hand. "It can be a great defense mechanism for smaller stations, but for one of Lagrange's size, it's a major inconvenience to all incoming and outgoing traffic. Iressa, he's the captain of the station, still complains about the time and costs associated with cleaning up after the last battle."

From thirty years ago? She squinted at the screen as something more organic floated by. Shannon gasped, shrinking back. "Please tell me they at least cleaned up the remains."

She shivered as her gaze followed a bit of body shaped space junk sliding by. The cool breeze from the door opening behind her not helping the situation any.

"Spare the dead your empathy," Q'aid spoke from navigation. "They knew what they were getting into when they signed onto a pirate brigade."

T'rev entered the cockpit tucking his shirt into his pants and filled the empty command station.

Q'aid glanced back at Shannon. "Every space station knows what would happen if pirates took over. They tend to murder and sell off a majority of the population before settling in."

Shannon's fist clenched on the back of D'lane's chair as her chest tightened. Her mental black box crept forward more than ready to accept her anxiety around death. She shoved it back. She needed to deal with this now—there was always the possibility of death in space—and swallowed hard. "Are there many pirates out here?"

"Not in the populated areas," T'rev said from the operations counsel, "but sometimes there's no escaping them."

D'lane wrapped his arm around her waist. The seat bit into her hip as she leaned against him. She wanted to crawl into his lap and accept the comfort he offered, but now wasn't the time. Their height difference allowed him to lean up and brush a kiss against her cheek. "The T'grevis is equipped with the latest scanners and weapons. We'll receive notice hours ahead of any pirate contact."

Her breathing eased. Shannon nodded as he slowly released her.

He caressed her hip. "If you take your seat, we'll start docking operations."

She sat in the middle seat and briefly fiddled with the harness. She left them off and leaned back to enjoy the relaxed synchronization of D'lane and his crew. Their voices twined together, the tones humorous and unhurried and a strong juxtaposition to the previous takeoff involving flashing alarms, incoming missiles, and the imminent threat of death.

The T'grevis sailed smoothly toward the hodgcpodgc of the behemoth space station in front of them. She couldn't have wished for a more boring and professional interaction, especially with the cold vacuum of space only a thin hull away.

T'rev's station dinged. "Communication coming through, commander."

"On screen."

The external view of the station and approach images shrunk to quarter screens as a green lizard being filled the other side. Panic spiked. Heart pounding, Shannon flailed upright. Her heel slammed into the metal under her seat and an ache settled into her calf.

The red door slammed open. Pain shot up her ankle with each dragging step. The two puncture wounds continued to seep through her swollen skin.

"What's wrong with you?" Her father slurred from the couch. Metal clattered on the floor as the can dropped from his limp fingers. "Can't you see I'm trying to sleep?"

His lashes fluttered as he passed out.

Gasping for breath, she limped over to his prone body, searching for the bulge of a phone tucked away in a pocket. Lashes wet, she dug the hard plastic out from under his hip and flipped it open. She stared at the flickering single bar.

Her nails bit into the flesh of her palms. The bright yellow eyes of the lizard scanned the cockpit, the same color as the one she'd ran into in the desert. Like back then, Shannon hunched into her seat and hoped they hadn't noticed her as their gaze settled on D'lane.

A forked tongue flickered into view. Was this the infamous Iressa, the pirate fighting captain of Lagrange One?

Their blurred background lacked any visual cues on their surroundings. Roughly humanoid in shape, the lizard had a large sagittal crest arched over the top of his skull. Varying shades of green scales covered the flat planes of his face and neck. A speckled pattern of lighter green scales gave way to darker ones, arrowing down the center of his forehead to stop at his nose.

Hissing filled the cockpit, almost overpowering her translator.

"D'lane, how nice to see you again." A nictitating opaque lid flickered down over his eyes. "I'm surprised My'len would allow you back into my nesting area so soon."

The reptile's 's' were drawn out, disrupting her ability to follow the conversation. She ran her finger over the bump behind her ear and glanced at D'lane, remembering his initial growling language when they'd first met before the translator successfully integrated.

Laughing, D'lane sat forward. "Iressa, you know My'len and Ssisster have already reached an agreement in regard to that incident."

"That doesn't mean Ssisster hasn't stopped complaining about how My'len shortchanged them."

Hissing filled the space. Was that a laugh?

"But Ssisster's always complains." Iressa's gaze settled on Shannon, and they went preternaturally still.

Shannon's palms broke out in a cold sweat. She dared not break the intense yellow eyed gaze. Who knew what relinquishing dominance meant to Iressa's culture. Although, she could also be instigating a situation as she continued to stare.

"Speaking of problems," Iressa hissed as they finally broke contact. "You seem to be carrying a nest mate not of your own."

D'lane's left ear flicked toward Shannon as he leaned back in his chair. "We have Kro-Gen *employees* aboard."

Iressa flashed a sharp smile. "I didn't realize My'len was playing chauffeur."

D'lane growled. "It's a mutual agreement."

"Ah," he hissed.

Sounds filtered in from outside the lizard's screen. How many other beings were around this male? He scratched his chin. A small scale dislodged from his forehead and fell off screen. Yellow eyes zeroed in on D'lane. What was it with his eerie irises that kept her locked on them?

"Did you want your normal port?"

D'lane tipped his chin. "If you could oblige us."

A smile flashed across the screen, sharp fangs exposed. "It isn't a problem, my friend."

D'lane shifted in his seat as his voice became formal. "I am afraid I will not be joining you for drinks this time around. Our stay will be short."

"I see."

"However, if you'd like to come aboard and view some of our ship wide improvements, I am sure T'rev wouldn't mind showing you around."

Shannon's fingers curled on her thigh, unsure how comfortable she'd be with Iressa aboard the T'grevis.

"I might take you up on that offer." Iressa glanced off screen and gave a sharp nod before returning their attention to D'lane. "I'll see what I can shuffle around on my schedule to take a look." Iressa's smile widened further, exposing another pair of fangs. "Have a pleasant stay on Lagrange One."

The screen returned to their approach. Lagrange One filled more of the free space. They were close enough she could see the pock-marked patches of mismatched plates welded together that overlapped without a single straight line in sight. Just how safe was this station?

The gaping maw of the landing bay opened wide to swallow them whole. The screen flashed bright white. She blinked to clear her vision and block the sharply shifting angles on screen as Q'aid navigated to their parking space—ship space? Landing pad? Whatever the hell did they call the literal spot the T'grevis softly settled on.

D'lane stood and checked his weapons. Her gaze followed each movement, making the routine action more suggestive in her mind as he settled each one into place. He turned and caught her staring. He arched a brow as he went over the last few guns in his arsenal. Was it her imagination, or did his hands linger now that he knew she watched? She swallowed roughly and forced her overactive libido back under control.

"Clamps engaged." Q'aid shut his screen down.

"Are you ready to see the exciting expanse of Lagrange One's landing bay?"

"Heck yeah I am." Even if she didn't get to see the rest of the station, off the ship was still something new. Shannon stood and gestured at his weapons. "Do I need protection?"

"We're armed enough per My'len policy."

She nodded at D'lane's arsenal. "How many weapons do you need? I've counted seven so far on you alone."

Not that she was complaining, or that she hadn't already picked out a favorite. It was the slightly curved blade strapped to his right bicep which snaked around his muscle.

"Why?" He stepped closer and tucked a curl back behind her ear. "Do you think I need more?"

"I mean, it has to be restricting your movements

with all those hard…" She flushed, hot cheeks prickling.

He chuckled, catching her fingers as she went to cover her face. He brought them close to his lips and brushed his cheek against the back of her hand. She twitched as the nerves on her arms reacted.

"I could manage at least one more weapon for you."

She glanced down with a breathless laugh and her gaze caught on the hard line of his penis. "I think you already have."

He laughed, and she pressed a kiss against his lips to try capture his joy, one meant to last a moment, but it turned into more as their tongues dueled. Pressed against his chest, she broke her lips from his and rested her head over his heart. The beat pounding in her ear.

He brushed a hand down the line of her back as their breathing slowed. "We need to get moving."

She found herself trailing beside D'lane, watching the sway of his tail.

After traveling down a ramp, they arrived at the back of the ship. A quick glance at her NIC let her know the station resided on the other side of the wall they faced. His hand hovered over the control panel she couldn't see. He searched her gaze. "The smell can be a little off-putting."

"Surely it can't be that bad."

He palmed open the door, and the stench hit immediately. Sour and damp, filled with burnt metallics and the hint of tangy organic scent of unbathed bodies seared her lungs.

The rotting scent of thawing earth and half frozen flesh bit sharply at her stomach with every breath. Straightening, she cleared the sweat from her brow and frowned at the other holes surrounding her. They still had two more weeks before they wrapped up at the dig site. Two more weeks of decayed earth and decomposing matter exposed with every shovel full of dirt. She climbed out of the hip high trench and headed toward the sled. The half-frozen caribou at the edge of the dig site needed to be moved before the smell got even worse.

He laughed at her pinched expression. "It gets better once you leave the landing zone, and it's practically nonexistent in the more affluent parts of the station."

Her heart sank as her expression sobered. From what he said, she wasn't going be allowed out of eyeshot of the ship.

He brushed a knuckle down her chin. "It's something we'll explore on our way back from the derelict."

D'lane walked down the ramp, tail flickering between his feet. She caught up with him as he paused at the end. They'd exited the ship facing the nondescript gray wall, which wasn't horribly exciting. A large yellow line on the metal floor wrapped around the sides of the ship likely denoting the ships parking space. He took her hand, and they rounded the edge of the ship together as the rest of the hangar roared into view.

Sound bombarded her ears. She flinched into D'lane's side as his ears flicked back, probably to try to dim the noise. She yawned and popped her ears. Sound rushed in with a clash of stomping feet, raised voices, and rumbling engines. It took a few moments for the stations chaotic roar to settle to a more manageable level.

Dozens of ships perched like birds of prey ready to launch into flight. Others crouched, crunched upon themselves reminiscent of dead arachnids. Smooth lines and sharp edges glinted under lights. Scorched and perfectly spotless surfaces probably hinted at the difference between atmospheric entry and purely space ferrying ships.

A pungent cloud of exhaust drifted past. She breathed into her shoulder until it passed.

D'lane patted her back as she coughed. "The smell from the older ships re-acclimating to atmosphere can be horrendous from the mix of ozone and elemental compounds they picked up on their trip. It's horrible to breathe but safe."

His gaze skipped from vessel to vessel. Was he searching for something?

"Do you recognize any of them?"

"No, but that doesn't mean trouble won't find us here."

Shannon hugged herself. "Perhaps I should have a weapon after all."

"Kro-Gen hasn't approved it, but I'll see what I can do to expedite the process." He settled a hand at the small of her back. The touch butterfly soft, her jumpsuit tickled the small hairs of her skin as he steered her further away from the T'grevis to the edge of the thick yellow line on the far side of the ship.

"Keep an ear out for high-pitched ringing." His palm slid down to the base of her spine. "It doesn't happen often, but ships weapons have misfired on unsuspecting victims in bays like this."

Shannon brushed a hand down her arm, smoothing the raised hairs underneath. How many of those deaths were planned? She shivered as the general's words of warning came back. It'd be easy to pick someone off in an open exposed situation like this and blame it on a malfunction.

He stepped closer, enveloping her in his heat. "We have a few moments before we need to return and help the crew."

Shannon struggled to keep her attention focused on D'lane or the sea of individuals milling around the docking bay of Lagrange One, gawking, like her, at the variety of ships. As much as she coveted her time with D'lane, she couldn't keep her attention away from the intense colors that flashed under the bright lights.

Her gaze flickered from body to body, trying to see everything all at once. A blast of exhaust tangled her hair in front of her face. The smell of ozone and oil was unpleasant as ever.

She shoved the curled locks back. "How many different types of beings are there in the universe?"

D'lane chuckled. "I can't speak for the entire universe, but there are many."

Clothing of every style imaginable passed by—and not, as she watched a naked alien stroll by. Aliens pushed and shoved their way through the stagnate groups of species that congregated near the open ramps of ships. Some aliens were remarkably similar to humans at first glance, but their coloring and shape was slightly off. Others had horns spiraling overhead in different orientations mounted above elongated faces.

Shannon watched as a race of bipedal amphibian's descended into a group of their peers. "More than there are here?"

"I used to think that there were too many to count. But over the course of my travels, I've found that at the larger stations like Lagrange One, it doesn't matter where one is from, but how they choose to interact with those around them."

"Is there a list somewhere that I can get on the social standards of this station to study for the trip back?" If she had the free time to do so, it would give her a step up in understanding any new cultures she would have to adapt to as she finished paying off her debt.

"I'll transfer the file to your NIC now." D'lane's head tipped toward his wrist, exposing the delicately shaped ears she realized weren't that different when compared to the rest of the alien population.

Shannon's wrist buzzed indicating the transfer was complete, but her attention remained on her surroundings. Skin types varied as much as body appearance. Some beings were spotted like cow hide, while others had a translucent shape of butterfly wings pressed against skin. Others were so dark, she only caught sight of them because the light had shifted just right. On the flip side, some had skin so bright they were translucent, making it easy for her to see what the interior of the species looked like.

Lizard species matching Iressa's visage wound through the crowd along with tall lean figures with bat-like wings that were given a large amount of room as they traveled. They traveled in pairs with ears flickering wildly in every direction. Current humans in various colored jumpsuits were sprinkled throughout the crowd along with a few Chriw'rian's as heavily armed as D'lane.

Shannon gestured after the last Chriw'rian passed. "Do you know any of them?" She immediately bit her lip. "Don't answer that. It's a silly question. If you asked me if I knew any of the humans walking by, my answer would likely be no."

"I don't recognize them, but they might not be

affiliated with My'len." D'lane chuckled as he bent to brush his cheek across hers. She cupped her cheek, taking comfort from the intimate action as he straightened. "We need to head back and help the crew."

Shannon was hesitant to leave the area they stood in, as this was the first real taste of the world she now lived in, but she'd still be able to see the crowd back by the rest of the crew. She smiled at him. "Will I be able to help?"

The doctor had approved her for light lifting, but if it required her to move heavy objects onto the ship, she wasn't sure what she could do to help.

His lip kicked up at the side. "Probably not, but you'll be safer next to us and within the defensive shield of the T'grevis."

Her excitement waned for a moment as they walked back to his crew, arms brushing with each step. Maybe she'd spend her free time on the flight back researching personal safety instead if just standing in a landing bay could get a person killed.

He gave her a squeeze as they neared the crew at the loading ramp. He stopped short outside of the few remaining containers that needed to be loaded. "One of us will be within shouting distance if you need anything."

She watched his tail sway as he walked away. He reminded her of her cat Kiki when he got the good treats. Shannon rubbed the center of her chest and stood off to the side and out of the way as D'lane jumped in to handling the pallets that had been dropped off.

Arms flexing, he loaded boxes onto the floating cart. J'rax said something, too far away for Shannon to catch. D'lane laughed, and soon the entire crew joined in. Her chest panged. Their comradery was something she deeply missed in her life. She turned away from the T'grevis to enjoy what little time she had left for sightseeing.

The hangar got uncomfortably hot when a few ships landed nearby. Perspiration dotted Shannon's face and rolled down her neck. She used her sleeve to wipe the stinging sweat from her face and turned back to the crowd.

Her gaze snapped to the right. Rich red hair flashed within the crowd. Was there another human from her time here? Excitement spiked, and she turned toward the T'grevis. "Did you see…"

They were too far away to hear her whispered words. Pivoting back, Shannon searched the crowd, attempting to catch another glimpse of the red-haired human. She stepped forward.

A wide pair of shoulders blocked her view. "I wouldn't do that if I were you."

She stalled at a leaner version of D'lane that had lines of white scars, likely made from a set of claws peeking out of the neckline of his shirt. Had he been violently rejected by a suiter, or picked a fight with the wrong person? The bright starburst scar cut across his cheek was new compared to the others. How many people had he managed to piss off?

She glanced over her shoulder, catching sight of D'lane hauling one of the boxes into the ship. She scratched her cheek, unsure what to make of this new Chriw'rian. "Do what?"

"Chase after that human."

She frowned, weaving back and forth on her feet, unable to see a thing. Damn this alien made a great wall.

"Who are you again?"

"I never introduced myself."

She snorted as she finally gave up on catching another glance of the red-haired human. "That must be why I don't care." She pivoted and headed back to the ship.

He followed hot on her heels. Irritation and fear straightened her spine as she strode toward the remaining crew milling outside of the ship. Her shoulders relaxed as J'rax called out to the stalker in greeting. His name was P'ret, if she caught it correctly, and had to be the brother D'lane mentioned earlier.

She should probably be polite to him seeing as he was a Chriw'rian, and related to D'lane, but something about him rubbed her the wrong way. She crossed her arms. It probably correlated to his belittling attitude and the slight sneer resting at the corner of his lips when he looked at her. She refused to be thought of as less-than, not after spending her teenage years fighting to make something of herself.

Chapter 13

Personal note: Re-check the images taken from Anunnaki crash sites.

Nerves still buzzing from being out in Lagrange One, Shannon took the seat next to D'lane and placed her tea atop the conference room table. "I wasn't expecting you to be here. Are you keeping me company while I research?"

"Sadly no." D'lane leaned back in his chair. His tail curled around her ankle. "I'm meeting with Iressa and some of the crew before we depart."

"Oh." Leaning forward she picked up her cup. "Give me a moment to clear up my research, and I'll leave you to it."

His hand stopped her. "I'd like for you to stay."

Warmth flooded her as she smiled. Cloth flickered at her periphery. She jerked her head to the door and swore under her breath as the scarred replica of D'lane she'd interacted with in the bay strolled in. Dressed in relaxed brown fatigues he lacked the assortment of weapons D'lane continued to display strapped to his body, and for that matter, what the other Chriw'rian's on the station had worn. If the arsenal was expected of all My'len employees when they were off world, as D'lane had stated, where did it leave this stranger? Was he employed by My'len, and if not, why was he on the ship?

"P'ret," D'lane said, standing. His voice, warm and

190

familiar. He rounded the table. "Settling in smoothly I hope?"

They embraced, pounding each other's backs as brothers often did. D'lane stepped away but kept ahold of P'ret's shoulder.

P'ret cut his gaze to her, his irises closer to Iressa's yellow than D'lane's gold. "I noticed I'm not in my standard room."

Shannon took a sip of her tea. Had she been placed in his usual room? Or did Hellen currently occupy it?

D'lane's fingers whitened where they rested on P'ret's shoulder. "We have others on board."

P'ret traced the scar on his cheek as he pinned her with a stare. The mark obviously held a deep meaning for him, but they were going to have problems if he continued to stare at her. She rolled her shoulders and tried to shake off her nerves.

It bothered her how similar P'ret and D'lane looked, and how different their personalities were. She needed to separate herself from placing any of her feelings for D'lane on P'ret and think of him as just another co-worker she needed to get along with.

D'lane frowned, narrowing his eyes as P'ret lingered on the scar. "Get it removed."

P'ret glared at him. "Not until I finish my mission."

Nodding, D'lane turned and headed toward Shannon, his tail brushing her leg as he stopped beside her. Her heart fluttered as he rested a hand on her shoulder. "This is Shannon, we'll be using her pre-revival skills on our mission. She belongs to the T'grevis."

There was the phrase again. *She belongs to our ship now.* It had to mean more than just the words, but what?

"Understood." P'ret's lips kicked up at the corner as he gave her a once over. "Kro-Gen couldn't spare us a real historian?"

Shannon's hands stilled on her lap as she bit back her reply. Their mission didn't have the time for whatever the hell it was that had P'ret trying to get a reaction out of her.

"None they could spare." D'lane retook his seat, his body a reassuring solid wall of warmth beside her. "Has Iressa boarded?"

"No." P'ret sprawled out in a chair near the head of the table, nose wrinkling as his gaze landed on her.

She arched a brow.

P'ret kicked his heels up to rest at the edge of the table, a small quarter size heel repair sat on the bottom of his back sole.

D'lane growled, and her shoulders relaxed. The familiar sound was the same one he'd given his crew when they sparred and one she'd associated with a vocal correction. P'ret chuckled in response. D'lane sighed as he tapped a rhythm out on the table. "Let's review the information you brought before Iressa arrives."

"Good idea." P'ret pulled a crystal from his pocket and placed it on the table. The dull green gem was no larger than the end of a pencil eraser. It liquefied into the surface. "I haven't had the chance to more than glance at the data myself."

Leaning forward, she brushed a finger over the smooth white surface where the gem had disappeared. "How do you get it back?"

"You don't." P'ret leaned back. "It's been internalized, downloaded, and dispersed within the T'grevis mainframe."

She glanced at D'lane. "What about viruses?"

P'ret snorted. "There are safeguards in place to neutralize them. Has Kro-Gen taught her nothing?"

Her hand curled into a fist. Breathe, she chanted internally, breathe. Now was not the time to start shit. She met P'ret's safety yellow gaze. After the meeting on the other hand…

A screen lit up in the middle of the table. Data scrolled across it. D'lane worked some magic and with a few movements, the information was in front of each of them. Her saved setting translated everything. "Most ships have a separate system that accesses the downloaded data and ensures the safe transfer between the main core and the crystal. Although our processer isn't impermeable—"

P'ret scoffed. "Nothing's impenetrable."

"—it would take something so outside of the norms to disrupt our system. We're more likely to find embedded sabotage incorporated into corrupt coding, than for us to have downloaded it."

Shannon squeezed his hand in thanks before leaning forward to read what had been shared. A few unfamiliar glyphs were scattered throughout the text, obvious words that had no direct translation. The data points were confusing. Her research provided some understanding of the coordinates system currently being used, but what they were identifying was outside her scope of understanding. Other untranslated lines might have been names or nouns if she was learning to read the sentence structures correctly. At his own screen, D'lane flew through the information at the pace of someone who knew exactly what they were reading.

A large screen rippled across the wall, the

transformation from blank surface to digital screen was something she was used to seeing by now. Figures ran down it in streams reflecting the untranslated version of what was on her screen. Had D'lane found something important?

P'ret leaned forward. "That's details on the size and placement of the derelict ship."

Her hand froze on the screen. "That knowledge was meant to be secret. Why was it on it on *this* crystal?"

"I also found names of suspected Anunnaki sympathizers." D'lane frowned, hand resting on the butt of his knife as if he could take them down from where he sat. "I am not surprised the information has already made its way to the more corrupt corporations and people in our galaxy; their bribes can be substantial." D'lane hummed as the data paused. "A few of the names are intriguing."

P'ret gestured at the wall. "Like the general Fernández for one."

Shannon sat forward and sifted through the information until she found the general's name, the only one listed under the League's insignia. Flabbergasted, she stared at the screen, unable to believe he'd be involved in sabotaging his own mission.

Her gaze clashed with D'lane's. "How accurate is this?"

If the general truly wanted to hinder their mission, they were in more trouble than she'd expected. She suspected they'd already be dead if he wanted them to be.

P'ret scratched the marred skin on his cheek. "Informants give bad information to remove rivals or distract us from the real moles. Others provide the truth knowing they can trust us not to rat them out." He leaned forward and pulled down the information from the wall. "The skill lies in knowing which is which."

"Is that your job?" She wondered anew why he hadn't been on Earth.

He flashed her a smile filled with teeth. "I'm not at liberty to say."

Unsettled, she glanced at the table and focused on the list illuminated in black and white. "Do we need to warn the general?"

D'lane snorted. "If I know him as well as I think I do, he'll already have protections in place for situations like this."

P'ret shifted in his seat. "It is interesting he's the only person listed at the League and Kro-Gen."

She scrolled past Fernández's name to search for more clues. "Perhaps someone wants him removed from the picture?"

T'rev chimed over the comm. "Commander, our friend is here."

She glanced up as V'ren entered the room and settled into the seat across from her. She gave Shannon and wink and dove right into the data on her screen.

"Grant him access to the T'grevis. He'll know where we are."

"Sir." T'rev signed off.

Iressa entered shortly after, bringing in the scent of hot sand and oil. They were clothed in a pair of tight-fitting pants, and long-sleeved shirt in a darker hue than his green skin, setting off the unusual shapes of their scales. The view screen in the bridge earlier did little justice to the intricate layout of Iressa's scales. Wider at his crown, they decreased in size as they traveled down his face. They were softer than she expected as they deformed into a smile when D'lane rose to greet him. Iressa's boxy body came to the center of D'lane's chest, which meant he was closer to her height.

Iressa shook D'lane's hand before catching sight of her. His smile widened, and she twitched as he revealed two sets of fangs.

"A human!" Iressa hissed as he took a step forward. Shannon pushed into the back of her seat. He stopped and stared at her head, likely taking in her hair. The soft arch of his nostrils flared. "And an ancient one at that. She smells different from the humans I have on my station, and her skin is darker." His nictitating opaque lids flashed down as he glanced at D'lane. "Is that normal?"

Shannon burst out laughing. Her tension broke, and she relaxed with his inquisitive innocent statements. She could tell there wasn't any malice behind his questions or motives. He was genuinely interested.

V'ren chuckled. Iressa's gaze briefly flickered to the Chriw'rian before returning to Shannon's hair.

P'ret sighed. "What information do you have for us?"

"Not much."

Iressa shifted into the seat next to V'ren. The action was frighteningly smooth and unhindered by Shannon's normal body physics, like hinging joints and bones. Her fingers itched to pull up information on his species.

"My sources are surprisingly tight lipped." P'ret rocked his chair back and forth, before stilling. "No one will be safe if the Anunnaki attack."

Fear was a great motivator to keep people's mouth shut. Her father had taught her that.

V'ren tapped out a restless beat against the table. "Are they planning on going on a harvesting rampage? They'll draw too much attention if they follow through with their plans and increase the likelihood of a mounting a combined counter attack."

"Rumor is," Iressa said sitting forward, "they'll move quadrant to quadrant, clearing everything in their path, sparing no one. Not even space stations will be safe."

D'lane body went rigid at her side. "Do you know where they'll hit first?"

Fear shivered down her spine. They suspected that the Anunnaki had already taken out the Gunnel station, but she had no idea where it resided in space or if it was considered an attack by them. She rubbed her eyes in frustration. Had she been awoken to die by the same hand that had killed billions of humans a thousand years before?

Iressa pulled a map up on the wall. "Latest data from Ssisster is they plan on taking the water world Aquiriana, and perhaps one of the newly developing planets in the delta quadrant."

V'ren quickly swiped through her data. "Looks like they're prepping for the Anunnaki interactions."

Did that mean they planned to fight them like we, the Chriw'rians, and the other aliens had in the past that managed to send them on their way? It seemed unlikely that the Anunnaki would use the ships that lost them the wars all those years ago.

P'ret swung his feet off the table and his boots hit the floor. "I doubt it will save them."

"Why not?" Shannon asked.

"They're not sending in a handful of ships as

before." D'lane turned toward her. "Those are easy to fend off. This time, they're sending out the full force of their regalia based on our data."

Iressa gave a shrug in a smooth ripple of a motion. "As for fighting them off, even a combined attack between distant planets would likely amount to loss. I'll be hard pressed to keep Lagrange One out of their path as they move through space."

Sucking in a breath, Shannon stilled her shaking hands on the table. This was not good. What would be driving them to destroy so many? She sucked in a breath, drawing the attention of those around the table. "Around my death, Earth had about a seven-thousand-year gap between their last harvest. This attack was roughly thirty-eight thousand years ahead of schedule. And with this upcoming harvest only two thousand years later, something else has to pushing them to deviate so much from their normal collecting tactics?"

D'lane's golden gaze pinned her in place. "Explain."

The fear hidden in his voice was almost subvocal, one she recognized from her childhood. That same primal fear that ran through her as a child. She pulled up her notes. "We need to understand why they are changing their attack schedule. Without this information we're not going to be able to stop them."

"You've been revived for how long?" P'ret crossed his arms, the My'len insignia bright on his chest. "These are questions that we've been working to solve for ages. How do we know if we can trust her? She could be a mole, involved with the Anunnaki for all we know of her past."

"She's not." D'lane squeezed her thigh under the table, the silent support settled her enough to know her concerns had been heard, even if P'ret doubted her. D'lane's thumb brushed her knee before he withdrew.

V'ren drawled, "Are we still expecting no help from any of the other planets or corporations?"

Iressa frowned, his face twisting into a hair-raising alien vestige. Shannon swallowed hard, happy to be on the other side of the table. A rattle overrode the hiss in his voice. "Most companies won't be bothered unless they feel they'll be targeted, and even then, there is no guarantee."

Her fingertips pressed into her thighs. "Don't they understand how many people will die?"

D'lane pulled up a painfully red-marked cost analysis sheet with Kro-Gen lettering at the top. "Planets will not risk speaking up to provide sanctuary without large scale corporate approval for fear of reprisal and lawsuits of wasted resources when refugees arrive."

"And," P'ret tugged down the end of his sleeve, "with corporations owning large swaths of land on those planets, they'll attempt to ride out the attacks and deem any damage as an acceptable loss covered by their insurance."

Horror filled her. How could the life of a person, and a population, be valued against the money made off their death? "That's barbaric."

V'ren shifted in the seat across from her. "It is about the response I expected from the League and others like them."

Iressa highlighted an egg shape space in the center of the map still on the wall. "We have some idea of the direction they'll take, between the Chriw'rian home world and Earth."

P'ret growled, "Chriw'r is not our homeworld."

Shannon sat up straight and swung her gaze to D'lane. His tail thumped rapidly against her toe before sweeping away. What did that mean?

Iressa corrected, "Sorry, your second home planet, but the rest is pure conjecture. We don't know how far they'll probe into any quadrant before turning back."

She fidgeted in her chair, uncomfortable with the list of planets running down the side of the screen. Beings were going to die if they couldn't figure out how to stop this attack. "Will they be able to evacuate with enough warning?"

D'lane frowned, drowning her hope.

"Everyone travels in space now, right?" She glanced around the table, "There must be enough spaceships to evacuate everyone."

P'ret laughed, the harsh sound echoing in the room. "Not everyone owns a ship, and those who do couldn't guarantee enough space onboard to get everyone off in time."

"We're talking billions of beings being moved from one place to another. Lagrange One has over a million beings populating it at one time." Iressa clenched his hand. "That's just a drop in a bucket compared to the populations that will need to be re-homed when they get off planet."

D'lane sighed. "This also assumes that everyone on the planet or station can afford the relocation costs."

"And where would they go?" Iressa said, the hiss back in his voice. "If the Anunnaki are hitting space stations, even with the firepower on Lagrange One I won't be able to fight them off. Nowhere is safe."

Heart pounding, the room began to tilt. She dug her fingers into her thighs, and she forced herself to breathe.

The painful truth of what could happen if they failed to find the information needed to stop the Anunnaki on the derelict began to settle in. The shear wake of death and destruction the Anunnaki would leave in their path would be soul destroying.

D'lane cleared the map from the wall.

Her fingers felt like ice as Shannon flexed her hands. "Is there anyone in particular who wants this mission to fail?"

"It'd be easier to ask who wants you to succeed," Iressa hissed. "Some corporations will consider the trade increase they'll receive once the Anunnaki finish their destruction as an acceptable outcome to the shortfall of production profits they receive in the interim."

Iressa rattled, "I know because Ssisster asked me for the same report."

V'ren tapped out a rough beat on the table. "And any surviving laborers will be glad for the opportunity to move up the corporate ladder."

With a quick glance at his wrist, Iressa stood. Shannon stumbled to her feet as everyone followed suit.

"I need to get back before Ssisster starts asking questions about my extended disappearance from the den."

D'lane gave a formal bow, V'ren and P'ret repeating the motion. She followed suit and straightened.

D'lane tugged his shirt into place. "Thank you for this information."

Iressa's head dipped in D'lane's direction. "Next time you stop by, I'll take you up on that drink."

"Be safe," Shannon said, retaking her seat. Iressa flashed her a sharp smile as they left.

She might still be bothered by their likeness to the

snake that bit her, but Iressa was one being who was ready to defend the population he served.

D'lane commed the bridge. "As soon as our friend leaves, prep for departure."

"Roger that," Q'aid said.

"I'm calling it a night," P'ret said as he pulled a handheld from his pocket and tapped it to the table. The screen flashed with data as he tucked it away. "I've been up for the last three rotations without any rest prepping for this mission. I'll continue reviewing the information in my room."

Shannon ignored the squinted glance he sent in her direction. For someone involved in the undercover work, P'ret didn't seem willing to go with the flow.

V'ren sighed and stood. "I'm headed back to work as well but will review what I can."

She tapped the table with her handheld to transfer the data before leaving a moment behind P'ret.

Shannon turned toward D'lane. "Will you share the data with the rest of the crew?"

She stilled as D'lane stood, his tail sliding against the inside of her calf.

"T'rev will receive the full breakdown. He's one of my top advisors, as is V'ren. Q'aid and J'rax will get an abbreviated version of the information. They don't need to know everything to do their jobs. As for Hellen." D'lane sighed. "I'll leave that up to Kro-Gen."

She brushed a hand up the long line of his back. "Do we even have a chance at stopping them?"

He glanced at her. "Who can say? We can only do what has been asked of us and continue on the path we've been sent on."

She tipped her head back as a heavy weight settled

deep in her chest. "What if we fail?"

He tucked a curl behind her ear. "In life, nothing is certain."

Chapter 14

Shannon: Double check the Gandaki reference regarding negotiations with the Anunnaki.

Blank search results stared back at Shannon. How the hell had she managed to find a question that returned nothing with three very large search engines at her disposal? Leaning back in her chair at the conference table, she erased the text, and tried another phrase which managed to get a few hits. She'd been studying the information on the remnants of the Anunnaki ships left after the war and had hoped there'd be a larger reservoir of images or recreations of their language in use. But there wasn't enough data to get a full understanding of their basic lettering system.

Shannan cracked her knuckles and deleted her last search. She'd already attempted the if's and then's used in coding commands back in her time for improved results, but it didn't have the same response on the T'grevis's NIC. Maybe they'd moved past this type of coding in the current systems?

She typed in 'conspiracy Anunnaki ships' and waited with bated breath as the system churned its way through her request. Gathing this data wouldn't be an issue if the Anunnaki interacted with others outside of war or if all the pictures taken during the wars weren't such grainy images.

She rubbed her temples as she replayed the blurred

image of an Anunnakian vessel taken from a passing ship during My'len's the last war. Could no one capture a clear image of their invaders?

She hoped to get a better handle on the Anunnaki before she arrived at the derelict, but when her search request returned only few results, her hope diminished. If she could understand why a culture chose to expend a vast amount of resources to harvest other planets, she could understand them a little better and hopefully work out a way to stop them.

One of the theories was the Anunnaki's home planet was dying. That one didn't fit as well as a reasoning for their actions as some of the other ideas. If their home world was failing to support life, why not instead move to a new planet, like P'ret had hinted the Chriw'rians had? Their entire society would need to accept the destruction of others to support themselves instead of using that same energy to rebuild anew? Or perhaps the majority of the population didn't know? Although that would be unlikely due to the sheer number of beings involved and the harvesting timeline.

She could say one thing after researching the Anunnaki; their tactics were predictable. They always arrived with force, armed with an armada of spaceships, and enough weaponry to disable and overtake an entire planet. They ripped what they wanted from the planets bloody grasp and never attempted to barter or trade for resources.

Like others, their actions left her with too many questions. Did they process or do anything to what they took on the ships? Maybe they had something like the recog on board that dissolved and stored what they took for easier transportation. Which led to the question of the energy consumption they needed to make the round trip worthwhile.

She rubbed her dry eyes and stood, ready to take her frustrations to the one person she trusted to bounce ideas off of.

D'lane sat alone. Dead center in the cockpit, he had complete control of the ship from his chair. The view screen displayed the black expanse of space around them with the occasional flash of light. She stopped next to his chair, resting a hesitant hand on the back of the seat.

"Sit with me," he said, tugging her willing body onto his lap. "We have a few minutes until the others return."

She snuggled closer, breathing in the smooth scent of hot sand and the sweet hint of dates that was uniquely his. Sometime between their meeting and now, he'd removed all his weapons, and she relaxed into the warm planes of his body.

She rubbed her forehead against his shirt. "I can't figure out what causes them to do what they do."

"The Anunnaki?" He stroked her arm. "Do they need a reason?"

"There's always a motive, or else why leave their home in the first place. It can't be for the power of conquest since they leave no markers of their passing." D'lane tensed under her. She caressed a random design over his chest, leaving the question on why that statement had bothered him for later. "In the past, we knew where the Romans were because they'd left behind aqueducts and monuments, and they enslaved those they conquered. Other than their destruction, the Anunnaki have only left one item behind, the communication device that called them to Earth a thousand years ago, the one Krogenic's sent my team searching for."

She glanced up to find his attention focused solely on her.

"Have you ever met one?" she asked, thinking of the two blurry outdated photos she'd found in the archives provided by Joseph. "Just one Anunnaki in all your travels?"

"No." D'lane ran a hand down the outside of her arm, his rough fingertips playing over the top of her hand resting against her leg. "I have not traveled often enough to see one. Our stories are focused more on our success in the last battle and less on the appearance of our enemies."

"Could we ask Iressa?"

"We're on restricted communication for the duration of the trip as a safety precaution."

"What about V'ren and P'ret? They've traveled and might have seen or met an Anunnakian." Even after her brief interaction with P'ret, she'd risk his grumpy side to find out if he'd ever laid eyes on one during his travels.

"Would they even know what they've seen? You asked earlier about how many species existed in the universe, and the answer is truly unknown. We'd also be making an assumption that anything seen during the war was their normal attire."

"Is there a place that keeps a running list of alien populations? They might have a list of unknowns I can research."

"P'ret would be a great resource for that research."

Shannon sighed. "I figured as much."

A bright light streaked across the screen, catching her attention. "The Anunnaki have been around for millennia. It's odd that no one has any idea about why they attack. We have recog's now, why shouldn't they be able to produce what they need for themselves if they're harvesting for nutrients. There has to be something I'm missing."

"Give yourself a break." D'lane hugged her closer. "You've sifted through a large amount of data in a short time."

"I've had lots of practice cramming." She shifted to rub her forehead against his neck. "Maybe it is a mating call?" Her arm arched across the screen. "See all the planets I have conquered. Do you want to have my babies now?"

He rumbled a laugh. "It would be one hell of a dry period between mating cycles."

"Unless they're harvesting somewhere else in the meantime."

He tucked her closer. His heartbeat was steady under her ear.

The attacks had to play some major role in their civilization. "Understanding why will help me to decipher their ship."

"The answer is there, and I know you'll find it."

His faith in her sent a steady pleasurable throb through her body. Her palm slid across the firm planes of his chest. His pulse quickened under her ear as her fingers explored his warm abdomen over his shirt. The black cloth was soft and silky, but the smooth skin of his neck drew her like nothing else. Taking her time, she made her way up to explore the firm line of his jaw. Their breaths were quick as the tip of her finger grazed his tufted ear.

His hands clenched at her hip and shoulder. He lowered his gaze to hers. The gold eyes turned molten as she wet her lips. She gripped his shoulder, leaning up and brushing a kiss across his lips. She pulled back slightly and got caught in his searching gaze. What was he looking for?

His nostrils flared as he sucked in a breath. His chin dipped, and she met him halfway. Her tongue swept into the damp heat of his mouth. Moaning, she leaned into him as they leisurely explored each other.

She angled her head to the side and caressed down his chest. He hummed, and the kiss deepened. The touch of his tongue was still rougher than she was used to as he tangled with her own.

They separated, breath panting and grips tight.

"I am trying to give you time to adjust." He leaned in and nuzzled her ear. "You've been revived, forced on this dangerous mission, and have no real family to fall back on." He kissed her cheek before moving to the other side. "If you were a Chriw'rian, I would understand your signals better, and you mine."

A hot damp lick to the pulse at her neck had her knees clenching. She tilted her head back, her thighs shifting as he hit a particularly pleasurable spot on her shoulder. "D'lane."

"Yes." His breath beat against her damp lips.

She leaned forward. "Stop thinking and kiss me."

Their mouths clashed. His chest pressed firmly against her breasts. The soft material of her shirt slid deliciously across her sensitive skin. His tongue swept in as he took control.

A rough caress skimmed down her sides and settled at her hips. She arched her back, pressing the beaded points of her nipples against the hard planes of his chest. He growled. The sensitive points tingled at the vibration.

A footstep fell heavy in the hall, and she jerked

back. His grip on her hips kept her in place. She wiped her damp lips and attempted to straighten her hair. She needed to stop kissing him in public places.

Q'aid ducked into the cockpit, flashing them a smile. "I see you're working hard captain."

D'lane chuckled and kept his golden gaze on Shannon. "I endeavor to meet your standards."

Q'aid lounged in the navigation chair, swinging the seat around to face them. "I'd say you'd already met them, and then some, but I prefer to keep our next sparring match friendly."

D'lane's grip relaxed, and she fought a shiver as he caressed the length of her leg. "Smart choice."

Her feet hit the deck as she stood from her spot on D'lane's lap. To say she was turning tail and running from the crew would be a moot point. "Do you know where V'ren is?"

Q'aid swung around to the table and images flashed across the screen. He pivoted back with a smile. "Looks like she's in Engineering, probably bugging J'rax."

"Thank you." She bent and pressed a quick kiss against D'lane's cheek. "I'll see you at the next meal." She needed answers, and she hoped V'ren had them. Otherwise, she'd have to brave P'ret.

****

Heart pounding, Shannon stared at the lithe Chriw'rian in front of her. J'rax had melted out of the shadows to block her path, wielding a wrench longer than her arm with an ease that meant they knew how to use it.

J'rax's bright blue eyes held her place as they spoke, "Welcome to my lair."

Laughing, Shannon pressed her palm against her

chest until the erratic beat calmed. "This is where you work?"

Large, dark machinery loomed overhead. Down in the bowels of the ship, the T'grevis finally felt like the spaceship she had been expecting. The wide metal track she stood on had yellow reflective lights lining the walkway. Further down the lane bright spotlights sat above several doors leading to unknown rooms.

J'rax hung the wrench on their belt wrapped thickly around their waist. The strap canted down at a sharp angle. "Exquisite isn't it."

Hands at their hips, one resting on the belt's black strap, the other atop the wrench, J'rax tapped out a slow steady beat. "So, what brings you down here this ship cycle?"

"Have you seen V'ren? I'm hoping to ask her a few questions."

J'rax arched a brow. "I might have."

Chuckling, V'ren stepped out from behind the machinery, and stopped next to J'rax, their shoulders touching. V'ren's southern accent came out strong. "How may I be of service?" V'ren glanced at her NIC. "I'm assuming it's not a medical need as I don't have any warnings of crew dismemberment."

"I'm trying to fill in some missing information in my research. D'lane said you've had travel outside of My'len space and I wanted to pick your brain."

"My experience is limited. P'ret would be the one you need to talk to."

Shannon grimaced. "I'd planned on it, once he's in a better mood but in the meantime, I was hoping you can tell me whether you've seen an Anunnaki in any of your travels."

J'rax slowly straightened, their stance rigid and gaze hard. "Are you suggesting V'ren wouldn't have reported it?"

Shannon took a half step back. "I'm hoping someone from the general population has had social interactions with them outside of planetary annihilation." She took in J'rax's clenched fists. "Is there something I'm missing?"

V'ren rested her hand on J'rax's shoulder. The sharp anger in J'rax's blue eyes dulled. "J'rax is worry about my honor, but to answer your question, no, I've never seen one. Just the slew of other cultures that make up the mass population on stations."

"Damn." Shannon sighed. Looked like she'd have to talk to Grouchy McGrouchyface after all. "Have you heard of anyone seeing one?"

J'rax shifted their weight as they traced the wrench with the tip of their finger. "No one knows what they're looking for."

"So I could have already seen one and not known it?" A machine clunked drawing Shannon's attention. "All the images I've seen lack the refinement to identify the race."

J'rax shifted closer to V'ren. "Not all aliens look the same."

Shannon flushed. "I know that."

V'ren curled her tail around J'rax's. "My'len may have a secret repository of these sightings."

"She'll need to be granted access." J'rax leaned into V'ren.

"Is that something D'lane could do?" It wasn't like Shannon could ask the general to grant her access, not with communications turned off. If D'lane hadn't mentioned these secret files, then he didn't know of their existence.

"I don't believe he has the authority," V'ren drawled.

"But P'ret does," J'rax said.

"His personality leaves a bit to be desired." Shannon tugged on her jumpsuit sleeve. "But I'm sure I can be polite enough to ask him a few questions before he runs away."

Shannon played with the NIC bracelet around her wrist and swallowed her irritation. "Do you know where I can find P'ret?"

V'ren waved Shannon over to a wall mounted NAV. "I'll show you how to find people on the ship."

Shannon snorted, glancing at the white bracelet she couldn't get off. "I knew this thing had a tracking device on it."

V'ren shrugged. "They all do. It's required in most corporations to have complete access to an employee's location. It increases safety and reduces danger."

"But what if we're boarded by pirates?" she asked, remembering the conversation they'd had approaching Lagrange One. "They'd know where everyone was."

"True." V'ren flashed a smile. "If they can get access to our locked-out NAVs, then we're probably all dead anyway. Now, this is how you go about tracking someone down. Just don't tell D'lane I showed you how."

Five minutes later she stood in front of P'ret's door, braced for the next interaction with a male that constantly put her on edge. She still hadn't decided if it was his attitude, his slightly off likeness to D'lane, or his personality, but there was something about him that bothered her.

Fist clenched around the cup of bitter stimulant she'd seen D'lane down like water in the mornings, she took a deep breath. Holding the breath, she waited a second before slowly letting it out. She knocked on P'ret's door. No one answered. Glancing down the hallway to her room across the way and to the right, there was no one to help her get P'ret's attention, so she repeatedly knocked without success.

Knuckles hurting, she growled and prowled down to the corner NAV and searched for P'ret location again. Maybe he'd moved from her last search visiting the recog... She flicked through the screens and found that he'd slipped past her somehow and now occupied the space in the conference room of all places.

Stomping down the hall, she fought to get her frustration under control. Why was this male so hard to pin down?

He'd left the conference door open, and when she stepped inside, she found him sitting in what she was starting to consider 'her' chair. Reading his PDA, he had his other hand on the table. His fingers twitched at her arrival even as he continued to ignore her.

She cleared her throat.

Clearly disgruntled, he raised his gaze and wiped the work screen on the table, not that she would have been able to read it in the first place.

"Was there something I could help you with?"

Her hand clenched around the cup, and she reminded herself she wanted to stay on his good side for the time being. Forcibly relaxing, she chewed through the meaning behind his tone, hoping her translator was mistranslating his attitude. She placed the mug next to his hand. "I brought you a cup of coffee."

"Thanks." He pushed the cup away and turned back to his screen and ignored her.

She cleared her throat again. "I have a couple of questions I was hoping you'd answer."

Arching a brow, he sat back and stared through her. "And what would that be?"

"Have you ever seen an Anunnaki?"

He stilled, expression hardening, the starburst of his scar bright white against his sandy cheek. "No."

She stepped closer and pushed the cup within his reach. His nostrils flared. "Don't you think that's unusual?"

He leaned back and crossed his arms. "I'll give you that."

His body language screamed to be left alone, but she wasn't going to leave until he answered her questions. "Look, I need your help, or I wouldn't be here bothering you. I can think of a thousand things I'd rather be doing than trying to beg for your attention, but I can't get all the answers on my own. I don't know this time, nor have the proper access, but you do."

He growled, "You presume to give me orders?"

"No." Muscles strained as her fist clenched, she slowly forced herself to relax. "But I am asking for your help in understanding how this would be possible."

Chapter 15

P'ret to D'lane: Don't let her sway you from your path.

Shannon's cheek rapidly closed in on the floor. The thick blue mat was a firm slap that did little to soften the pain from the fall. "Damn it!"

D'lane chuckled from his position propped against the wall. "You're getting better."

V'ren offered Shannon a hand up. "You almost blocked my last attack."

"Go me!" Shannon cheered as she took the offered assist. Her muscles screamed in protest as she straightened and wiped the sweat from her face. "At least I'm getting better."

She'd wandered down here to work off her frustration with P'ret and found D'lane and V'ren sparring. They'd left her alone for a handful of bouts before pulling Shannon in for the next round of lessons. She appreciated the opportunity to focus on something else for a while.

V'ren passed over a folded black towel. "Little by little we'll get you up to scruff."

Shannon perked up. "How much longer?"

"If you practice every day," D'lane said as he pushed away from the wall and stepped onto the mat, "It should only take a few years."

Shannon's heart raced as he prowled closer.

Excitement and fear warred at the possibility of physical contact. "Are we sparring?" Shannon's voice cracked. She cleared her throat. "I don't know how much more fight I have in me."

V'ren chuckled. "I'm sure you could go for another round or two."

Shannon narrowed her eyes in response as V'ren collected her shoes from the lockers on the far wall. Shannon's muscles were limp noodles after training with V'ren. D'lane could topple her with a slight shove. Not that's she'd mind as long as he fell with her.

His lips kicked up at the side. "We won't be sparring."

She sighed in relief. She tugged the front of her jumpsuit away from her chest. The cold air felt good against her warm skin. The wet fabric was unable to keep up with the amount of sweat she produced.

D'lane's tail brushed her ankle. "But we are going to work on your form."

"Crap," Shannon groaned.

"See you two in the mess for end of shift meal," V'ren tossed over her shoulder as she headed toward the door. "And Shannon, be sure to use the massage setting in the shower afterward."

Unsure about what V'ren meant, Shannon released the jumpsuit and braced her feet shoulder width apart. Her thighs twitched as she recalled the conversation at the end of their last lesson at Kro-Gen "Are we working on falls?"

"No," D'lane said as he walked around her. "You've worked enough on those with V'ren. We're work on striking combinations."

"So, first position?"

"It's always best to start there."

She sat deeper in her stance and swallowed a groan as her thigh muscles trembled with fatigue. "Hands open or closed?"

He ran a finger down the outside of her hand. Her fingers tingled.

"I'd like them to be loose but not relaxed. You want to be able to easily translate between a fist, open hand strike, and a block."

Shannon wet her lips. "Right, that makes total sense."

Shaking her hands out, she worked on following his directions to improve the strength behind her punch, and how to put her weight behind a palm strike. Her thighs jerked with each twist and crouch. The involuntary movements grew stronger with each movement.

"Good," D'lane said as he stopped in front of her. "Keep practicing these moves and we'll work on transitions next time."

"Thank you," she said, standing and shaking out her rubbery legs. She hadn't wanted to call a halt to their lesson as she enjoyed being the center of his attention, but she wouldn't have lasted for much longer. Already her mind was shifting back into research mode and what she needed to do before they arrived at the derelict.

"The lesson isn't over."

"It isn't?" she squeaked, fingers gripping her thighs.

He chuckled. "Go ahead and stretch while I go over the more vulnerable points of the body."

She sprawled out on the mat and waited for her heart rate to calm before starting the cooldown routine they'd walked through pre-workout. She groaned when her twitching muscles finally relaxed and reached for her toes.

"There are many points in the body that can cause great pain or loss of limb strength. It's key to understand how those areas vary from being to being."

She glanced up at him as the colorful aliens from Lagrange One's hangar filtered through her mind. "They'll be in different areas depending on the shape of the person."

"And locomotion." He turned to the side with his tail slightly held out from the rest of his body. "The vulnerable places on your body are most likely the same on mine, excluding any internal locations." He lifted a knee, "Joints are the best point to start if you're trying to keep your distance. Watch which way their limbs move and a well-delivered punch or a kick in the opposite direction should work to disable them."

She felt at the back of her elbow and brushed over the bulge of her ulnar olecranon where it cupped the humerus to stop the over extension of her arm. Of firm hit there could cause serious pain.

He squatted in front of her. "Depending on the skeletal evolution of the species, this tactic may not always work. Exoskeletons and bioengineered joints are usually reinforced and become virtually impossible to displace."

The images of some of the other races that the Anunnaki had attacked hinted at the possibility of aliens with plated skin and thicker bound joints. "What do you suggest if none of their joints are vulnerable to attack?"

"Go for the soft features or orifices, like the eyes and nose." He curled his fingers and angled his open palm up before striking up into the air. "A palm strike to the nose, a cuff to ears, and jabs to eyes are great ways to defend yourself."

"But I'd have to be close to do so."

He sighed. "Yes, and in a very dangerous position. That's why we'll work on breaking holds next time."

"Great."

Chuckling, he stood and offered her his hand. "Don't worry. I'll let you recoup before beginning the next lesson."

"Thanks." She slipped her hands into his, surprised once again at the slightly rough texture of his fingers. He tugged, and she flowed up to her feet. Her poor abused muscles strained to keep her straight, and she stumbled into his chest. On accident. Totally unintended. Or that's what she was willing to tell herself.

His grip settled on her hips. "Steady."

"I haven't been this exhausted since I volunteered on my first dig. They'd had me driving markers into the ground and shoveling pits all day."

A sharp ping stung her ears as she hammered yet another stake into the frozen tundra, arms aching with every swing as her limbs twitched. Steven worked on her right, doing the same. His shoulders were visibly slumped. The darkly cloaked Kro-Gen agent stalked between them muttering to himself and growling up at the sky. His head jerked in her direction. She glanced away, swinging the hammer down on the next horrible spike, unwilling to call his attention to herself. Not after what happened last time.

"Shannon?"

She blinked rapidly. His face came into focus a few inches away from her nose. She swallowed thickly. "Yes?"

His finger traced the arched length of her eyebrow.

"A memory?"

She cleared her throat. "An unpleasant one."

"I am sorry for that."

His arms wrapped around her, tentative and uncertain of his welcome. Sighing, she leaned into him and returned the embrace. His tail curled around her calf as he brushed his hand down her spine, slowly working his way back up and massaging every knot and tight muscle he found until she was a limp noodle within his grasp.

"You'll want to take a hot shower tonight." D'lane repeated V'ren's earlier statement, "Do you know how to turn on the message setting in the shower?"

She moaned when a knot in her should tingled as it let go. "I'll NIC the directions. I need to figure out how to get the water to go above freezing anyway."

His hands stilled. "I can walk you through it if you like?"

She nodded, trying to keep the drool from escaping the edges of her mouth and wetting the front of his shirt.

"And ask Dr. Grates for some pain meds."

"I will." Shannon sighed as his hands traveled up to her neck.

"Did Kro-Gen not walk you through how to use our technology?"

Shannon went rigid. D'lane's hand froze. She debated staying put and riding out the heat flushing her cheeks, but she stepped back. She stared over his shoulder at the wall holding the weapons she hadn't been allowed to touch. "Kro-Gen's bathroom had clear indications on temperature settings. The room provided to me was prepped to be closer to my time period then this one."

What she didn't add was that Hellen had walked her through how to use the shower when she'd been assigned her room.

"So the failure is mine."

Her eyes jerked back to him, surprised that he'd admitted it. She hadn't expected it, especially with his position of authority. "I could have NIC'd it at any time."

"That is not acceptable. I will rectify this now."

He grabbed his towel and walked out of the room, his tail snapping back and forth.

She plucked the top of her jump suit and fluttered it open and closed, forcing air over her skin. "I should probably follow him," she said to the empty room.

She ran after D'lane, her exhausted muscles making the movement more of a stumbling gait as she forced herself up two flights of ramps and caught up with him as he neared her door. Mentally she replayed what her room looked like. Fortunately, she didn't have to worry about underwear on the floor, but she questioned whether she'd made her bed earlier or left the blankets flung about.

He stopped, and she leaned against the wall, hoping her legs would keep her standing a bit longer. "What are we waiting for?"

D'lane cocked an eyebrow at her. "For you to open the door."

"Right." Of course the room was locked to her hand print now that she was in T'grevis's system. Laughing under her breath at yet another reminder that she did not know how anything worked, she palmed the door open. He remained in the doorway. She straightened, all her muscles complaining in the process, and entered her room.

Thankfully her bed was made with her red pillows tucked under the top blanket. Everything else she had stowed after his previous statement about keeping things put away.

He stepped inside and stood shoulder to shoulder with her. "How'd you sleep last night?"

Shannon stared at the bed and struggled not to think about how it would look with both of them on it. Her thighs twitched, and she locked her knees. "I will say this, the beds in this time are definitely better than anything I've slept on in the past."

"I'm glad you find them comfortable. The crew's already complained that they're not as comfortable as the ones we have on Chriw'r." He moved forward. "Let's get you situated with the shower. I'm sure, like me, you're ready to wash the sweat from your body."

"That would be nice." Although a cold shower right about now might cool down her overheating libido.

Shannon followed him into the tiny bathroom and stopped at the imaginary point on the floor she'd created to demarcate where the water would start and stop flowing. She groaned and palmed her forehead. "Is there a line on the floor?"

"Right here." He tapped his toe about an inch in front of her feet. "Ah, I understand the problem now."

Frowning he stared into the vacant space. She caught the glance he sent her out of the corner of his eyes before he tugged his shirt out of his pants. "I'll need a towel."

Her attention was riveted on the smooth expanse of skin being exposed to her. She fanned her face and stared. Wait, he'd said something. "What?"

"A towel. I have to reach into the stall to show you

how to operate the controls."

"Right." She dampened her lips and mentally traced the line of his chest down to his abs. This close she could identify the smooth edges of the starburst scars on his right shoulder. Mouthing the word towel repeatedly, she reluctantly pulled her attention from the dull belt buckle on his pants and wandered back into the room. She snatched the towel out from the cabinet and jogged the five steps back into the bathroom, all of her aches and pains forgotten.

He hadn't moved, except for the small smile hovering at the edge of his lips. She propped her shoulder against the wall trying for a nonchalance she didn't feel. Arms crossed, towel hanging loosely in her grasp, she waited for the wet chested show to start.

"There are two main settings. One," he ticked off on his thumb, "controls the temperature of the shower, and the other," his first finger uncurled forming an L, "the pressure of the water. Both settings are located near the center of the main wall."

He shifted forward, the toe of his boot staying rooted on the far side of the shower line. His arm crossed the invisible edge. Freezing water poured from the ceiling instantly pebbling his skin. She knew intimately how that felt. He grimaced.

"You see why I'm asking you to show me the controls."

He palmed the wall, rotating his hand to the right. The room warmed as steam rose on the floor. She still didn't understand how the ground absorbed the liquid without any visible holes. Her gaze traveled back up to his dampened chest. Although the why of it wasn't important right now.

He shifted slightly and kept a finger against the off white surface. "Rotating as I did to the right will warm the water. Cooling is the opposite direction."

He double tapped the wall. The curtain of water morphed to larger droplets. A tap again and harder rain pinged against the floor. A third touch returned it to the original setting. Leaning back, he brought his arm back to his side. The shower flickered off. Dampness clung to her face and neck, and she stared at the trail of water that slowly made its way down the wide expanse of his chest.

His lips kicked up at the corner. He ran the palm of his hand down the long line of his abs. Water dampened the top of his pants. Her breath held as he fingered his belt, the tease, before he held out his hand.

Snapping the towel clean, she handed it over to his waiting grasp. "Thanks for walking me through the shower," she said, watching every smooth swipe of the cloth.

"I should have ensured the room was fully prepared for you. Or at the very least, that the water was set to a temperature a bit above freezing."

She gave a small nod and crouched to pick up his black shirt off the floor. She breathed in the warm scent of D'lane and fingered the cloth. Maybe she wouldn't give it back. She'd love to sleep in something he owned. "Everything's good now that I don't have to take the icy plunge just to wash."

Her fist clenched as he stroked the towel down his chest.

"Is there, ah, anything else I need to know about the shower controls?"

He paused, gaze searching hers. "There are several message options built into the system that cycle through when you hold your palm against the pressure setting." He maintained eye contact as he reached out and touched the far wall to indicate its location. The water cycled as he pulled his arm back. "The NIC will have a description of each of the options."

He was quick to get the rest of the water off his arm, and she exchanged his shirt for the towel, the damp fabric still warm from his skin. He was shrugging into his shirt when she asked, "Which one do you recommend."

His abs flexed as he forcefully tugged his shirt into place. His tail twitched erratically at his feet. He opened his mouth. Closed it. Dragging a hand down the front of his face, he sighed. "I prefer option three, but you may find you prefer something else."

His gaze darted across the length of her body in a quick caress. "I've heard that option one and five are preferred by those of your body shape."

She followed him out of the bathroom and into the bedroom. "I'm sure I'll find one that works for me. I'll let you know which one I decide on."

D'lane stumbled, righting himself before he slammed into a wall.

She stilled. "Are you alright?"

How could one conversation about shower massage settings cause this much drama? It wasn't like they had a removable shower head to make things interesting.

"Yes," he straightened and refused to make eye contact. "Thank you for your concern."

"Great." She hugged the damp towel to her chest. Lips pursed, she looked him over. He appeared fine. "How many times do you recommend I use it?"

He choked, taking half a step away from her.

A flush rode his cheeks. She frowned and reached for him. "Do you need to see V'ren?"

He stepped out of reach. Her fingers curled into her palm, as her arm dropped. What exactly was going on? She searched his body, stalling at the hard length of him pressed tight against his pants. He took another step away from her, and she smiled. What was involved in this massage option that he was thinking about?

His hand shook as he swiped across his bottom lip. "I'll see you at the evening meal."

Chapter 16

Personal note: More research needed on language structure used by the Anunnaki.

Buckled into the seat at the back of the bridge, Shannon stared at the screen as the T'grevis aimed for the Anunnaki derelict. Bits of debris orbited the oblong craft whose exterior was interrupted with metallic boils. It looked like a lumpy sausage.

Unlike Lagrange One, the ancient derelict vessel hung lifeless in the center screen. The vacant ship the a silent monument to the thousands of Anunnaki who'd occupied it until its destruction. The heat map in the upper corner of the screen reflected nothing but the radiation of the cosmos. All the heat had been sucked from it as it equalized with the universe. The T'grevis's exterior lights were the sole source of illumination in the dead of space. A large gouge ran down the length of the ship, almost as if a claw had caught on the edge and parted the flesh with ease as it then plucked the organs from inside it.

Her research said it had floated into League space, but perhaps it moved into their space if it still held any velocity.

"Captain, scans of the exterior hull confirm the only access into the vessel is the open orifice on the far side of the ship." Q'aid rotated the image of the derelict around until it reflected the screen. "I've confirmed no major changes to the structure since the original scan by the Fritdz."

D'lane opened the file on the arm of his chair. "Have we been able to confirm the bulges on the exterior of the ship are by design and not the result of stress to the hull?"

"Not at this time captain," Q'aid said. "I can confirm they've remained largely unchanged since the scan."

"To what percentage?" D'lane flicked through the data.

"Five percent." Q'aid flipped through multiple live feeds of the derelict. The drones J'rax deployed when they'd arrived to surround the ship remained steady. The images on the screens were ones she'd seen in her research several times before.

Shannon did some quick math. A five percent change in volume could mean an expansion of over seven thousand square feet. She rubbed her temples. Prior to revival she hadn't been able to handle that level of mental math. On a ship that size, was the resolution tolerance an acceptable value? "Is that good or bad?"

D'lane's nails scratched across his armchair. "That resolution is a dangerous level to have their scanners set to. It would get the job done, but with the vessel of this caliber, you'd lose all ability to detect concerning volume changes." D'lane tapped a nail on the arm of his chair. "The Fritdz must have wanted to get in and out as quickly as possible."

D'lane spun his chair around. His golden gaze locked onto Shannon. "Do the files mention the metallic nodes in the original discovery of the ship."

Shannon mentally ran through the images she'd been studying over the last twenty-four hours. "They do, but I don't know the answer to whether it's part of the original ship design."

Q'aid said, "We'd have to get onto the ship's exterior hull and confirm the location of each node. The nodes are close enough in size to fall either way if it was a uniform material failure."

"We don't have time for that." P'ret walked closer to the screen.

"If they are from stress," Shannon played with the tip of her finger, "It happened a long time ago, before any images in my files were captured."

"True." D'lane flashed Shannon a quick smile before turning back to the screen. "We've got a 15% chance the ship will rupture while we're there."

"Or we might push the vessel to failure just by boarding," P'ret said.

D'lane's tail flicked at his feet. "Full safety precautions will be taken until hull integrity can be determined."

"*If* we can access the ship," P'ret said.

Shannon sucked in a breath. Rising panic soured her stomach. She hadn't thought that would be a problem.

D'lane's ear flicked back. Shannon's shoulders tensed. She waited for him to disagree with P'ret, but he didn't. Her hands clenched at her knees.

D'lane's ear slowly rotated forward. "We'll deal with that issue once we land."

What would happen if they couldn't get into the derelict? They'd have come all this way to crawl into a ship that did its best to keep everyone out. How much time would they waste trying to move into the derelict? She slowly let go of the breath she held. One problem at a time.

"Take us in T'rev." D'lane cleared the data from his

screen.

"Yes captain."

Q'aid settled the main display on the large tare as the hull looming closer. "Should we pull the deployed drones back in before we land?"

"No." D'lane shifted in his seat. "I want them out there monitoring the surrounding space. We only have a short period of time to gather data, and I'd like to know about any potential problems before they happen."

Sharp metal gleamed in the T'grevis's forward lights. The exposed edges of the derelict's hull curled into its shell where the ship had been punched into by a large object.

The jagged hole drew closer as the T'grevis came in for landing. Shannon fingered the safety belt hanging at her side. "Are we sure we're going to fit?"

"We have plenty of clearance." D'lane's fingers danced across his armchair. A red tinted rendering of the Anunnaki ships interior flickered on half of the screen. "It's finding an area clear of metal debris large enough for us to land and access to the rest of the ship that'll be problematic. The space needs to be large enough to fit the T'grevis but contained enough that we can activate the shields to retain the atmosphere."

T'rev smoothly guided the T'grevis into the derelict. "I want to set us down near the back of the exposed space, near the partially destroyed wall."

"Scanning landing zone." Q'aid's screen filled with a rough map of debris scattered across the floor. Did that mean there was some form of gravity acting on the ship?

The red triangle flickered rapidly over each object before expanding and multiplying. The warning color flashed to yellow or green until the image reflected a kaleidoscope of primary colors. "Possible landing configurations being transferred to T'rev now."

"Got it." T'rev spun the T'grevis.

The image rotated on the screen. Shannon swallowed the acidic bite of bile climbing up her throat and glanced away from the front of the room to focus on D'lane. His stable, non-moving body centered her mind. She cleared her throat. "Will the floor hold the weight of the ship?"

"As long as we don't set down too close to the broken ledge, we should be fine." D'lane glanced back at her. "J'rax will take additional material samples once we land to confirm the integrity of the space and determine if we'll need to move the ship."

The T'grevis jolted. Shannon slapped her hands out across the seats for stability. Bracing herself was a reflex from poor driving choices, but no one else in the cockpit seemed phased by the sudden movement. She slowly slid her arms down from their spread position and into her lap. The screen flickered black before filling up the display with playbacks from the exterior drones.

D'lane stood, and she admired how the long lean line of him prowled within his domain. He moved to stand behind Q'aid's screen. "Re-map this entire room with digital marks on all doors and accessways. I want to know every viable way into or out of the derelict before we disembark."

"It'll be ready for you in under an hour, sir."

Shannon sighed and slouched back against the seats. They had finally arrived. Her work would truly begin once she had access to the derelict. She'd need to work with J'rax to get the derelict's exploratory drones ready for mapping the rest of the interior of the ship if—no, she corrected—*when* they got access. Once she got access, the bulk of her free time would be spent researching the areas of the ship she deemed important.

She had a laundry list of potentially high interest locations that might yield the most information on the Anunnaki, based on her research across cultures. With the help of the drone mapping, she'd could focus directly on the areas of possible significance. Across cultures, community congregation locations usually looked like large mess halls or hallway junctions. If she could locate those, they should guide her to the more important areas of the ship. Hopefully her search criteria was accurate, and she'd be able to get access to them on this and other floors. They still had no idea what the inside of the ship looked like and how much damage had been done to it over the centuries.

She smoothed imaginary wrinkles on her jumpsuit as she stood. "I'll be with J'rax if anyone needs me." Shannon doubted they would, but the information was more for D'lane than anyone else's.

His ear flicked toward her; his golden gaze followed shortly after. "I'll check in with you before the next ship meal."

Shannon nodded her agreement and descended into the lower deck. She found J'rax on the engineering floor, past the exercise room and propped against the wall, flicking through the NAV in their hand. The mapping bots spread out before J'rax in ever increasing rings. In a wave of pulsing red, their power lights blinked eerily in sync. At J'rax's feet, the last bot unfurled its six legs and rose from the ground like a reanimated insect.

"Give me five more minutes with these bad boys and I'll have an army of drones ready to be unleashed upon the derelict."

"Thanks, J'rax. I appreciate your help. I doubt I could have got these up and running based on the instructions alone."

J'rax chuckled. "You could have given enough time and familiarity with the system. Hell, without V'ren's quick help finding a usable integration system, we'd have had to program each drone with a different ship location and task. She's the one we should be thanking."

"I'll have to bake her some cookies next time I'm in the kitchen." Or figure out some way to do it with the available kitchen equipment. She didn't remember seeing a stove tucked away in the mess. It'd take the fun out of the surprise, but she'd have to ask V'ren how best to use the kitchen to make them. "Is there anything I can help with? D'lane will be summoning you soon to help evaluate the landing site."

"I'm waiting for all the lights on these spider bots to turn green, and then we'll be ready."

Shannon glanced out again at the web of robots, their long limbs missing that extra set that would officially make them an arachnid, but J'rax's description wasn't wrong. If Shannon had come across one of those things out in the wild, a large dog sized spider would have definitely been her first description. Tiny lenses covered the front of their bodies with one large red light in the center. A handful flickered green from one blink to the next. "Are any of them giving you trouble?"

J'rax skimmed through the data. "No more than a handful, which is to be expected with a group of drones this size. Most can be fixed with a reset, but two will need more invasive work."

"Which ones?"

"RT1F2 and Z9."

Shannon gazed out at the rows upon rows of machines. "And they're…"

J'rax looked up from her screen. "They're the ones with the steady red non-blinking light."

"Right." They should have been easy to see. Should being the operative word here, but there was so much red. "I'll be right back."

A quick trip to the mess and she came back to find a sea of pulsing green. Shannon uncorked the thick paint pen, and she searched for the problematic drones. They sat poised in the middle of the group, the red light easily seen now that she didn't have to search for it. The paint pen slid smoothly across the boxy surface and left behind a bright yellow F2 and Z9 on the respective units. The expected paint fumes were missing, even as she recapped the pen.

"Should I mark the more problematic ones as well?"

"Not yet." J'rax tapped the data pad against her thigh. "We'll attempt a hard reset on all five before you mark any new bots."

"What about the two I already did?"

"They'll be our special pair until the paint wears off. Now, I'll run through this quickly in Cass'iva on the tablet before having you translate it to your language for a review." J'rax raised the handheld until Shannon could see the screen. "The buttons should all be in the same locations, so you should be able to repeat everything for each unit while I meet up with D'lane and the others."

Shannon glanced up. "I didn't hear a call over the comms."

J'rax nodded toward their wrist. "They pinged me on my NIC."

The steps J'rax ran through were pretty straight forward, and once Shannon translated it to English, they were able to stay for Shannon to run through a quick fix for an error on one of the bots.

J'rax nudged their hip into Shannon's side. "You can always ping me if you have any issues. I should be able to respond within a few minutes and hopefully walk you through the steps."

"Gotcha."

"Let me know if they're still giving you problems after the reset. You can leave the tablet here and I'll attempt to fix the more difficult ones when I return."

Shannon tapped the PDA against her thigh. "Do you know how long it'll take to confirm the landing zone is safe?"

"The vids didn't provide the best imagery of the floor layout, but I expect once I start sampling, it should go pretty quickly."

"Then I'll try to hustle through the fixes to get these bots ready for action."

J'rax chuckled as they straightened. "P'ret and T'rev still need to work on acquiring access to the interior of the ship. Assuming this ship's technology reflects our knowledge of the Anunnaki systems and not something entirely different from the machines we've cannibalized in the past. You'll be able to launch the spider bots then."

Shannon looked at the drones crouched in the dark, green lights blinking as they waited for the command to deploy. "Should I power them off or charge them after the reset?"

"Nah." J'rax waved over their shoulder as they hit the ramp. "For our uses, their battery life exceeds the length of our mission."

"Good to know." She waited until J'rax cleared the ramp before turning back to the bots. Shannon wasn't sure if she felt more like a general preparing to lead her troops into battle, or a villain ready to unleash her minions for destruction.

Chuckling, Shannon settled on a general as she selected the problem drones from the screen and followed the prompt request sequence for reboot. After a few moments, it was as she expected, the original two tagged bots remained problematic. Flipping through the program J'rax had installed, Shannon read through the coding command structure, thankful for the notes the original programmer kept on each line. The language hadn't translated well into English, but it provided some insight into how it worked.

Hitting figurative brain melt after a handful of minutes of reviewing the layers and layers of loops and additional program callouts, she turned the device off and left the data pad atop the last bot by the door. Her idea of trying to resolve the problem on her own was laughable when she had no real idea what she reviewing.

She notified J'rax of the bot reboot issues and hit the mess for a cup of coffee. Steaming cup in hand, she wandered down to the cockpit to catch a glimpse of the work going on outside the ship.

She stalled in the doorway, unsure if she wanted to enter.

P'ret sat in the captain's chair watching the screen. She must have made some noise because he turned around, mouth open for a greeting that never came. He frowned, the scar on his cheek kept both lips from hitting the full pout and turned back around without a sound. It looked like their earlier conversation regarding the

Anunnaki hadn't changed anything between them. Not that it had been a pleasant interaction in the first place.

She took a sip of the coffee she'd meant for D'lane. "Not who you were expecting?"

"No." He took down one of the screens scrolling with data before enlarging the image of the crew outside. "I hoped to finish my conversation with V'ren before she returned to work, but it looks like that won't be happening any time soon."

Shannon propped her shoulder against the door, focusing on each Chriw'rian suited up in grey outside until she settled on the one to the right. His build becoming as familiar to her as the back of her hand. "I can leave if you want? I'd hate to be the reason you couldn't focus on your work."

"Don't think so highly of yourself."

She dragged her gaze away from D'lane's figure outside and locked eyes with P'ret. "In that case, could I get an update? I have no real idea what's going on out there."

P'ret muttered under his breath, too low for the translator to pick up other than an underlying rumble.

She straightened away from the wall. "I'm not asking for much, just an update. I'd like to know when I get to go out there and do my part in all this."

P'ret growled, frustration pulling his brows down. "J'rax confirmed we won't need to move the ship, but we're still locating an appropriate ingress point on top of ensuring radiation around the T'grevis is at acceptable levels."

"Are they still trying to connect to the derelict's computer to get in? Or have we moved on to looking for a good wall to cut into?"

P'ret's tail flicked at his feet. Irritation likely added that extra snap to his voice. "Both? The problem with cutting an access hole is the sheer number we'd likely need to do on a ship this size to get into every nook and cranny within the derelict. Each cut would lead to another obstacle until we have a tunnel of open holes that lead without purpose. It would severely delay and restrict the bots scanning progress. It's also better to work on keeping the ships system in place as it continues to keep any emergency ship wide procedures up and running."

"Like fire suppression?"

"And hull rapid depressurization protection. I wasn't sure if you noticed but hull integrity on this ship is pretty damn low. Be careful where you travel and keep your NIC on you at all times."

She wasn't sure what to think of P'ret's current concern for her safety. She rotated the thin bracelet at her wrist. "You can track me?"

"And notify you when you're entering a dangerous area of the ship."

"Ah." She refused to feel shame for questioning his motives. He hadn't given her any reason to trust his emotions where she was concerned.

"What do you have against the NIC? We all have one and are readily tracked down with a single request." He unbuckled his bracelet and held it up. "Just take it off during your down time like everyone else."

Shannon shrugged. "I can't get mine off."

"Here." He put his NIC back on and gestured her forward. "Let me show you how to unclasp the band."

Shannon hesitated, unsure of his motives. His hot and cold attitude left her little stability whenever their paths crossed. She sighed and stepped forward with her wrist held out. She wanted this bracelet off, at least for a little while.

P'ret's fingertips brushed her skin. She jerked her hand out from his grip. The sensation of his touch was unpleasant, even though she'd expected it.

"What are you doing?" D'lane growled.

Startled, she glanced over her shoulder and frowned at D'lane from where he stood at the door. "P'ret's walking me through how to remove my NIC."

D'lane's gaze was locked on her as he prowled forward. "Your NIC needs to stay on at all times."

"Why?" Shannon huffed, dropping her arm to her side as she turned to face him. "It isn't like I'm going to run off anywhere."

P'ret grunted, likely covering a laugh. She couldn't see him anymore, but it sounded like he returned to his screen.

D'lane stopped a hands-breadth away. "I'm more worried about you *disappearing*."

"We're basically in the middle of nowhere on a ship most beings aren't aware even exists." She fiddled with her NIC. "Who the hell would be out here with us, and why would they kidnap me?"

He brushed a stray curl from her forehead as the stiff points of his ears softened. "Did you forget we were shot at as we left Earth, or that everything we've done so far needed to stay under the radar? We're out here, far from any support, trying to stop an attack that could wipe out billions. There are too many unknown players who would do everything in their power to ensure this attack occurs."

"Not to mention," P'ret added, "we're so far out from our galactic base, by the time any of our distress signals were responded too, we'd all be dead or destroyed anyway."

"Thanks for the uplifting information P'ret," Shannon said.

"Any time."

D'lane took Shannon's hand and drew her further away from P'ret. "You see now why it's important to have the NIC on you and active at all times."

"I do, but I want privacy at some point. Some time to myself without others having immediate access to me."

"I hear you." D'lane's thumb ran over the top of her hand. "But, until this mission is completed, all crew members are required to keep their NICs on at all times."

Her shoulders slumped. "Damn it."

"Tell me you will obey my order." His tail caressed her ankle.

Irritation gnawed her gut. The NIC suddenly a heavy weight at her wrist. Back home she'd been able to turn off her phone or leave without it. She hadn't owned any wearable personal electronics or anything else that would track her unless she wanted it.

She fiddled with the circlet. If she had stepped away from the T'grevis on Lagrange One, she would have been lost in a sea of other. Why did his request have to be so reasonable? "I will."

D'lane tucked her hand into his elbow. "How about a tour of our new operations bay?"

She perked up. "We got access to the ships computers?"

The countdown to leaving had begun as soon as they landed. The longer it took to get access to the ship, the less time they had to collect data, and they were already six hours into day one.

"Not yet, but we've cleared the surrounding vicinity for crew traffic."

Finally, she'd get to do something other than electronic research. "Do I get to wear those nifty spacesuits?"

"Only if you want to live."

She tugged him toward the bottom of the ship. "Then let's get this show on the road!"

As much as she loved the T'grevis and being out in space, she was dying to explore the derelict and get away from the same three floors she wandered since they'd left Earth.

She hurried him along past the exercise room to the large closet beside the cargo bay door where the unused suits were stored.

The door was a manual, the first she'd come across one the ship, although there had to be more in case of emergencies. A quick twist and Shannon had the locker open. A handful of white spacesuits hung from a crossbar.

D'lane reached past her, his warm scent a soothing balm on her rising tension, and pulled out the smallest suit she'd seen. He held it up to her at shoulder height. "I used the data in your medical records to fabricate an appropriately sized suit before we left Kro-Gen."

Shannon froze, one foot half out of her shoes. "Excuse me?"

She wasn't sure if she should be offended he had access to her personal health information or grateful that she had a suit that fit.

D'lane toed off his boots and stored them in the small bench cubby beside the closet. "The suit should fit now you've put on weight."

Choking on her own saliva, she fell against the wall. "You shouldn't say things like that."

His head cocked to the side as his ears swiveled forward. "Why not?"

"It was not commented on during my time." She straightened as curiosity peaked. "Do you know if it's more common now on Earth?"

"You'd have to ask Dr. Grates. It's generally a positive thing in Chriw'rian culture, especially when you've put on more muscle tone after your time spent in cryogenics."

"It's all those sparring lessons." She toed off her other shoe and placed it next to D'lane's. "And likely the supplements in the food and water."

"It's not uncommon for Chriw'rian's returning from missions carrying more muscles than when they left."

"It's likely because all your free time on the ship is spent either working out or zoning out to media." She struggled to slip a foot into the pillowy spacesuit material designed like a newborns onesie. Her jumpsuit was more of a hinderance than she expected.

Their eyes connected. His golden irises turned molten. "Or partaking of other exhilarating activities."

Her cheeks heated. "You'll have to show me some of those activities later."

With both feet in the suit, Shannon slipped her hands through the sleeves and into the gloves. Bending, she grasped the zipper and pulled it up over her calf and hips, across her chest, to stop on the opposite side of her shoulders. At her neck a rigid ring clicked together.

If she remembered the technology in her time correctly, spacesuits contained structured frames with sliding rotation joints with the fun benefit of climbing in through the back. The current suit she wore remained loose and nonbinding over her silver jumpsuit. The boxy helmet rested on the center of her shoulders on a ring that let her see in 180 degrees. "I thought this would be more constraining."

"Kro-Gen's suits are designed for a relaxed fit to aid with the temperature and pressure regulation layer." Barefoot he curled his fingers inward and motioned to follow him as he headed to the back of the storage bay.

"My suit is still in the containment room." His soft tread was virtually silent compared to the slap of hers. "Follow me and I'll walk you through decontamination, run through safety procedures, and how to select the appropriate channels for communication."

He stopped next to a glass cabinet with two suits hanging with long tails limp on the floor. The matching boots and gloves were mounted within.

"How do you get your tail..." Shannon stuttered to a stop.

D'lane unbuckled his belt, his pants sagging on his hips. He tugged his shirt out from his pants and casually tugged it off. The dark gray fabric pooled on the floor. He unzipped his pants and hooked his thumbs into the waistband.

She licked her lips. "What are you doing?"

His ear flicked toward her. "I'm getting into my suit."

She cleared her throat. "And getting naked helps?"

"Unlike Kro-Gen's unitards, the My'len uniforms don't fit under the suits." His lips kicked up into a smile. "You can always look away if it bothers you."

There was no way in hell she was looking away. He

slowly pushed his pants down. She dampened her lips as the lines of his hips came into view. Black cloth pooled at his ankles. Her brain short-circuited as D'lane stood naked in front of her.

Warm sandy stretches of muscles filled her vision. She struggled to keep her attention at his feet and the tip of his tail that lazily swayed back and forth, but it was a losing battle. Strong ankles led to well-muscled calves that flexed when he stepped free of his pants. His thighs bunched as he bent to pick his freed clothes off the ground. She followed the long line of his thighs as he stood, her gaze stopping on that part of him she was most interested in. His uncircumcised length hid the rings she remembered from the anatomy videos, with his balls just visible from behind his thick girth.

He chuckled. Her gaze snapped to his. He winked and strode into the cupboard to retrieve his suit and boots. Naked ass flexing with every step, she zeroed in to where his tail met his back at the top of where his cheeks met, and like the tip of his tail, his skin darkened where it transitioned at the base of his spine.

She wet her lips. "Do you walk around naked in front of the rest of your crew?"

"Nope." He closed the door. "Just you."

He casually sauntered back to her, his lean, long body on display with his semi-hard penis getting harder and starting to rise as the tip edged out from its foreskin.

She fidgeted with the need to reach out and touch this virile alien male. "It's not nice to tease."

He closed in and stopped only when they were pressed together from chest to hips. The spacesuit kept her from feeling the heat of his body, but it did little to hide the hard planes of his chest and firm length of him at his hips. "Who said I was playing nice?"

He cupped the back of her head and slanted his lips over hers, driving his tongue into her mouth in a powerful back-and-forth dance. Her hand dug into the hair at the back of his neck. Moaning, her body was a tingling bundle of nerves under her spacesuit as he pulled away.

Her core pulsed with a need to be filled. She wet her lips and took a deep breath. They didn't have time for sex right now as much as she desperately wanted to jump his bones.

"Why?" It was such a loaded question. Why now? Why here? Why wait until she was stuffed into a suit that she couldn't easily get out of?

He brushed a kiss against her lips. "Wouldn't want you to get bored."

Chapter 17

T'rev comm to D'lane: Object spotted at edge of scanners, likely a passing comet.

Shannon clicked her heel into the hard rubber over sole that covered the bottom of her foot. Her gloves flexed as she tugged the last bit of fabric at her wrist straight.

"You're not afraid of nicking your suit?" she asked as he tucked a knife into a thigh pocket of his grey spacesuit. That along with the guns holstered at his hips, thighs, and lower back made him a walking risk for punctures.

"The suits are sturdier than they appear."

Box helmet already in place, she joined D'lane at the exit as he finished attaching the last of his weapons, suited tail extension still at his ankles.

She rocked back on her heels to check out the back of his suit, enjoying the snug fit across his hips and the hard length of tail snuggly wrapped within his spacesuit. His tip twitched at his feet.

The sleekness of the suit wasn't the only difference between them. His air tank was tight and high on his back, more like a kid's knapsack than anything else, while hers was loose and situated at her lower back and shoulders.

Unlike her boxy helmet, My'len supplied a trapezoidal helmet that offered a greater field of vision, sat closer to the head, and kept the Chriw'rian ears visible. That and his being armed to the teeth, she'd counted five weapons at least, made him a being to be reckoned with.

She didn't want to complain but it was clear she had the short end of the spacesuit stick. "Why is yours so much tighter than mine?"

"I can provide you a complete breakdown of the variances, if you like?"

"Maybe later if I want something to put me to sleep." Although if he was lying next to her giving her the rundown on equipment differences, other options to sleep would be going through her mind.

"If I was trying to exhaust you, I'd have a more pleasurable way in mind."

She flushed. "I'll have to take you up on that."

He palmed open the first outer door. "You remember what channel I'm on?"

Shannon glanced at the black comms case cuffed around her arm, a stark difference in color to the white of her suit. "You're on one. V'ren's on three. I'm five."

"And P'ret's on two," D'lane said as they stepped into the secondary stage of doors, the first ones closing behind them.

She doubted she'd be touching that channel anytime soon but nodded anyway.

He opened the outer door. A dark and drab warehouse-like space sprawled out before her, occasionally broken up by patches of light. P'ret and V'ren were already out, the lights from their helmets sweeping across the floor.

"Be careful where you step," D'lane said as he lifted his foot. "The slipcovers for your shoes will help prevent punctures, but it doesn't stop everything."

"How do I know what's okay to step on and what isn't?" She'd obviously stay away from anything sharp and pointy, but with the dark piles of unknown material spread about on an alien ship she'd never heard of prior to a week ago, how was she to know what was dangerous and what wasn't?

"Just be careful when you're exploring the space. We haven't documented all major dangers, but we could use your help to clear the floor."

"Point me in a direction and tell me what to do." She glanced around, her helmet giving her a great view of the floor. Q'aid worked at the vessel's door, large tablet in hand. J'rax slipped in and out of the light at the far right of the space like a specter in the night.

She trailed behind D'lane as he rounded the back end of the ship. V'ren stood amongst orderly piles of debris. D'lane called out as they approached, "I've got you those extra hands you were asking about."

"Thanks, captain." V'ren tapped a few more commands out on her handheld before looking up. Her grey gaze was crystal clear as she met Shannon's through the visors. "Hope you're ready for some work."

Shannon rubbed her hands together, the gloves thick and pliant against her palms, and ensured channels one and three were lit up on her wrist cuff. "Yes Ma'am."

"Great." D'lane patted Shannon's shoulder, the touch firm through the layers of fabric. "I'll be by to collect you for your meal break."

The white frame of her helmet beside her ear blocked D'lane's body from view. Shannon's turn was halted by V'ren's palm on the clear visor. "Enough ogling the captain," V'ren drawled. "We've got work to do."

Shannon laughed and gave a rough solute. "Yes, Mame. What's the first item on your list I can help with?"

The list was long and lengthy, and also how she ended up in the far corner of the impromptu hangar space with a trash cart trailing behind her. She still wasn't sure how the gravity worked on a ship this size, or how it continued to maintain itself after the derelict was out of use for so long, but she'd been assured that it wasn't going to cut out any time soon.

Shannon's helmet light flashed on yet another piece of ragged twisted metal. "Whatever the hell it was, it tore through this ship and did a lot of damage."

V'ren's voice cracked over Shannon's intercom. "Running theory is the damage was caused by a series of attacks involving targeted radiation and chemical bombs. There doesn't appear to be any residual chem spheres left intact, but keep an eye out for them, and notify me immediately—"

"If I come across one," Shannon finished in unison.

V'ren laughed. "Can't stress that statement enough. Once you've seen what one of those spheres can do, I'd hate to be around when a whole payload is deployed."

Shannon grasped an arm size piece of metal and tossed it on the cart. "I read after the last Anunnaki war, they were banned from use."

"Doesn't mean people aren't selling or using them," V'ren drawled. "Caches still make the news every now and again, frequently enough for me to worry if we ever come across pirates."

"That's the third time pirates have been mentioned. Are they that common?"

"More so in the outer reaches," V'ren grunted, a loud clang carrying over the speaker. "Which we currently reside in."

"Great." Shannon reached for another piece of debris. "Just what I wanted to hear."

"Better aware than not is my motto," V'ren drawled.

Shannon chuckled. "I totally agree."

Three filled carts later, the trash pile sat sharp and dangerous in the corner, with Shannon staring at a reflective heat warped scrap of metal. The reflection of her helmet wavered in the distorted square as D'lane joined her.

"What have you got there?"

"I'm not sure. It's not one of those spheres I was warned about, but I don't think it's part of this ship either." Shannon turned it over, the backside was a flat black with a streak of grey. "Perhaps it belonged to one of the original ship's crew or one of the ships that attacked the derelict?"

"It's a possibility. I've caught the odd reflective bit of metal while moving about." D'lane tapped the piece in her hand, the tip of his gloves slightly sticking to it. "It has some magnetism to it if my gloves are reacting. Let's bring it back to the T'grevis to have it analyzed further."

Shannon placed the bit of metal into a pocket on her belt and pushed the cart to the next area of debris. D'lane trailed ahead. His suit pulled snug over his flank when he bent to pick up trash, his tail lifting slightly to help maintain his balance.

She hadn't thought of herself as much of a tail and ass gal, but D'lane's derriere occupied way too much of her attention. He lifted a long black twisted bit of metal stretched to a breaking point. He tossed it on the cart where it joined countless others.

He bent and reached for another bit of metal. "How's your suit?"

Shannon hummed as she picked up her own piece of garbage. "I keep hitting my helmet on the cart. How much damage can it take before it cracks?"

He straightened and ran a finger over her clear visor. "They can take quite a beating, but I don't see any damage." He stepped back. "Any other problems?"

She tapped the outside of her helmet over her ear. "For the most part I can hear what everyone else is saying, but if the voice drops to just the right pitch, I can't make out a thing."

"We'll have J'rax take a look at it once we've gotten access into the derelict, although that might be a hearing problem rather than a suit issue."

"Are you saying we humans don't hear as well as you Chriw'rians?" His ear rotated within his helmet. She chuckled. "Don't answer that."

Shannon tossed another bit of trash on the cart. "Do you think they'll have time? We still have the reconnaissance drones to take care of."

"They're pretty much self-sufficient."

"Captain." Q'aid's voice crackled over her comm.

D'lane turned toward Q'aid's position in the far corner of the impromptu hangar. "I'll be right over."

Shannon chuckled. "You're still on my channel."

He flashed her a smile. "I'll see you in a couple of hours."

Pushing the trash cart around the pile of debris, Shannon moved on to the next square on the grid previously set up by P'ret. Thankfully she and V'ren were only clearing the larger pieces the cleaner bots weren't able to pick up. Plucking the fist size metal off the floor, she tossed it onto the cart with a muted clang.

Out of the corner of her eye, Shannon kept an eye on P'ret. It was the fifth door he'd been working on since she first started cleaning. A growl crackled through her helmet. She glanced at her wristlet. Channel 2 was lit, and she knew that wasn't a mistake. "Was there something I could help you with?"

P'ret tapped aggressively on his handheld. "A majority of the doors in this area have been damaged beyond our ability to power open. I've spent way too much time wrestling with them when I should be opening them."

"Is cutting through them an option now?" Way too many sci-fi movies with laser cutting through safety doors flashed through her mind. "Or blast?"

He straightened. "That is never an option on a ship you plan to occupy. You're basically removing all emergency systems."

Shannon scanned the ship. "So, any fire or explosion—"

"Or atmosphere," he added.

"—wouldn't be contained?"

P'ret's hands fisted. "We'd all be fucked."

She rubbed her arm, the touch muted through her suit. "I hope it doesn't come to that."

"I doubt D'lane would let anything but drones through the ship as our last resort."

Shannon glanced over to where D'lane stood talking with Q'aid. "Would the bots be able to get enough information to help stop the attack?"

P'ret turned and gave her a once over. "I've met some desperate revivee's who would do just about anything to get out from under Kro-Gen's corporate thumbs."

She scoffed. "What does that mean?"

"Don't think I don't know what you're playing at, getting D'lane all emotionally wrapped up in your problems. I know you're only here because you were given no other options to repay your debt. He won't be able to save you from Kro-Gen indentured service, there is nothing he can do, and he won't take you with him when he leaves. His life's mission means too much to him."

Pain knifed through her chest from his ugly words. "You're a real piece of work. I'm out here trying to use what little knowledge I have that is useful in this time to stop the murder of billions of people, and I don't need your conspiracy shit on top of it trying to destroy anything that D'lane and I are building. So you can keep your fucking thoughts to yourself!"

Shannon pivoted on her heel and headed toward the dump pile, more than ready to take her anger out on inanimate objects.

She tossed the first piece of junk against the wall. The shriek both satisfying and frustrating. "What the hell is his problem." She slammed another piece down. She reached for a third. Static crackled through her comm. She flushed. The comm for P'ret still blazed active. "Fuck."

A gloved hand wrapped loosely around her wrist as D'lane tugged her around. "Take five."

Shannon's hand clenched. "Why?"

He tugged her closer. "You're endangering yourself with your actions. You're likely to puncture your suit at this rate."

She pulled at his hold. "Give me a few moments and I'll have my head back in the right space."

"No." He stepped closer and leaned down until their helmets tapped. "I want you to do this now."

Opening and closing her hand, she held his gaze. Her breath was amplified in the enclosed space making it difficult to think. She closed her eyes as she sucked in a deep breath, followed by a second. On the third, she consciously relaxed the tight grip of tension in her neck. Her hand went limp.

She cleared her throat and lifted her lashes. D'lane's face remained close through the clear panes of their touching helmets. "I'll take a break."

The relief in his expression was clearly visible as her answer sank in.

His hand slid down her wrist to capture her fingers. The squeeze was comforting through the layers of fabric. "Find V'ren. She'll tell you where to go to take some personal time without un-suiting." The helmet reflected the room when he tilted his head toward P'ret. "I have other business to attend to."

Shannon found herself parked on the inside of the ship, unable to see anyone or anything except the ten-foot space that represented the pressurization room between the outside of the ship and the T'grevis. She ran through everything that had happened since they picked up P'ret and the anger she consistently felt whenever looking at his face.

She had delt with enough egotistical people in her life, that adding one more to the mix shouldn't have been a problem. Although P'ret wasn't a direct reflection of D'lane, he resembled D'lane enough that P'ret had quickly become the focus of all her insecurities in regard to her and D'lane's relationship. Her fear of not being enough, and how D'lane might treat her once this was all over played into her rection to P'ret. Otherwise, why would she be affected by someone who she really didn't know?

Determined to not let her insecurities seep into her reactions, Shannon exited the ship and returned to garbage duty. She wasn't sure what D'lane and P'ret's conversation had consisted of while she was gone, but P'ret ignored her for the most part after she rejoined the group.

Shannon was helping V'ren clear the trash carts for the next quadrant when P'ret called them all over. He'd managed to partially hack into the derelict system and open a door with the help of a cobbled together power bank.

They all stood in a semi-circle about ten feet from the door. Shannon excitement surged as she moved closest to the door and across from P'ret. J'rax and V'ren stood on either side of D'lane who had a direct view into the guts of the derelict.

"Power's not going to last long." J'rax propped her fists on her hips. "Maybe a handful of hours to a full cycle before the derelict sucks the power from the system."

Shannon stared into the dark maw of the ship. Muscles twitching, she clenched her fists to still the movement. Creepy wasn't a big enough adjective to describe the reaction flowing through her.

"I want this door manually propped open and drones sent in for reconnaissance." D'lane made eye contact with everyone in the group. "No one goes in until they've done an initial sweep of the area."

"If we're doing a quick mapping of the immediate area," J'rax said, "I can get them in and working in under 20 minutes with the help of Shannon."

"Do it." D'lane's ears flicked forward. "When we enter the ship, if it's deemed safe, we'll be exploring in pairs until further notice. I don't want anyone inside the derelict alone. P'ret, where do we stand on gaining access to the derelict's mainframe?"

P'ret shifted his weight. "I'm still searching for an undamaged terminal. We have the general coding structure mapped so using our system to break into theirs should go more efficiently once we find a usable access point."

"V'ren will help once we get the all-clear from the bots." D'lane tapped a few times on his suit's NIC. "In the meantime, let's stabilize the power on this door and set up a game plan for when we head into the ship."

Shannon cleared her throat. All the Chriw'rians gazes focused on her. "What if it's unsafe?"

"We'll let the drones do their work and return to Kro-Gen and report what we've found." D'lane's tail twitched at his feet.

"If nothing else, the bots will have some information for me to study on the trip back." Shannon sighed.

P'ret nodded at Shannon. "I'll keep an eye on her captain."

Shannon scoffed. "What for?"

P'ret's gaze narrowed. "Wouldn't want you sneaking into the derelict on a last-ditch effort for data collection. I'm sure of all of us, the captain wouldn't want you getting left behind or killed."

Shannon's anger spiked. She opened and closed her fists, and she counted to three before answering,

"Whatever."

"P'ret." D'lane's hand flexed, suit pulling tight against his forearms. "We discussed your attitude toward my crew earlier today, *and* the repercussions if you failed to adjust."

Shannon's brow arched. It wasn't just her P'ret had problems with?

"She," P'ret pointed a gloved hand at Shannon, "should not be out here helping or in this meeting."

"If I had wanted Shannon safely inside and away from this," D'lane growled, his body rigid, "I would have asked her to leave. If you have issues with how I handle my mission, this is not how you express it. If you are unable to follow proper paths of communication, disciplinary actions will be taken regardless of our kin status. Do I make myself clear?"

P'ret's chin raised.

"I said," D'lane stepped closer to P'ret, "Is that clear?"

"Yes, sir," P'ret bit out.

"Good." D'lane turned toward the group. "I want the bots up and running on the remote work by next meal."

Chapter 18

Personal note: Review Namegiver legacies.

She tugged at the sleeves of her silver jumpsuit. The sparring mat was soft and pliant under her feet. She'd debated accepting the tank top and pants V'ren had offered when she first boarded the T'grevis, but with limited clothing on board, she didn't want to take something V'ren might need later. Maybe next time they stopped at a station she could pick up something that wasn't owned by Kro-Gen or My'len. All she'd need to do was figure out how to pay for it.

She settled back into first position and spun into her next series of moves. Shannon's anger still simmered from the earlier incident with P'ret. If she wasn't willing to get into a verbal sparring match with him, then she'd work off her frustrations here, free from the prying eyes of the crew. Her chest heaved as she punched her first through an imaginary face.

She stilled as D'lane sauntered into the room sans shirt and dressed in loose black pants that she'd never seen before. Shaking out her limbs she took the time to appreciate the sexy being that was D'lane before blurting, "What is P'ret's problem?"

Body poised, she flexed her toes as D'lane prowled around her on the right. "It has nothing to do with you, and everything to do with the practice of revival."

She stilled. "Was he denied the process to save

someone?"

He sliced a hand through the air. "It's his Namegivers legacy." He stopped in front of her, exquisite bare chest in her face. "Eyes up here."

She cleared her throat and met his gold gaze. "Are you saying I'll have to deal with him and his problems for the duration of the mission?"

"Not if I can help it. Now, let's start our next lesson."

"Do we have time for another lesson with everything going on?"

"I wouldn't have offered it if we didn't."

She saluted him and flowed into first. She bit her lip as his warm hand altered her stance with small nudges. "Today we're going to work on throws."

She smiled and eyed him. "I get to toss you around the mat?"

"Nope." His 'p' popped. "You'll be learning to land softly today. We'll need to go over in more detail alien body types and points of balance before we have you throwing other beings."

"Any references you could recommend."

He stepped behind her. "I'll forward the list."

She shivered as he moved up against her back. The heated contact relaxed her stance. "I thought we were practicing throws?"

"We are." His hand skimmed down the top of her arm. "I'm attempting to decide if I should walk you through a landing or—"

She slammed on the ground, breath frozen in her chest. Adrenaline spiked through her veins as sharp needles of pain riddled her body. She gasped, head rolling to the side to catch D'lane's toes. Her palms stung. She flexed them against the mat. "Ouch."

He leaned over her, golden hair draping to frame his face. "Walk me through what happened."

She shifted her bent legs, tailbone still aching from the fall. Stunned, but not really hurt, she blinked up at him. "I'm not getting up."

"That's fine."

She closed her eyes, blocking him out even as his weight dented the mat at her shoulder.

His palm had been warm and firm at her hip and shoulder as he hooked his foot around her heel. After that... Her eyes popped open. "Did you use your tail?"

He flashed a smile. "I did."

She sat up with a groan. "I can see why you wanted me to wait on the throws."

"We always start with falls."

She took the hand he offered. "Then why did I eat asphalt."

His brows turned down. "There is only a mat here."

She rose as he tugged her up. "Was there a reason to drop me so unexpectedly?"

"To remove any anxiety you might build during our lesson. Now," he crouched beside her, "the stance you have when you're thrown isn't important as you'll have no control over it when it happens during our sparring. Instead, I want you to focus on using the energy you've been given to flow with the landing."

Fall after fall after fall, Shannon rolled, tucked, flopped, and spun her way across the mat. Swimming in sweat, she propped her back against the cool metal wall, legs sprawled out in front of her. A clear sphere landed in her lap. Plucking it up, rind cold in her hand, she bit off a chunk of the skin and sipped.

"You did a fantastic job today." D'lane sat down beside her, long legs stretched out to match hers. He rubbed her thigh and her tight muscles relaxed. "Give me some more time and I'll make an excellent fighter out of you."

His touch lingered. Hesitant, she traced the tendons on his hands when what she really wanted was to twine her fingers through his. "Do you think we'll actually get into the derelict?"

"We've already ventured farther than any other crew thus far."

She tipped her head back against the wall. "But what if we get nothing from those reconnaissance bots than a scan of a hallway before we hit another dead end?"

"Then we leave knowing we've done everything we can to learn from this derelict."

She slumped further down. "It won't be enough to help stop the coming attack."

"Who's to say what we do discover *will* or if we'll understand what we're looking at to stop it from happening again?" He turned his hand over and wove their hands together and warmth spread within her chest. "We'll do everything we can to salvage this trip. Even if we left right now, we'd still have more information than we did before."

She played her fingers off the tips of his digits.

"He is not angry with you."

She tipped her head to look at him. "P'ret?"

D'lane squeezed her palm. "He's always hated it when I maintain a calm voice while he loses his."

She laughed. "I'd say that's true for most people." She cleared her throat and glanced at their interwoven clasp. "How do you know it isn't me?"

D'lane kissed the back of her hand. "Because you're mine."

She rolled her eyes as she adjusted to a crossed position. "It isn't like one precludes the other."

"Knowing my destinies and the possible paths it may take going forward, it does."

She leaned her shoulder against his. "If I'm linked with your path, what does it mean for your destinies, the ones you mentioned at Kro-Gen where you tended to die at the end?" She opened her fingers to take back her hand but stalled when he gave a soft squeeze. "Does my destiny become yours?"

"It doesn't work that way." His tail curled over her knee, the tip settling in the open space between her legs. "Your own path might travel alongside mine, but it will never be exactly the same."

"For how long?"

"As long as we both desire it to be so."

Her lips pulled down at the corner. "It can't be that simple."

"Why not?" He leaned over, hand braced on the floor by her opposite knee and invaded her personal space.

She waited a breath before leaning in and kissing him. His skin was salty from their session. When he angled his head, the soft hair on his face brushed against her cheek. Heat spread deep in her body, and when his tail flicked between her legs, she shivered. He bussed swift kisses across her lips. She followed his every move, fighting for prolonged contact. Finally, desperate for more, she turned and wrapped her arms around his neck, swung her leg over his hips and mounted him.

She deepened the kiss, having missed the texture of

his tongue brushing against hers, and the unique taste that was D'lane filling her senses.

His hands settled at her waist. The press at her hips had her shifting her weight from her knees to rest in the cradle of his lap. His tail stroked up her side to curl around her arm.

The hard length of him a bar pressing against her clit, she rocked against him. Pleasure spiked in her core as he arched hips. Groaning, he pulled her closer, hugging her tight as she ground down on him, one arm across her back and the other twining through her hair. His hips meet her grinding pulses, lengthening the friction with every movement.

She gasped as his hand tightened in her hair. A tingling wave washed over her scalp as he arched her neck to the side, his lips sucked and nipped their way down her vulnerable skin. The fine hairs on his face raising goosebumps in their wake.

Moaning when he licked the sensitive skin where her jumpsuit met her neck, Shannon fisted her hand in his silky-smooth hair, pulling him closer. She trembled, warmth spreading through her as her core grasped at nothing. She looked up as pulled back. Her protest died as his lips closed on hers.

Their kiss was raw, wet, and heated. His rough tongue a counter stroke to each of her glides. He groaned. The vibration stimulated the hard points of her nipples all the way to her core. Shuddering, she tore her mouth away for some much-needed air. He palmed her ass, fingers caressing the seam where her thighs ended. Desire dampened her suit, creating friction against her sensitive skin and the hardening numb it contained. She fought to get closer.

Breathing harshly, he kissed and licked his way down her neck. He pulled her jumpsuit tight against her clit. She rocked back. Static short-circuited her brain as a wave of sensation swamped her.

"You haven't agreed."

Teeth nipped at the sensitive arch where shoulder met neck. She tilted her head to the side, to give him better access. Shannon tightened her grip on his hair, holding him place. The rough slide of his tongue against her vulnerable flesh and she clamped her thighs tight around his waist. She gasped. "What?"

His tail forced its way between them and glided up her stomach. A quick wiggle and it pressed across the aching point of her nipple, shooting sensation through her with every breath.

"Your future," he breathed against her ear, "next to mine?"

She whimpered and stilled. Both hands now fisted in his hair. "For how long?"

His hands slid up her hips. He brushed his thumbs against her abdomen and pushed her down against him as he ground up. Lightning flowed through her.

"For as long as we need."

She locked her gaze on his, the gold in them almost molten. She took a shuddering breath and ran a finger over the tip of his ear. "Yes."

She leaned back and opened the seam of her suit. He helped free her from the damp cloth. Breasts free, she pressed forward, grinding her nipples against the fine hair on his bare chest. Each was a soft caress against her skin. His fingertips skimmed up her ribs to palm her breast. He pinched her nipple. Sucking in a breath as pleasure spiked, she grasped his other hand and guided his fingers up to her neglected point. Nerves strung tight, her body clenched on emptiness.

"Please," she whimpered.

"I've got you." He pushed forward.

Her legs slid from his hips as she scrambled back and fought to get out of the remainder of her clothes. He helped tug her legs out of the pants, tossing the fabric aside, and prowled up her bare body.

"I want you naked," Shannon said.

He licked the fragile skin where her hip met thigh. He hovered over her damp curls, chest expanding with a deep breath. "No time."

She arched her hips with a soft laugh. "Somethings got to come off if we're going to do this."

He stared at her damp nether lips. "Not necessarily."

She groaned. "It better." She tugged him up. "Not after all this."

He rose over her, eyes bright as he met her gaze. "You're right. It's time."

She slipped her hands between them, running her palms down the long length of his chest until the metal of his belt stalled her progress. With one hand she cupped him, watching his eyes close as she stroked him through his pants. She explored the raised rings through the thin material, each a solid ridge around his length with the second slightly larger than the first.

She ran her thumb across the smaller one near the tip. He groaned, flexing against her grip. She flicked the belt open, and slid her hand beneath his pants, palming him. With her other hand she skimmed past his dick and found his balls. The hot globes soft and she cradled in her palm before giving them a light squeeze.

He growled in her ear as she stroked up his firm

length with both hands. A second pass and he nipped her neck. Impatient to see him, she worked the top of his pants down enough to see what she was handling. Propped on his elbows, he helped her, letting out a small groan as his tail slipped free of his clothing, instantly coiling around her calf.

With her hands back on his penis, he was long and just the right amount of a handful, the tip of him pointed more than she expected. Instead of bulbing down into a thinner shaft like she was used to, his dick thickened into the first ring that dipped into a slightly thicker second, before smoothing out.

With a sigh of appreciation, she let go of his length and gave his bare hips a squeeze. "Condoms?"

He propped himself up on a palm beside her head. His muscles flexed as slick fingers caressed her folds, before zeroing in on her clit. Her breathing sped up. Pleasure coiled tighter as she rocked her hips.

"Chriw'rian's are all on birth control and have been medically cleared prior to each mission." He leaned down and lapped at her shoulders. "I'm more than happy to share your pleasure in other ways until we can replicate a sheath cover."

She wasn't on any birth control, not yet anyway, but as long as one of them was on something…he stroked a hand down her side and cupped her. She gripped his biceps and arched into his touch. "I want you inside of me," she panted.

The tip of his finger dipped into her core. She clenched and rocked up, trying to pull him deeper into her aching depths. He retreated, and she slid her grip to his wrist. The tendons flexed as he sliding deeper. His palm, and the hairs on his hand stimulated her sensitive skin to the point of breaking.

"I meant your dick." She clenched around him as he brushed his thumb across her clit. She teetered on the edge of the abyss, and she wanted to come around the full length of him when he settled deep.

She lost her grip as he pulled away. She cried out at the loss of penetration as his damp palm settled against her ass. Her core flexed on emptiness and her knees clamped his sides to keep him in place. He tipped his chin down and he reached for her lips. "Why didn't you say so."

The kiss was deep and frantic. Her knees relaxed, and he dipped down, using a hand to notched his cock against her slit. Her swollen flesh hugged his curves as he pressed the hard full length of himself into her core. He shifted his hips and pulled back. She groaned, biting her lip as the two rings pulled out before he pushed back in. Coated in her softness, each pump was slicker than the last. The rings slid past her entrance in a repeated burst of sensations that coiled tighter in her core.

His tail coiled around her waist as he palmed her breasts and played with her nipples. She gasped as electricity coiled in her core. She his biceps as he slid deeper. D'lane growled and tipped his head back. She stared at the long delicious line of his neck as he surged into her again and again. She wanted to bite it, lick and suck at his flesh as the fine hairs covering his body stimulated the sensitive skin everywhere they were joined. She widened her thighs and clenched around his length, fighting to keep pressure on just the right spot. She slid her fingers into his hair and fisted his silky strands. Gold gaze snapped to hers and he slammed home. Wound tight, nerves rioting, she exploded. Crying out, she arched wildly as her climax peaked.

He pumped a few more times, his swelling rings sending zinging sensations through her before he buried his chin into her hair and groaned. Heat flooded her core. He melted against her, a pleasant weight to take on as his breathing slowed.

She rubbed his upper back as her core occasionally flexed on the solid length within her, enjoying the slow flicking of his tail against her ribs. "Wow."

She groaned as he pulled back, sliding from her one ring at a time like a finger pressing all the right buttons. She bit her lip and stared at his semi-hard length between her splayed legs. His cock didn't look that different then a human's, but he worked it to give her some amazing sex unlike anything she'd had before.

"I'll get us a towel." He brushed a kiss over her lips and stood before heading to the corner. Popping open an alcove, he crossed back with a black towel and helped her clean up before taking care of himself with a few passes of the material before snapping it clean.

It took her a moment to realize he was cleaning the damn thing and not flinging the remanences everywhere. Muscles sore from everything, she lounged where she was and watched him as he put the towel away and began dressing. As interesting as she found it to see him tuck first his tail, then himself back into his pants, she would have liked some more post sex skin on skin time. Had he not enjoyed their sex as much as she had?

He tipped his chin toward her. "Did you need some help?"

"Just enjoying the show." She stood, muscles complaining, and watched as he snapped clean her jumpsuit before handing it over. Their fingers brushed as she took it. "Thank you."

He leaned over and brushed a kiss over her lips. "It is a little thing."

She stepped into her jumpsuit and shimmied the material up. "Where does this leave you and your life's prophecy?"

After all the discussion about their tangled paths and the physical and emotional connection they'd explored, he must have changed his mind about what version of his namesake he was living.

"What do you mean?" D'lane asked as he tightened his belt.

She closed up her suit, suddenly thankful for the extra layer of protection for this difficult conversation. "Have you determined which D'lane you'll follow now that you've given up the king's path."

He frowned as his tail twitched at his feet. "I haven't deviated from my chosen prophecy. Why would you think that?"

"Oh I don't know." Shannon paced away before pivoting back to face him. "Perhaps it was when you asked me to walk beside you. That generally implies that you aren't hurling yourself toward a lonely premature death."

His hands clenched at his side. "When I spoke of how our paths would diverge at some point in the future, your affirmation meant you understood we wouldn't be spending our entire lives together."

"I understood it was in a more 'our old age and different species could dictate how long we have together' kinda way." She crossed her arms. "Not that you expected me to watch you die."

"You'll leave me before then." D'lane prowled

around the room. "Once you've settled into your new life."

Shannon gasped as pain stabbed deep. "I expected we'd have some trouble trying to see each other after this mission was over because we worked for different companies, and likely at different points in space, but to imply that I'd *leave* you once *we* became an inconvenience?"

Her hands clenched. "After what we just shared, how could you think so little of me?" Anger raged. In three strides she stood in front of him. "You know what your problem is?"

He crossed his arms over his chest, his tail twitching erratically at his feet. "Please enlighten me with your ancient knowledge."

Shannon's teeth clenched. "You are terrified to let anyone close, to truly feel an emotional connection to anyone. Don't think I haven't noticed how you hold everyone away at arm's length."

"I respect my crew."

She tossed her arms up in the air. "And that's it. You don't let yourself step over that line into friendship. You even do this with me. I'm emotionally safe for you. I know nothing of what's going on with you outside of this little slice of time, and you know I can't use you to gain anything in my current position."

"You think you have nothing to gain from me?" D'lane flashed a fang. "I didn't take you for a fool."

Shannon sucked in a sharp breath. That he thought she was using him at all dug bloody claws into her heart, but that he still chose to be with her regardless spoke to his delusion of grandeur on his life's destination. How could he be so reckless with his soul? She blinked rapidly to clear her gaze and met his defensive golden gaze. "You have everything I ever wanted in life. You're surrounded by people who love you and want to be with you for who you are, and yet you throw it away every chance you get."

His hands clenched, and his tail stilled. "And what about you?"

Shannon wet her lips as trepidation set in. "What about me?"

"You grasp desperately at those around you, terrified to be yourself for fear of rejection. Do you think we haven't noticed how little you try to interact with us? Instead, we have to approach you one by one to make you feel safe." His expression went hard. "Your fear of abandonment turns you into a liability."

****

Shannon hid her anger behind a nonchalance she didn't feel and sipped her tea while flipping through the latest images from the derelict's interior. D'lane had sat across the table from her when he came in, and she wasn't petty enough to move just to spite him. They hadn't spoken since his last parting words, and she'd been able to avoid the pain of his accusation by reviewing the drone information.

D'lane finished the last few bites of his meal. The vibe between them was tense and unpleasant. She'd wanted to ignore him, be anywhere but here, but work trumped personal life, especially when so many lives were at stake. "There isn't enough useful data here to stop an attack."

The cold derelict's interior read as more of a warehouse building than a living space. Infrared was of little help as the ship had equalized to the external temperature some time ago. The only source of heat was a small plume mid ship where D'lane thought the gravity well might be located.

The low-level lights from the bots showcased rooms with doors permanently ajar and sealed hatches at the end of hallways. The open spaces were no larger than a closet and held nothing of note except shattered pieces of metal that at one time could have been shelves or hooks.

She sucked the rest of liquid from the ball and added it to her empty plate. "Do you think there's any chance of cubbies in these rooms the bots failed to pick up on?"

"It's likely," D'lane set his utensil down and barely met her gaze, "but doubtful. If we did find any and figured out how to open them, the dimensions of the rooms indicate they wouldn't hold more than the T'grevis's does."

Which meant towels and cleaning supplies were all they'd find if they weren't already cleared out. Shannon tapped the table with her free hand. "Is there full power to the terminals on the hatches?"

If they could manually open more doors, then the bots scanning area would increase tenfold if the derelict's floor plan continued on as it did.

"P'ret believes so. Given enough time, he thinks he can get enough power to open the doors."

"How long would they stay open?" They were already at least halfway through the estimated power needed to prop the single door open. How much more would they need to operate them all?

D'lane stacked their trays and stood, heading toward the recog. "J'rax says they can change one, maybe two of our larger power packs out to give us the time we need to do a small reconnaissance, but it would be cutting it close if we needed the packs for the T'grevis in an emergency."

She swung a leg over to straddle the seat and keep him in sight. "What can I do to help?"

She knew he could throw his liability comment back in her face with her request, but she refused to sit back and relax while their departure clock continued to counted down.

"Not much other than review the video from the drones, which you're already doing." D'lane inserted the trays into the recog for material reclamation. "T'rev is helping with the last sweep of the debris from the platform while everyone else is assisting P'ret."

She tipped her chin back as he stopped beside her. "I'm worried about the doctor."

He reached to brush a hair from her face; she leaned back away from his touch. His hand clenched. "V'ren?"

"Hellen. I haven't seen her in a while, and she hasn't been in the sickbay any time I've passed it." Shannon glanced at the door. "Have you seen her lately? It's weird to go from seeing her several times a day, to no interaction at all."

He smiled weakly. "She did clear you for longer durations between checkups, if you don't recall."

Shannon pressed her lips together to keep her snippy response to herself. "You didn't answer my question."

D'lane sighed. "No, I haven't seen Dr. Grates since our interruption."

Heat rose up her neck as she remembered the cleared throat while they'd been making out in the hall. Shannon fingered her jumpsuit collar and waited for the flush to dissipate. "Is that normal?"

"The interruption?"

She glared at him. What else would she be referencing other than the subject at hand? Was he purposely being obtuse or trying to get a reaction out of her?

"You are her only charge on the ship." D'lane propped his hands on his hips, the tip of his tail rapidly flicking at his feet. "What else would she have to occupy herself with when she isn't waiting on you?"

She sat up straight as his tone rubbed her the wrong way. How was she supposed to know what anyone did on a ship during a mission when she had nothing to compare it to? She pressed her hands flat against the table. "Can we at least pretend to be civil toward each other?"

Did he think that she wanted to be sitting here, next to the male she'd been falling for, who continued to fight tooth and nail in order to keep their relationship as nothing more than fuck buddies? She'd rather go through the whole painful revival process again than be trapped in this awkward situation with him.

"I apologize." D'lane sighed. "I was out of line when you were obviously concerned with Dr. Grates. Have you stopped by her room to inquire about her health?"

The tension melted from her shoulders, and she accepted his apology. "I could try again? The last time she didn't answer."

"Let me know how it goes. I need to ensure the mental health all members aboard the T'grevis." D'lane gave her an informal bow.

Pain bit into her chest as his action cut deep. He'd just set a new level of emotional distance between them, even if the respect remained.

He straightened. "Until our paths cross anew."

"To seeing you again," she returned the traditional Chriw'rian parting call.

She turned back toward the table and blinked repeatedly to clear the tears from her gaze. She had work to do and focusing on how her and D'lane's relationship was falling apart wouldn't solve anything.

She played with her handheld. There wasn't much to review in the reconnaissance drone logs, other than making notes on possible locations of interest that were few and far between. Congregation areas at hallway junctions would be a good place to start looking for ways to deepen her knowledge of the command structure of the Anunnaki.

Her fingers twitched with her reluctance to check on Hellen. The doctor-patient relationship had never moved into any type of genuine friendship, mostly because Shannon hadn't allowed it, but her worry for Hellen was real.

Shannon sighed and stared at the blinking curser. She wouldn't forgive herself if she didn't check in on the doctor. A few strokes later she had the locations of all the crew members visible on the ship displayed on her PDA.

D'lane, P'ret, and J'rax were marked as outside of the ship, likely working on improving the power source and getting access to the derelict. T'rev was in the cockpit. Hellen remained in the room marked as hers while V'ren was headed into the med bay.

At the recog, Shannon grabbed the tea that Hellen preferred and made her way to the doctor's room. After a quick search of the wall, Shannon pinged Hellen. A few moments later Hellen answered the door in an oversized shirt that Shannon hadn't seen on any human before.

The doctor yawned into her hand as the chaotic state of Hellen's room came into focus. The blankets and pillows were half on the bed and strewn across the floor. Clothing was scattered across the floor, more metallic than anything else. She scraped a hand over her head. "Was there something I could help you with?"

Shannon's hand tightened on the warm globe careful not to burst it. "I'm sorry if I woke you. I wanted to check in and make sure you were okay. I know I'm getting twitchy being on the ship with nowhere to go until I'm allowed to explore the derelict."

"I wouldn't want to step foot off this ship even if I was offered the opportunity." Hellen accepted the coffee and smiled. "I have you to look after, but other than that, I've been treating this trip as a bit of a vacation. I haven't been on one since my last trip to the Grandiose system five years ago. They may have some shady business deals in that district, but their spas are amazing."

Shannon glanced back at Hellen's room. "I've never had a spa day, let alone traveled to another planet."

"We'll have to go sometime after all this business is over." Hellen popped the drink sphere into her mouth and bit down. She somehow managed not to spill a single drop, a feat that Shannon hadn't quite perfected yet.

"That sounds like fun. I can't remember the last time I had a vacation and I know I could already use a break from all this high-level anxiety."

"It definitely builds on you, the stress of revival and integration." Hellen propped her shoulder against the doorframe. "A nice relaxing trip is always recommended once a revivee has settled into their new life."

"Hopefully that happens soon." Shannon smiled. The edges of her lips wobbled as she struggled to maintain the expression. "I'll let you get back to sleep."

Shannon turned back toward the ship's mess.

"Hey."

She pivoted back. "Yes?"

"Let's take our next meal together. We can chat and you can fill me in on what you've been up to. I promise," Hellen held up her hands, "No health questions from me the entire time."

Shannon chuckled. "That sounds great. It'll be a few more hours, but I'll come get you."

"Or better yet, we can crash in my room, and I'll get you started on the vids of the era. There's a new retelling of *Beauty and the Beast* and I've been dying to watch it."

Shannon's painful smile warmed. "That sounds great."

After all, it wasn't like she had anyone else to spend time with now.

Chapter 19

Anonymous Memo to P'ret: Five days to derelict departure.

Shannon's helmet light flashed through the empty doorway leading into the bowels of the derelict before she turned back to D'lane. He'd ruled the ship safe enough for two small exploration teams to enter. They stood in a semicircle with P'ret and D'lane across from each other. Shannon stood next to D'lane and J'rax stood between Shannon and P'ret. The remaining crew were back on the T'grevis.

She wasn't surprised the Chriw'rian's were armed to the teeth. They did not know what to expect once they got into the ship, but they weren't going to get caught unprepared. She however, had been denied a weapon, again. She pressed on the edge of her comm. Her suits gloved fingers were a stark white against the case's black.

She hadn't explicitly asked for one, but she'd assumed she'd at least get a stun gun or something along those lines. D'lane's hands had been tied since My'len hadn't approved her use of defensive equipment, and Hellen wasn't able to submit the request to Kro-Gen with their radio silence. What Shannon did have was control of the spider bots clinging to the walls and ceilings, their green lights active and bright beams illuminating the hall. She could always order these six-legged guard dogs to swarm someone or something.

At this point, everyone's channel remained open, and Shannon could hear the cross conversation between P'ret and D'lane even if she didn't understand the technical aspects.

She bent slightly at the knees to sneak a peek through the break in bodies. The three lights at the top of the data pad connected to the derelict's hatchway still remained a steady green. Shannon shifted her weight and glanced at the rigged-open door. The darkness was soul sucking and captivating at the same time.

J'rax tapped her on the shoulder and pointed at the comms. Shannon closed all of them except for two.

"What are you looking at?" J'rax's question caused Shannon to jump.

"Something about long dark hallways, hastily propped open doors, and unknown spaces screams horror movie and impending doom for us all."

"That door isn't going anywhere. I rigged it with a brace from of the T'grevis just to be sure. But I totally agree with you." J'rax laughed. "There's this slasher film scene that keeps playing out in my mind. I keep seeing my tail pinned to the wall in some sicko's collection room."

Chest tight, Shannon released a strained laughing-cough. "I never watched those types of movies myself. My imagination and general human nature are enough for me."

"It'll hold." J'rax patted Shannon's shoulder.

Shannon quickly flicked open all the channels and pivoted. A wave of noise slammed through her helmet. She stumbled back gripping her helmet. A hand gripped her arm and pressed on her comm. The volume died down to a more manageable level.

Shannon stared at her wrist and noted only two channels were lit. She followed the grounding limb back to its owner. D'lane. "I shouldn't have turned the volume up."

"Probably not a good idea," D'lane said with a smile.

Shannon halfheartedly chuckled. "I'll keep the volume turned down."

She patted her pants pocket where her handheld resided. "When did you want the rest of the bots sent in?"

"Let's wait on that." D'lane nodded toward the door. "I'd like to keep the hall lit before we send them on their way."

"Great idea."

Even though the helmets came outfitted with lamps of their own, their battery life was nowhere near the length of the bots. The headlamps would last maybe two or three hours tops at full lumens while the bots could go days.

D'lane's head tipped to the side. "Are you ready to enter?"

Nerves tingling, she opened and closed her hands. "Yes?"

D'lane gently squeezed her wrist, a supportive action she chose to allow, before he turned back to the open door. "Let's move out."

She followed behind him, grateful for the emotional support but unsure how she felt about it. They still hadn't spoken about the conversation that divided them. She'd deal with it after they left the derelict.

At the hatchway, Shannon stepped to the side at D'lane's request and waited; she'd be bringing up the rear of the expedition. Both D'lane and P'ret paused for a moment as they reached the other side. Equal measures of excitement and fear flowed through her. What was so unexpected even an experienced crew would linger at? Where there bodies in the hall?

Shannon's fingers twitched.

Once J'rax was clear of the opening, Shannon stepped forward. The door slid shut as something flickered in Shannon's periphery. D'lane was on the other side of the hatch, trapped inside the derelict. Her helmet light flickered everywhere. Panic breaths echoed inside her suit. Her hand slammed against the door. "No!"

Shannon steadied herself against the wall. She flipped through all the comms, turning everything off and then on again. "D'lane?"

"Shannon," D'lane whispered through her comm. "Can you hear me?"

"Yes!" Heart racing, she pressed her palm on the door. A slight vibration beat against the surface. Were they attempting to break the door down? "I can hear you. Can you hear me?"

"I can. Now listen closely. I need you to use the mounted data pad to key open the door."

She slid sideways, keeping her palm against the door until she stood directly in front of it, and paused.

"Should I get T'rev?"

"Let's see if you can get the door open first, and then we'll try T'rev."

Shannon took a deep breath and open and closed her hands to fight off their trembling. "What do you want me to do?"

"Can you confirm all the lights are still green on the

data pad?"

"They are." A steady set of green lights, three in a column, stared back at her. The door shouldn't have closed under power, especially with it propped open. But where was the bar J'rax had used?

Shannon twisted and looked back. A bot just to her right had been impaled to the floor. A shiver racked her frame. That rod had flown right past her head.

"I'm going to call out a combination sequence for the keypad." D'lane's voice soothed her over the comms. "Once you enter it, the door should open up again."

She pulled her attention away from the dead spider bot and back to the door. There were two pads one atop of the other, with the green lights in between. "Am I using the handheld hijacked into the system or the door pad for this sequence?"

"The handheld."

Her hand hovered above the electronic surface and took a steading breath. "Ready whenever you are."

"You're going to punch in the following characters. *Bi, en, vi, oo—*"

"D'lane?"

"Do you need me to go slower?"

She swallowed hard. "It's not that. It's just that the PDA is in the Chriw'rian language, not English. And I haven't been able to full memorize the Chriw'rian alphabet and corresponding sounds with the other research I've been doing, so I only know about half of the letters you're saying." She bit her lip to stop rambling. "Is there any way I could change the language setting on the pad?"

"One moment." D'lane cut the channel. Her helmeted breathing was exceptionally loud to her ears as she waited in silence. Why couldn't she go get T'rev? Surely this would go quicker with someone familiar with the language.

"I talked to P'ret," D'lane's voice startled her as it crackled over the comms, "There's no converting it. The language software in the pad would fail and we'd be locked on this side of the ship until we can be cut out."

"I know your scared. I can hear it in the tone of your voice." D'lane's voice was soothing despite her frantically beating heart. "You have this. I know you can get the door open again."

"Why can't we comm someone from the ship to come down here?" Shannon gestured at the T'grevis even though no one could see her do so. "That would ensure success right from step one?"

"We're having trouble raising them right now. It could be any number of reasons, but I've decided to try this first before additional measures are taken. Now, are you ready to try to input the code? I'll pause to describe what the letter looks like when you don't know it."

Shannon shook out her hands. "Let's give that a shot."

"Good. If the first attempt doesn't work, P'ret is working on a layout of the pad to help tell you the row and column location of the letters."

She wet her lips and stared at the pad. "How many tries do we get?"

"I don't have an answer for you with the derelicts system. It'll depend on their security protocol."

"Sò, no pressure."

D'lane chuckled. "None at all."

She went to move a curl stuck on her lashes and slapped her helmet instead. "Give me a moment." She tipped her head back and closed her eyes tight. No matter where she stood with any of them, Shannon didn't want to leave them trapped on the other side of the door, in an unknown ship, with limited air supply. She could help them if she stayed calm and collected and worked through the Chriw'rian script on the pad.

She took a handful of deep breaths, the tight band around her chest easing. She could do this.

She focused on the pad again. "Let's give this a go."

A tense handful of minutes stretched to eternity. Shannon methodically typed out each letter D'lane described. Finally, they reached the last symbol D'lane defined. "I know that one." It belonged to the coffee icon Shannon regularly used. "Here we go."

A press later and the door opened. Shannon was blinded by someone's helmet light. She blocked the beam with her hand and blinked to clear her vision. "D'lane?"

The light dimmed. "Shannon are you okay?" D'lane asked.

"I should be asking you that. I wasn't the one locked inside a foreign ship." Shannon lowered her arm and moved to the side as J'rax pushed past. "But the bots have all failed."

"Don't worry about that now." D'lane guided her further out of the way as P'ret passed. "I'm sure we can get them back up and running shortly. Do you know what happened?"

"You know as much as I do." Shannon tensed as J'rax returned holding a rod, bits of bot stuck to the end.

"Looks like the jam failed."

"Are we…" Shannon coughed. "Are we going back into the ship?"

"Yes," P'ret said as he stopped beside them. "We don't have time to wait for better prospects. We should do some scouting while the bots are getting rebooted."

"I agree." D'lane fingered the knife sheathed at his hip. "Standard protocol still stands. No one goes anywhere alone."

"Are we going to use the rod to keep the door open in case the keypad fails again?" Shannon asked. "Not that it worked so great the last time…"

"We'll attempt to keep it open, but we'll plan for extraction from the derelict by the T'grevis." D'lane nodded a J'rax. "Are the bots all in the green?

"All except for the one impaled," J'rax said as they tossed the bar from hand to hand.

Shannon leaned against the wall. "How long are we planning on exploring the interior?"

"Eight hours." D'lane met everyone's gaze. "Anything more than that and we risk endangering ourselves with reduced oxygen and degrading suit power if rescue takes longer than planned."

"Then let's move out." J'rax jammed the rod back into the doorframe. "Time's a wasting."

Shannon waited for the group to enter again before she stepped over the doorway. This time if the doors closed, they'd be trapped inside and forced to worry about their exit strategy later.

"We'll assign one bot to shadow each group," D'lane's voice commanded over Shannon's comms.

D'lane dimmed the light on his helmet as the two remaining spider bots headlights brightened. The rest of the bots had already passed through the doors to scan ahead of them. "Use the bots to mitigate external power use on your suits. It'll buy us some time if we run into additional problems."

Shannon tapped her handheld on top of the closest bot. A drone shimmied over to P'ret and another to D'lane. "They're ready to go."

"Shannon and I will explore further into the ship." D'lane's tail flicked at his feet, just missing the bot that waited next to him.

Shannon fought back any unpleasant emotions D'lane dragged up. With the amount of time they'd be spending alone together exploring the ship, now wasn't the time to wage a mental battle on whether they'd have a future together and what that might look like. She shoved all her insecurities and relationship unknowns into her mental black box to deal with once she was back on the T'grevis and done with the derelict.

P'ret propped his hands on his hips, just above the weapons holstered there, and glanced at D'lane. "J'rax and I will remain near the hatch and search the local area for anything of interest."

J'rax bumped Shannon's shoulders with her own. Shannon shook her head to move a curl back out of her face and opened J'rax's channel.

"We don't know how far our comms will travel through the derelict." J'rax tapped their wrist. "It's better to keep all lines of communication open and discover where our comms get thin as we explore rather than when someone's lost."

Shannon opened every channel on her NAV and glanced at the bot near D'lane's feet. She'd programmed it to follow his every step. "Can we use the bots as relay stations if the suits can't communicate?"

"We can," P'ret answered. "But we'd be sacrificing the bots ability to continue mapping the rest of the ship by forcing them to stay stationary and within comms range."

"Let's assess the issue when it arrives." D'lane pulled his handheld from his suit pocket and tapped a few commands. "I expect routine updates from both of you on the quarter hour, with more thorough updates on the hour."

"Yes, captain," echoed from both P'ret and J'rax.

"Good. Stay safe." D'lane gestured for Shannon to follow him and started down the dark hall. Shannon waved a goodbye to J'rax and followed.

The bot at D'lane's feet illuminated the corridor in front of him. Her own dim helmet light added a small percentage to the overall glow but lit up the back of D'lane when she looked forward. The sound of three sets of breathing and occasional swallow seeped through the open comms.

Her nerves spiked as darkness crawled up behind her, an ever-moving wall of blackness nipping at her heels. She shivered, feeling the spirits of the ship rush up behind her. The hair along the back of her neck rose as she waited for them to reach out from the dark alcoves and grab her. Shannon hurried to D'lane's side, her gloved fingers twitching.

"Why aren't there any bodies? Shouldn't we find *something* on this large of an abandoned ship?"

D'lane wiggled his handheld. "If there were any corpses aboard, we'd have captured minute traces of them."

Shannon noticed he'd sidestepped the answer. "Would their recyclers or version of a recog remove all organic waste?"

"It depends on the type of scrubbers," D'lane said as

he passed another open doorway. "Perhaps they evacuated after an attack and took their dead with them?"

Shannon peeked into a room that led to another set of chambers. "This ship is a maze of empty interconnected storage spaces." She turned back to D'lane. They walked a hands width apart. If they were back on the T'grevis, she'd be able to feel the heat of his body radiating against hers. "Are we sticking with the larger hallway or diverting to one of the smaller offshoots?"

D'lane gestured forward. "This main hall is our first check." He held his handheld toward her, a partial map of the interior ship sprawled across its screen, a larger depiction of the one she had on her wrist.

"I'd like to stay in a straight line with easy access back to P'ret and J'rax. I don't want us to get too comfortable just yet."

Shannon zoomed out on the partial map on her wrist which was constantly updating from the scanning spider bots. Two sets of red dots moved away from each other that depicted the two teams exploring the ship. All around the map were splattered green dots representing the bots. The image was a labyrinth of halls and small rooms that hinted at a repetitive design that could hold the key to the entire layout of the ship. The bots continued to expand at the edges of the screen, depicting more twists and turns.

She followed D'lane at a slow place, the assigned bot crawling at their heels. The urge to stare down pitch black hallways kept her eyes focused forward. She knew nothing would come crawling out at her from those passages, but her visceral fear of complete darkness kept pulling her mind from the task at hand.

She crept closer to D'lane's side, brushing up against him occasionally as she peeked into every room, terrified of what her brain might imagine jumping out at her. Her dim helmet light diffusing into nothingness a few feet from the doorway did not help. "Do you think they left voluntarily?"

"It would seem so."

Shannon checked the power on her suit. An urge she'd fought since they first entered the guts of the ship five minutes ago. The battery image on her wrist was green and full. How confident was D'lane on the eight-hour operation? Her suit wasn't My'len made. Had he taken that into account when he measured their remaining time?

She lowered her arm and immediately raised it to check the power again.

The weight of D'lane's hand settled on her shoulder. "I have our power levels programed in my handheld. We'll have more than enough time to explore and get back to the T'grevis before it becomes an issue."

Her shoulders sank. "I'm new to all this."

"I know." He gave her shoulder a squeeze. "And you're doing a great job keeping up with me and asking all the right questions. But Shannon…"

Her heart thudded in her chest as she glanced up at him, her helmet light causing him to squint. She wet her lips. "Yes?"

"You need to trust me."

The answer was easy. "I do."

"Captain?" Shannon twitched as J'rax's voice whispered in through her comm.

Shannon cringed. She'd forgotten they all had their comms open and knew both J'rax and P'ret had heard their entire conversation.

She went to step back, but D'lane kept her there. "Here."

"We found another locked door. The pad looks usable. We're going to cobble together a few bots to see if we can't replicate the power chain at the main access way to open it."

Excitement spiked through Shannon. Every unknown area of the ship held the potential to unleash the knowledge they needed to stop the Anunnaki attack. And as of yet they'd found little to be of any help.

D'lane's helmet tapped against her own as he looked down and focused on his PDA. "How many bots will you need?"

Breathing filled the air between J'rax's statement. "Minimum five, max seven."

D'lane typed out a command on his handheld. "I've rerouted the closest ones to your position. You'll see them as yellow on the map once they're linked."

Shannon zoomed out on her map. A handful of green dots flashed yellow where they clustered around the red pair representing P'ret and J'rax. The remaining bots shifted around until they filled in the gaps missing in their scanning network.

"Keep me informed." D'lane slid his PDA into a hip pocket.

"Yes, sir."

D'lane's low headlight flooded Shannon's vision. She blinked repeatedly until her eyes readjusted and his face came back to focus. His brows pulled down. "Keep an eye on our surroundings and let me know when you want to stop and investigate, otherwise we're following this main corridor until we hit an end."

Shannon nodded. "I'll let you know."

It was hard to say when she wanted to stop and look at *everything*. Like the T'grevis's main deck, nothing decorated the derelicts walls, and the bare rooms left a lot to be desired. What was she expected to find to help save billions of lives if she couldn't discover a working information pad—assuming she could even read it? Did the League expect them to get what they needed by just *walking around*?

In the end it didn't matter what the powers that be expected, they'd been assigned a single project, research the site in a short period of time, and it didn't matter how bare of artifacts it was, she'd do her job to the best of her ability.

Shannon glanced at the map, checked her power yet again, and stepped in front of D'lane to take the lead. The bot at D'lane's feet kept the light steady. Her body blocked a chuck of the light and stretched her shadow out in front of her.

Bots crisscrossed their path as they crawled up and down the walls to their next scanning location. She wasn't sure if being the first to walk into the unknown was any better than shoring up the back end. She'd never been surrounded by this level of darkness. Even when she camped outside during digs on moonless nights, stars still lit up the sky.

Steady breathing echoed in her helmet. She gestured at the retreating metallic bot. "Were these the best designs available for the bots?"

"Why do you ask?" D'lane asked.

Shannon shivered as a spider bot skittered around a corner halfway up the wall. "They're…creepy."

D'lane chuckled. "They mimic a predator from

Chriw'r that drags its pray deep into its forested den and devours them."

"Lovely." Shannon glanced at her wrist and noted a void in the bots map. She took a right toward it. "Exactly what I want to hear as they skitter past us."

D'lane brushed against her arm. "At least they're smaller than their namesake."

She tipped her head back to keep her headlamp out of his eyes. She cleared her throat. "Smaller?"

D'lane chuckled. "The ke'lar's stand at waist height and are around six feet long."

Shannon brushed a hand over the arm of her suit. "Remind me to never venture into their territory."

D'lane fell behind her. "You won't have to worry about that."

His comment cut to the bone. Did he mean to imply they had no future together? She needed their conversation to take the edge off the disturbing factor riddling the ship even as the lid on her black box let the most recent emotion seep out. She hedged, "They're extinct?"

"It's a protected species." D'lane cleared his throat as his helmet light scanned the hall. "Besides, My'len doesn't allow non-Chriw'rian's outside of the designated landing zone."

The tension in her chest dissipated as she realized she'd misunderstood him. The hall opened up to a large open space. Shannon stopped and turned. "What if someone's there to visit family?"

D'lane hesitated. "Even then."

"I see."

But she didn't. If it involved pandemic security, wouldn't this time period have inoculations for that?

Perhaps Chriw'r had extreme security concerns? But who would attack an entire planet? She scoffed and looked around. The answer obvious as they currently explored their ship.

She had questions, but they could wait. Shannon pivoted back to the space and moved forward.

The area held two rows of tables that lined the central passageway to the back wall. Hip high, they left sufficient space between their edges for multiple bodies to move around.

"What do you think about this?" D'lane's helmet light cut across the space. "They don't appear computerized."

"Why would you think that?" Shannon stopped next to a large tabletop and rapped her knuckled on the hard surface. Not that she could hear the response, but it felt solid.

D'lane crouched at the end of the table. "It'd have a box or some other primary control if it was." He stood and walked the table's length in five strides. "Older interactive units aren't uncommon to find especially in the less affluent areas of the galaxy, but this is nothing more than a null surface."

Shannon chuckled at that statement.

"What's so funny?"

"Every surface was a null surface in my time. Digital table tops were only starting to permeate the market before I died."

Shannon walked the length of the room, occasionally taking a note on her NAV about an interesting dent or divot on the table, but there wasn't much to record in the room.

D'lane's headlamp landed on her. He'd been

following a few feet behind her as she grumbled through the mic. "Tell me what you think."

Shannon checked the map and pivoted on her heel to face him. "This could be the mess if not for the lack of chairs."

D'lane wandered over to the table, the spider bot following at his feet, and took most of the light with him. "And the recog's?"

Shannon scrolled through the map illustrating the connecting halls. "I'm not seeing another void for a kitchen like the T'grevis."

"Maybe the service trollies are hidden inside the walls?" D'lane tapped a nearby panel.

Shannon chuckled. "I keep tapping surfaces, expecting to hear something through my helmet."

"I have the external mic on."

Shannon stilled. "You didn't mention that channel before."

She flicked through the comms options loaded to her NIC. Was there a button she failed to push to activate hers?

"Your suit doesn't have that configuration."

Shannon huffed as she crouched at the next table. Yet another reminder of the difference between them. "Do you hear anything interesting?"

He gestured to the nearby bot moving along the deck. "Just clicking."

"Exciting stuff."

He flashed her a smile. "I wouldn't want to hear anything else."

An eerily true thought.

D'lane stilled. Shannon's comm light clicked off of line one. He'd muted her line!

She stood and focused on his helmet as his lips moved rapidly. She zeroed in on his still tail as he hit a few more buttons on the additional comm she noted on his wrist. She caught his deep breath before he glanced her way. Was something wrong?

Shannon dragged a gloved finger across the next table as she walked to the far end of the room and waited for her line one to light up again. "Any updates from P'ret and J'rax?"

She hoped the conversation had been about the pair making more progress. D'lane stalked the perimeter with an occasional stop to rap on the wall. His body language remained tense despite his calm tone. "They're still stringing together the bots."

She hit the end of the room and took a right. She searched for a lip, handle, or some other marker on the wall to indicate a hidden compartment. "How many have they done so far?"

"J'rax is working on the third now."

She couldn't hold back her desire to know who he'd been speaking to. "Why'd you mute my line?"

He stilled. "You caught that?"

"It was kind of hard to miss when you're the only other person in the room." Shannon moved on to the next section of the room and found nothing. Her shoulders slumped. They needed to move on to a new location and hope for something more interesting.

"I'm having trouble reaching T'rev."

She stilled. "When did you last talk to him?"

"Five minutes ago."

Was he worried? The emotion in his eyes was hard to read through the helmet.

Shannon leaned against the first table and reviewed

the expanding on her wrist. "If we continue through to the end of this hall, we'll be running parallel to the T'grevis. It could get you in a better position to talk to the ship."

D'lane stopped beside her. "That would be a good idea."

She flipped her comms channels back on.

"We're ready to switch on our power banks." J'rax cut into their conversation.

D'lane asked, "Any reason to rethink opening the door?"

"Negative," P'ret said.

"Then proceed."

J'rax whooped. Shannon braced herself against the table, her own excitement prickling her nerves. She observed D'lane's tense stance, unsure when he would notify them of his concern with the T'grevis.

"It's open." J'rax's excitement evident in their voice. "I'm calling the local bots in for mapping now."

J'rax's breath came over comms "I've sent three bots in…Data coming in now. It doesn't look like much yet, but the layout is different than our current quadrant of the ship."

Shannon wanted to ask if they should shift their search area but D'lane cut his gaze to her. "P'ret, see if you can touch base with the T'grevis for an update."

Shannon bit her lip.

"I spoke to T'rev a few minutes ago, but I can't reach him now. The derelict may be interfering with my ability to reach them." D'lane's tail flicked back and forth at his feet. "Once you've reached T'rev, have him run one of the T'grevis's larger generators to your position to help keep that door open."

"Can do captain," P'ret said.

Shannon crouched to look under the table and sighed when metal legs stared back at her. Still nothing of note. She glanced up at D'lane. "Do you think P'ret will be able to reach T'rev without traveling back to the ship?"

"Captain?" P'ret's sharp voice cut harshly over the comms. "We have a problem.

Chapter 20

Internship comm: We've found them.

"Close the door. Now," D'lane commanded.

Shannon's adrenaline spiked as she straightened next to a table. "What is it?"

"Working on it," J'rax commed.

D'lane gold gaze met Shannon's. "Our distance from the ship isn't why I'm unable to reach the T'grevis."

Shannon's hand shook as she went to move her curl from her face. She jammed her fingers into the helmet instead as she stepped closer to D'lane. "Why wouldn't the ship answer us?"

J'rax's quick breaths crept into Shannon's comms. "I can pull power on the rig? It's the quickest way to close the door, but it'll damage the bots and take time to reconfigure once we're back in touch with the T'grevis." J'rax's breathing evened out. "We'll also be out another bot when we re-rig the power."

"Do it." D'lane stepped forward and leaned out into the hall.

"Yes, captain," J'rax said.

"I checked the path back to our landing bay," P'ret's voice cut in. "The T'grevis is gone."

"As I had hoped." D'lane unholstered the gun on his right thigh. He tilted it left and right. A light at the end of the gun flashed green and flickered off.

Shannon wet her parched lips. "Why would you want the T'grevis gone?"

How would they survive on a derelict with only the air stored in their suits? She checked her power. The green light was strong, but how long would that last for? Shannon took a step. "What are we going to do when our oxygen runs out?"

D'lane halted her forward momentum. "We'll follow standard protocol."

"Right." She took in his strong unfazed stance and reminded herself that this wasn't a new situation for D'lane, especially if contingency plans were in place.

A drop of sweat collected on her temple. If the ship was gone, they had no way off the derelict. "I don't want to die here. Not Now. Not after—"

"Shannon, look at me." D'lane set his gun on the table and gave her shoulders a small shake. "No one is going to die. It means my crew is alive."

Shannon rubbed the back of her neck over her suit, the fabric incapable of providing the grounding skin on skin contact she needed.

D'lane stepped closer. Her eyes met his before darting around the room. She needed to get out of here. "I still don't understand why your ship abandoning us is a good thing?"

"If the ship remained on deck and we'd lost communication, then we'd have more pressing concerns."

She needed to focus on D'lane and how they were going to survive without his ship. She called forth her mental black box and shoved her rioting panic inside. The pressure in her chest eased. "How can you be certain?"

"The T'grevis's flight system lock-out procedure keeps non-crew members from operating the ship. The only way my ship would have left was at the decision of one of my crew."

"That doesn't mean T'rev wasn't forced to move the ship under duress." Shannon took a handful of steps away before pacing back to D'lane. She glanced at the table and what it held. "I want a gun."

"I've got the door closed," J'rax cut in through the comms. "We're on our way to your position."

"P'ret," D'lane growled as he drew another firearm from the back of his belt and checked it over. "Were you able to get a read on what we're dealing with?"

"There are at least two ships in the derelicts bay. They're part of the Zu-Ki clan," P'ret answered.

D'lane added the weapon to the table. Shannon's hand clenched. She would wait and see if he offered her one before she took a gun for herself.

"The latest intel doesn't have them venturing this far in the sector," P'ret continued. "They usually can't afford the fuel."

D'lane grunted and pulled a third weapon from his left thigh holster, this one long, thin, and tapered with a trigger at the other end. He checked it over. "You disabled our exit?"

"Yes, they won't be able to get our entry point open," P'ret answered. "I don't know if their ships sensors caught my activity. It would depend on what scrap components were used to rig their ship together."

"Let's assume they did." D'lane's tail flicked at his feet when the weapon flashed green. He offered the gun to Shannon with a nod.

Shannon accepted the weirdly shaped thin weapon

and lowered it alongside her thigh. "Who are the Zu-Ki?"

"They're a pirate clan that normally run in smaller familial groups consisting of a handful of ships." The weight of D'lane's tail settled around her calf.

Her stress morphed into a twitch in her knee. "I thought pirates wouldn't be out here?"

"They usually salvage junkyard ships and the occasional lone, unsuspecting vessel they come upon." D'lane pulled another gun from his double right hip holster and checked it over. "Thoughts, P'ret?"

D'lane had at least three more weapons, including two blades sheathed on his biceps, her favorite curved blade and the black handled one he usually wore at his hip to check over before he'd gone through the arsenal Shannon knew about. And all she could do was watch him check every edge, his fingers caressing the handle as he went over every single one and try to convince herself she shouldn't be turned on.

"The Zu-Ki ships are held together by spit and sheer luck, and they normally work alone. This feels like a larger operation." P'ret's voice echoed over comms. "I think we're either dealing with a bigger family group or they've combined clans."

Shannon tapped the gun against her thigh. "Are they here to scavenge the derelict?"

D'lane pulled the last gun from its holster. "T'rev wouldn't have pulled the T'grevis back for that alone. The exterior drones likely tagged incoming vessels."

Shannon wanted to ask if D'lane thought they were going to survive this but blurted out, "What would it take for T'rev to leave?"

"Pirates." D'lane's gold eyes locked eyes with Shannon. "Lots of pirates."

"They could have the derelict surrounded and we wouldn't know," J'rax said.

"How many is a lot?" Shannon asked as her twitch grew into a shake. D'lane's tail caressed her thigh, and she settled to wait for more information.

P'ret grunted over the comm. "I'd bet my lucky boots they were paid damn well to jump all the way out here."

"Intent?" D'lane asked.

Shannon swallowed thickly as D'lane placed the fifth gun beside his remaining three on the table. Did he hope to hold off a number of Zu-Ki crew with only a handful of weapons and sheer luck?

"Unknown at this time." P'ret's breathing hit at an increased pace. An indication that he'd started to run deeper into the ship. "Likely capture or neutralize."

"Convene on us." D'lane pulled a blade from his arm sheath.

Shannon eyed the stylized machete with a black handle. He'd worn her favorite weapon. Not that it mattered, but it was either think of that or focus on how the bot's light cast skeletal shadows across the room where they broke against any vertical surface.

The blade flashed in D'lane's helmet light as he pulled it out and reseated it in its sheath. "Once we regroup, we'll decide on a new path forward."

"Yes, captain," J'rax said.

The line went silent, except for the sound of breathing. She checked her power as D'lane re-sheathed the knife. She was down one green power bar. D'lane's gloved hand covered her wrist and blocked the display.

"We have plenty of time left," he soothed.

Shannon's laugh rang sharply in her ears. "Was that

before or after the pirates? Or perhaps when the T'grevis sat on the other side of this wall."

He gave her wrist a squeeze. "And it'll be the same after we take care of the Zu-Ki."

She wanted to believe him, but she was entirely out of her comfort zone. Shannon shifted her weight. The urge to move crawled up her spine. They'd solve nothing by staying here, easy pickings for murderous pirates. Her toe tapped against the floor. She met the intensity shining in his golden gaze.

In the end, she didn't have a choice. It was either trust D'lane or panic, and panic would get them both killed. "Should we recall the bots? Possibly use them as backup in case we're attacked?"

"No." D'lane released her and holstered two of the three guns from the table. "Leave them. We'll use them as alarm triggers for when the pirates break into the derelict."

"I'll activate the setting on the bots to trigger a warning when they detect non-mechanical movement."

"Excellent." D'lane stroked a hand down the last weapon of the table, the first he'd checked over before tucking it away. She knew it was his personal favorite. It was the gun he always touched whenever he crossed his arms.

"I want to walk you through what's going to happen next," he said. His arsenal was now complete, except for the empty holster on his left thigh, where her gun would have resided.

Shannon shook her head as a shaky laugh escaped. She feared his information would lead to more questions, and she'd sink into a rabbit hole of unknowns instead of focusing on the here and now.

D'lane closed the distance between them and leaned down until his visor tapped hers. His golden eyes locked on hers as his tail curled around her ankle. "Knowing what may happen will help reduce your stress response."

"I have a pretty good idea of what's going to go down." She'd suffered through enough action movies to guess the basics of a cat and mouse game when guns were involved.

"It's different when you're in the moment." He settled his hands on her shoulders. She'd give anything to be able to feel the heat of his touch right now.

"Captain," J'rax's voice strained over Shannon's comm. "Looks like we won't be joining you."

D'lane's hand tightened on Shannon as he straightened. "Update."

"The Zu-Ki aren't as hesitant to cut into the derelicts hull as we were." P'ret's breathing picked up speed. "We're still a few corridors away from your location, but bots are lighting up from bogies all around us."

D'lane's lashes came down over his golden gaze as he stepped back. "Can you evade?"

Transferring her gun to the opposite hand, Shannon zoomed out on her NAV. The pair of red dots that were P'ret and J'rax moved at a rapid clip away from them. She tapped her screen to refresh it. They were down too many bots.

"Negative, captain."

"Do not engage. Gather data and stay free of capture. Notify us as soon as you're in a secure location," D'lane said over the comms. "We'll be doing the same on this end."

"Stay safe captain." J'rax clicked off.

Shannon turned toward the unexplored dark hallway

behind her. Her helmet light permeated a few feet before hitting a wall of darkness. Would they come this way as well?

"P'ret?" D'lane pulled Shannon back the way they'd entered, the spider bot trailing behind them a few feet away.

Shannon tripped over the bulky toes of her boots and D'lane's grip on her hand was the only thing that kept her up and moving.

"Yes, D'lane."

"I'm trusting you to keep J'rax safe."

"Understood." P'ret signed off.

Throat dry, Shannon swallowed. Her headlight scanned from wall to wall. "Where do we go now?"

"We get as far away from the pirates as possible." D'lane released her. "Stay close."

Shannon's hand shook as she stayed tight on D'lane's heels. "And then what?"

D'lane's smiled back at her, his canines flashing in the low light. "We get rid of the vermin on this ship."

With a mission to focus on, Shannon's hand steadied as she flicked through the updated bot map on her wrist. D'lane led them toward an uncharted portion of the ship. "What can I do to help?"

"Keep me updated on the bot motion alarms." D'lane slowed as he neared a junction. A raised hand indicated he wanted to stop.

The halls of the derelict were pitch black and silent except for D'lane's breathing. Her eyes flicked to the right and stared down a corridor. A dark mass slid from one side to the other. She blinked rapidly and focused back on her wrist. "Are you sure no one died on this ship?"

"I never said that."

Chest tight, she kept her attention glued to the map and D'lane and ignored the ghostly tricks her mind played on her. A handful of bots flashed yellow down the hall on their left. Shannon sucked in a breath. "Take a right."

He tucked her hand into the back of his weapons belt, her fingers clenching around it on a death grip so tight the stitching in her glove dug into her skin as he took the turn.

"Have your gun ready but keep your eyes on the map."

"I can do that." She took a steadying breath and readjusted the weapon in her free hand. The uncharted space on the NAV rapidly closing in. "What happens when we run out of map?"

His tail tapped the side of her calf. "We wing it."

"Exactly what I wanted to hear."

He chuckled as they continued moving. Shannon gave him directions whenever needed and D'lane continued to lead the way until they walked into the unknown. No additional bots in sight. They were blind to any pirates that might be in front of them.

D'lane followed the closest wall until they hit a corner. "Arc P'ret and J'rax close?"

Shannon scanned the map, zooming all the way out. Yellow lights flickered on and off as the bots stumbled upon the Zu-Ki even as she noted their decreased numbers. "The pirates have moved further into the ship and are destroying any bots they come across."

D'lane grunted. "That's to be expected."

"P'ret and J'rax have deactivated their trackers." Shannon's head brushed the back of her helmet as she looked up at D'lane. "Should we turn ours off?"

He shook his head no. "Let's try comms first." He activated the two additional lines on his wrist's NIC. She glanced at her forearm, noting he'd turned her channels off at some point too. She quickly opened them.

"Captain here."

A breath hit before anyone answered.

"Good to hear your voice, cap," J'rax said. "We're still trying to stay out of the pirate's range, but they're moving faster than we can secure ourselves." Their harsh breathing cut in and out over comms. "It was a great idea at first, but we're practically surrounded."

"Location?" D'lane demanded.

"Not recommended over the unsecure channel," P'ret cut in.

Shannon searched back to the collection of yellow lit bots. "They're back where we started if the rapidly decreasing number of bots is any indication."

"The Zu-Ki started taking them out as soon as they realized we were using them for intel," J'rax said. "We lost our personal bot a few minutes ago."

"I can reroute a replacement?" Shannon's finger hovered over a stalled bot.

"Don't waste bots on us." J'rax chuckled. "Capture is imminent, and I want to keep as many active as possible just in case."

"Aren't the bots armed? Why not use them to hold back the pirates?" Shannon pulled up the global spider bot command structure.

"Wait." D'lane gently moved her hand from the gauntlet. "We don't have our suit IDs stored in the program. If you activate the command on them all at once, they'll shoot at anything that moves, including us."

Shannon's hand spasmed as she met D'lane's gaze. "Is there nothing we can do?"

"P'ret, keep trying to reach T'rev on the T'grevis." D'lane's ear twitched. He turned toward a door. He must have picked up movement with his external mic. "We'll do the same. Captain out."

D'lane hustled them deeper into a room. "Let's hope there's an exit at the end of this space. We're about to get company and I'd rather not have to fight our way out."

The room opened up in a reflection of the previous tabled room.

The strong line of D'lane's back stiffened her own. She needed to do something else to help protect them. "I'm recalling another bot."

They hit the end of the room at a jog, passed through an unknown doorway, and kept on going. Arm moving with every step, she scrolled back to their section of the map and selected the closest bot. Her hand clenched on her gun as she focused on D'lane's form. "Backup bots should be along shortly."

D'lane's ear flickered in his helm. "Not if the Zu-Ki have anything to say about it. That's the second one I've heard them destroy in the last five minutes."

"Should I call additional backup?"

D'lane nodded. "Spread the selection out. We don't want a stream of bots leading the pirates right to us."

"I'll widen their motion detection field too." Shannon flicked through the controls. "We'll lose some of our fine data collection, but surviving this is more important."

"Agreed."

D'lane stopped. Shannon came up short, her NIC tapping against his back. She peeked around his shoulder. The hall went on about a dozen more steps before taking a hard right. Their bot crawled to a stop at their feet. It's light not quite stretching to the corridors end.

He reached behind him and held her arm. "Remember that hallway a few yards back."

Shannon squinted at the wall. "Yes?"

Did the hall get brighter?

"Move and be quick."

Shannon spun on her heel and took off after D'lane's strong lean frame, her gun held at the ready. D'lane's even breaths regulated her own.

Close on his heels, her headlamp brightened the back of his grey spacesuit. She stifled the urge to grab his tail and hold on to the lifeline. She glanced at her wrist with the schematics of the ship still pulled up. Somewhere along the mad run, they moved to cut a new fresh path into the unexplored part of the ship. Their suits provided the charting algorithm with data after each new step.

D'lane's body braced left. She turned to follow except he took a right. Shannon cut the sharp corner and lost traction. Her hands opened to brace herself as she slammed into the wall. The fingers in her hands ached from jamming into metal.

She struggled to keep her emotions under control as she righted herself. Escaping the pirates, abandoned on a ship with limited air, and D'lane somewhere behind her descended into a dark coil of panic. Her free hands clenched on air as her frantic thoughts placed him halls away even as his helmet light brightened her feet. Breaths short, she focused on the end of her dim light and kept running.

"Shannon!" D'lane's voice cut through her throbbing temples.

She stumbled to a stop. The bot at his feet cast her frame in shadow.

He captured her arm and circled around in front of her. The weight of his tail settled against her ankle as his golden eyes searched her own. "Are you hurt?"

"No." She sucked in deep breaths to calm her pounding heart. Her eyes scanned up and down the hall. "Did we lose them?"

He squeezed her hand. "I think we've run far enough."

She closed her eyes and slowly blew out her held breath. "Okay."

She wanted nothing more than to take a moment and press herself against his warmth as he wrapped her tight in a hug. Instead, she was forced to hold everything together until they fought themselves free of this pirate situation.

Her hand shook as she raised her NAV. The maps progression began in a straight line as she'd followed in D'lane's footsteps, and then shifted to erratic when she made the wrong turn and suddenly became the leader. Zooming out, she noted the three reconnaissance drones headed in their direction.

Her voice shook as she said, "ETA of bots is ten minutes."

He gripped both her shoulders. "Now tell me how you're doing."

Her gaze scanned the dark space, searching for any movement that might herald danger. "Why is that important right now? We need to keep moving, the Zu-Ki could find us at any moment."

He gripped her helmet and forced her to remain focused on him. "I called your name repeatedly. You didn't answer."

She went to step back, but he held her in place. She wet her lips. "I was focused on getting out of there."

"You were lost in your own fear."

A hair tickled her check. She scrunched her nose to dislodge it. "I led us to safety."

"But not where we were meant to end up."

She shoved his hands off her helmet. "Then you should have said where you wanted to go!"

"Why else would I have taken the lead?" He turned away from her. "I have no idea how far away we are from P'ret and J'rax now."

"With their trackers off they could be anywhere."

D'lane grunted as he faced the wall, tail still at his ankles as his hands fisted. She stared at his back. She'd lost any chance he had of finding his crew before the Zu-Ki did.

"You were right earlier." A heavy weight settled in her chest. She glanced at her empty hands and blinked away wetness. "I am a liability."

"I never wanted you to be in danger." His hand covered hers as the tickle on her cheek returned. "You should have stayed on the T'grevis."

Pain bloomed as her pulse pounded in her head. She could do nothing right. Why was she even here? D'lane and his crew could do everything without her. She pulled from his grasp. She was never good enough for the task at hand. Mistake after mistake piled up until she became a colossal failure.

Her free hand knocked into her helmet as she went to brush her hair from her face. Anger spiked. "Damn it."

She jerked her head up. "I want out of this fucking suit."

She dug at the latches at her neck. She needed to get this helmet off and get rid of that god damn itch.

"What the hell are you doing? Are you trying to kill yourself?"

D'lane's hands slammed down on hers. His grip bit into her collarbones at the edge of her helmet as she struggled to get free.

"Listen to me." He gave her a shake. "Take a deep breath."

Her vision darkened at the edges. She needed to get away. She raised her foot and slammed it down, skimming the side of his boot.

"Fine," he growled. "We'll do this the hard way."

She was hauled tight against his chest. Their helmets smacked together face to face. He pinned her arms to her side as she struggled to break free. Why couldn't she get control of herself? It wasn't like she had anyone in either life. She sobbed, body going pliant.

"Listen to my breathing." D'lane's voice penetrated deep. She blinked the fuzzy world into focus.

"You are valued. Prove your demons wrong and come back to me." He slowly inhaled through his nose.

She closed her eyes. His breathing consumed her. Her chest compressed, ribs holding her lungs tight. Chest rising, she followed his lead until she breathed in sync with him, pulling her from her pain.

"There you go. Match my breaths."

He slowly slid her down until her feet hit the floor. Every joint in her body ached from stress and she desperately wanted to wipe the water from her eyes. He took her hands in his. "We need to move again."

She pulled back from beneath his grip. Her eyes

were swollen and gritty. "Okay."

He straightened and unholstered the gun at the base of his spine. He checked it over before handing it to her with a half-smile. "Try not to lose this one, I only have a handful left."

"I don't remember dropping the other one. Perhaps when I ran into the wall?" She took it from him. Her fingers flexed on the hard metal as his tail gripped her calf. She slowly raised her gaze to his and searched for some sign of pity or frustration. Instead, she found strength and resilience. Her shoulders straightened. She could do this.

His looked her over and nodded. "Let's go."

Shannon shadowed D'lane's every step. With her hand tucked into his belt, she kept one eye on the map and the other on her surroundings. "First bot is now three minutes away."

D'lane grunted. "The sooner the better."

Shannon hummed. "It's acting funny. I can't tell if its malfunctioning or if it's something else."

He stopped. "How so?"

"Its motion detector is constantly tripping." They usually flashed twice and held a steady light for a beat or two before starting again when the pirates passed one.

"Send it somewhere else. Fast."

Breath hitching, she released his belt and typed a rapid command across the NAV. "You think the Zu-Ki are using the bot to track us?"

"It's likely one of the methods they're using to determine our location."

She rerouted all three to take the scenic route to their position. "How close do you think they are?"

D'lane's tail twitched at his feet. He tipped his head

to the right. "A few halls that way if I'm estimating the sound reverberations correctly through the open doorways."

"We've been here"—she glanced at the remaining power on her suit—"two hours and they're already ahead of us in this maze."

"They likely entered the derelict through several locations. It's what I would have done if I had more crew."

D'lane tensed. His tail tapped her shin. She re-checked the map. "A bot is creeping up behind us. Motion sensor is non-reactive."

He led them into an open room. A small table sat off to the right in a space no bigger than the mess on the T'grevis.

Shannon moved to the table and ran her hand over the surface. Her light caught on something odd. She focused on what her glove had revealed under the thick layer of dust. "D'lane, you need to see this."

Chapter 21

Mental note: Six hours till our oxygen supply runs out.

"Cap." J'rax's tense voice cut through Shannon's comm. "Capture imminent. Activating our trackers now."

"Shit." Shannon scanned her NAV. Two red lights flickered on at the opposite end of the derelict's map. They'd traveled far from P'ret and J'rax.

"What will happen if we're captured?" Shannon asked.

"Likelihood of aggressive interrogation or immediate death is low with the Zu-Ki." P'ret's voice cut through Shannon's comms.

Shannon froze. "That was an option?"

"They don't like getting their hands dirty." D'lane's golden eyes met hers. His anxiety for his crew clear in his gaze. Her chest panged in sympathy. She didn't want anything happening to J'rax either. And she knew if either were injured D'lane wouldn't forgive himself.

"The Zu-Ki enjoy being the middle being," P'ret said through the comms.

"Take caution all the same," D'lane ground out, brows drawing together in concern.

"Copy, sir," P'ret answered. "Going silent."

D'lane stalked to Shannon's side, stance rigid and tail straight. "Tell me about this table."

Shannon understood his frustration wasn't directed at her, but the situation they were in. After her panic attack, she'd do anything she could do to help take his mind from his powerlessness with what was happening with his crew.

She turned toward the table, the first object they've crossed that wasn't just a flat surface. A set of keys were grouped together in sets of twelve and fifteen. The layout likely indicated the Anunnaki operated outside of a base ten numbering system. The arrangement their version of a QWERTY keyboard.

Shannon set her gun on the table and wiped another layer of dirt from the keys surface, another sign this room wasn't the same as the dustless others. "I believe we finally found a system console."

"I wonder why this isn't a digital pad." D'lane leaned over the table and touched a key. "I can't read any of this."

"Neither can I." She bussed a thumb over a hatched symbol, removing more grime. "Does the layout or color choices mean anything to you?"

"No. Even our older systems had fewer keys." He pressed a swirled circle symbol by his thumb. She held her breath. The tables surface remained dark.

"How about you?" he asked.

"With the last Anunnaki attack occurring after my death, it's unlikely I'd have ever come across anything like this in my research on their attacks. If I did, it was likely buried in the online space alien propaganda discussion board.

"The language on the table is a complicated mix of syllable and logographic symbols. The cryptology is closer to the older languages I've studied since being revived." Shannon touched a key. "I recognize familiar stylized lines and basic shapes. That doesn't mean much when circles and triangles are involved."

D'lane depressed another key. "Can you decipher it?"

"Not without references and time, neither of which we have on hand."

D'lane glanced at his NAV as the bot they requested ages ago skuttled in and settled next to their original drone. "Prepare yourself. We're about to get company."

"Scan what you can and let the NAV help you detect any patterns." D'lane unholster his gun. "I'd be happy if you'd turn the damn thing on while I and our bot friend give these pirates some of our attention. If we're lucky, we could figure out how to use that table to arm the ship against our unwanted Zu-Ki friends."

"I can try." She took a snapshot of the board before peeking under the table. Straight lines and smooth surfaces stared back at her. Its legs reached all the way to the floor. "Assuming there's power, and it's still connected to any weapons we could activate."

"I'll give you ten minutes to figure out if you can get it working." He headed to the doorway. "After that, you'll have your hands full helping me clear a path out of here."

"What happens after ten minutes?" Shannon pressed the first exterior righthand button. Nothing happened. She selected symbols up and around the side of the board. Power buttons were usually at the edges of the keyboards.

"We go to Plan C." He readied his weapon. "And blow up this ship."

She paused; her finger was poised above the last

key. "What happened to Plan B?"

"It died a quick death when P'ret and J'rax were cornered." Braced in the doorway, he leaned around the corner and fired. Blue flickered at the end of the weapons barrel. His features were set and focused on the trouble at hand. The battle had begun. Her heart rate kicked up as her hands shook. What would happen if them if they were captured by the pirates?

D'lane ducked back in, fiddled with the NAV, before leaning out to fire again. Both bots scuttled to his feet and fired intermittently down the hall.

She pulled her attention back to the table and pressed the last button. The tabletop remained dark. "Crap."

D'lane's slow exhalation every time he fired, synchronized her breathing to his. Every breath he took, she followed suit until her helmet began to fog at the edges.

Shannon checked the power reserves on the bot's defense system. Both spider bots power now stood at fifty percent and continued to drop steadily. She scanned the table, looking for any clues she might have initially missed. She had little time left.

Shannon ran her flat palm across the keyboard's surface, the raised ridges snagging on her gloved hand. No change. She changed tactics and pressed three buttons at a time, a 'ctrl' 'alt' 'del' callback to the laptop she'd had back home. Nothing.

D'lane ducked back into the room. A barrage of yellow flashes lit up where he'd stood. The weapon strikes splattered like broken paint balls before dissipating. Black smoke rose from where the metal had melted. D'lane flashed her a smile. "Waiting for the wall to cool before returning fire."

When it reverted to its dark gray color he moved back into position, braced against the wall, and took aim.

Shannon braced her hands on the table and bit her lip. Why wasn't this ridiculous ancient table working? No matter what she did, the table remained dark. Frustration bit at her. She swiped her arm across the keyboard hoping to activate a screen. Gray stared back at her. She leaned back and rapidly punched every single button independently.

No reaction.

She slammed her palm down on the table. "Why won't this damn thing turn on?"

If the T'grevis door keypad and the control systems on the derelict were able to communicate in order to grant access into the ship, surely there had to be something similar between the two systems? But she couldn't see a way to pry anything up or hook a power source into.

She leaned over the surface and studied the keys. The symbols blurred together. She blinked rapidly and took a steadying breath. A brown lock fell across her vision. She jammed her fingers into her helmet to move it. "Damn it!"

"How's it looking?" D'lane leaned into the hall and squeezed off a few more shots, before ducking back inside. The bots at his feet shot in response.

Shannon pressed another sequence of buttons. "I'm not going to get anything from this relic any time soon. The NAV is still deciphering the language, and assuming there's still enough power in their systems, I'm unable to type in the activation sequence."

"As I expected with this derelict." D'lane ducked

back into the room. A burst of light hit the frame above where he'd stood. He headed toward the table and rested his hand on her arm. "Time to go."

Shannon straightened from her hunched position and arched her twinging back. "What should I do?"

"Watch my back."

"So, the same plan as before." She palmed her weapon she'd left on the table and eyed the door. She faced him as she tightened her grip on the hard metal. "Did their backup arrive?"

D'lane moved them toward the back of the room. He kept his gaze focused on the only exit and the remaining bots rapidly firing away. "Quicker than I expected."

Shannon scanned the map on her NAV. A green dot crawled along the hall behind the solid wall in front of them. On the screen, the pair of bots in the room flashed a lower power warning even as the proximity alarm flashed. "We're locked in."

The weight of D'lane's tail settled around her ankle. "We'll have an exit shortly."

A white-hot dot glowed in the far corner of the room and rose in a straight line leaving behind a melted valley of metal behind. Her brow arched. "Clever."

The spider bot on the opposite side of their shared wall used its weapon to cut through the metal starting where wall and floor met. When the white dot rose to knee height it took a hard ninety-degree turn, traveling straight across for three feet before taking another right. By the end, a glowing square of cut metal pulsed near their feet.

D'lane smirked, turned his back to the wall, and raised his knee. He heel kicked the cutout. Metal slammed against the floor. D'lane winced, his external mic likely cranked high, magnifying the sound it would have made when it hit the ground. She glanced at the door. Could the Zu-Ki hear it too?

"Hurry." D'lane pushed her gently down to the floor. "We don't have much time."

Shannon pocketed her gun and crouched to belly crawled through the opened space. Her suit caught on the edge as sweat dripped down the front of her face. D'lane's shove helped her scramble free of the thick wall until she gained her feet. The steady light from the firing bot back in the room flickered into the hall.

Weapon in hand, Shannon scanned the passageway for motion and moved out of D'lane's way. The bot that had supplied their exit folded into a ball a few paces away. Its energy reserve depleted from carving out their escape.

She crouched to pick up the square cutout from where it landed and waited for D'lane to clear the tunnel. Flashes of light pierced through the opening as the remaining bots traded fire with the encroaching Zu-Ki in the vacated room.

Shannon pressed the metal square into the opening, the hallway darkening. "We should tack this into place. It could buy us some time."

"Good idea."

She moved her hands to free up one side of the metal sheet. "How much longer do you think the bots will survive?"

D'lane fired a few bursts from his weapon and pinned the metal in place. "Hopefully long enough for us to be a few halls away once they find our makeshift exit."

"One can hope." Shannon stood and scanned her map on her NAV before nudging the dead bot with her foot. "This was the closest one who could help. The next drone is too far away to get here any time soon."

"We'll have to make do without one." D'lane took off down the hall. "Keep close."

Shannon hurried to catch up. "Where are we going?"

"To find P'ret and J'rax."

"Finally." Shannon glanced down a vacant hall. "How do we find them?"

D'lane unholstered a fresh weapon as they moved and checked it over. "There's nothing these pirates can do to stop me."

They slowed when they neared a four-way intersection. His tail flicked at his feet. "I'm impressed with how you've handled yourself. I know trained grown beings who've fled at the first sign of distress."

She rolled her eyes as warmth bloomed in her chest. "I'll be sure to add calm under pressure to my list of qualifications on my resume."

D'lane chuckled as he slid around the corner. She kept close on his heels, her attention acutely focused on his stiff tail and tense stance. They were a clear indicator that trouble remained closed by.

When his stance relaxed, she crept closer and squeezed his shoulder. "Thanks."

He didn't have to offer reassurances, but it meant everything to her that he took the time to check in.

A flicker from an unknown light source hit one of the halls. Shannon glanced at her NAV, there were no bots nearby. She gripped her gun with both hands. "D'lane."

"I see it." He crouched and led them away from the incoming light. "We're close to my crew's location."

Shannon checked her map. The dots of J'rax and

P'ret were stagnant a few halls away. "Why would the Zu-Ki leave their locater beacons on?"

"They don't have access to our mapping system."

She stilled. "Or are they letting us think that?"

He held up his hand. Shannon froze, her breath held. A moment later, he waved them forward again. "Unlikely with their tech."

She glanced at her oxygen levels. The indicator light remained green, but she'd lost another power bar. She eyed the strong line of D'lane as he led the way deeper into enemy territory. Anxiety clenched around her chest. "When do we discuss the rescue plan?"

D'lane's tail flicked.

Shannon's eye twitched. "We're winging it?"

"With no real intel, it's all we can do." D'lane slowed as they neared a corner. "Weapons at the ready."

"Locked and loaded." Sweat stung her eye, another sign that her suit was losing power. She blinked rapidly to clear it.

"Be sure to unlock it." He raised his weapon, his canine flashing in the low light from her helm. "Or else I'll be fighting them all by myself."

An unsteady chuckle escaped her. She rotated her wrist and checked the power light on the weapon. Fully charged. She wet her lips. How many shots would she have before the power ran out? D'lane had fired repeatedly for minutes with his gun, but that didn't mean hers held the same energy load.

D'lane's ear twitched as he checked his weapon. "Expect heavy resistance."

Breath shaky, she raised her weapon. "Ready when you are."

"On my mark." D'lane rotated his wrist, and she

caught the flash of yellow for his power level.

"Mark."

He slid around the corner. His tail flicked and then the shooting began.

Fingers tingling, she tightened her grip on the weapon, and waited for a pause in the action. She took a bracing breath and stepped around the corner and into chaos.

D'lane wove back and forth across the hall, his aim true as he shot at the brightly colored Zu-Ki scattered down the hall. Their boxy light green spacesuits were easy targets as Shannon took aim.

Lights flashed down the hall. The weapons fire splattered against walls and floors. The only sound Shannon could hear was D'lane's measured breathing. She squeezed off a few shots before ducking behind him.

D'lane worked his way down the hall, gaining ground with each pirate taken out. She trailed behind D'lane and somehow managed not to shoot him as he repeatedly wove in front of her. At some point D'lane had set his headlamp to full power. She upped hers in response to remove the target from his head.

Her hand shook each time she raised it to fired. Three shots later, she hit her first target, dead center. A spray of bright light ate through the pirate's suit and into their flesh and skin. Another five shots, and her second target hit the floor.

The Zu-Ki retreated through an open doorway. D'lane reached backward from where they crouched and patted her on the thigh. "You're doing well."

"Thanks." She tried not to think about the missed Zu-Ki's shots that dissipated down the hall. Any one of them could have killed them if they had landed. She also had a new fear unlocked; blindly stepping around a corner on a spaceship and getting taken out by a rogue energy blast.

A pirate leaned out and aimed at D'lane. She shot. Light exploded on their helmet. Arms flailing, they fell backward as their visor disintegrated.

Shannon shoved the crippling visual of their horrifying death deep into her black mental box to deal with later and shot at another Zu-Ki. "What the hell do they want so bad that they're willing to risk their lives to retrieve?"

"Whatever their financers want. Likely to keep the information held on this ship from ever getting out."

"But we've found nothing."

D'lane's tail flicked. "They don't know that."

They continued to move down the hall. She followed close to his heels and shot over his shoulders at visible targets. She noted the smoldering carcass of a dead bot taken out by the Zu-Ki and glanced down the hall where more pirates waited. Was this ship worth anyone's life?

She cleared her throat. The tension from waiting for the pirates to peek out again tightened her spine. "Do you think there's a backup plan if the Zu-Ki fail?"

"Definitely."

Three more shots by D'lane and they had the hall cleared. D'lane glanced into the defensive room the pirates had squirreled away to and sighed. "All clear."

Stance relaxing, D'lane looked over his shoulder. His gaze was bright, flicking back and forth, likely checking her over for injuries. "You good?"

Her heart raced but she was in one piece. "My nerves are buzzing."

"Let me know when you crash." He moved up the hall to the first victim, a Zu-Ki he'd shot in the face. D'lane rapidly searched the pirate's pockets. "The first time in battle can be rough."

Her fingertips tingled. Nerves rioting without a source of action. Shannon leaned on old coping mechanisms and focused on her breathing. Her frantic pulse steadied. "I'm fine. I'll save my mental breakdown until after this is all over."

"You'll have to share with me how you compartmentalize." D'lane paused and looked up at her. "I might need a moment to collect myself after how close you were to being hit."

"I would never have guessed." Her hand shook as she checked the map for P'ret and J'rax. Their dots flickered three halls away. The lines on her suit battery flickered yellow. "You were so calm and collected in the face of danger."

His gold gaze captured hers. "It was the only way I knew to keep you safe."

She bit her lip and focused on D'lane as he pulled a handheld from the dead pirate's pocket and placed it on the square torso box of the suit. The Zu-Ki's gun landed there shortly afterward.

The intensity of her feelings rose. She opened her mouth but thought better of sharing them while surrounded by death. Instead, she looked away. Shannon caught the shape of a pirate's chin and lower lip through the melted metal hole in their suit. Was this her victim or D'lane's? Either way they were no longer a danger to either of them. "I understand what you mean."

She eyed the hall of bodies in singed green. Their helmet lights were spotlights scattered down the hall, occasionally muffled by the floor. The alien spacesuits unaware that their occupants were dead. She swallowed the lump in her throat. Faceless and nameless made it easier to deal with their death, but that didn't mean that someone wouldn't be missing them. Family would morn. "Do we leave them here?"

D'lane squinted at a Zu-Ki NAV on their right gauntlet. He cycled through the screens, gun still in hand. He dropped their wrist and pocketed the handheld. "We have no place to put them, or the free time to do so."

D'lane picked up the weapon he'd left resting on the pirate's chest before moving to another body halfway down the hall.

She crouched next to D'lane. She was pretty sure this was one of the Zu-Ki she'd killed sprawled in front of them. She forced herself to think of the body as a mannequin as she followed D'lane's lead and patted the pirate down, searching for hidden pockets. "Are we looking for anything in particular?"

"A ship-to-ship comms. Their lead didn't have it." D'lane tilted his head toward the first body he searched. "I expected their communications expert to have one. But neither they nor their team leader"—He tapped the small insignia of an 'X' on the Zu-Ki's chest—"are currently keyed in."

Shannon lifted the arm of the body next to her and eyed the NAV interface. "Can we remove the device from one of their suits?"

"If it was just one pirate ship that boarded the derelict, yes." D'lane rolled the team leaders body over onto its back. "But with a number of ships involved, the only way we'd know what they're planning is ship-to-ship comms."

He searched the last pocket and leaned back on his heels, his tail tucked around his ankles. "Nothing."

She glanced down the hall and noted the spots of green. "What about the other bodies?"

"They were nothing more than cannon fodder." D'lane activated the comms on his wrist, and Shannon followed suit. "Report."

J'rax replied, "We need to hurry Captain."

Shannon stood. "Why?"

J'rax's grunted. "They've got detonators hidden all over the ship."

A hysterical laugh bubbled out of Shannon as she took a step back. "They can't blow the ship up. We're still on it."

"They'll take a financial hit." D'lane checked the charge on the Zu-Ki's weapon he'd picked up. "But still come out on top if they've fulfilled a clause in their contract."

"The payout must have been high for them to attempt to capture before kill." P'ret said through the comms.

Shannon glanced at the hall of still bodies. If only one was still alive, they might be able to find out where the explosives had been placed. "Can we disarm the bombs?"

"It's unlikely given the time frame." P'ret grunted, his dot still too far away from their current position to meet up. "We pilfered a comm off one of the pirates."

"Good." D'lane stood. "First order of business is to find one of those explosives and determine a time frame." Shannon followed hot on his heels as he moved to a bend in the hall that would lead them closer to his crew. "J'rax, spend a few minutes listening in to the pirates before using the pilfered comms to contact the T'grevis."

"I'll try to get what information I can before they discover we're listening," J'rax said.

D'lane turned to Shannon. "Escape is now our current priority."

Yellow splattered across his shoulder.

He grunted, taking a half step forward.

Pain brightened his gaze before the gold dimmed to a dull yellow. The shot ate through his suit to expose the golden skin underneath. "Shannon."

She caught him as he collapsed.

Chapter 22

T-minus five minutes.

"D'lane!" She slapped her hand over the hole in his shoulder in a desperate attempt to close it and searched the hall for the shooter. Nothing moved. Muscles straining, she pulled him back around the corner and placed him flat on the floor. At this angle she could put all her weight on the suit's hole, but it had already dissolved through to the other side.

Dropping her gun, she leaned over him and pressed her helmet against his. Dim yellow eyes met hers. His lips were tinged blue as his skin began to gray.

"D'lane." She shook him when he didn't respond. "Tell me what to do."

The arm she'd pinned to his side flexed. She gave him some room and his fingers twitched toward a pocket.

Orange moved in her periphery. She grabbed for her weapon. A heavy weight slammed into her shoulder. Crying out, she sprawled across the floor. Her gun slid down the hall. She scrambled for it.

A foot pinned her in place, the sharp edges digging into Shannon's side. Trapped against the ground, the suit forced her neck to a painful angle. Her helmet scraped across the floor as she turned her head to look for D'lane.

Her light hit the top of his head. His face was turned away from her in his helmet. She reached for him. The tips of her fingers skimmed his slack arm.

"D'lane!" She squirmed closer. The foot pressed harder into her ribs to hold her in place. The familiar tufted point of his ear remained still and unmoving.

Hands bit into her shoulders. Hauled upright, she struggled to break free. She *needed* to get to D'lane. They forced her arms in front of her. Heavy circlets cinched around her wrists as a Zu-Ki in a bright orange suit crouched and rifled through D'lane's pockets. Why weren't they wearing green like the other pirates?

Shannon kicked out. Her boot missed their bright orange shoulder by inches. "Leave him alone."

The pirate took their time standing. Visor dark, they turned to Shannon and kicked D'lane.

"No!"

D'lane's body twisted away from her from the force. His helmet slammed into the wall. The back end of the hole was visible on his grey suit. The skin she could see through the cavity was graying at the edges. If Kro-Gen revived her after being dead a thousand years, surely My'len could breathe life back into D'lane's body after such a short period of time?

The orange helmet turned toward her. Shannon fumbled for the NAV on her wrist; her cuffed hands restricted her movements. Why had D'lane kept closing her comms off from the rest of the crew? If she could reach P'ret or J'rax, they could come and save D'lane.

The tip of her gloved finger stretched for the channel further up her arm. Her wrists strained to make the correct angle. A palm slammed into her helmet. She staggered into the wall.

Grunting, Shannon braced her back against the solid surface. "What the fuck was that for?"

Three Zu-Ki wrapped in orange suits crowded

around her. About Shannon's height, their dark helmets made it difficult to get a read on what they looked like.

The one that had kicked D'lane hand chopped sharply through the air. Was he saying something?

Shannon shook her head. "Mother fucker, I can't hear you."

The Zu-Ki shoved her down the hall and further away from D'lane, back through the green suited dead Zu-Ki in the hall. She turned around and cut her helmet's light to D'lane, still on his side half against the wall. She focused on his tail, the one limb that was always moving. The tip remained still.

Forced back around, she was pushed along in the wake of the lead Zu-Ki. The hand on her shoulder stifled her ability to escape.

"Shannon." P'ret's voice cut through into her comms.

She fumbled to activate her NAV in response. Her fingers locked, but she managed to press a handful of buttons.

"I'm here." She kept her lip movements to a minimum encase they were looking at her. The pirates pushed her further down the ship as additional orange suited Zu-Ki joined them. "But I don't know for how long."

Shannon tripped over a body she hadn't been expecting. Her helmet light landed on a Zu-Ki she was sure D'lane nor her had killed. Did these pirates kill their own men? Her heartbeat pounded in her ears. "D'lane's been shot."

"Is he alive?" P'ret asked.

Throat tight, Shannon said, "I don't know."

The silence stretched on so long Shannon feared

they'd been disconnected.

"Where are you?" J'rax cut over comms.

A roughly cut hole in the wall came into view. The metal surrounding it melted in immense, jagged tares. A long gray tube extended outward from the derelicts hull and into the vacuum of space. A bitter laugh escaped as her foot lifted over the roughly cut ship threshold and landed on a grated umbilical conduit funneling her to a different location. Hazmat scenes flashed through her mind.

Shannon glared at the pirate shoving her forward. "I'm being escorted off the ship by our new friends."

"Where's D'lane?"

Her chest clenched. She stumbled, wrenched back upright by her guard as they neared the pirate leader. She glanced backward, her headlamp hitting the dark exterior of the derelict ship.

"He's three halls away." She bit her lip, tasting blood. "With a laser eating through his shoulder."

She was jerked forward as the hull of the enemy vessel came within sight. Her light hit a scorched patchwork of the Zu-Ki ships exterior.

D'lane's chest had been so still. His gold eyes glazed as they stared into nothingness. She stepped over the bulkhead. A sob escaped. "I couldn't save him."

"We'll find him." P'ret's voice echoed with the oath.

"Hurry," Shannon whispered.

The gangway door closed.

Grey walls surrounded her. The paint peeled away from the walls exposing rusted metal underneath. She searched for a weapon, anything she could use to fight for freedom, but everything was bolted down. Her hands clenched, the cuffs around her wrists pushing her spacesuit into her skin.

The lead Zu-Ki spun Shannon around. The dark globe of their helmet consumed her reflection. Her wrist was jerked to the side, forcing her to twist at the waist to remain standing as the Zu-Ki guard kept her standing with a firm grip to the arm of her suit. The spacesuits NAV crumpled under the guard's grip. The metal pressed hard into the flesh of her wrist. She rotated free of their hold and cradled her hand against her chest. She fingered the grooved indents left behind on the crushed comm as her shoulders slumped, any chance of communication with P'ret and J'rax destroyed.

The lead Zu-Ki's hand pointed at Shannon's head before cutting sharply to the side. Was this some new salute she needed to know? Not that she could return it with her hands bound in front of her.

Off balance, Shannon jerked back, forced against the chest of the guard who crushed her NAV. "What the hell!"

The hand tightened on the back of her suit and lifted. Her heels left the floor. She pointed her toes to maintain contact with the ground. The leader reached for the external latch on her helmet. Panic set in. What if the air on the ship wasn't breathable?

Shannon batted their hand away. "This is staying on."

The lead Zu-Ki lunged at her. Shannon kicked out. The pirate spun away, and her leg met air. They grasped her helmet and the spacesuit material tightened under Shannon's armpits. She strained against their grip as they tugged. Material ripped.

Shannon sucked in a breath as the pirate jerked the

helmet off her suit and held it aloft. Soft white material dangled from the metal ring that had been draped around her shoulders. Her chest remained still as her spacesuit slipped off her shoulder.

Her heels hit the floor as the lead Zu-Ki flipped up the visor on their helmet.

The pirate flashed a predatory smile surrounded by purple lips and gray skin. The lead's voice was a soft juxtaposition against a face that hid nothing of the violence from their past. "Now we can talk like the civilized beings we all pretend to be."

Chest burning, Shannon stared ahead. Her next breath could be her last. She cut her gaze to the hatch over the Zu-Ki's shoulder. D'lane was back there, his life taken from him before he'd fulfilled his destiny and there was nothing she could do about it.

Her fingers brushed the mutilated NAV. She was alone and only had herself to rely on. She swallowed the lump in her throat. She needed to survive for him, and for herself.

Shoulders squared, Shannon glared at the captain of this ship and slowly exhaled. Her next breath filled with the taste of damp sweat and mold. It flooded her lungs. She choked.

"Such drama." The lead Zu-Ki rolled their brown eyes and laughed. "You *popsicles* are all the same, terrified the slightest inconvenience will kill you. Kro-Gen really hasn't improved their release program over the decades."

The lead shoved Shannon's helmet at her. It dropped to the floor. Her arms were still bound in front of her and unable to catch it.

The lead sneered as the smaller third Zu-Ki trailing

the group scurried forward and picked up her helmet before disappearing into the bowels of the ship. The lead resettled their gaze on her. "As long as you've got a bit of oxygen and nitrogen in the air you'll survive, and fortunately for you, we Zu-Ki need it too. Not as much as humans, but you'll live…for now."

"Why am I here?" Shannon struggled to make her voice even in the thin air. "If you've captured me for information, you'll find I know virtually nothing."

The lead removed their helmet and shook out their shoulder length jet black hair.

"Silly human." They smiled again, the knife scars on their face drawing off in every direction. "I don't care what you know. I'm just completing a job."

"The bulky Zu-Ki behind you is going to be your new best friend." The captain nodded to the silent guard beside Shannon, the only other Zu-Ki armed in the group aside from the captain. Which of them had killed D'lane? "You won't be able to breathe, let alone sleep without Klick glued to your soft human hide."

The cuffs pulled at her wrists. Their weight disappeared as Klick cut her free. She rolled her wrists to relieve the tingling as blood flow returned to her fingers, and glared.

"Come along ageless human," the captain said. "I need to head out before more trouble can be found."

Klick's finger dug into Shannon's back. Forced forward, she stomped after the captain. "What else could go wrong that you haven't instigated?"

The captain glared over their shoulder. "A lot. Now keep up."

"Who are you?" Shannon followed at as slow of a pace as she was allowed. She didn't want to get too far from the ship-to-ship umbilical. Any chance she got, she was making a break for it back to the derelict.

"How callous of me." The captain turned and offered a flourished bow at the waist. "You can call me Axe, the captain of this ship and your savior from those hideous Chriw'rian's."

Shannon scoffed. "You believe that lie?"

Klick shoved her forward. She caught herself on the wall and glared back at the suited Zu-Ki. She straightened and wiped the gray flaking paint on her suit leg. With the patchwork hull and the corroding walls, her fear of unexpectedly meeting the cold vacuum of space retched up to the forefront of her mind. How was this ship still livable?

Axe flashed wide bright teeth. "I'll believe anything for the right price."

The captain hung their helmet on a row of rusted hooks and opened a metal door. They peeled off their bright orange suit exposing a patched-up vest made up of all manner of material and colors that led to a loose pair of black pants cuffed above their well-worn boots and was so many times it had faded to dark grey.

Shannon's eyebrow rose at Axe's exposed gray chest. The skin between the open panels of their vest was riddled with scar tissue and pucker marks. Shannon didn't know anything about the Zu-Ki culture, but with the healing cream availability and medical advancements in this time, the scars must be a badge of honor, that or they couldn't afford the cream.

Following the captains lead, Klick, pulled their helmet off and de-suited. Exposing purple irises and black shaved close to their head. Their vest pattern and colors clashed against their skin as scrap pieces of fabric smaller than their captains had been sewn together to make a semblance of a vest.

Humanoid in proportion, Klick had mismatched squares sewn over their knees. She bit back a snort. It looked like Axe got all the good pieces if their uniforms as a visual representation of the rank on the ship.

Axe's purple lips kicked up at the corner. "Remove your suit."

Shannon froze. "Why?"

Axe smirked as Klick crossed their arms across their wide chest. "Don't tell me that you followed Chriw'rian traditions and went naked under there?"

Klick snickered. Shannon's cheeks flushed with anger when Klick waved off her concern. "You don't have anything we haven't seen before and passed on."

Shannon knew they were fucking with her since her silver jump suit had been exposed when Axe destroyed her spacesuit.

She fingered the loose spacesuit fabric around her neck. It was the last line of defense protecting her from the outside world. Her jumpsuit wouldn't protect her from anything other than heat regulation. She couldn't escape with it in its current state; she'd need a new spacesuit for that. The protective layer was more than a failed escape opportunity, it was her last link to the T'grevis and D'lane.

Klick loosened their stance. "We can do this the easy way"—they cracked their knuckles—"or the hard way."

Shannon stared at the crumpled NAV on her wrist. "Give me a sec. I'm going to have trouble getting this off now that the metal is destroyed."

Any time she could buy was another moment the

Zu-Ki stayed attached to the derelict.

Axe raised a brow. "We can always cut your hand off."

"That won't be necessary." Without the helmet metal lock ring on her suit, it was easy to shrug off the suit fabric.

She took off her hard soles, slipped out of the suit, and stepped back into the space shoes. The white suit hung from her wrist, the crumpled NAV hindering her from removing it completely. She pushed on the cuff. It slid an inch before catching on her palm. She touched her thumb to pinky and relaxed her muscles. The metal slid another inch, now caught around the thick part of her hand.

Axe sighed. "Klick, you still have that machete on you?"

"Always." They bent and pulled a calf length blade from their boot, excitement bright in their purple eyes as they held the weapon aloft.

Though not as cared for as D'lane's blades, it still sent panic down her spine. Shannon pushed harder on the broken cuff. Panic spiked as it failed to budge.

"I'll hold her." Axe stepped closer. "You were always cleaner with your swings when the victim's flailing limbs were controlled."

"No, wait!" Shannon shoved down on the metal. Skin tore. Pain spiked as the suit hit the floor. Breathing through clenched teeth, Shannon cradled her hand to her chest as blood seeped through her fingers and dripped to the floor. She'd taken off too many layers of skin where the destroyed NAV dug in.

Axe's smile exposed wide teeth. "That wasn't so hard."

"Leave it." Klick stopped her from gathering the destroyed spacesuit. "One our crew will take care of it."

Shaking off Klick's grip, Shannon glared at the guard. "It's mine."

"Not anymore." Axe grabbed her wounded hand. Pain spiked as he dragged her down another hallway deeper into the ship. Shannon bit her lip, tasting blood, to keep from crying out. She didn't want to appear weak in this unknown situation.

Axe pulled her down a hall and released her after she tripped over a makeshift threshold with a tisk. She caught herself on the wall next to a set of overlapping plates and continued after the captain, Klick tight on her heels.

The Zu-Ki's ship was a hodgepodge of components patched together as much as their clothing had been. Unlike the seamless walls of the T'grevis, the metal was held together with endless welds. She leaned in and brushed a finger over a discoloration. It came away wet.

Klick pushed her forward. "Don't touch."

She brought it to her nose and sniffed. Sulfur and gasoline hit her senses. She wrinkled her nose. "Afraid I might damage the ship further?"

Shannon wiped what she hoped was grease on her thigh.

Klick's purple eyes flashed. Their arm tensed. She flinched, reflexively bracing for a cuff. Her response was one she'd thought banished years after her youth. Her shoulders relaxed as the possibility of violence passed and she tried not to read too much into the emotion in Klick's gaze. They were still part of the problem of her being kidnapped and on this pirate ship.

"We frown upon abuse within our clans." Klick

nudged her after the captain. "Now move."

She followed the stout frame of the Zu-Ki captain. The urge to regress into her reactionary childhood habits of coping was hard to reject, but it was a sure-fire way to get hurt on a ship with crew that cared nothing about her safety. She needed to focus on buying time for her to escape and not push the crew into violence.

The ship rolled under her feet. She stumbled into a wall and straightened. Clumps of dust and who knew what floated past, likely dislodged from the ship's movement. She sneezed as her heartrate spiked. "I thought we were waiting to detach?"

The Zu-Ki captain chuckled. "What gave you that idea?"

Her hands clenched, an ach settling into her cut hand as she stepped over a hand-width wide hose on the floor with a filter taped to the end. Questions about air quality were shoved aside so she could focus on what the hell was happening and plan. Knowledge was power, and she could desperately use some right now.

Axe ducked through the rounded hole cut into the side of the wall where a door should have been.

Shannon touched the edge of melted metal that reminded her of the spider bot's escape cutout on the derelict. "Did you get locked out of your own ship?"

Shoved from the back, Shannon stumbled after the captain. She bit her lip to keep from smiling. Klick was easy to piss off.

She stepped over the rounded threshold and surveyed the bridge. The tight space was filled with 1960s style hard plastic seats worn to a shine. Three Zu-Ki were crammed against the far wall, huddled around a large console. With their backs toward her.

The rest of the room was packed with mismatched cargo containers and various metal sheets all held in place by black cargo netting. It looked like the beginning of a hording addiction. A small portion of the wall at the far end remained clear of storage and projected the view outside of the ship. The dark universe stared back at her.

With the patch worked hull, constant interior repairs, and makeshift air cleaner, how did this Zu-Ki ship survive in space?

"Umbilical successfully detached from the derelict, captain, and the ship is rotated for departure," the Zu-Ki in the middle said, vestless their body lightly scarred from blade wounds.

Shannon searched the pirates for visible blades and found none. Did they sew sheaths into their patched-up vests and pants or were the captain and her guard the only two allowed weapons?

The captain slipped their feet into a metal looped foot hold in the center of the space and grabbed for the 'Oh Shit' handle, as her father called it, above their head. "Pull up a feed on the rest of the Zu-Ki ships. I want to keep an eye on where they are."

Shannon wove her way across the floor, looking for a place to safely jam herself into in case shit got weird. Klick followed close at her heels. She finally settled on wrapping her fingers through the dark cargo netting keeping cargo off the floor.

Klick chuckled and braced their feet. "That rope won't do much good. Not with the youngen flying."

Little dots were fireflies that circled in the blurry and did little to help her decipher anything aside from the large derelict hogging the screen. Shannon tightened her grip further on the netting and searched for the T'grevis among the specks. She frowned when what the captain said finally clicked. "I thought you all were working together?"

Axe flashed a smile. "Finders keepers has always been the rule of the trade."

That would explain their complete lack of hostility toward Shannon over their dead comrades in the hall. Or perhaps their dead was something they were used to seeing. "If you return me to the Chriw'rians, I'm positive that Kro-Gen or the League would pay the same rate as your contract."

At least she hoped they would. The cost would likely be tacked onto what she still owed the League, but better the entity she knew then the one she didn't.

A beat of silence.

The Zu-Ki roared with laughter. Some bent over at the waist while Klick slapped Shannon roughly on the back. She grunted and fell into the netting.

"You are hilarious." Axe wiped their eyes. "What era were you revived from?"

Shannon struggled to untangle herself from the mesh. "Like I'd tell you."

"I'll have to get me a human with the same pizzazz." Axe's brown gaze looked her up and down. "And hair."

"Captain," a young voice cut through the laughter. "The remaining Zu-Ki are pulling away from the derelict."

Axe snapped to attention, all humor gone from their voice. "Are they following us?"

"No," the Zu-Ki underling in the middle answered.

The captain frowned. "I don't like this."

Shannon's breath sped up as her body shook. She took a step forward. Klick moved into her way. She

leaned around them. "Wait, you don't know about the—
"

The derelict buckled. Flashes of white escaped from the newly shorn seams. The Zu-Ki's ship lights flickered as proximity alarms sounded.

"—bombs."

Chest tight, her heart pounded as the derelict splintered apart. On the screen, three sections grew into six, then eight, until it became too many for her to count.

"D'lane." A heavy weight settled into the depths of her chest. Her gaze tunneled to a small sheet of metal glistening in space.

"Well, that was unexpected." The captain wandered over to the Zu-Ki that had reported before. "Let's be off before they discover we have the *Find*."

Her soul shattered. Thousands of sharp fragments ripped her heart to shreds. She dropped to her knees and screamed.

Chapter 23

Axe to contact: Find acquired. In route now.

She was alone, alone on a ship filled with pirates who weren't afraid to kill to get their job done. Shannon's eyes stung, but she had no tears to give. D'lane and the T'grevis were gone, along with any hope she had with escape.

"I thought you wanted us alive?" Shannon whispered as she looked up at the captain. Her knees ached from where she'd collapsed. Her body cold as the metal floor sucked the heat from her.

Axe shrugged. "The initial extraction team apparently had other ideas."

Shannon climbed to her feet. The view screen dark as Axe's ship traveled further away from the derelict. "Where's the T'grevis?"

T'rev should have been there, should have stayed to fight off the twenty ships that were now headed this way. If he hadn't fled, then maybe she and D'lane could have escaped from the derelict together, and she wouldn't be here, captive on a Zu-Ki ship.

"We're too far away now to tell apart the wreckages from the explosion," Axe said. "With any luck the Chriw'rians were taken out with a few of my competition."

Shannon rubbed her dry eyes. If Axe and their crew were any indication of the Zu-Ki factions fighting over this *Find* they mentioned, she might be able to use the lack of information sharing to her advantage. If she had the chance. But it didn't matter now. Everything she had built for herself in this new life lay spewed across an uncaring universe unable to be revived. Her breathing remained a struggle either from the low oxygen on the ship or her building rage at all that was taken from her.

Her hands clenched. "What are you planning to do with me?"

"You're the most valuable commodity on this ship." Axe strode closer as the ship continued to increase the distance between them and the other Zu-Ki vessels. "Klick is going to take you to our storage room and keep you company until payment is made."

Shannon took in the rusted paint and patchwork repairs scattered within the helm visible under the rows of cargo netted boxes. She lifted the lid of the closest gray box to test their limits. "I have a right to know who wants me."

Klick slammed their hand down, closing the box before she could get a good look inside. "You have only the rights of a *Find*, which is basically nothing."

Klick took hold of her injured hand and Shannon winced.

"Oh," Shannon said as she was forced out of the room. "Any rights in particular?"

Klick growled, fingers digging into the flesh of her arm and pulled her close to their purple lips. "Keep giving me trouble and you'll arrive with a few less fingers."

A chill raced down her spine. Shouldn't she have learned by now to keep her mouth shut?

Klick hauled Shannon close. The Zu-Ki's breath

was a mixture of bitter tea and egg. This close Shannon noted that their pupils were a darker brown than the captains, even surrounded by the same purple iris.

"I'd take your trigger finger first." Klick's lips quirked revealing their square teeth. "I'd rip the nail right out with my favorite pair of pliers just to make sure you were awake. Next, I'd separate your first knuckle from the rest of your finger. My blade's a bit rusty and dull, but it'd eventually make it through the joint."

Klick leaned over her. Shannon arched her neck to keep her lips from theirs. "I'd do the same with the second knuckle, but that last joint I'd grab that remaining shred of exposed bone and tare the phalange right out of your hand."

Shannon swallowed thickly. "Fantasize much?"

Klick's smile sharpened. "Never enough."

"You should get out more."

Klick shoved her away. "I get out plenty."

Shannon stumbled. Her arms swung out for balance and her hand slammed into metal. Dust and who knew what floated through the air. Flakes of gray paint fell to the ground as she straightened. At least the wall itself had felt solid even in its rusted state.

Klick arms folded. "If you're done mouthing off?"

Shannon nodded and wiped her palm on her suit. The dark streak on her leg grew.

Klick prodded Shannon down the hall. "Come on."

The corridors of the ship were dark. The lights had burned out or possibly turned off to save energy for more important things, like air purification. She rubbed her temples. She needed to get out of this mess.

With Klick trailing behind her, Shannon was free to evaluate the NIC D'lane had gifted her. She'd tucked it up her sleeve when she'd stripped out of her spacesuit before Axe had noticed.

Her dried blood coated the surface. A quick brush of her thumb revealed a dead screen and dented sides where Axe's finger had crushed it when he'd destroyed her suits comms. Shannon's shoulders sank as she tucked it back under her jumpsuit. She wasn't sure if it'd work since she was off the T'grevis, but assumed it'd still light up when touched. So, it was either dead from the damage, or the screen was busted but she was too far away from the T'grevis for it to work. There was no way she could tell which it was. She'd have to hope the T'grevis was able to locate her some other way when she freed herself.

Shannon scanned every room they passed. The dim lighting, corroding gray paint, and wall to wall netting made it difficult to catalog anything that might be of use. Her current escape plan involved locating a weapon, knocking Klick out, and heading back toward the Zu-Ki spacesuits. Assuming she could make the suits work, she'd be in a better position to get off this ship and free from her kidnappers.

"In here tiny human." Klick pushed her toward an open doorway. The dim light made the room a gaping black hole.

"Dude, we're the same height." Shannon braced her hand on the doorframe and peeked inside. She had a brief glance of overstuffed boxes before a firm hand shoved her the rest of the way into. Shannon stumbled over a raised pipe. "I was making my way in."

"Not quick enough," Klick said as they stomped in after Shannon.

Once her eyes adjusted, Shannon reassessed the

space. Clear of much of the hording in the other rooms, the storage space contained only a handful of boxes off to the side secured with more cargo netting. The length of a long hallway, and three times as wide, bare piping broke up the room as it elbowed out at random intervals on the walls and into the ceiling.

Klick ducked under a pipe and circled around her left.

Shannon shifted to keep Klick in view and searched for a weakness. "Are we on a timetable I'm unaware of?"

With their wide shoulders and heavyset frame, the pirate moved decisively through the hold. If Klick had a limp or injury, they hid it well. She touched her neck and the bruise that was likely forming there. That combined with Klick's strength meant her best chance of escaping her guard was a surprise attack and a run for freedom.

"There are a lot of things you don't know." The Zu-Ki pulled out a metal fold down chair from a dark corner. They planted it on the ground and shoved it a few feet away from Shannon before pulling out a second for themselves. "Sit."

Shannon dragged the chair closer to the wall and sat, playing along with this little game that wasn't a game. She kicked her heels up on the nearby pipe. A dust cloud lofted into the air as the pipe groaned. "Why did you all laugh when I offered to have the League buy out the contract?"

Klick leaned back. The chair groaned as their vest slid open and exposed a well-worn knife handle. That brought the weapons Shannon knew up to three including the gun on their hip and the calf length blade strapped to their leg they'd threatened to cut her arm off with.

They smirked. "Who do you think paid us to pick you up?"

Shannon reeled. She planted her feet on the floor to keep her balance. "That can't be possible. They're the reason we're here."

Klick chuckled. "It's not up to us to figure out who wants what or why. We only provide the *Find* once payment has been made."

Shannon settled back into her chair, gaze unfocused on the drab wall in front of her. The only answer that made any sense led to more questions. Someone at the League, and possibly Kro-Gen had set them up to fail. Were all of them in on it? During the meeting she'd only met three, but they'd implied there were more. But how many more where there and what about General Fernandez?

She pulled her attention back from the unknowns and focused on Klick. "Where are you taking me?"

"To meet our patrons now."

Shannon arched her brow. "So back to Kro-Gen?"

Klick shrugged. "The League own many things and Kro-Gen is only one spin-off."

Shannon leaned forward. "But which one is it?"

"It matters little which head of the beast we deliver you too. Credits have been paid, the contract signed, and the *Find* will be delivered as promised."

"Aren't you bothered by the fact that through my capture you'll be contributing to billions of beings losing their lives when the Anunnaki rampage through the galaxy?"

"Why should I or my clan care about the lives of those *cranks*?" Klick stood, looming over her. Shannon shrank back in her chair. "Where was this charity when my family was killed by pirates paid by the League to eradicate our home ship? Or when my tribe excommunicated me when I wanted vengeance?"

"Can you live with yourself knowing you could have stopped it?"

"Of course." Klick's anger subsided as quickly as it rose. "Why else would I be here babysitting you instead of at my station on my mother's ship?"

Shannon touched the crushed NIC tucked under her sleeve. She had little hope of convincing Klick to help her escape and was rapidly running out of options. "What do they plan to do with me?"

Klick lifted a shoulder and dropped it. "You'll likely be sent to a mining camp circling one of the many unhabitable planets in their sector."

Shannon grasped her wrist. "They don't plan on killing me?"

"Oh, you'll die, just not from their hands." Klick snorted as they circled around their chair. "No one in this sector likes to get their hands dirty."

The Zu-Ki's purple eyes stared at her from where they stood methodically cracking each knuckle on their hands. Shannon's knee bounced. Klick exposed wide teeth in a predatory smirk.

Nerves tingling with the urge to move, Shannon stood and explored the boundary of Klick's range. If she couldn't get Klick to convert to her way of thinking, it was back to her initial plan, and she needed the pirate close.

She needed to get off this ship and now was as good of a time as any. Shannon headed toward a particularly rusty wall, and the only thing she'd been able to rile Klick up about. "What's the name of this ship?"

"Why?" Klick grunted.

"So, I'll know it's this ship on news bulletins when it rapidly decompresses. It'll be a shame when it kills everyone within." She ran her finger over a particularly heinous weld.

They tensed. "What did you say?"

"How is this vessel even flight worthy?" Shannon picked at the edge of gray paint and pealed it back. "I didn't think spit and sheer will could hold this piece of shit together, but here it stands."

Klick took a step forward. "Do not utter another word."

Shannon bared her teeth. "Okay."

The cuts on her hand reopened as she picked at another piece of paint. The small paint chip turned into a dinner plate slab as a large section came away from rusted metal.

Their hands fisted. "Don't you dare."

Decision made, she tugged. The crack spread down the wall. "Shit."

Three feet of paint crumbled to the floor.

Klick roared and lunged. She ducked to the side as Klick slammed into the wall. Dirt and debris rained down, coating their shoulders.

"Look at that imprint." Shannon danced back and pointed to the humanoid shape now inlaid in the paint. "It's like you're trying to prove my point."

Klick shook their head as they stepped back. Chunks of gray paint dislodged from their black hair.

Nerves tingling, she shook out her hands. She needed to be threatening enough to engage with Klick, but not too threatening that they'd pull a blade or the gun at their waist and consider her a serious threat. On top of all that, she would need every scrap of martial arts knowledge she'd gained from D'lane, and then some to Klick them on.

Shannon shifted further away from Klick and closer to the chair they'd given her. It was the only weapon she had at her disposal. She'd seen the strength the Zu-Ki possessed. They'd torn through her spacesuit as if it was paper and crushed her suits metal NAV without flinching. Hell, Klick had lifted her up by her neck, single-handed. It'd only take one solid hit to knock her out for the remainder of the trip.

"You're going to regret destroying my home."

Klick stalked toward her, each step eating up more distance than the last. She was within touching distance of the chair when the pirate charged.

Shannon screamed and danced out of reach. Klick's fingers grazed her shoulder. Dragging the chair with her, she turned to face them, breath frozen in her lungs.

Purple gaze locked on her, Klick lunged. Shannon spun and slammed the chair into their head. Metal thrummed. The impact vibrated up her arms as Klick crashed into the deck.

Dropping the chair, Shannon leaped forward. She slammed her heel down on the outside of their knee joint just like D'lane described. A pop sounded and Klick roared.

Shannon fumbled for their gun. She brushed metal as Klick rolled onto their back and she jumped out of reach. She mentally berated herself when she realized she should have gone for the chair and knocked them out when they were down.

Klick clambered up to their feet, favoring their left side. "I'm going to kill you." They pulled the short blade from inside their vest. "I don't care what the captain says. We can always do this with you dead."

Shannon laughed nervously as she kept out of reach. "I'd rather you didn't."

Klick limped forward. "You should have thought of that before attacking me."

She bumped into the cargo netting. "Shit."

She'd walked herself into a corner. Desperate, she grabbed the top of the nearest metal box and threw it at the Zu-Ki. The pirate blocked the lid with their arm, a gash dripping blue blood down their arm as they limped closer.

Klick lunged. Their blade flashed as Shannon stumbled back. The mesh tore and boxes tumbled to the surrounding ground.

She turned and followed the length of the wall, throwing anything within reach at the pirate, but they crept closer. Klick lunged, slicing out with their knife. Shannon jerked to the side. The pirate punched through a metal storage box. Arm swallowed by metal, they struggled to free themselves.

She pressed against Klick's side and patted them down, aggravated to find their gun was holstered on the other side of their body, outside of her reach. Shannon lifted the metal lid of the container Klick's knife had lodged into. Their eyes locked. This close, Shannon could see the darker dots within their iris.

Klick leaned back and struggled to free themselves. Shannon couldn't let the pirate escape. Her fingers tightened on the lid, and she slammed it into Klick's head.

Klick grunted and tipped to the side. Shannon swung again. The lid warped in her hands. Klick wrenched their arm free of the box and stumbled back, blood rolling down their face. A slow blink covered blown out pupils. She swung again and the lid split in two. The pirate collapsed.

Gasping for breath, Shannon dropped the lid and crouched beside the pirate. She searched for the gun, finding the grip tight against metal. They'd fallen on it, pinning the weapon to the floor.

"Damn it!" Shannon shoved Klick's shoulder. Their dead weight was unmoved from the action.

Sitting on the floor, she braced against the dirty metal and propped her feet against Klick's side. "Why can't anything be easy?"

She shoved with her heels. Klick's body tilted. Her bloody hand slid out from under her. She stood over the pirate and glared. There wasn't anything else in the room she could use as a lever to move their heavy weight off of her preferred weapon of choice. She was left with the knife strapped to Klick's calf. She had no training in knives and was more likely to cut off her own limb than hurt someone else.

Shannon kneeled and fished around Klick's thick legs until she located the hilt. With her good hand, she took a firm grip, unlocked the latch, and slid the blade free. Her arm dropped from the weight of it. The sword tip bit the floor inches from her toes. Damn, these Zu-Ki were strong.

"What do you think you're doing?" Axe said as they entered the room.

Jerking, Shannon slowly turned toward the captain. "Leaving?"

"The hell you are!" Axe charged.

Shannon stood and tugged on the weapon. Nothing.

Axe closed in. Planting her feet on the floor, she pulled. The tip jerked free. She stumbled back, and the blade swung wide.

Arm reaching for her, Axe's gaze widened. The sharp edge arched up, hit little resistance, and sliced through their forearm. The blade and dismembered body part hit the ground at the same time.

Blood pumped from their wound and splattered to the ground.

"You little shit." They reached for their elbow, clamping down on the raw end with their hand. "You made the wrong choice."

Releasing their wound, more blood spilled to the floor as Axe went for their knife. Shannon took a step back and bumped into the dented chair she'd hit Klick with earlier. She grabbed for it as Axe swooned and dropped to the ground.

Releasing the chair, Shannon ran for the door. She stilled, foot hovering over the threshold. She couldn't leave like this, wondering around the ship unarmed and vulnerable to the pirate crew.

Shoulders bunched, she stalked back to the captain and kicked their knife away. Careful of the blue blood seeping across the floor she crouched next to their sprawled body and did her best to ignore the dismembered limb that lay at the toe of their boot.

Using her good hand, she unholstered Axe's gun and stood.

Axe's lashes fluttered and their stump twitched. "Hclp."

She fingered the trigger on her gun. Although these pirates didn't plant the bombs on the derelict, they were responsible for killing D'lane. What did she owe them after they kidnapped her? She sighed and kneeled next to Axe as they continued to bleed out all over the floor.

She set her weapon within reach and rifled through Axe's pockets. She pulled a dirty scrap of fabric she'd noted the entire crew pilfered it wherever they could from their pants.

Using her medical field training from dig camp, she created a tourniquet just below their elbow. Axe winced as Shannon cinched the knot tight. "Be grateful I'm even offering you this level of care, pirate."

Their lashes fluttered. "You must stay."

Shannon flinched when their brown eyes met her own. Their head tipped to the side. Cloudy and unfocused, the pupil briefly separated into two before rejoining. Was that natural?

"Why?" Shannon desperately needed answers.

They wet their lips. "Need the money."

They coughed and didn't elaborate further. Shannon sighed. "I should have asked a better question."

Shannon placed her palm on Axe's forehead, their scars raised and rough against her skin. Their skin was warm to the touch. She slid her fingers into their black hairline.

"Wait, there's more."

"No time." Shannon slammed Axe's head back against the floor.

They groaned, body going slack.

Shannon grasped the Zu-Ki gun and stood. Her hand throbbed from reopening the wounds during her fight, but she tuned it out and checked the power on the weapon.

A blue light blinked back at her. "Okay, no idea what that means."

She headed back to the door and stepped through. She had two choices: to go back the way she'd come or try a new route. Her hand panged in protest as she gripped the gun tighter. She turned right and readied herself for confrontation. She needed to get off this damn ship, by any means necessary.

She crept from room to room, searching for anything that could help her escape be it a spacesuit, an escape pod, or plans to take over this musty ship. Her nerves a rioting shock of distress as she waited for an alarm to announce her escape.

She'd seen five crew members, and Axe probably had one or two more, if they followed the T'grevis crew model. Two were out of commission, at least for the time being.

She ducked around a corner into a room packed with more boxes.

That left potentially five more crew. The three pirates who'd been on the bridge when she arrived would likely stay there. She had two unaccounted for on a ship too small for comfort for a game of hide and seek.

Approaching footsteps echoed down the hall. Panic spiked as Shannon pressed herself flat against the wall. A weak beam of light swept the room. The pirate's flashlight landed on a dark corner. Her lips kicked up. She was in luck. Two escape pods stared back at her.

Another footstep landed closer to the doorway. She pressed herself harder against the wall. Were they looking for her or just patrolling the ship? Her hand clenched around the weapon. Her flesh itched as blood oozed from reopened wounds. The crewmember crept closer.

They paused for a handful of heartbeats before the

beam cut away as the pirate continued on their path. Shannon released the breath she was holding and wove her way through the minefield of boxes.

Even in the dark, the fractured glass on the escape pods was hard to miss. Her shoulders sank. The damn things were useless. She glared at the coffin-like tubes. Why would they use glass on an escape pod?

Her head fell back, and she sighed. She wasn't getting off this damn ship.

The lack of solid, unpatched clothing, and failing equipment did nothing but prove Axe's statement right. This group of pirates were in desperate need of credits.

With the clock counting down to a personal delivery she wasn't looking forward to, this left her with one option. One she didn't think she'd survive.

No longer concerned about stealth, Shannon strode out of the room, gun at the ready. She continued down the hall until she looped back to the exterior hatchway and the lockers filled with the Zu-Ki's orange spacesuits. The hooks on the wall were filled with garments exactly as she expected. The lock on the other hand, was a surprise. Were they expecting one of the pirates to make off with the bunch? Or had they expected her to escape and try to make a break for it?

Shannon tucked the gun inside her neck of her jumpsuit and jimmied the lock. The latch bent, but the soft metal remained whole under her hand. She planted a foot on the wall. Paint flaked as she shifted it into a comfortable position, braced her weight, and pulled.

The lock shattered. She stumbled back and hit an exposed pipe mid-back. Grunting, her muscles stinging, she rolled her shoulder as she stepped back to the shelf. The bar holding the suits in place slid free.

The ship rolled under her feet. She crouched as one spacesuit after another slid to the floor. Her gaze lingered on the captain's orange suit. She fiddled with her broken NAV wishing she had access to the ship's information to find out what was going on.

Barring that, if she could get the hatch open, there was a slight chance the T'grevis could find her before the borrowed suit failed and left her to the endothermic whim of space. That was if P'ret and T'rev were searching for her after what happened back on the derelict, and if the NIC on her wrist was still working. She placed all her hope into the T'grevis following hot on Axe's tail. Otherwise, from what Klick said, she was only changing up the time and place of her death.

Her fingers brushed the captain's orange suit as the ship shuddered again. Axe had the best of everything on the ship, the newest pants, the biggest scraps of clothing, and a weapon. Their spacesuit was the best choice of the lot.

Beeping started up behind her She swung around to face the hatch. The previously dark pad had a handful of hashmark flickering through some type of count down.

"Damn it." Someone was trying to break into Axe's ship. Who would want to do that? "Whomever they are, I doubt they're the friendly types."

She grabbed the captain's suit and helmet and bolted to an empty room a few compartments away. She needed to hide until she could assess the situation and decide on a new plan. Shannon shimmied into the orange suit. The gloves were a nightmare with the still bleeding cuts on her hand, but she managed to keep silent as she bit through her lip and arranged the digits to slide the rest of the way in. The suit sagged at her shoulders and the attached gloves stretched beyond the tips of her fingers, but it was on.

Rapidly scanning the area, she maneuvered herself behind the exposed pipes near the doorway and out of eyesight, afraid the bright orange suit would give her away. She'd placed the helmet atop a nearby stack of boxes and kept her gun firmly in hand. Sweating, she sagged against the wall and caught her breath.

The hiding spot had a great view of the hall, but if anyone glanced into the room, the orange-colored suit would give her position away. Why didn't any of these rooms have doors?

She fought the urge to move as time stretched to the breaking point.

A raised voice filtered down the hall.

"Where is that bastard?" A Zu-Ki in a lime-green spacesuit walked into view putting a face to a voice. Their spotless suit and helmet loosely grasped in their hand but did little to detract from the lack of scars covering their face. "Axe has stolen from me for the last time."

Her hand clenched around the gun as she realized who this Zu-Ki pirate represented. They belonged to one of the ships that fired on her, rigged the derelict to blow, and ripped to shreds any hope she had on having D'lane revived.

"Round up that wannabe captain and their crew and lock them all in storage. We'll space them when all once the *Find* has been located. I don't want a single crew member alive after I turn this ship to rubble."

A lime green Zu-Ki followed closely behind. "Won't the High Console take offense captain?"

The new captain pivoted and glared down at the

other Zu-Ki. "I'll worry about them."

"Order received." They crossed one arm over their chest and bowed. "I live to serve."

The captain laughed. "You're lucky I like you." They turned and headed toward the cockpit. "Or else I'd kill you where you stand for questioning me."

"And the *Find*?"

"Bring it to me."

Shannon released the breath she'd been holding as they disappeared from sight. She waited until she could no longer hear the clank of their footsteps before working her way out from her hiding spot, grabbed her helmet, and held her gun at the ready.

She crept to the open hatch and the sleek metal intership umbilical. Shouting echoed from deep within Axe's ship. They must have found the cockpit.

A quick check confirmed Shannon was alone, and she stepped over the hatch and into the thin corridor that connected the two ships.

The metallic musk and taste of sweat dissipated as she moved further away from her kidnappers. The hull of the new captain's ship peeked out from under the gangway with not a welded patch in sight. A good sign for the quality and repair of their ship. She held her breath and stepped through the hatch as she exchanged one Zu-Ki ship for another.

Stale air greeted her with a layout that was a direct reflection of Axe's, minus the hording. There were a few small areas of rust in the corners of the ceiling where it had eaten away the paint, and the metal floor had been worn to a shine, which she hoped meant they had money to maintain the ship and all its equipment.

Shannon turned back to the hatch and fiddled with

its controls. If she could close the door and get it to disengage it from Axe's ship, she'd have fewer pirates to deal with.

It flashed yellow. An alarm blared.

"Shit." She crouched and pivoted from the hatch.

Steps light, her gun at the ready, she traveled deeper into the bowels of the new ship. She paused outside the doorway to the room with the escape pods. She held her breath and peeked inside. Purple lights blinked above the pods. Hope rose as solid clear glass staired back at her.

She glanced at her gun. The same purple indicated the charge level, but what did it mean? Her toe tapped. She could leave now, get into an escape pod and jettison out into space with the hope of the T'grevis finding her, but where were the rest of the crew? Her grip tightened on the gun. Perhaps she didn't have to leave the ship.

She crept to the cockpit. One Zu-Ki manned the bridge. Did that mean there were three more unaccounted for crew on the ship or had Axe overstaffed his ship? The bridge pirate's breathing was loud enough to cover any noise she made crossing the metal floor. She stopped right behind them and scratched an itch on her neck. D'lane would be yelling at her right now to go back and take the escape pod, but he wasn't here, would likely never be here, and she wanted to do this her way.

She sized them up. Seated, the pirate's shoulders were no wider than her own. The muscles in their arms, twice as thick as hers, flexed as they reached across the counsel. Could she take them?

She'd beat Axe and Klick. Admittedly by sheer luck, but how hard could it be to take on one lone Zu-Ki with her gun and the element of surprise? The likelihood of success weighed in her favor. She glanced at the helmet and decided she needed at least one hand free. She leaned over to place it on the ground and lost her grip. It slipped from her fingers.

Chapter 24

Two hours since D'lane's death.

The Zu-Ki pilot spun around. The screen behind them gave a chest cam view of Axe and Klick being subdued on their ship.

The pirate reached for the weapon at their waist as they stood. "Are you the *Find*?"

"Fuck." Heart pounding Shannon fumbled with her gun. Her hand shook as she aimed. "Not today."

She pulled the trigger. The Zu-Ki flinched.

They patted down their chest and glared. "Hey!"

Panic rose. Had her gun failed or maybe she'd missed them? She searched for a safety. When she found none, Shannon shook the damn thing and aimed again. Breath held, she squeezed the trigger. They winced.

Nothing.

The pirate drew their own weapon. "Enough of this."

She threw her gun. They ducked. Shannon bolted. Heavy feet pounded after her as she ran down the hall of the ship. Shannon gripped a doorframe, rounded a corner, and slid into the room with the escape pods.

She slapped her palm on the raised keypad on the outside of the pod and glanced over her shoulder. "Come on, come on."

"Wait!" The Zu-Ki froze in the doorway. "That isn't—"

The escape pod opened. She squeezed in and slapped the interior of the pod until the door closed. The Zu-Ki ran at her. Their fingers grazed the glass as the door shut. The launch sequence activated with her touch.

They pounded on the clear surface, wide brown eyes met hers. "You must stop."

Shannon glared at the electronics next to the window. The countdown had begun. She fisted her shaking hands. "Any time now."

If the new captain was willing to kill Axe and their crew, she wasn't interested in being interrogated by them. At least Klick had been all talk until she started shit, she doubted it'd be the same here.

The Zu-Ki slipped from view. Shannon's quick breaths echoed in the chamber, and she focused on slowing them. She settled back into the coffin sized pod and rested her head against the mat. With her eyes closed, she waited for the jolt of disengagement.

A tapping sounded. Her lids flicked open. That pirate was back and this time they were attempting to break the window. The implement was a mix between a safety hammer and a punch. The tip dug into the glass.

The countdown flashed red. A metal shield closed across the window blocking the pirate from view. A tone sounded and her stomach dropped out from under her as the pod shot her into space.

The interior of the pod blinked with small lights, partially blocked by her curls floating in front of her face. The padding at her back did little to protect her head when she hit the roof of the small chamber. Her injured hand bumped into the wall. Flinching, Shannon held it against her chest and pulled herself back down to the floor where she tucked her toes into the foot notches at the bottom of the pod, similar to the ones Axe had used on the bridge.

She shivered, no longer able to hide from the vacuum of space outside her window. A handful of breaths later, she looked out. A relatively small piece of metal and glass kept her pod pressurized against the icy death of space. The metal that slid across the window when the escape pod launched hadn't come with her.

An unpleasant view of black consumed everything. A dark so deep her pupils hurt looking at it. The Zu-Ki pirate ships were not in view. Although that was with an assumption that the ship's exterior would be lit. She could be flying beside it and not even know.

The pods light caught on a smudge. The pit holding the colors in a way the rest of the window wasn't. Her hand shook as she brushed her thumb over it.

"Fuck." That pirate had damaged her pod after all. Was it getting bigger?

Shannon focused on the chip in the glass. It was all she could stare at. A thin line grew from its center, and then another until a spiderweb of cracks radiated from the chips center. She traced the longest line and shivered, her breath a visible puff in front of her. Perhaps she'd finally catch a break, and the glass would remain whole? The interior of the pod remained smooth. She exhaled and settled more comfortably into the foot holds.

The pad next to the door flashed yellow. A new countdown had begun. But for what? She had no idea what any of the Zu-Ki color coding meant. Her gun light had been purple but didn't fire, and there'd been no blaring alarms or warnings of impending doom when she climbed into the pod. Perhaps yellow meant that a suitable location had been found for landing the Zu-Ki pod, but would she be able to survive on it?

She tucked her floating hair behind her neck and into her suit and messaged her temples. "I really wish I'd managed to keep that helmet with me."

She closed her eyes briefly before tucking her scratched hand between her knees and unlocking the extension of her glove. One hand free, she pulled back her sleeve and brough her wrist up to her face to tap the NAV with her chin, unsure if she could activate it through her spacesuit. It was her new worry stone while she remained free floating as she traveled to an unknown destination.

The screen remained black, as expected, but it was comforting to have something from D'lane here with her in this cramped pod surrounded by the vast emptiness of space. She tipped her head back and glared at the bare metal ceiling. She'd given up any hoped of the T'grevis finding her, although she imagined they pursued her, and were moments away from intercepting the pirates who were no doubt getting ready to re-capture her pod.

A loud snap stung her ears. She flinched and her gaze tracked back to the window. Her heart rate kicked up as more cracks crawled out from the center of the chip mark.

It continued to creep outward in erratic bursts.

"Well shit."

She locked her glove back in place, not that the pressurized suit would help without a helmet.

The fracture spread to the corner of the window with each breath she took. The pad's icons rapidly flashed. The end of the countdown was close. A new splinter started in the opposite direction.

The pad flashed blue and a soft voice overhead

notified Shannon her sleep cycle had started. She had no way to stop it, and honestly didn't know if she wanted to. She pictured D'lane with his golden eyes and deep wounded soul that wove so well with her own. She struggled to catch her breath. She wished it was him cradled against her and not the oversized suit.

The new line spread across the crystalline surface. Sweat trailed down her temple as Shannon gasped for air. If she ever found out who decided to put a window on an escape pod, she'd kill them. Cold crawled up her arm, and she lost all feeling in her fingertips. Her vision tunneled and a low oxygen warning sounded. Her lids were heavy. The muscles in her body went lax. Her arms floated away from her as she drifted up. A whistling started, and she blacked out.

A heavy boot slammed into her chest. Bone snapped as her breath was forced out. Pain engulfed her. Whimpering, she clutched her ribs as she lay on the hardpacked icy tundra. Every inhalation brought a fresh wave of agony.

A pillar of light shot into the dark sky.

She wet her lips and rolled her head toward the pit she'd spent the last few hours digging. It tripled in size in mere seconds. The bright light originated from deep within.

A man stood in the center of it all, feet braced apart, the relic held high. Her breath caught as Steven slammed into him. The relic flew out of his hand.

The earth quaked. Ice ground against itself as eerie shrieks filled the air. Fissures radiated from the pit. The tundra ruptured. Large chunks of earth thrust up. Arms flailing, she rolled closer to the light.

The relic slid by her. She grasped for it. The hot

metal ate through her glove. Searing pain bit at palm as it branded her hand.

The ice tipped out from under her. She fought for purchase as the edge closed in. Her cleated feet swung into open air. She slipped. Arctic water engulfed her. Her diaphragm locked. Unable to breathe, unconsciousness pulled at the edges of her mind. Her mouth opened, liquid flooded in.

****

Shannon jerked her eyelids open. Crushing white light bit into her pupils. Her lashes fluttered before settling into a squint. Her chest hurt, each breath a painful fight for air. She groaned. The overhead light dimmed. Her mind raced. She should have woken floating in the escape pod, but gravity held her to the bed. Had she been recaptured by the Zu-Ki? A hint of mint in the air indicated otherwise, but the surface she lay on felt unfamiliar.

She licked her lips, the cracked skin rough against her tongue. She'd kill for some water.

She cleared her throat and called out in a dry whisper, "Hello?"

"Shannon?"

Hope rose. The voice was familiar. Shannon rolled her head to the side. Above her a slim body in silver swam in and out of focus. "Hellen?"

The doctor leaned over her and fiddled with the bed. Something tugged at Shannon's side. "Nice to see you again."

Relief crashed over her.

"Am I back on the T'grevis?" Shannon frowned as she struggled to sit up. "P'ret. D'lane—"

Hellen's hand pushed her back down. "Lay still or

371

you'll ruin all my hard work."

If she was on the T'grevis, that meant… Shannon's blurry gaze searched the room for the one individual she was desperate to find.

"What happened? How am I here?" Shannon blinked to clear her vision, but the clouded distortion remained. "D'lane?"

She swallowed, unable to get rid of the metallic taste in her mouth. "I need to find D'lane."

Shannon went to roll over. Rough straps tightened on her wrists. She froze as her heart rate sped up. "Why am I restrained?"

Hellen's face came into focus as her breath puffed against Shannon's cheeks. "You need to stay down."

She whimpered. "I need to know what happened to D'lane."

Hellen stepped aside. "He's right here, sedated and on the mend."

Shannon shook, using her shoulder to wipe the tears from her eyes. She struggled to get him into focus. D'lane lay across the room from her. His chest rose and fell at a steady rate. His tail still. Her eyes burned, and she blinked rapidly but the finer details of his body remained distorted. What was wrong with her eyesight?

Her fists clenched as she tested the slack in her restraints. She needed to get over there, to touch him, to lay her head on his chest and feel his warmth and to see if he was real. "How did they get away from the derelict before it exploded?"

"It's a story that will have to wait until after you're healed." Hellen stepped back.

Shannon kept her gaze glued on D'lane. She was afraid that if she looked away too long, he'd disappear, and she'd be left in a universe without him in it. A familiar clicking hiss of a shot being loaded drew her gaze back to Hellen's distorted image. Hellen pressed the hard tip of the inoculator against her neck.

Shannon flinched. "What are you giving me?"

Hellen's thumb turned Shannon's chin away from D'lane. "A dose for pain management and a light sedative. You died again in that pod, and your body still needs time to reconcile all the new pieces."

Shannon strained to get out from under Hellen's grip. "I don't want to go back to sleep."

Terrible memories waited for her there. Ones that left her dead and alone. She wanted nothing more than to lay beside D'lane, his tail curled around her ankle as she traced the soft skin of his chest until he woke.

Hellen gave her shoulder a squeeze and Shannon turned back to D'lane. "I know, but your body still needs rest. I had to do a lot of repair work to get you back up and running and your body hasn't fully healed."

Shannon focused on Hellen. "Can it wait a few moments?"

Hellen's grip on her shoulder tightened. "You shouldn't even be awake now."

"Please."

Hellen's gaze firmed. "No."

A buzz cut through the room that almost sounded like an intercom. Hellen frowned as her hazel eyes rapidly flicked back and forth. She straightened and placed the hypospray on the edge of the bed. "I'll be right back."

Shannon waited until Hellen entered the office to make her move. Step by painstaking step she tugged her wrist loose of the straps. The burn and scrape of freedom added fresh injuries to her healed hands.

She sat up and reached for the broken NIC. She hit bare skin. A quick glance confirmed it was missing from her wrist. A pang of regret flashed in her chest. As silly as it was, she'd wanted to keep it as a sign of all she'd lived through. Instead, all she had was memories and a story to tell, but as long as she had D'lane, then every would be alright.

She swung her legs off the bed and hopped down. Her feet connected with the floor. Her knees gave out, and she caught herself on the edge of the bed. Pain radiated up her body in waves. Shannon sucked in a handful of breaths before straightening. When she was sure she wasn't going to fall, she took a weak step. Shards of agony radiated up her heel, hips, and spine. Her vision grayed, but she remained vertical.

She grit her teeth. "I will not pass out."

It became her mantra with every stride until she crossed the room.

Her fingers brushed fabric. She looked down and D'lane's beautiful face lay before her. Her breath shuddered, and she leaned over and pressed her ear against his chest. His heart beat a steady rhythm beneath her.

"You're alive." Eyes wet, her hand fisted the blankets as she sobbed. "How did you survive?"

She laid there for moments, his lungs lifting her with each breath, as she absorbed the fact that he was real, alive, and beneath her fingertips. Leaning up she brushed the golden hair off his face and traced the line of his brow to the pointed curve of his ear. The skin on his neck was discolored with speckled patches of lighter skin that trailed down to a starburst of damage on his shoulder.

She still didn't understand how he had gotten off the derelict before it exploded, but she didn't care.

She traced the edge of the healed wound. The skin covered in baby fine hair stood up on its end. Afraid she'd wake him, she lifted her hand.

"Don't stop." He pressed her palm back down.

Shannon's gaze jumped to his. His voice was a low rasp she could barely understand. "You're awake?"

His golden gaze was clouded from medication even as the corner of his lips kicked up. "It's either that or I'm dreaming."

A sob escaped. "Or I am."

D'lane pressed her palm harder against his chest. His warmth seeped through her icy fingers. "You're here and safe."

She wiped the wetness from her vision. "You were dead."

He chuckled. "That's something we now have in common."

She looked at his hand atop hers, warm, soft, and filled with life even as they covered the mark death. "That's not something to laugh about."

"Of course it is."

She smoothed the blanket at his hip and did the hardest thing she'd ever done in life, something she should have done before they even stepped foot into the derelict. "I'm sorry for how I acted. I shouldn't have assumed that you'd change your life after being with me. Can you forgive me?"

"No."

She sucked in a breath as the pain settled deep. "Did I ruin everything between us?"

"Shannon…"

His hand rose from atop hers and her heart stopped. She'd done it again. Even now, centuries away from her past, she kept reading too much into relationships. Wanting too much. Needing too much from them.

He cupped her cheek. "I'm the one who erred. The one who should apologize for keeping parts of myself hidden and away from you."

Relief left her weak, and she leaned into his touch.

His thumb brushed over her cheek. "I was afraid of what might happen if we got too close. If I cared too much for you." D'lane's tail brushed her thigh. "Keeping myself locked away from the world and from those I love isn't the answer."

She bit her trembling lip.

D'lane tugged her close. "I love you."

"What?" She pulled her hand out from under his. "You don't have to say that to make me feel better."

He struggled upright as his blanket pooled in his lap. "I don't have to say anything, but I am telling you that I love you."

Shannon leaned away. The distance blurred D'lane's face and the raw emotions there. "It's the concoction Hellen gave you."

D'lane tugged her closer. "V'ren is the only doctor seeing to my health."

She freed herself and stepped back. The pain from her injuries made itself known. "Near-death experiences make people feel all kinds of untrue things."

"I'm deadly serious." He growled, "Now get back here."

Something slammed in Hellen's office. Shannon turned and squinted to bring the glass enclosure into focus. Hellen's muffled voice rose in anger. Shannon caught a fragment of a word. Was Hellen in distress?

D'lane gripped her wrist. "Don't go."

She patted D'lane's hand. "I want to check on Hellen. Make sure she's okay." She shifted toward the office. "I thought I heard—"

"I'll go with you." D'lane winced as he struggled to sit all the way upright.

Shannon guided him back down. "Stay here. I'll be right back."

"I don't want you going alone."

She caressed his shoulder and the vivid scar there. "What could possibly go wrong in the twenty feet between you and the office?"

She crept toward Hellen's desk, each step a painful reminder she was still healing. Her muscles strained with each careful heel placement, but she needed to remain silent if she hoped to check on the doctor without Hellen catching on. Otherwise, Hellen would sedate her and Shannon would lose the chance of discovering what angered the doctor, a state Shannon hadn't seen her in during the entire trip.

Hellen paced in front of the NAV on the far wall. Shannon cursed her eyes as the image blurred, but Shannon could make out a bald head and the distinctive coloring of the League's copper body suits. But which one was Hellen talking to?

"I'm sending our coordinates now." Hellen said from the desk.

"Good."

A familiar voice hit Shannon, one she'd heard before. She just couldn't assign a name to it yet.

Shannon leaned against the wall beside the door. Hellen pivoted as she paced her desk and her shadow pointed directly at Shannon. Shannon ducked, her knees collapsing out from under her from the sudden shift in weight.

"Shannon," D'lane whispered.

"I'm okay. Just moved too fast." Shannon tried to be quiet as she whispered back, but she feared Hellen still heard them.

The longer Shannon sat and listened to the continued conversation, the closer she got to remembering the League members name. Shannon turned toward D'lane as she remembered the block on communication. "Did the security protocol on calls get lifted?"

D'lane shook his head. "Not until we return to Earth."

How had Hellen gotten around security?

"I'll give them our new position." Hellen argued through the wall. "The Zu-Ki will come and take Shannon and be done with it."

"It'll be too suspicious this close to her rescue." The voice returned. "They'll know you did it."

"It's too late for that." Hellen laughed, and the screen went blank.

Shannon crawled back toward her bed. Her heart pounded as her hands went out from under her. Her cheek hit the floor. The slap echoed and D'lane flinched.

The office door opened, and Shannon froze, only halfway to where she wanted to be.

"What do we have here?" Hellen's feet came into focus. They crouched and fisted the back of Shannon's jumpsuit. "We can't have you wandering around the med bay like this. You could get hurt."

Shannon's feet dragged as Hellen forced her up.

Shannon fought the doctor's grip as anger overrode her fear. "Who did you give our position too?"

Hellen hauled Shannon forward. "You're smart enough to figure it out."

"My crew will fight the Zu-Ki off." D'lane grimaced as he struggled to sit half-way up. "You won't get away with this."

"I always do." Hellen dragged Shannon closer to her bed.

The hypospray Hellen had prepped earlier lay only a few steps away. Everything boiled down to keeping Hellen from that hypospray. Shannon went limp and took them both to the ground.

"Shannon!" D'lane fought to sit up on the bed.

Hellen slammed her elbow into Shannon's chest. Shannon grunted into Hellen's face and wrapped her arms around Hellen waist and locked her hands together. Her arms shook as she clung to Hellen as the doctor struggled to free herself.

D'lane slid off the bed with a grunt. Hellen wrenched away, slipping from Shannon's grip. "No!"

Hellen jerked upright, and Shannon went feral. She dug her nails into Hellen's arms. When that failed to keep the doctor in place, she climbed up Hellen's suit and went for the eyes.

Her thumbs brushed Hellen's soft orbital flesh and pushed. Hellen seized Shannon's hands. Her nails bit into Shannon's fingers as she wrenched them back, stretching the tendons to the point of pain. Crying out, Shannon used Hellen's grip against her and pulled her off balance. Hellen let go and caught herself on the floor.

D'lane trapped Hellen's calf. His hard black nails disappeared into the silver bodysuit. Hellen yelped, lifted her free leg, and kicked at D'lane.

Shannon struggled to her feet. Pain pulsed through every joint. Braced against the bed, she leaned over and picked up the hypospray. The metal was cold in her grasp as her legs were kicked out from under her.

She slammed into the floor. Agony spiked through her hip and head as she rolled on her stomach. The hypospray landed a few feet away. Dry heaving, Shannon crawled toward it.

"Shannon!" D'lane called out. "Watch out."

Hellen grasped fistfuls of Shannon's jumpsuit and yanked herself up Shannon's back. The fabric tightened against Shannon's throat. Gasping for air, Shannon twisted and threw her elbow back. Pain radiated up her arm as it connected with Hellen's chin.

Hellen's weight lifted and Shannon twisted free. She scrambled for the spray.

"Come back here you little shit." Hellen's punch landed in Shannon's back.

Ribs locked, Shannon gasped for air as she reached for the spray. Her fingers brushed metal.

"No!"

Shannon slid backward. Hellen's weight settled on Shannon's hips. The doctor's thighs squeezed tight as her hand fisted in Shannon's hair. She was pinned in place. Her neck arched, painfully pinching her spine.

"I don't understand why you're fighting me." Hellen picked up the hypospray. "I'm only looking out for your health."

She gritted her teeth. "Because you're a traitor."

"Don't say that." Hellen leaned down until her lips brushed Shannon's ear. "You might hurt my feelings."

The hypospray pressed cold against Shannon's

neck. Shannon closed her eyes. She pictured D'lane's face as he said he loved her. She wanted the last thing she saw before being revived on a pirate ship to be the fierce passion bright in D'lane's eyes. Shannon's lids flashed open. "Where's D'lane?"

The hypospray lifted from Shannon's neck as Hellen shifted her weight. She twisted. "Don't—"

The doctor slid off Shannon's back as D'lane fell to his knees beside her, a different hypospray in his hands. Shannon scrambled free. A quick glance at Hellen confirmed she was out cold, cheek smooshed against the floor.

"D'lane." Shannon caught him as he toppled sideways. "Are you okay?"

"Are you in this much pain all the time?" he huffed out as he leaned into her.

Shannon laughed weakly. "It gets better."

He lifted the hypospray in his hand. "It should keep her out for an hour."

A throat cleared. Shannon's grip tightened on D'lane as she jerked toward the hall.

She squinted as a blurry P'ret stood in the doorway, gun in hand. "What the hell happened here?"

The rigid tension in D'lane's body dissipated. Shannon leaned into him as he settled more of his weight against her. She repositioned her hands on the floor and landed on his tail. He grunted, and she moved her hand to a different spot. "Sorry."

D'lane wrapped his tail around her wrist and glared at P'ret. "Took you long enough to get here."

"The NAV is still on the fritz from our shootout with the Zu-Ki. We mistook your bed's distress call for a system error." P'ret holstered his gun. "Besides, it appears you had everything in hand by the time I arrived."

"We need to move the T'grevis." Shannon glanced between the two. "Hellen sent our location out to the pirates."

P'ret entered the clinic. "Already done when we captured a copy of her outgoing message."

Shannon shifted her weight. D'lane's gold eyes locked with hers. His tail tapped her hand. "Out with it."

"I don't understand how you were able to get off the derelict before it exploded."

P'ret cleared his throat as he knelt beside Hellen and checked her pulse. "The Zu-Ki began to clear out when we lost communication with you. That left J'rax and I free to get to D'lane. By that time, the T'grevis was back in range. It was a close call, but we got everyone off before the damn thing exploded."

Shannon ran her fingers over the short hairs on D'lane's tail. His warm soft silky hair another reminder that he was alive and next to her.

Metal clinked together as P'ret pulled a set of cuffs from his pocket. "We ended up taking on three Zu-Ki ships before they ran off to join the rest of the group."

Shannan leaned into D'lane. "Likely because they realized that Axe had me on their ship and not yours."

D'lane's golden gaze met hers. "Or to keep us from following."

P'ret rolled Hellen onto her stomach and clicked the handcuffs closed. The smile he flashed Shannon showed fang. "You'll have to explain how you managed to escape."

D'lane growled, "Some other time."

P'ret dipped his head in a bow.

"I've paged V'ren to look you two over." P'ret grunted as he hefted Hellen over his shoulder. "While I take our prisoner here to the brig."

"Is she on her way?" D'lane wobbled upright.

"Likely." P'ret chuckled as he stood, the doctor's weight did little to hinder the movement. "You'd better hurry if you hope to escape her wrath."

"Why?" Shannon rearranged her legs into a more comfortable position on the floor. "It's not like she can put you in time out, you're the captain of this ship."

"We need to be in our beds," D'lane said as he wobbled on his feet.

Shannon glared as P'ret headed toward the door. "Thanks for leaving us to struggle off the floor by ourselves."

"Anytime little sister." P'ret gave her a mocking solute. "Better hurry and get back to your beds before she revokes privileges."

D'lane tugged on Shannon's arm. She pushed up to her knees and stood. "You're the captain, how bad can it be?"

"She revokes her freshly made food." D'lane leaned into her, his weight settling against her side as she struggled to move him to his bed. "Last time I had to eat from the recog for a week."

Shannon chuckled. "Poor D'lane, missing out on his sweets."

She got him close enough that they managed to collapse half on half off the bed. A steady set of foot falls crept closer.

He lifted first one leg and then the other, his chest heaving from exertion. "I do like my sweets."

"I don't think I've heard you speak so candidly

before," Shannon said as she crawled up beside him.

D'lane settled back on the bed, his body pressed tight against hers. He tucked her even closer and curled his tail around her calf as she wrapped her arm around his chest.

"Perhaps now you'll believe me when I say I love you."

Warmth filled her as she pressed a kiss against the bare skin of his throat. "I love you too."

"Thank the Namegivers." D'lane brought her palm to his face and rubbed his cheek against her hand. The small hairs on his skin tickled her flesh. "I thought I'd have to spend the next few days sweettalking you into believing."

She smiled and traced the fine line of his pointed ear. "You can do it anyway."

D'lane's eyes closed, and he groaned. "If V'ren doesn't revoke our skin privileges."

"Maybe she'll be kind to us." She cupped his neck and brushed her thumb across his jaw, content in a way she hadn't been at any point in her previous life. "After all, we *were* hurt."

V'ren flashed Shannon a smile as she came into the room. "It won't save you."

Shannon brushed her thumb over D'lane's bottom lip. "Damn."

Chapter 25

Four days until arrival

Shannon woke with the delicious weight of D'lane's torso draped across her chest. His breath puffed damply against her neck. The dim overhead light did amazing things to the long line of his body. She trailed her fingers down the deep curve of his spine stopping just before the start of his tail. He arched into her touch. She caressed the round shape of his ass as he resettled against her, his tail flicking lazily between their feet.

It'd been three days since the incident with Hellen and the T'grevis was on its way back to Earth. Today was their first day off bedrest, and after dinner last night, they'd showered and collapsed on the bed, putting off getting dressed for passing out. The result coalesced into the pleasure of extreme skin to skin contact. Something she wasn't going to complain about, no matter how hot his body ran. They'd spent most of their days recuperating together, re-establishing trust and emotional safety when they weren't forced to sleep by their healing bodies.

Their greenlight for more intimate activities by V'ren couldn't have come at a better time. The NICs had kept them from being able to even fool around without being ratted out, and she could really use some unmonitored alone time with D'lane. He shifted his arm. The action raised her breasts as he nuzzled into her neck.

She lifted her chin to grant him more access and the small hairs covering his face tickled her skin. She shivered as nipples tightened.

She rested her hand at the base of his spine and brushed her thumb over the firm skin covering the start of his tail. The tip twitched with her every touch. "Are you awake?"

"Mmmm?" He flexed his arm again.

"Stop that." She laughed and the pat she gave his butt turned into a caress. His tail went erratic, a sensitive spot she'd need to remember later. "I need to talk."

"Okay." He tugged her closer and tucked his nose behind her ear. His rough tongue brushed her neck. "But you need to stop doing that, or else it might be awhile before we do."

He pushed his hardened length against her thigh. She sucked in a breath and debated the idea of discussing her concerns to after more pleasant interactions, then she moved her hand to safer territory. She needed to face this issue head on. If she locked it away deep in her mind, it'd become a behemoth of a monster eating away at her soul.

Silence fell. The hum of the ship filled the space. He didn't rush her, or push her to speak, instead he placed a warm hand at her waist and ran his nails lightly over her skin.

She shivered and combed her fingers through his silky mane. His tail brushed up and down her calf, matching the rhythm of her hand through his hair. This male loved her, had come back from the dead to tell her so. She could count with one hand the number of people who fell under that umbrella, and she really only needed two fingers to do so. "We know the Zu-Ki were paid by the League—"

"Or Kro-Gen."

"Right." Shannon sighed. "If only I could remember which one I heard talking."

She shifted up in bed, dislodging D'lane who followed suit, and picked up her handheld. She reopened her last tab. If she could solve this one puzzle then maybe their time spent on the derelict wouldn't have been in vain.

D'lane pushed the handheld back on the bed. "Obsessing over their images isn't going to help."

"We have to do something!"

"We've done what was asked of us," D'lane squeezed her thigh, "explored and mapped what we could of the derelict. And now we head back to report on what we learned."

"But not the entire ship, and we won't get a second chance seeing as it's gone." Shannon ran a finger over the veins atop his hand. "I doubt we've discovered enough information to stop an Anunnaki attack or how much value they'll place on the information we did provide."

Or how much she'll remain in debt.

He pressed his shoulder against hers. "There's no guarantee even if we had mapped everything, it would be enough to save us."

"Are we still sure that going back to Kro-Gen and requesting the relic is the best plan of action?"

"It's the only action we can take to try to shift the attacks." He flipped his hand over and captured her fingers in his. "We've been over this before. What is really bothering you?"

She flinched, gripping his hand tighter. She rubbed

her temple, and worked up the courage to start the conversation that kept her from enjoying the male next to her, the one where he would leave her once it was over. She stared at him, cataloging every feature from his golden eyes, sharp chin, and lips you wouldn't expect to be soft. The tuft on one ear peeked out from his hair when he tilted his head, waiting for her to speak. She loved this man, and refused to be anything but truthful to him, even if it meant losing him. "I'm not the same person I was before."

"Of course not." D'lane brushed a curl off her forehead. "Nor am I. Every day brings us something new, something different that causes us to rethink what we were before and brings us one step closer to our destiny."

"You don't understand," she whispered. "I'm not talking about small changes." She released his hand and turned to face him. He did the same until their knees brushed and the tip of his tail rested over the top of her thigh.

She cradled her head in her hands, tucking her fingers through her curls. "The past me was a coward. I was weak, unable to stop the man who called the Anunnaki attack."

"What could you have done?" He gently tugged at her wrists.

She dropped her hands but refused to meet his gaze. "I knew something wasn't right with the trip, but I still went along with it. I thought it was nothing more than a very unpleasant client, the usual pompous type I didn't like."

He crowded closer.

"But it was more than that." She focused on the cut

healing over his brow, the cut he obtained wrestling Hellen wasn't deep enough to warrant using the healing cream. "The rules were to stay together, so I had my doubts when Steven woke me up, but I trusted him. He had us drive out into the middle of the frozen tundra in the dark of the night, while the rest of our crew was sleeping. We dug for hours."

"He was your mentor. I would have trusted him too in the same situation."

"I keep thinking back and wondering if Steven had a choice to bring me along, or if the Krogenic's representative had forced his hand." She bit her lip. "I went quietly, even with my reservations. I think I hoped that if we took care of the mission that night, we could head home and be done with this job. So, I grabbed what little gear Steven let me have, and we left. I expected we'd find a bone carving or tusk, some eccentric's desire for the hard to obtain for their collection. Instead, we discovered something worse."

He grasped her shoulders. "You couldn't have guessed that aliens were going to attack."

Her chest tight, she wiped wetness from her eyes. "I could have guessed he'd kill us."

"No one expects murder." Leaning forward, he rested his forehead against hers. "That's a shock no matter what situation you're in."

She closed her eyes and breathed in his warm scent. "I'm directly responsible for the decimation of my planet."

"You cannot say that."

A sob escaped. "What else would you call the person who helped the alien's locate my planet?"

"The only person responsible for their attack is the

man who called them back to earth." He placed his palm in the center of her chest. "You need to trust me. I know you and the person you are. You would have done everything possible to stop that male."

"How do you know?" Her hand shook as she pressed on her lips. "We've only known each other for a sliver of time."

"Who is seated in front of me desperately trying to solve a mystery to a voice that doesn't affect her debt to Kro-Gen? Or who repeatedly put her life on the line protecting me on the derelict?"

She plucked at invisible link on the bed. "I could have been protecting myself."

"Then you would have stayed hidden and out of sight until the firefighting died down. You've spent so much of your time and energy researching a history and a time that isn't your own to help save the lives of billions."

"That's self-serving." She sighed. "I'm doing it to decrease my debt. I didn't even choose this situation."

"Exactly, and yet you've done everything you can to be the best being for this situation. You've spent countless hours poring over endless data looking for some sliver of information that could alter the course of the galaxy all for beings who don't even know you exist. You do this out of the goodness of your heart, out of a drive to do what's right. That along with many other reasons, its why I love you."

"I love you too."

She shifted his hand to cup her breast. His touch was firm as he palmed her flesh. His thumb brushed over her nipple. The tip hardened as she gasped. She lifted her lashes and met his gaze. He still loved her after everything; a warmth settled deep in her chest. She wanted to express all the ways she cared for him, but the rush of adrenaline from finding out he still wanted her short circuited her brain.

The heat traveled south, and she eyed his bare flesh. "And now I really need you deep inside me."

D'lane's golden eyes gleamed as he leaned in and kissed her. The meeting of their lips was powerful and searching. He delicately nibbled on her bottom lip. The touch was not deep enough for what she desired. She swept in and dueled against his rough tongue. She needed him closer and tunneled her hands into his hair, demanding more. His grip settled at her back, and she arched, pressing her breasts against his unforgiving chest. The small hairs covering his body lightly pricked her sensitive skin.

She pushed him onto his back and stared down at him sprawled out before her. Chest broad and abs slightly defined, he was covered in a layer of fine hair that darkened into a line that led to the thick length of him. He was hard and ready, the dual rings halfway down his dick partially engorged and pulsed with his heartbeat. Her hand clenched with the desire to fist him and guide him to her wet core. But she wanted to savor this, to tease him and draw out their desire to a breaking point.

She trailed her gazed down his lean hips and well-defined legs before following his twitching tail back up. In the dim light, she studied the solid length of his cock. The hair at the base of his penis was dark, but not much longer than what covered the rest of his body. For all the intensity of his gaze, his arms remained at his sides, hands fisting the sheets. She touched the soft skin at the tip of his dick. It twitched. "Are you okay with this?"

He ran his palms up his chest and back down again before fisting his length. His fingers covered up the pair of rings near the hilt. "I'm a hair trigger away from unloading just from looking at you. I've been reciting My'len's code of conduct to keep from throwing you to the bed and fucking you into oblivion."

She smiled, joy settling deep as she wrapped a hand over his remaining length. His warm flesh flexed in her grip. "Has it been helping?"

He threw his head back as his fingers whitened. "No."

Her smile turned feral as she brushed his hand off his cock. "Good."

Palm tingling at his moan, she stroked down as he pressed up into her grip. Solid and hot under her touch, she used the drops of pre-cum to lubricate her hand as she pumped up and down on his penis. She wet her lips as his restless movements egged her on.

His molten gold eyes met her own, hunger heavy in his voice. "Enjoy teasing me while you can."

Joy settling into her soul, she swayed forward and licked up along his chest to latch on to one of his nipples. His strong heartbeat drummed in her ear. She stroked his length, fingers massaging the rings every time she stocked up to meet the head of his cock. Groaning, his tail brushing her knee as he swept a hand through her hair.

She leaned down at his tug, her breasts grazing the top of his thighs. The points tight and stiff as she inhaled his musky scent. She licked hot skin, tasting salt and the unique flavor of D'lane. He cursed and his fist tightened, tugging deliciously at her scalp.

Body tingling, her mouth slid down his length, her

lips bumping over each engorged ring. The texture was rough compared to the surrounding skin and called her back time and again. Sucking, she pulled up until the tip rested behind her lips, pulling in a deep breath before taking his length again. She set a steady rhythm, needing more of his taste, his groans of pleasure, and craving a closeness with him.

Her body ached. Desperate for more contact and his cock still in her mouth, she climbed over the top of his thigh and ground down on his tense leg. His nails scraped her scalp as she lived the throbbing vein running down his shaft. Sucking in a breath, she released his wet length and sat up. He gripped her thighs where she straddled his leg and slowly circled her hips as sharp desire nipped her in the core.

D'lane's abs flexed as he jackknifed up in a powerful move until his chest brushed the sensitive points of her nipples. Grunting, he squeezed her waist and helped her straddle his hips. The tuft of his tail brushed her lower back and she shivered.

His cock, trapped between them, glistened from her saliva. The damp head brushed her belly. She gripped his silken hot length, raised up on her knees, and positioned the tip to take him inside her. She coated him in slick as she played the edge of him through her folds.

He tugged her forward with the hand at the back of her neck. Abs flexing, she bent at the waist and followed him down as he devoured her lips. Nipping and sucking at them as he followed the line of spine to knead her ass. She wiggled her hips, fighting his grip to push back and fill herself with his hard length, but he kept her there, poised at her entrance.

She tightened the grip she still had on his dick. He

growled, and the tips of nails pressed against her skin. She met his gaze and waited for him to take her in one bold stroke. Had hoped for it actually. Instead, the bastard released her and lay back, chest heaving, and golden eyes bright as he reached for her breasts.

"Whenever you're ready love." He pinched her nipples. Nerves spiked. Her eyes closed, and she moaned at the added simulation. "But I beg you let it be soon."

She wanted to glare at him for making her do all the work, the jerk, but a smile spread as rose up to her knees, widened her stance, and notched that ribbed cock right at her core.

Lowering, the tip of his penis slid in, spreading her sensitive passage. She whimpered as she encountered the first ring. Rising, she pushed down again, slipping past the second ring, before rising a third time to push down until their hips touched.

She panted, core pulsing and feeling perfectly stretched as his base parted her folds and firmly pressed against her clit. "We need to talk about your dick."

He rocked her slightly. "There's nothing wrong with it. It works just fine."

Breathlessly laughing, she shook her head and decided the time for conversation was over. Leaning forward, she braced a hand beside his head and ran her fingers through his hair as he slid a few inches out of her sheath. She wanted all of him back inside. She arched her hips and met the upward rise of his own.

Gasping, she spread her knees as far as they'd go, and moaned as he pulled out of her before thrusting in with one long stroke. The rings stimulating her clit from the inside as waves of intensity rose over her. His tail brushed her foot. Startled, her internal muscles clamped hard on his length. Groaning, he slammed up, each ring forcing its way into her core. Thighs weak, she collapsed atop him, blindly searching for his lips. They met in a wet clashing of tongue and teeth as he continued to pump into her.

This new position slapped her clit against his hips, the sensitive point stiff and unable to escape the scrape of his body. Her nipples grazed across his chest with every rock forward, tightening her ring of delicate flesh below. She froze on the cusp. The sound of wet flesh meeting flesh ignited her further. She arched hard and ground against him. His tail flicked up and brushed her thin skin stretched tight around his penetrating length. She tore her mouth from his and cried out. Her body trashed as she crested, pulsing rhythmically on his knotted length.

He propped his feet against the bed, changing the angle of his cock within her, and thrust repeatedly into her clamped sheath. Body climbing toward a second climax, she cried out. She slapped her palms on the bed next to his head, and braced herself from hitting the wall before meeting his every thrust.

Gnashing his teeth, he buried his head at her neck and snarled as his tempo went erratic. Warmth flooded her from the inside. His rings swelled further, stretching her sensitive skin. She lost control and fisted his hair, grinding against his hips. A second wave of pleasure washed over her in a surge of ecstasy.

Panting, he slowed as his breath beat against her ear. His kissed her shoulder and kneaded her ass. She unclenched her fingers, joints aching as his strands slipped from her grasp.

"Wow." Shannon stretched, shivering as her nipples

brushed over his chest. His hard length remained locked within her, a location she wanted to keep at least for a few more moments. She wasn't sure, but he felt larger than last time. It took him two attempts to get the blanket up and over them. She wiggled to get more comfortable, and he twitched inside her.

"D'lane?" She didn't think she was anywhere ready for round two.

"Don't worry about it." He brushed his cheek against hers. "It should only be a few moments before the swelling should go down."

She propped herself up on her elbow until she could meet his golden gaze. "You've heard?"

His cheeks reddened as he brushed a curl off her forehead. "This is a first for me. Something I thought you'd guess seeing as this didn't happen the last time we had sex."

She lifted up and discomfort pulled low within. Shannon hummed as she draped herself over him until they could separate. "I can see this getting uncomfortable in certain positions."

He chuckled and pressed a kiss against her temple. "I love you."

She snuggled deeper into him, tucking her head against his shoulder. "I love you too."

****

Tension rising, Shannon flicked through the screen on her NAV from where she sat in the mess. She knew her research led down the right path, even if it was one she detested. She looked up as D'lane sat beside her.

His tail wrapped around her waist as he leaned over and kissed her. His lips were soft and warm, and hinted at the intimacy spent in his room a few doors away.

He straightened and placed a cup before her. "Your stimulant refill."

She pressed a kiss against his cheek. "Thank you."

Shannon's gaze caught on P'ret as he entered. She debated asking P'ret to join them since he needed to hear this information too, but D'lane took the choice out of her hands.

"Update?"

"I've got a lead," P'ret said as he sat.

D'lane straightened. "On which one? We have feelers out on who organized the missile attack when we left Earth, who is working with Hellen, and discovering how pervasive their ideals are within our corporations."

P'ret leaned back in his chair. "It's an intermediary between the Zu-Ki and the Earth contact."

D'lane straightened. "When are you leaving?"

"Within the hour."

Shannon cleared her throat, waiting until she had both their attention before hesitantly pulling up her saved file. She projected the information onto the wall. "Then I think you should see this before you go."

"What exactly are we looking at?" D'lane asked as he shifted in his seat, his tail tightening around her waist.

She'd finally had time to review the full file General Fernández had given her before she left earth. The relic from her memories had been found near her body when she was recovered. The item made her want to vomit every time she looked at it.

D'lane ears flattened. "Who is that?"

She flipped to the next screen and the zoomed in on their face. The man, human in origin, had dirty blond hair sharp blue eyes, and a mouth pressed into a thin line. In his mid-forties, he was whipcord lean, and wore the dark signature Krogenic's shirt he'd had on the entire time on the expedition.

She glanced at D'lane. "He's one of the reasons I'm here." She changed the image to the next slide, unwilling to look at the man who had murdered her entire crew. "He's the security agent Krogenic's, that's what Kro-Gen was calling itself back then, sent on my dig."

P'ret's yellow eyes flicked to her. "You got your memories back?"

"Most of them. I remember Krogenic's demanding our group take one of their leads with us on our trip to the artic, and that I was against it."

"Why?" D'lane leaned forward. "Security details are a standard element on all trips."

"Even trained in cold weather survival, it's a dangerous landscape out there. Hell, you're lucky if you could communicate with the rest of the world from those remote locations. But no matter how hard I fought against his problematic addition, we couldn't walk away from what Krogenic's was offering to bring him along."

P'ret frowned. "Why?"

"We were failing, and they offered a large sum of money and were refusing to give us the exact location of the dig. And now I know why." She shifted to the next page. "At the bottom of the page on objects found near my body you'll find the note: *Female grasps a five-inch diameter metal disk a quarter-inch thick.*

"All I have is one blurry photo taken when they broke my hand to remove the relic and the brief image I have in my new memory of what it looked like before I grasped it. But the stylized symbols match up to the images recovered by the bots of the table we were trying to activate before the pirates attacked."

She still didn't understand why it had remained in her belongings back at Kro-Gen during her time on ice, seeing as they'd sent her team out to the tundra looking for it in the first place. It was almost as if someone had deliberately left it in there, or they didn't know the value of it even now.

P'ret leaned forward, his gaze intense. "Do you have any idea what the image says?"

"The NAV is still compiling the data."

D'lane stroked a hand down her spine. "If the relic is still at Kro-Gen, we might be able to sidetrack the Anunnaki ships to a new location if we can use it to call them there."

"There's a lot of ifs." P'ret stood. "And something I'll have to leave to you two to solve while I hunt down that pirate lead."

D'lane stood and Shannon followed. "Standard mission protocol?"

P'ret nodded. "No contact until mission completion."

The brothers met in the middle of the mess, slapping shoulders, and hugging each other. D'lane tweaked his brother's ear. "Take care and keep the new scars to a minimum."

P'ret laughed. "I can't promise that. I'll be paired with Tala. You remember what happened the last time we were together?"

Shannon stopped beside D'lane, as he spoke to his brother. "The other human from Lagrange One?"

D'lane turned, one hand still on P'ret's shoulder as he answered her unasked question. "She shot him."

"More like winged." P'ret laughed. "Believe me, if Tala wanted to shoot me, she would have."

"Fortunate for you," Shannon said.

"I'm sure someone agrees." P'ret turned back to D'lane. "If you don't hear from me, you know where to check."

D'lane nodded. "Understood."

A word about the author...

E.L. Roux is a Science Fiction and Fantasy Romance author who writes about finding love in all the wrong places. E.L. uses their knowledge of everything from prosthetics to the sport of fencing to weave together complex romances you can't put down.

E.L. Roux lives in Washington State with their artistically inclined family, an indoor street cat, and a terror of a Bosten Terrier.

Thank you for purchasing
this publication of The Wild Rose Press, Inc.

For questions or more information
contact us at
info@thewildrosepress.com.

The Wild Rose Press, Inc.
www.thewildrosepress.com